RESURRECTION OF GRACIE

978-1-64367-030-0

A coming-of-age story and history lesson, *Re   y Gracie MacDougal*
dignifies everyday characters living through extraordinary times.

In Linda Buxbaum's sweeping World War II-era historical novel, *Resurrection of Gracie MacDougal*, a young woman's Montana ranch life runs parallel to events on the world stage.

Between 1939 and 1945, the MacDougal family loses one child to kidnapping, one to death, and one to the Merchant Marines. The family also adds new livestock, grandchildren, and in-laws. Through it all, Abi MacDougal, the book's narrator and one of the family's middle children, keeps close tabs on America's involvement in World War II. As victory approaches for the allies, Abi chronicles her family's own closures with their series of extreme ups and downs.

The book creates satisfying symmetries: between Abi's coming of age and the world's reckoning during the war; between good and evil. It moves chronologically, with even-keeled language and a mix of modern characters.

Six sections—one for each year of the war—are divided into several short chapters. Each chapter covers one or two defeats or wins for the family, keeping the story focused, succinct, linear, and fast-paced. Clever segues, as when the latest Nazi atrocity leads into a story about Abi's violent older brother, link family tales to current events. The book's climax follows the climaxes of the war. The family's suspense is the world's suspense; its fate lies with the outcomes of key battles. With the end of the war, the family's story concludes happily, in delightful contrast to its ominous start.

As the book's narrator, Abi is a voice of reason amid her stubborn and sometimes brash family members. She writes as she would speak, describing her many chores alongside brooding pubescent thoughts. A bright student who reads a lot, she skips grades, entering high school as barely a teenager. Her father surprises himself by listening to her counsel on how to forgive a wrong done against the family, and she establishes a trustworthy and capable tenor, even as she tells about her encounter with a "spirit bear," a relationship that develops beyond plausibility. Her attempts to reconcile her religious foundations, her mystical experiences, and her literary inquiries set a balanced and easy-to-read tone.

Abi and her family members are as varied as the Allied and Axis powers. Her "crazy" Aunt Peggy dresses like a man. Little Gracie bears the virtue of her name. Her sister Blair has a child at fifteen. Twins Callum and Cameron are as different as night and day. Abi names her favorite horse after Larry, an enemy later treated as a family member.

Along with references to *Time* and *Life* articles and radio shows, the family tracks the war through letters from its parachuting brothers, Colin and Craig. The book captures a variety of personalities in a variety of forms, resulting in a tale that is much larger than Abi herself.

A coming-of-age story and history lesson, *Resurrection of Gracie MacDougal* dignifies everyday characters living through extraordinary times.

Review by Foreward Reviews/Clarion

RESURRECTION OF *Gracie MacDougal*

LINDA BUXBAUM

ISBN: 979-8-88640-836-2 (sc)
ISBN: 979-8-88640-837-9 (hc)
ISBN: 979-8-88640-838-6 (e)

Because of the dynamic nature of the Internet, any web addresses or links contained in this book may have changed since publication and may no longer be valid. The views expressed in this work are solely those of the author and do not necessarily reflect the views of the publisher, and the publisher hereby disclaims any responsibility for them.

One Galleria Blvd., Suite 1900, Metairie, LA 70001
1-888-421-2397

CONTENTS

1945

SYNOPSIS FOR RESURRECTION OF GRACIE MACDOUGAL

Abi MacDougal lives on a cattle ranch in a pristine valley of the Rocky Mountains in western Montana. While she and her family are at her brother's funeral, someone steals her six-month-old baby sister, Gracie. Abi and her family spend the next seven years searching for Gracie and praying for her return. Without fail, the MacDougals receive a picture of Gracie every Christmas. "How cruel and yet kind," Abi's father, Angus, declares after receiving the first photograph.

Angus hires private eyes to search for Gracie. Abi keeps a journal in which she records details of their daily life. From her writing, she discovers three childless couples who have stayed at the ranch during the past year that could be suspect in stealing Gracie. Abi also targets a former neighbor, now living in Seattle, who has lost her husband and baby after which, Abi's mom, Nora, invites her to come stay with them until she recovers from her terrible loss.

Abi's story begins in 1939 just before the outbreak of World War II. Abi is heartbroken after losing her sixteen-year-old brother to a ranch accident. When she places her rose on his coffin, she silently promises him she will always remember him. Abi can't bear to watch as he is lowered into the ground and runs down the hill to be with her baby sister, only to find her missing. Abi feels lost. When she is in the house, she misses Gracie, and when she is outside, she misses her brother, Ian, whom she followed around like a little puppy ever since she could remember. He was seven years older, and she looked up to him, admiring how he understood animals.

One afternoon, she goes to their little graveyard to talk Ian. She is finally hungry and brings a peanut butter and honey sandwich. She sits on a boulder next to Ian's grave, telling him about his funeral and how many people came to honor him. When she begins to tell him of Gracie's abduction, she breaks down, crying. She hears a rustling in the grasses growing between the Aspens and sees a white bear coming toward her. She is frozen stiff with fear, thinking that she might be the third tragic loss in her family. The bear begins licking the trail of salty tears from her face while making a m-m-r-r-ing sound which Abi likens to the murmurs a cow makes to her newborn calf. She remembers her sandwich and cautiously offers it to the bear. He takes it, and she runs like mad down to their ranch yard.

Abi rereads a paper she had written about bears just before school ended. She is sure this bear is a Spirit bear mysteriously sent to her "to give her strength and confidence to stand up to adversity. . . and if she believes in and befriends this Spirit bear, she will be healed and become grounded again."

The next day she returns to Ian's grave, armed with peanut butter and honey sandwiches, which she offers to the bear when he reappears. She names him Ian, and they begin a lasting relationship. Abi discovers that Ian is a she when the bear returns the next spring with two cubs. Abi, though only nine, has an old, wise soul, which she bears to Ian in his grave and to her bear. She finds talking to them helps her heal and find the courage to fulfill her dream of becoming as great a horse whisperer as Ian had been. She begins training young colts born on the ranch, and when she turns fifteen, her parents give her a stud and mare they have purchased from the King Ranch in Texas, which is famous for breeding fine horses.

The MacDougal family is large—Abi has three sisters and six brothers. She is just eighteen months younger than her twin brothers, Callum and Cameron. Cameron constantly does things *accidentally* to cause harm to family members and nurses a particular disdain for Abi. Cameron also spends his free time in the woods, shooting small animals. Even though Angus and Nora ground him and punish him with extra chores on the ranch, Cameron continues his loathsome behavior.

When Abi discovers Cameron's place in the woods where he stores traps of all kinds, including three very large bear traps, she puts an end to that, realizing he is responsible for her bear coming back some springs without cubs. She is appalled when she finds piles and piles of furs and among them, three small bear skins. When the twins are away at football camp, she donates all of Cameron's traps to the scrap drive. She tells her father about her discovery. He is infuriated since he has forbidden trapping on the ranch, considering it to be inhumane. He and Abi burn down the old shack where Cameron had been doing his evil work, without saying a word to him. Angus feels that losing the shack and traps is punishment enough but promises to protect Abi if Cameron ever discovers her part in putting an end to his obsession.

Months later, Cameron hears of Abi's donation and comes home, furious, and nearly strangles her to death. Callum saves Abi, and there is a vicious battle between the two brothers. Angus comes home to find a bloodied Callum and a duct-tape-bound Cameron. Abi never knows what was said between her father and brother, but the next morning, he is gone. Later they discover he has joined the Merchant Marines. Now the MacDougal family has four children to worry about. Gracie is still missing, and Abi's two oldest brothers are with the 101st Airborne, constantly in harm's way fighting Germans in Europe.

In the end, Abi's dreams and hopes all come to fruition, but not until she faces her revenge-seeking brother, Cameron, who nearly kills her again. He does kill Abi's Spirit bear; whose grown cubs then kill him. Gracie is returned, Abi's two older brothers come home safe and sound, and the boy she's had a crush on all her life returns home safe and begins courting her. Most of all, Abi, in her own right, has become a proven horsewoman—a horse whisperer.

1939

Spring

....

After the rampage of season-changing winds, winter comes—silent, still, menacing, deadening all life that recently basked in Autumn's sunlit-warmed reaping. Shorter days, cool, frosty mornings, and dusk stealing in a bit earlier each evening should be warning enough of what is to come, but we choose to forget. Winter makes his appearance, and we still find it shocking. We have dismissed the memory of the old man's fierce, painful hold just as a mother fails to remember the agony of labor pains.

It's unfathomable to think of how one colossally tragic week can clutch a family in something akin to winter's silent, frigid grasp. Your father no longer whistles as he washes for a meal. Your mother no longer sings her happy songs when doing household chores. Your brothers and sisters no longer squabble good naturedly as they settle around the kitchen table. Your dog no longer thumps his tail, waiting for a good rub.

After that awful week, I abandoned the thought that Mom and Dad could shelter us from the woes of life, especially death. The knowledge that life is tenuous, fragile, and can be taken from us in a moment became embedded in my soul. Not only would I grieve Ian's death and Gracie's disappearance, but I would also lament the loss of that snug, safe feeling my parents had previously instilled in me.

I realized they could not save us from much—we are, every human being, basically on our own, and that is one of the loneliest thoughts I have ever had. We can all be together as we were during Ian's funeral and burial, tightly holding hands, but we are essentially alone—isolated from others because we cannot always save one another or share each other's travails. We come into this world alone and we leave alone.

The week before these epochal events, high winds and a thunderstorm plagued our valley. Nature ushered in Summer and left us with a pout. She stirred up the heavens, mixing together the perfect ingredients for a maelstrom.

The summer before there had been a drought—no rain for months. Forest fires raged, eating up all they could—gluttons gobbling away at what nature had kindly given man and beast. Where fire hadn't prevailed, native grasses, usually prevalent and bountiful, dried up to nothing but forlorn sprigs, peeking hopelessly out of the earth, looking for redemption. Wildlife came down from the mountains, hoping to find sustenance. All life seemed to have withered, including the people who made their tenuous living relying on rain to water the plateaus and valleys below. That summer everyone performed their own rain dance.

The redeeming moisture did not come until late December, dumping two feet of snow on the valley floor and three to four times that in the high mountains. January began softly with temperatures warm enough to melt a bit of snow, leaving a skin of ice on everything after nature cursed us with a few days of eighteen-below-zero temperatures. February lovingly granted ranchers warmer temps and hardly any snow, making calving season tolerable despite the tenacious ice clinging to everything. In April, the rains came. The land became drenched with water. Ranchers up and down the valley struggled to keep their newborn calves alive in the wet while thanking God for the much-needed respite from drought.

May came warm and sweet with sunny days that urged new grass and wild flowers to burst from the ground. Our valley looked like paradise. As the earth slowly warmed, melt-off from the mountains crowded streams with icy, clear water, causing every creek to swell and blossom. The source of all life ran from the creeks and into the reservoirs, lakes, and rancher-made ponds, replenishing them. Then came the storm of all storms. People still talk about it to this day.

Short-lived, benign thunderstorms brought beautiful, soft rain at first. Our black Angus herd, washed by the rain, became shiny-clean and beautiful. After branding the calves, we began herding our cattle to mountain meadows where they would graze and raise their babies, chomping away at the exuberant foliage. They would return in the fall, fat, sleek, and smug, bringing home equally fat, satisfied calves.

The day of the storm, our family's mission was to take the last of our pairs to their summer pasture. We began early, knowing that this would be the longest ride of the season. We rose before the break of dawn, ate a big breakfast, brought our sleepy horses into the barn, and brushed them as they ate their oats. After saddling them, we gathered our cows and calves and hit the trail. Mom rode that day, along with Dad, Ian, Callum, Cameron, and me. Blair stayed home to clean up breakfast, finish Mom's household tasks, and watch baby Grace.

Once we started moving the herd and they figured out what was happening, they joined us in our early morning enthusiasm, and moved out willingly with the usual bawling of the calves and the cows screaming instructions to them: *Don't you dare leave my side. Just stay with me and everything will be okay. Follow me, and whatever you do, don't wander off the trail or fall back. Soon we'll be in a beautiful place full of nice, green grass.*

I imagined the calves protesting, "But I'm scared! Why can't we just stay here?"

Just wait and see; you'll like it up there. Just stay by my side and you'll be fine.

The day started as a Garden-of-Eden day. Birds and squirrels chirped and fluttered about as we made our way through the woods. There was a slight breeze that carried the scent of pine and the verdant, earthy smell of decaying undergrowth found among the cast-off pine needles and the deciduous leaves from summers past. A few foxes ran off, and a small, black bear lumbered away through the woods, its bubbly behind bouncing.

"There's that damn creature that's been stealing honeycombs from our hives," Dad groused. "I'll have to shoot her one of these days, I suppose."

I sat up straight, "No, Dad, don't do that. What's she hurting?"

"Oh, I don't care about her harvesting some honey, but she does make a mess."

I sighed, knowing he would never do such a thing. Dad worshipped nature—it played a large role in our livelihood. He gave us many lessons about her ways, and all the life that fell under her control, and had us devouring books on the subject as soon as we could read. Gathered around the supper table each evening, he lectured us on that subject and more—the husbandry of cattle and horses, human history, and politics.

Before noon, we stopped to allow the cows to graze while they mothered up, letting their calves suck hungrily from their engorged teats. As we ate our lunch, we watched with amusement as the baby bovines wandered off drunkenly to sleep, their little black faces dripping with mother's milk.

We hit the trail again with the usual bawling as cows reclaimed their babies, admonishing them with their same, previous warnings. When we reached the high, open meadows, we noticed storm clouds building. Lightning and thunder began in the distance and soon the gentle breeze became a howling wind, furious as colder air bullied its way into the mix. The warm, moist air of the morning had become cocky, exuberantly forcing its way upward to form the dreaded cumulonimbus clouds that preceded a bad thunderstorm.

The previous warm humidity became a penetrating cold. The formerly innocuous clouds hurried frantically to gather and make weather. The sky became dark as the clouds collected and came lower. We finally reached our destination, and as the pairs mothered up, it began to rain with soft pattering drops.

As the storm continued to build, the cattle became agitated. Every cow but one had found her calf. Dad decided to take the rest of the family home, leaving Ian and me, the better riders, to wait until she found her baby. He instructed us to come home as soon they paired up, and if that didn't happen within a half hour, to just come home.

They left, and Ian and I felt free. We loved thunderstorms and had to be coaxed inside when they began to rage. There is nothing like thunder in the mountains. The sound of it echoes for miles and miles from one slope to another, and from a distance the lightning bolts look like simple flashes. But when you are in the middle of it, you see the lightning in bolts and then hear the deafening boom of thunder.

We watched as the storm came closer, still not feeling alarmed. But then, just as our wayward pair found one another, we watched in horror as lightning struck the mother. Her body hit the ground, smoking. Burnt flesh sullied the sweet, rain-rich air. Her baby stood bawling, confused and wanting his mother. Ian and I looked at one another, wide-eyed, at last fearful of the storm.

"We'd better catch him and take him home and get out of here as soon as we can!" Ian yelled into the charged air.

He roped the calf, who was still small, since he had been born late. We tied his legs and threw him over Ian's saddle. The calf thrashed his head around, bawling weakly, but soon succumbed, lying still, making the ride home easier.

The storm bullied us all the way home, drenching us as we fought to keep to the trail; the mean, fierce wind jerked us around, taking our breath away. We jumped each time we heard a thunder bolt even though we knew the worst danger, lightning, had already struck close by. Without a herd of cattle to trail, we made good time, and in less than an hour, we arrived home. We put our unfortunate orphan in the barn and fed him a bottle of milk replacer. Later, we would put him out with the milk cows, where he would soon be adopted by all of them. He would never go hungry or be without mothering. We unsaddled and brushed our horses as they ate their well-earned oats, and then headed for the house, where our relieved family made a fuss over us. Mom had us strip out of our wet clothing, urged us into dry garments, gave us hot chocolate, and sat us in front of a warm, comforting blaze in the parlor's fireplace.

We only lost that one lightning-struck cow, but many families did not fare so well. The wind ripped off roofs and uprooted trees up and down the valley, hitting the Petersons' apple orchard hard. Ranchers who had hay land along the creeks lost acres of their first-hay cutting. The Millers lost one milk cow and most of their laying hens and all their young fryers. The wind destroyed their chicken coops while their milk cow drowned as a flash flood raced through their pasture. Wind toppled the big circus tent in town, along with gypsy wagons and stands belonging to carnival people.

Old Man MacPherson was swept away in a wave of water that took him and his house, dumping them nearly two miles away in McGregor's meadow. He had drowned, or was it a heart attack? Years after, we would herd our cattle, stepping around storm-felled trees in the lower meadows, and someone would say, "Yup, that's from the storm of '39." We would nod. Yes. And then that memory would bring us to thoughts of what followed, and we would become silent.

Summer Solstice

··

Everyone loved and adored my third oldest brother, Ian, at school, at church, in town—everywhere. These days one would call him a horse whisperer. He could train any horse, even those "bad" ones—those too stupid or too stubborn to remember what they were supposed to do and what not to do. Ian had his way with them, turning them into viable, working ranch horses. Before Ian was old enough to work with them, Father sold those "bad" ones, with most of them going to the glue factory.

Ian fared equally well with bovines. If a cow balked at her motherly duties, he could fix that. Sometimes if a mother had a difficult time birthing her calf, she would refuse to let it nurse. Ian had the patience to calm her down, using a gentle voice urging her to be a "good mama," and along with a set of hobbles and a head catch, she would soon accept her baby, allowing it to suck her dry. After that she would be devoted to her baby and never let it out of her sight.

During calving season, from sunup to sundown, Ian watched the herd with hawk-like eyes. Dad watched them at night despite Ian's protests. Dad was firm. "Son, you're still a growing boy and need your sleep. You'll have plenty of night-calving when you're older."

Every fall when the calves were weaned from their mamas, Ian would comfort me. "Don't you fret, Abi. They will soon forget that baby and look forward to taking care of the one kicking inside them." When he wasn't busy, he would sit on a straw-bale or an overturned bucket in the barn, meditating, absentmindedly caressing one of the barn cats or our cow dog, Charlie. Those creatures would trail after him as he went about his maternity checks and other chores. I often unloaded my school girl troubles on him when he had time to listen. He made me feel better while at the same time admonishing me. "Abi, you are just too sensitive. You've got to get thicker-skinned."

Along with every girl in town and out in the country, I worshipped my brother Ian. His eyes were a warm hazel that looked out from his handsome face with an openness that reflected his easy-going nature. His wavy hair matched his honest, honey-colored eyes and made him stand out in a family of mostly dark heads.

I followed him like a little puppy as soon as Mom would allow me to be outside with him. He was seven years older than me and managed me with the same level of patience as he did animals. But once I learned to read, I began to leave Ian to himself and his husbandry passions. But then Father assigned barnyard duties to me. He knew what good help I was since I had tagged after Ian for so long and felt I would be best put to work helping him.

It wasn't until I was eight that I could ride out to the boulder pasture and help Ian bring in the milk cows each morning and evening. I rode well, and had learned to ride bareback. But each time I left the yard, Father insisted I saddle my horse. He told me it was good discipline to always use a saddle. When I asked him why, he told me it was just safer when riding in the meadows, in the mountains, and especially in the boulder pasture.

Our father held us to rigid rules of conduct. His way of meting out punishment was unyielding—lickings with his big, leather belt kept us in line and always mindful of his expectations. Only once did I receive a licking and that was once too many. I had told a blatant lie.

Dad had a scale to which he adhered. For a sloppy mistake or not paying attention, causing someone—even ourselves—to be hurt while doing chores or playing, we received four hard licks. We received six for telling lies, and eight for fighting unnecessarily.

I say unnecessarily because our parents would allow us to carry on a dispute within reason, and we nearly always had enough sense to know when reason ran out. I guess our parents wanted us to learn how to argue and stand up for ourselves, preparing us for the outside world when Dad could no longer play the arbitrator. We were also rewarded eight licks for fighting at school, or perpetrating any sort of bullying. Ten licks were reserved for out-and-out disobedience and for cussing or talking back to either one of our parents.

The evening before our troubles began, Dad had dealt Ian ten licks for running his horse in the boulder pasture. Ian seemed fine with his punishments. He would move on, cheerful, and as if he hadn't just bent his long and lanky sixteen-year-old body over the edge of the couch. Our father, quite utilitarian, made us all watch, putting the fear of God in us, making us feel somewhat punished. The humiliation it created for the perpetrator was thrown in for good measure. After my one and only punishment, I wouldn't talk to Dad. Ian, despite having the biggest heart of all of us children, received the most lickings. He was just too open and honest; he certainly was not sneaky, and perhaps running his horse gave him a thrill worth the punishment.

The next day was summer solstice, a beautiful first day of summer. I had saddled my horse and waited outside the barn for Ian to finish saddling his. A gentle breeze wafted over me, cool and crisp, bearing a mixture of heavenly scents—lilac, pine, the earthy smell of freshly turned garden soil, and horse. I have always loved the smell of horses— their coats, their breath, and even their dung, steaming fresh or days old, and have never minded mucking out the horse barn. I kissed my mare's soft, gushy muzzle, inhaling her heady, equine scent, while scratching behind her ears and the underside of her long neck. She reciprocated by blowing out her warm, horsey breath, tickling my neck, and then she whinnied, anxious to move out. I squinted my eyes and looked up toward the sun, thinking this would be our first hot, hot day of the season.

Ian came charging out of the barn.

"What are you doing?" I yelled, hoisting myself into the saddle, urging Moriah to gallop.

"One of my stupid stirrups is messed up. I'll fix it later. Let's just get the milkers in. I've got a lot of calves to doctor today; it could take all morning."

Since Ian kept his horse at a gallop, I kept Moriah in a run until I was in shouting distance.

"Ian! Stop running your horse! You're gonna get another lickin' if Dad sees you! Ian, stop! And you're bareback, too. You're gonna be in trouble!"

I grabbed another lungful of air. "Don't you ever get tired of lickings?"

Ian raced on and I gave up trying to talk sense to him. I soon lost sight of him because I had slowed down to a walk so Moriah could pick her way around the chunky rocks and boulders that littered the ground. I implored our Maker that Dad hadn't seen Ian's exit from the barn or his race across the stony meadow—bareback of all things.

Moriah and I came up over a small rise, and I strained my eyes to find the other horse and rider. I caught my breath as Ian's gelding came moseying toward me. I kicked Moriah's side until she reached a slow canter, my eyes scanning the trail while I prayed that Ian was okay. As I crested the next small incline, there he lay, sprawled out on the ground with blood oozing from his head. I jumped from my horse, and running to him, saw that his beautiful eyes were wide open and glazed, as if he wasn't seeing anything.

I ran to Moriah and threw myself into the saddle, kneeing her sides until she was in a gallop. I didn't care if this would earn me a licking. Ian needed help. But my young mind already feared the worse. I had seen dead animals, and my instincts told me Ian had already left this world. But I still had hope. The idea that our parents could fix everything and protect us from the worst still lived in me, and I rode like a fury from hell to fetch them.

I reached the yard to find Dad finishing up saddling our stud, Henry. Dad began admonishing me for running in the boulder pasture before I could utter a word. Then he became quiet, seeing the panic in my eyes. I took a deep breath and began to tell him what happened. I hadn't even finished when he was up in his saddle and flying out of the yard, just as Ian had done not a half hour before. But then he reined Henry in short and turned to yell, "Get Mom to help you hitch a work horse to the wagon."

Mom and I worked feverishly. I ran out to the horse meadow and coaxed our best work horse into the yard with a pail of oats. I could see Mom's hands shaking as she hitched him to the wagon. She had me run into the house for an armful of quilts, and joining me on the porch, she gathered them up and clutched them to her chest. Then she stood waiting, hesitating. Should she start out now, or wait for Dad to return? Perhaps Ian had recovered by now and would ride home with him.

Just as she ordered me to spread the quilts on the bed of the wagon, Dad entered the yard, leading Henry with Ian's body lying over the saddle. My mother clasped my hand and told me to pray.

I had never heard her take our Lord's name in vain. "God, damn it, Abi. Pray! Pray like hell that your brother is okay! Pray, Abi!" She gripped my hand until I thought she would break it, and she swore again softly, "Jesus, Mary, and Joseph! I wish that boy wouldn't be so bull-headed and reckless!"

Mom has always told me that she doesn't recall much of that awful week. But I remember. At the age of eighty, I can still close my eyes and see the entire travesty play out in cinema technicolor. My father coming slowly into the yard with Ian's body draped over the saddle. How he carefully gathered Ian into his arms, bringing him to the porch, shaking his head slowly back and forth, tears running down his face, while my mother looked at him with wild eyes full of denial.

Dad finally spoke, his voice cracking as he swallowed down the emotion surging from his chest. "We've lost him, Nora. He's gone."

He held Ian out to Mom in supplication as if she could miraculously bring him back. She began to scream and beat on Dad's chest, and when she looked as if she planned to shove him off the steps, I intervened, trying with my slight nine-year-old strength to stop her. Blair came out of the house just then and wrapping her arms around Mom's waist, pulled her from Dad, who perched precariously on the steps with Ian clutched to him. Mom and Blair both went tumbling backward, landing on their backsides.

Mom continued to screech at Dad while Blair's eyes widened as understanding came to her. She turned and knelt before Dad.

"Is he . . .?"

Dad simply nodded. Blair began to sob as she stooped down, using her apron to wipe at blood still oozing from Ian's head.

Dad seemed to pull himself together and told me with a shattered voice, "Abi, go into the house and call the sheriff's office. If someone is using the line, tell them what happened and they'll make the call."

I nodded and went inside, glad to be away from the screaming and crying. I lifted the phone from the hook and felt relieved when I heard our neighbor and Mom's best friend talking. "Jessie!" I sobbed into the phone. "Ian has had a bad accident. Could you please call the sheriff and have him come out?"

"What happened, Abi? Will he be okay?"

"No! He'll never be okay because he's dead. He was running his horse again in the boulder pasture. Now, please call the sheriff and then come help Mom! She needs you!"

When I went back out, I watched Mom pick herself up off the porch floor and charge at Dad, who toppled topsy-turvy off the steps, still holding Ian. Mom raced down the steps and wrestled Ian from my father's arms, screaming like a banshee. "Give him to me! He's not gone! He can't be. Just give him to me! I'll take care of him!"

Mom grabbed up Ian's body and began shaking him, making his blood splatter everywhere. "Ian! Wake up. Come to, my boy! Ian! Ian!"

She kept yelling out Ian's name and when she realized it didn't do any good, she gathered him into her arms, rocking him, humming his favorite lullaby from long ago. When the sheriff arrived, Mom would not give Ian up, fighting off the poor man as if he were the devil. Finally, Jessie drove up our driveway, stopped her car, and came running. She calmed Mom down some, but she still refused to give up Ian's body.

When the sheriff, who was also the coroner, urged her to hand Ian over to him, Mom continued to screech swear words and insanities at him and would not let Ian go. Finally, Jessie went into the house and came out carrying Gracie, whose hungry mewl quickly became a loud insistent cry at the sight of our mother. Jessie leaned down to Mom. "Nora, your baby needs you. She's hungry. Don't forget, you have eight other children who need you. Come in the house and nurse baby Grace. She needs you."

Gracie, by then, was crying her pathetic hungry cry she had perfected very well by the age of six months. Mom stopped rocking for a moment, just long enough for her youngest child's needs to register. She pulled Ian to her and kissed him all over his face, promising him she would be right back, laid him in Dad's arms, and walked into the house to nurse Gracie, a macabre sight with Ian's blood speckling her bodice, face, and lips.

Dad handed Ian to the sheriff, and walked aimlessly to his horse. He leaned his forehead on his saddle for a bit, lifted his head, and then squared his shoulders. I could tell by the movement of those wide-set, strong shoulders he had let out a big, breathy sigh. I ran to him. "Dad, what should I do?"

He sighed and mounted Henry. He looked at me with the saddest look I have ever seen. "Go in, Abi, and take care of your mother."

I stood a moment, watching him leave the yard and enter the boulder pasture. I imagined he was going to bring in Ian's horse and the milk cows. I felt relieved to see at least one parent act normal, and I admired him for keeping on like that just doing the usual things.

I turned back to the sheriff who had just laid Ian in the back of his hearse. I ran to him yelling, "Wait!"

He had just slammed the back hood shut when I reached him. I looked up at him. "Please."

Without a word, he opened it again and stood back. I crawled in beside Ian and laid my head on his chest. He was still warm, and the tears began to flow. Our kind, patient sheriff left me alone in my grief. When I crawled back out, he gave me an awkward little half-hug, gruffly saying, "It'll be all right, honey, don't worry, people don't get over these things, but they do go on. Your mother and father will be okay. Just give them time."

I stood back, watching the sheriff drive slowly down our drive, taking Ian with him. We would never have our dear Ian at home again until we laid him to rest on the hill above our house. My throat closed at the thought, and I struggled to breathe.

Dad returned, leading Ian's horse. He tied him to the hitching post outside the horse barn and strode quickly into the house, coming back out with his 30 caliber Winchester rifle, walking hard and fast toward Joe. Realizing his intent, I ran after him, screaming, "Dad! Don't you do it! It won't change a thing!"

I reached him just as he had his gun up, siting its barrel just behind the horse's ear.

"No!" I gave him the same vicious shove he had received from Mom earlier. He went flying and the gun went off with a bullet hitting a rock pile nearby. Shards flew, showering both of us with tiny bits of stone. We would both sport small, hard scabs on our faces and necks during Ian's funeral and burial.

Dad grabbed his rifle again and aimed, and before I could get to him, he had accomplished his grief-frenzied mission. I ran to Ian's horse and prostrated my body over his head and neck, sobbing until I ran out of breath. I thought I had run out of tears while weeping over Ian's body, but I hadn't. When I finally stopped crying, I saw that Dad was still standing close by, holding his rifle limply in his right hand with the end of its barrel embedded in a fresh pile of horse dung. Serves him right, I thought, as I walked toward him. I grabbed the rifle and threw it as hard as I could, not caring where it landed, and stomped across the yard and into the house. Ever since then, the sound of a gunshot ringing through the air brings me back to that insane scene.

Mom had just finished nursing Gracie. She sat there, still as stone, staring into Gracie's beautiful baby face, still humming that lullaby which I would forever hate. I gathered Grace into my arms and lifted her to my shoulder to burp her. Mom sat lifeless in her rocking chair. Jessie came from the kitchen with a cup of tea.

"I put a little laudanum in chamomile tea. That should help her settle down."

"Where's Blair?"

"She shut herself in your bedroom and won't come out." Jessie sighed as she took Gracie from my arms. Gracie was heavy with milk-induced sleep. Little drools ran down from the corners of her pretty little lips, and I kissed each one of them as I handed her over to Jessie, tasting the sweet milk mixed with the salt of Ian's blood. Tasting Ian's blood made me want to cry again. But I just stood there, feeling lost.

Jessie tiptoed into the nursery just off my parents' bedroom and tucked Gracie into her crib, and when she returned she gathered me into her arms, gently forcing my head onto her shoulder, and holding me close, smoothed my hair. I suffered her embrace knowing that she did so out of empathy, an emotion she could rightly claim because of her own terrible losses.

Finally, she let me go. "Honey, what can I do for you?"

I sighed. "My head hurts really bad and my eyes are sore." I collapsed, feeling as if my knees had turned to rubber. Jessie helped me to the big stuffed chair across from Mom, walked into the kitchen, and came back with a glass of water.

"Here, drink this down, and I'll go find the aspirin tablets."

She came back with the medicine and another glass of water, promising me a cold cloth for my forehead and eyes. By the time she returned, I was nearly asleep, but I still remember her soft prayers for our family as she gently bathed my face with that cool, calming cloth.

When I woke up, Aileen, Craig, and Colin had just arrived. Aileen and her husband, Kendall O'Leary, the science teacher at the high school, lived in town. He had volunteered as a leader at 4-H summer camp and would come later, bringing Callum and Cameron home with him.

Craig, studying Forestry in Missoula, had just purchased an older 1929 Phaeton Essex, and upon arriving in the valley, went straight into town to pick up Aileen and Colin. Colin, aspiring to become a writer, worked for the town newspaper. The newspaper editor, sniffing a story, came out to the ranch. Friends and neighbors had shown up with vast amounts of sympathy and food. Party lines up and down the valley must have been zinging with the news of our tragedy.

As the day went on, it became complete mayhem as more people poured in with solace and hot dishes. I ran up to our room to check on Blair and get away. My mother had slept after Jessie's tea concoction, now surprising me with her calm collectiveness as she played hostess to our caring guests. Jessie had gone home to collect her suitcases. Mom and Dad had just purchased her ranch, and she planned to leave for Seattle in a couple of days to begin a job at a munitions factory. Since the moving men had emptied Jessie's house, Mom had invited her to stay with us until she left.

At first Blair refused to open the door for me. "Please, Blair, let me come in. Everybody's worried about you," I lied.

I heard her sniffling and blowing her nose. Finally, she unlocked the door. She grabbed me close to her, almost breaking some ribs in her fierceness. We clung to one another without saying a word. When she let go of me, she burst into tears, exclaiming with broken sobs, "I feel so. . . g-g-guilty. I have always been so m-m-m-mean to Ian, and now he's gone. Just . . . t-t this morning I called him a stinking hog because he asked for m-m-more pancakes, and when I finished putting them on his plate, I hit him a good one with the spatula." She heaved a heavy sigh, rubbing her red-rimmed, swollen eyes, and asked in a whiny voice, "Why am I so bad?"

I stepped up to her and grabbed her around the waist, hugging her to me, feeling her twelve-year-old pubescent girl's small and pointy-tipped breasts. I was in such shock I forgot our troubles for a moment. "My Gosh! Blair. You have boobies already." She stopped crying and reached up to feel them. "Oh! I know! I hate them! They always ache. I don't want to grow up just yet. I don't want to become a woman! I don't deserve to live. I am an awful person."

"Don't say that, Blair. You'll be a beautiful woman someday with your lovely face and splendid, dark hair. And you're gonna be tall with gorgeous legs because they're already so pretty. I bet you'll get nicer, too." I held out my hands and asked, somewhat sheepishly, "Can I feel them just this once?" She laughed shakily and turned as red as a sunset. "Okay, just this one time. In a few years, you'll have your own little things to feel." I stepped closer to her and cupped each one of my hands around them, marveling at how womanly they made my sister seem.

Just then Aileen stepped in and gasped, "What in the world is going on up here?"

I burst out with, "Blair's growing breasts! I think she likes them and hates them at the same time because they hurt."

Aileen shook her head. "Well, if you think growing breasts hurts, wait until the skin on your stomach and hips starts to stretch. I know it's for a good reason, but I am still getting used to the idea of how much bigger I will get. My friends say that stretching pains go away, but I don't know about that."

I looked at my oldest sister closely and noticed the small bump underneath the belt of her dress. "May I feel your belly?"

She nodded, and as I felt her precious little baby bump; I began to cry, remembering how happy Mom was when carrying Grace, and I hoped then that Aileen's baby would bring us some happiness after this.

Aileen slid her arm around me and then Blair stepped into our hug, swinging Aileen's free arm over her shoulders. We stood there for a while, taking comfort in one another's warmth and presence. Finally, Aileen spoke. "We better go downstairs. Mom needs us."

I have often wondered about our sisterly but peculiar intimacy that day. Ever since that time, I have noticed that people grieving do and say odd things. I guess that is our way of coping with our most painful times.

We went downstairs to the crowd of people. I acknowledged and responded to those who I instinctively knew held genuine sympathy and worry for our family. The ones I believed to be there for the drama, to watch us all suffer, I coldly ignored. Our house had become, indeed, a house of theatrics as some people put on a show with their fake compassion. I resented every single one of those who were simply there to see how the MacDougals dealt with such a blow.

As people, at last, began leaving, I searched through the diminishing crowd, but could not find Dad. I went outside to look for him, wondering why he wasn't with Mom during this awful time. She was beginning to tire of people and needed some sort of something—I don't know what exactly—but some help to go on. She needed him. I knew Jessie would take over while she was still with us, but I worried about how Mom would make out once she left. Jessie had already told me she had to leave in two days as planned or she would lose her new job.

I ran out to the horse barn. Joe lay in the barnyard, his lifeless carcass beckoning to every fly, crow, and magpie in the area. I chased them off angrily but they returned the minute I turned my back. The sun was high and hot. I shaded my eyes and looking around, I saw a movement up the hill where our parents had, years before, designated a family burial site. I ran up the slope only to find Dad furiously digging a huge hole in the ground.

I stopped and stood staring at him, still angry about his needless shooting of Ian's favorite horse. "What are you doing?"

My father grunted and kept on digging, sweat pouring off his face. I heaved a big sigh, not just from the effort of climbing the hill, but also for the exasperation I felt over his craziness. I took my stand, still glaring at him. I felt bad. I knew, deep down, that I was being a brat, but I was still furious with him for killing Joe. Wasn't losing Ian enough?

Finally, I asked again, "Dad! What are you doing?"

"Digging a hole for Joe. He can rest in peace here with your brother. I'm sorry about shooting him, but I knew I could not stand . . . bear, to see that horse every day; I would always think of Ian, and right now I can't do that without feeling crazy."

"Father, Ian's accident is not your fault. Just quit. You're gonna hurt yourself. Mother needs you."

He ignored me and kept on digging.

"How are you gonna get that horse up here, Dad?"

"I will. I can. Just wait and see."

I shook my head, frustrated, and ran back down the hill. I went into the house to find the last remaining neighbors standing around. I saw Pete McGuire, my father's good friend, and asked him if I could talk to him on the porch.

He gave me the mandatory hug and then asked what he could do for us. I told him about Dad digging a grave for Ian's horse, which he had shot dead after the accident, and that I assumed he would try to haul Joe up the hill all by himself and bury him.

Pete shook his head. "I was wondering where Gus was and why he wasn't here with your mom. Don't you worry, hon, I'll get a bunch of us men together to help him. Poor man! I bet he regrets shooting that fine horse, but you know, dear, I would have done the same thing considering the circumstances."

I nodded my head in thanks and gave Pete a quick hug. "Thanks, Mr. McGuire. He needs his friends right now."

Saying Goodbye

While I remember every minute detail of the day Ian died, his funeral is a blur to me. I detested the attention focused on our family. We knew the turnout for Ian's funeral would be enormous and that the church my mother attended wouldn't be big enough. She was a staunch Catholic while my father was Presbyterian. We children usually attended services with Mom since Dad was not as devout as she. When planning Ian's funeral, my parents decided on the First Presbyterian Church for the funeral service with the Catholic priest officiating, and then out at the ranch, the Presbyterian minister would officiate at Ian's interment.

Our family decided we would all ride in the hearse so we could be together as we made our final trip with Ian, with him lying in his coffin and us crowded into the first three seats. We younger children sat on laps and could easily see out the windows. The streets were lined with people as our procession slowly passed. I could identify many of them—Ian's classmates and teachers, townsfolk who knew us but who were not close friends, local business people, many Civilian Conservation Corps boys, and even members of the circus and their followers, the carnival people and the gypsies. I could see the red-headed circus lady who had wanted Gracie the night we went to the circus, as well as her husband and numerous other performers and carnival people. I saw the gypsy woman who had told my mother's fortune. As we passed by, she pulled on her pipe as if her life depended upon it, smoke circling her head like a swarm of angry bees.

Numerous family members had come from all over to be with us and our procession was long. Both sets of grandparents had traveled here by train all the way from Ohio. Our aunt and uncle had driven from Eastern Montana, as had some of our older cousins living there. My father's sister, Crazy Peggy, came, too. Everyone called her Crazy Peggy because she was. She never seemed to mind. I think she ate up the attention she received because she seemed intentional about her odd ways. Indeed, she steeped herself in strangeness, wearing men's clothing—always a big, white shirt tucked into baggy trousers, topped off with an ancient, ratty, brown felt fedora. She wore a just-as-used pair of men's wingtip shoes, drove an old, old car, and smoked a pipe. She talked out of the side of her mouth like some men do, and when I asked Aileen why she dressed like a man, Aileen just shrugged her shoulders and rolled her eyes. Crazy Peggy had been visiting the relatives in Eastern Montana or she would not have come at all.

All our friends and neighbors joined our funeral parade as it headed out to the ranch. We had left baby Gracie at home under the care of the McGregor's' oldest daughter, Faith. Ian had shown her some interest, escorting her to several dances in town, and she had decided she could not bear to attend the funeral.

My behind became stiff and sore as I balanced my boney butt on Dad's legs as we made our snail-paced, sad journey to the ranch. It was only four miles but seemed to take forever. My heart beat wildly, full of dread of what we had to endure next. We felt numb, and the ride was a silent one. I shot out of the hearse as soon as it had wound its way around large rocks and boulders, stopping at our family burial plot. The sun shone bright and there was a soft breeze carrying enough cool to make the hot sunshine bearable. The day seemed traitorous in its inherent beauty. Lying on top of the mound of dirt beside Ian's grave was a large bouquet of roses from which each of us were to take a stem and place it over his casket before it was lowered into the earth. There also were fresh-picked lilacs lying there in a bunch which I knew Faith had brought up there—they were tied together with one of her favorite hair ribbons.

The finality I felt upon seeing the open grave hit me hard. I decided I didn't want to be there. "Can I go back to the house and stay with Gracie and Faith?"

Mom, still in a zombie state, just shook her head, and I turned to ask Dad. He said, "absolutely not" but that I could go down later. I stood holding his hand, willing my mind to be somewhere else. I thought of Ian and me arriving home safe during that awful storm and how we had hugged each other with Ian saying, "We're alive! We made it! That's a story we'll share with our grandkids someday."

I fought tears, but finally, I couldn't hold them back any longer. I turned my face into Dad's suit jacket and cried. He stooped down and held me tight. "You'll be okay. Just cry."

He rubbed my back, and soon I stopped crying I whispered into his ear, "Dad, I can't watch while they put him in the ground." My voice broke, and I waited for a few moments for it to come tip-toeing back. "Please let me go to the house when that happens. Please?"

He let me go and whispered, "After you put your rose on Ian's coffin—I'll let you go first, and then you may go down to the house to be with your little sister."

I nodded and smiled up at him while wiping away my tears. It took a long time for the crowd of people to come up the hill after parking in the yard with the latecomers parking along our driveway. Our drive was nearly half a mile long and soon it was completely lined on one side with autos, trucks, and some horse and buggies. I stood shifting my weight from one leg to the other, feeling as if I needed to pee while my stomach churned. I thought I would be sick any minute. I tried again to put my mind somewhere else, so I thought of how good it would feel to hold Gracie when this was over—I would snuggle her warm little body to mine, kiss her all over her face, and inhale her sweet baby smells.

Finally, the service began, and that too became nothing but a cloudy memory. I was glad we didn't have the Catholic priest officiate because that would have made it much longer. The Presbyterian minister got right to it, and soon after his short sermon, I could feel my father pushing me in the small of my back, signaling me to step forward. I kept my sore, swollen eyes down and slowly picked up a rose stem. I kissed it and with a trembling hand placed it on Ian's coffin, promising him silently that I would never forget him and that I would come often to visit him and share my troubles with him like always. I turned, and when my father gave me a nod, I ran down the hill as fast as I could.

In the yard, I had to wind my way around the mess of autos, buggies and horses to reach the house. I ran up the porch steps and threw open the screen door. "Gracie! Faith! It's me, Abi!"

When there was no response, I ran to the nursery, but Gracie wasn't in her crib. I stomped through the kitchen and into the parlor. No one was there, not even Faith. I checked my parents' bedroom and the downstairs bathroom. Then I ran up the stairs to check Blair's and my room. Empty. Then, as I approached the boys' room, I heard crying. Faith was curled up in a ball on one of the lower bunk beds, weeping and holding one of Ian's shirts, which was wet with tears. I ran to her, not caring a bit for her grief. "Where's Gracie?"

She looked up at me with her big, brown, tear-stained eyes, and startled by the question, shook her head in confusion and insisted that Gracie was in her crib.

I huffed, "No! She isn't! Where is she?"

Faith sat up, alarmed now, her eyes wide. "I put her down for a nap an hour ago, and went out to pick lilacs, and before I ran up the hill to Ian's grave, I checked on her. When I came back into the house, I checked on her again before coming up here. She shook her head, bewildered.

"She's got to be here," she said sitting up, ducking her head so she would clear the top bunk.

We ran down the stairs and through the house, searching for Gracie as if she could have escaped her crib and made her way somewhere on her own. We concluded that perhaps one of Mom's friends felt that it would be good for Mom to have Gracie while they buried Ian. We ran out of the house and up the hill, and when we reached the burial site, we frantically looked through the crowd. Mom did not have her! My heart stopped, and I struggled to find some sort of control over my trembling body and befuddled mind.

"Where's Gracie?" I started screaming. "Who has Gracie? Where's Gracie? Who in the Sam heck has Gracie?" Everyone turned to look at me, and I searched their arms and then their faces—no Gracie anywhere. And then I vomited and everything went black.

When I came to, my father was holding me. "Did you find Gracie?"

He shook his head and then comforted me. "Everyone is looking. We'll find her. Don't you worry, my dear."

A long search was conducted with people looking through every car, buggy, and truck, but no one found her. They scoured the barn and every outbuilding, including the two outhouses behind the house. Dad called the sheriff. He had led our procession to the ranch but had gone back into town to oversee the loading of the circus and its animals and trappings onto the train.

The sheriff phoned the deputy in charge at the police station and ordered him to go down to the depot and stop the train from departing. His other deputy was already there overseeing the loading process. Sheriff Monahan deputized all the men involved in the search at the ranch and ordered them to go into town and search each boxcar, even the ones holding animals. They left immediately. He announced that he wanted anyone with any idea of what could have happened to Gracie to remain at the ranch and join our family in the parlor for questioning.

Dad thanked everyone for coming, for the support, the condolences, and the food and then asked them to go home and pray for our family. "Please pray that Gracie will be found soon and with no harm done." His shaky voice betrayed his devastation, and I felt tears rising again.

Since the men had carpooled into town, the remaining women and children did the same going home. Soon we MacDougals were nearly the only ones left to gather in the parlor, except for Faith and her family, our relatives, and a few nosy women from town. Sheriff Monahan questioned the women first and sent them on their way. He did the same with Faith, who was still sobbing and barely able to speak except to repeat again and again, "I should never have left Gracie all alone."

Suspects and the Long Search

After the McGregor family left, the sheriff then turned to me. "So, Abi, why do you think circus people could be responsible?" I had pulled on his arm as soon as he mentioned questioning us. "I have an idea who may have taken Gracie—circus people."

I sat for a moment, going back to the night before the big storm. I hesitated because I didn't want to miss any information that could help. Finally, I jumped up. "Just a minute, Sheriff. I wrote it all down in my journal because it was so strange."

I ran up to our room and fetched my journal from its hiding place between the mattress and box spring of my bed. I ran back to the parlor and handed it to Sheriff Monahan, opened to the page that I had dedicated to our night at the circus.

He started to read but then shook his head and handed it back. "Dear, I can't make out your writing. You'll have to read it aloud to us."

I turned to the right page in my journal and realized that with my eyes so worn out from crying, and my voice hoarse from yelling and vomiting, I had a difficult task ahead of me. I started to read, but my voice was barely audible, and I had to cough. Grandma Callaghan bustled into the kitchen and brought me a glassful of some extra sugary lemonade. I drank it down gratefully and started reading.

Tonight was very exciting, but scary. We went to the circus and watched all the circus peoples' daredevil performances and the animal acts, which were not as exciting, but were in a way, cause when do you get to see elephants, tigers, lions, and such beautiful ponies? I loved the magician and his monkeys and their tricks the best, but for animals I loved the elephants, not because of their tricks but because of what happened after.

Mom, Dad, I, and Gracie in her buggy walked around the grounds after the show. We looked at the fat lady. I can't even imagine how she can live since her fat rolls are gigantic. I know she can't ever lie down because then she would never be able to get up again.

We walked past the food booths full of cotton candy, ice cream, fried dough, and caramel apples. We had cotton candy, my favorite, and when we let Gracie taste it, she made a funny face and bounced up and down until we gave her more. I watched her suck on the sweet and almost burnt tasting threads of sugar, gumming it with delight. She laughed after her second helping and held out her chubby little hands, begging us for more.

We stopped at some of the game stands and watched as people competed for prizes. Ian and his friends haunted the Crossbow Shoot, the Balloon and Darts, and the Stand the Bottle booths, trying to outdo each other. Callum, Cameron, and Blair ran around with their friends in mischievous packs. I love that word—"mischievous." We just had it on our last spelling and vocabulary list before summer vacation. I think it sort of sounds just like what it means.

We walked on to where the animals were kept, and saw the elephants arranged in the strangest way. There was one in the middle of them, lying down, straining like she was trying to calve. The other five all stood with their backsides pointing toward her. Then, suddenly, the standing elephants all began making loud, joyful sounding noises through their trunks, and that's when we saw the baby come sliding out, just like our baby calves. Everyone cheered and those elephants answered back with more trumpeting like they had done during the show.

We left the elephants and Dad left us. He said he wanted to go check something out. Mom and I laughed, because he always needs to win a stuffed toy for her. When we got to the gypsy section, Mom made a joke. Should go have my fortune told. Oh, do! Mom, do it. I'll watch Gracie. She winked at me. Okay, you talked me into it. I stooped down beside Gracie's carriage and made funny faces so she wouldn't cry. Then I stood and watched as Mom walked up to the gypsy woman who stood outside her tent smoking a pipe. I watched them go inside and had the strangest chill go through me and became nervous, wishing I hadn't talked Mom into seeing her.

Then this red-haired lady came up to Gracie and me, the one who stood on the ponies as they ran their circle in the big top's middle arena. She smelled funny, like Dad does sometimes after seeing the boys in town, and she didn't look pretty like she had when performing. She stumbled and almost fell on Gracie and her buggy. She turned to this man. Look she has my hair. She should be mine. She gave me a funny look and grabbed for Gracie. The man told her NO!! She looked at me. Please honey? I just shook my head and pushed the carriage as fast as I could toward the gypsy's tent. The circus lady followed but her man pulled her back. He looked at me and said, "She's sad 'cause our baby girl just died."

Mom heard me yelling for her and raced out of the tent as I trundled Gracie and her carriage toward her. I felt stupid since I was crying, hard. That lady scared me by her wanting Gracie so bad. Mom told me everything would be okay. Then, when she told me what the gypsy said, I got another chill. She laughed and I could tell it bothered her too what that gypsy lady had said—Soon you will lose something very precious to you but it will be returned someday. I shuddered (another favorite new word) and I made a quick prayer to God for Mom and asked that it would never happen. What kind of people would want to take Gracie and who was this odd person telling Mom such a strange fortune?

After that I just wanted to go home. Dad brought Mom his prize from the Target Shooting booth. He won a huge stuffed elephant, bigger than Gracie, and Mom giggled. I felt better especially after Jake, Ian's best friend, gave me a stuffed monkey he had just won. I hope that someday he will want to marry me. What the Sam heck! I can dream, can't I . . .

The most surprising thing after Gracie's disappearance was how Mom transformed from the walking dead person she had been since Ian's death to the fierce, persistent, and alert mother bent on finding her missing baby. Her energy frightened us as she began her planning and organizing, bullying everyone to do this and that. She never gave up, reminding us continuously of the prophecy the gypsy lady had laid on her. She knew she would get Gracie back. She always believed it would only be a matter of a few days, weeks, or even months, but it would happen; it was just a matter of time.

Because of Mom's behavior, we became agitated and nervous in her presence. Blair and I were jumpy when we worked with her in the kitchen. One day I dropped Mom's favorite bowl, breaking it into a dozen pieces. She came as close to striking me as she ever would. She came at me with her hand raised, and I cowered, waiting for her anger to land on me. But after a few moments, I dared look up and saw that she was crying, her hand held over her mouth, appalled at what had almost happened.

I stepped around my mess and hugged her around her waist, crying, too. She gently wrapped her arms around my head and neck, pulling me close to her, kissing me all over my head. I hadn't seen her cry since that first day when Ian had died. She hadn't shed one tear when she realized that Gracie was truly gone—that someone had taken her from us. Her grief had become anger, making her crazed. Now, finally, she wept, her body becoming soft and yielding again.

As she crumbled to the floor, I heard her saying, "I'm so sorry. I'm so sorry." Her crying became loud sobbing, but she kept it up. "I'm so sorry. I'm so sorry. Please forgive me." And I wondered, who was she saying that to—Ian? Gracie? Me? All of us? Herself?

I knelt beside her and took her head, laying it gently on my shoulder. I fussed with her rich, dark hair that had escaped her usual pulled-back bun. I buried my face into her bosom. She still smelled like Mom, like gardenias, but I knew she would never be the same, and I hugged her as hard as I could. "It's all right. It'll be okay someday. You'll see. We'll find Gracie."

Even though Mom had become more approachable after her long cry, mealtime that noon was still silent and subdued, with us almost whispering as we passed the meat platter and bowls around, politely asking to be passed the salt and pepper instead of reaching across one another which had been our way before. We had become restrained, cool strangers, after being so emotional, with so many people around.

Our relatives had finally gone home, realizing they could do nothing for us. The sheriff and his deputies came out often with more questions and possible leads. The two private detectives Dad had hired began coming out with their own queries and clues. Mom and Dad attempted to join them in following many of those leads, at least to nearby towns.

They traveled to Butte and Anaconda many times, only to be disappointed. The policemen and deputized men from Philipsburg, as well as the police forces in both those cities, haunted the circus as it traveled from town to town, always looking to find some sign of Gracie. They would act as regular people attending the performances, but would snoop through the tents and boxcars during the performances. They would harass the gypsies, entering their wagons and tents, searching for Gracie. Mom and Dad had hundreds of their favorite photo of Gracie printed onto missing child signs and posted them everywhere. Since Butte and Anaconda were both Irish towns, there were many little girl babies with auburn, curly locks just like Grace.

They also went to Missoula where there were several sightings of red-haired, baby girls who people thought could be Gracie. Dad's private eyes went everywhere in Montana and the surrounding states showing Gracie's picture. Because of newly-paved roads, whoever had taken her could have easily and quickly driven a good distance away, or they could have taken the train anywhere.

Sheriff Monahan went back to questioning our family, telling us to think hard. "Try to go back for months, even months before Gracie was born. Was there anyone in your lives, or people you encountered that could have possibly been crazy enough to steal your child?"

I raised my hand as if in my classroom at school.

"Abi?" Sheriff Monahan said, as he raised an eyebrow.

I looked at my mother, my eyes beseeching hers for forgiveness and understanding before I spoke. "We had Jessie Aiken living with us for a long time after her husband died. When Mom began to show that she was going to have Gracie, Jessie would look at her funny—sort of like she was jealous."

I looked at Mom. She had her head down, thinking, then she looked up at me. "Go on, Abi. Is there anything more?"

I had broken out into a sweat, tightly wringing my hands, which had become red and throbbing. I took a big gulp of air and went on. "I am probably wrong because I didn't really like her much . . ." I looked up at the sheriff, and he nodded for me to continue. "She lived with us for a while and I . . . I . . . well I, I had this feeling that she wanted everything Mom has, since, well, since her husband died and her baby, too. After Gracie was born, she would look at Gracie like she wanted her bad." I let out a big breath, inhaled, and swallowed hard. "She would look at Dad that way too, sometimes, like she wanted him for her own, but not as much as she did Gracie." I offered those last few words, hoping it would make what I had said sound more reasonable.

Now my face burned as much as my hands. I looked around the room. But for my mother's gasp, it had become completely silent. Blair looked at me with her mouth hanging open, understanding the sexual implication of what I had just said more than I did myself. Dad looked at Mom with a look that was both wary and searching. The twins had stopped fidgeting, and looked down, embarrassed, as did Craig and Colin, whose faces were flaming like mine.

Aileen stood up and chastised me. "Oh, Abi, you can't mean that. You can't believe she would be that way. Not after how she helped those last two days before she left. She took such good care of Gracie, of all of us, when Mom was so, so . . . devastated and helpless."

Her hesitation alerted us. Everyone stared at her as she stood there realizing where her mind had gone, and we followed her down that path. I couldn't help but reinforce that now-shared suspicion, "Yes!" I shouted as I stood up, pointing at Dad. "I know she wanted Dad because I saw her trying to hug him one night just after she moved back to her own house.

"She came for supper, and Mom went to bed early 'cause the baby made her tired. It was just before Gracie was born. Dad had gone out to the porch. I went up to our room to get ready for bed, and when I came back down to say goodnight to him, Jessie was on the porch with him. I heard her telling him how lonely she was, and that's when she tried to put her arms around his neck. He pushed her away, in a nice way. 'Never do that again, Jessie. Never. Just go home now.' When Dad headed for the door, I ran up the stairs without saying goodnight. I didn't want him to know what I had seen and heard."

Mom stood up, shaking like a leaf. "Is that so, Angus?" Her voice sounded hard and sharp, making me think of the end of our shovel grating on a rock that had been turned up in our garden. We knew she was upset because she had used his proper name.

Dad stood and walked toward her. "Nora, there was no need to tell you—no reason at all. She had already sold us the ranch and had decided to move to Seattle. I knew she wouldn't be here much longer. Please forgive me for not telling you about this. Please? I would never . . ." he added, shaking his head.

Mom sighed. Then she went to him and gave him a hug. I could see the relief flood his face, not just about this, but also for the fact that this was the first show of affection we'd seen Mom give Dad since Ian died. Our parents had been acting as if they were complete strangers, let alone not married to each other. Mom had been making her plans with Dad, bossing him as if he were just another police officer or private investigator. We had seen Dad trying to hug or kiss her, but she would just turn away, taking his hands off her, as if she blamed him for everything.

Cameron stood up, and in his usual demanding voice, said, "Can us boys leave now? I want to go fishing since it's Sunday and we don't have to work all day."

Mom and Dad, with their arms draped around each other's waists, turned to him. "Yes," they said in unison. "Just be back in time to milk the cows." The twins and I were now responsible for that chore and nearly all the others Ian had performed with my help. It made me miss him even more. Cameron was surly and cut corners, while Callum meekly followed along. I knew so much more than both of them put together, but they didn't listen to me. I knew that Dad was disappointed in how things were going with them, but he didn't say a word because we had enough ragged, raw emotions plaguing our family.

Everyone grieved for and missed Ian, even Blair and Cameron, the most self-centered of us children. We each separately and privately nursed our own sorrowful thoughts about Gracie's disappearance, keeping the worst of our fears to ourselves, but openly voicing Mom's conviction that we would soon find our little Grace. It was just a matter of time.

After the sheriff left, I snuck out without a word. I don't think Mom and Dad noticed—they had so much to make up for. My oldest siblings all went their way, Aileen and Kendall had gone back into town along with Colin, and Craig had headed back to Missoula. Blair's closest friend's mom had taken them to a birthday party. Finding myself alone, I could think of nothing to do but visit Ian.

It was the third week in July already, nearly a month since Ian had died. Time passes whether you are happy or sad. They say time heals all things, but our wounded hearts, seared with two such dreadful, shocking losses, needed much more time to scar over. And all of us knew, instinctively, that we would never be completely healed. Nothing would ever be the same. When I was in the house, I missed Gracie. When I was outside, I missed Ian. This empty feeling made both places unbearable. I would wander in the woods above the yard, picking flowers, listening to the stirrings and the sounds of the creatures who made their home there. The peaceful flow of life around me would soothe my aching chest and throbbing mind. The terrible, tight feeling in my breast would lighten, and my pounding head would stop hurting for a while.

I had been up to Ian's grave with bouquets of wild flowers every day, but today would be different; I would talk to him about everything that had happened since he left us. I have always imagined Ian up in heaven watching over me, and that has kept me doing the right thing most of the time. I have never wanted to disappoint him or shame myself.

Spirit Bear

....

Bear lifted me up so I could see all the Earth.
He said I may jump high among the cliffs,
And live forever.
Full Mouth (Crow)

That afternoon I finally felt hungry, and seeing the mess of peanut butter, honey, and bread left out by the twins, I made myself a sandwich for my trek up the hill. Outside, it was hot with no breeze. I found refuge from the scorching sun under the quaking aspen that sheltered our little graveyard. There under the tall, slender, speckled trunks that housed millions of tinkling green leaves, thick as coins in the bottom of a fountain, was a boulder perfect to sit on, and close enough to Ian's grave so I could easily talk to him. Several large Douglas fir trees hovered on the other side of our plot, providing a partial screen. I was completely secluded from our house and yard below.

I plunked down on top of the boulder and brought my legs up, crossing them so I could sit like I had when I used to sit on straw bales talking with Ian. I took a bite of my sandwich but when I began to think of the things I needed to tell him, it stuck in my throat. I dropped the sandwich into the big pocket of my jumper and struggled to swallow that sticky, sweet bite. I told Ian about his funeral and how many people attended, how many came for his burial, and how Faith had laid a bouquet of lilacs near his grave. *Everybody thought so well of you, brother. You left a lot of love and respect behind for someone so young. Everyone said so.* I told him every nice thing people had said about him, and about how many women brought dishes they knew were his favorites and how we couldn't eat much of the food we received. Aileen and Kendall had taken most of it to the Catholic mission in town.

When it came time to tell him that someone stole Gracie during his burial, I stopped talking. Each time I started to tell him, a lump the size of a grapefruit, it seemed, clogged my throat and made my chest ache. I began to cry and could not stop. The events I needed to share with him overwhelmed me, and I thought—Did someone really take our baby during our already sorrow-stricken time? I thought about what a cruel and heartless thing that was to do to our family. I became angry and began sobbing out loud. A funny little half-moan, half-scream escaped my mouth. It felt good to do that so I kept it up, making those strange squawks until my voice wouldn't work any longer and my throat ached.

Then I sat quiet, listening to nature's sounds. A small breeze stirred the aspens and their quaking leaves tinkled like change in a pocket. I became mesmerized as I watched them twist and turn in those tiny gusts of air. One side of each leaf was green and the other silver. The soothing sounds of the aspens calmed me, making me feel sleepy, and in a stupor, my mind allowed tiny little thoughts to flit through my mind like butterflies in a garden. I thought of Gracie and prayed that she was happy and healthy. If someone took the risk of stealing her, never asking for ransom, only seeming to want her as their own, they must plan on being good to her. I thought of the places they could have taken her and how far away they could be. How would we ever get her back? All I could do is pray for that miracle.

Tears rolled again, wetting my face, my neck—even my ears felt wet. This time I wept silently. Everything was quiet; the breeze had left and the leaves hung silent. Suddenly, there was a rustling, and I turned to see a white bear rambling toward me. I turned back around and sat as still as possible. My heart raced, and my ears buzzed. I could only think of what people had been saying about our two losses: *These things come in threes. What will be the third tragedy that strikes the MacDougal family?* I sat statue-like, quaking inside like an aspen leaf, thinking, Oh

God! Please don't let me be the third, and I prayed. I prayed hard that I would be saved.

I heard myself moaning as the bear sniffed me, giving out little huffs of breath in between his inspective snuffs. He began moaning, too. He sounded like a cow talking to her newborn calf. Then everything went black.

When I woke up, lying face-up beside the boulder, the bear was licking my face, and when he moved down to my neck, I whispered," Please?" It sat back, looking like a huge teddy bear sitting in a store window, watching me, turning his head sideways as if he was trying to figure me out. His soft brown eyes looked at me with such sadness and concern, that I whispered, "Ian, is that you?" It turned its head to the side again and then came down on all fours and began licking the inside of my ear and I giggled—I couldn't help myself—and the bear sat back. My heart still beating in my throat, I settled down enough to think, and then I slowly reached into my pocket and pulled out my squished peanut butter and honey sandwich. I raised my arm, slowly, offering it to him. He took it gently into his big white claws, and I sat up carefully, got to my feet, and ran like hell down the hill.

When I had almost reached the yard, I turned just in time to see him run off into the woods. I went to the outdoor pump and washed my face, neck, and ears, remembering the sweet, green smell of his breath. His fur had smelled like last year's leaves. I walked up the porch steps and sat down on Mom's big rocking chair to pull myself together. I thanked God that he hadn't made me the third, and then I thought of the bear species and all that I had learned about them just this spring. I had written my first paper on them—white spirit bears, mostly. I remembered the belief that in bad times, people who became friends with or believed in spirit bears could be healed and helped by them. Hope rose inside my heart. Perhaps he could take my ache away.

I ran into the house, where Mom and Dad were sitting side by side on the davenport in the parlor, made a breezy wave to them, and said, "Hi!" My happy mood made them smile at one another. They had been so worried about me. I clambered up the stairs and raced into my room. I searched for my essay, which I had put in the box of my favorite school work. I found it and reread my teacher's comments and once again swelled with pride at seeing the A++. She had told me that I had potential to become a great writer, just like my older brother, Colin. Mom and Ian had been the only ones interested enough to read my paper, and they both thought it was good. Ian and I talked a lot about bears after that.

A white spirit bear is a rare black bear with white or off-white fur, brown eyes, a dark nose, and white or nearly white claws. As I reread my paper, I thought of Ian—that is what I decided to name him—and I realized, that, yes, he was truly a spirit bear, not an albino and certainly not a polar bear. I recalled the beautiful golden hair that lay across the top of his back and down onto his face, which was another strong trait in a spirit bear's coloring. The more I read, the more I thought this bear had been sent to me. These bears are usually native to British Columbia, but can be found further south. They are so rare that scientists believe there to be only about a hundred existing at one time. Even where they habitually roam, they are hardly ever seen, prompting many people to call them ghost bears. How had my bear come to be so far out of his natural habitat? I took in all this information with a new perspective, taking it as a sign.

My interest and excitement swelled when I read about their personality traits—shy and naturally afraid of humans. They prefer to be alone except when they are raising their babies, which takes two years. They have only black-haired off-spring. They are born white because of a recessive gene that is carried by only 10% of the Kermode bear species. They eat salmon, berries, green plants, insects, and nuts. I knew there was plenty of berries, plants, and insects in the area to satisfy him, but salmon and nuts? I smiled and thought of the fresh trout the twins brought home after they went fishing. My Ian bear would have to eat trout and forget the nuts. Their hibernation lasts from November to March, which made me sad. I would have to be without him for five months out of the year. By now, I truly believed, I knew, he would come back to see me in that same spot time and time again, and I felt joy for the first time since Ian's accident.

The entire mealtime that evening seemed lighter and happier. Mom and Dad were a loving unit again, and I was excited by the prospect of having a spirit bear. I couldn't stop thinking about him. I recalled how after I finished sharing my bear-paper with my class, our teacher gave us a lecture on the meaning of spirit bears and their history, along with the many Indian beliefs concerning bears.

The bear of any color and species has always stood for courage, strength, protection, and life in many cultures. Vikings wore bearskins into battle, believing it would bring them a proper warrior spirit and the courage to fight. In ancient Greece and Rome, the bear was associated with the fertility goddesses, Diana and Artemis. The Celts used the bear to represent the sun. Miss Cunningham told us that the natives here in the United States used the bear often as a totem but with different meanings and stories, depending on the tribe or clan.

A popular belief was that the white spirit bear had been made by the Creator to remind people of past hardships during the Ice Age. Some simply believed the white bear to symbolize harmony and peace, and since the bear lives a mostly solitary life, they offer people balance and comfort. Totems, she explained, can be spirit beings, sacred objects, or a symbol that serves as an emblem for individuals or for groups of people, and it is important to feel a close connection to your natural or mythical animal or totem.

Miss Cunningham passed around pictures of native men and women, especially shamans, wearing bear skins with the head intact, riding atop their heads. Shamans, she explained, were the natives' doctors, their healers. In Siberia, the name for a woman shaman is the same word used for "bear," and the Inuit people in Northwestern America believe there is a strong connection between their female shamans and the bear. She pointed out that any bear can inspire people who worship them, giving them the strength and confidence to stand up against adversity. She finished by saying that embracing the bear's close connection to nature and knowing the importance of restful solitude will bring healing and grounding in times of trouble.

The next morning, I woke up feeling happy and hopeful. At first, I couldn't think of why I felt good about life, but then I remembered my spirit bear. I crawled out of bed and ran down the stairs, feeling hungrier than I had since before our trials began, and I started breakfast since no one else was up. Mom and Dad could finally sleep again and were making up for many sleepless nights, and I knew that since school would be starting soon, my brothers and sister would stay in bed as long as they could. Even on school days, they had a difficult time getting going. Ian and I had been the only two who were eager to start their day.

Thinking of Ian, I felt alone again, my joyful mood dissipating, I carelessly turned the first batch of bacon, splattering my wrist with hot grease. I ran cold water over it, and determined not to let Mom see it. She came down to join me in the kitchen and when she tentatively smiled at me, I knew she was searching my face for the same cheerfulness that it had held last night. I didn't want to disappoint her, so I put it back on and gave her a big hug. Her pats on my back and my smiles allowed us to reassure one another that, yes, we would get through this, and we cooked breakfast in silent commiseration.

As I flipped the pancakes, I thought of how I could help my parents more. I certainly could not let them know anything about my bear. That would be apple-headed, and I certainly wouldn't let them know that I planned to finish training the mare Ian had gotten started a few months before. I had watched him for hours and knew I could do it. But at the same time, I could imagine Dad's horror if he saw me saddle that horse and ride her. But the next time they left to check out a lead, I planned to do just that—get on Jewel and fine-tune what Ian had begun. I grinned at the thought, and Mom, infected with my new joy, beamed back at me.

After breakfast, I went upstairs, made my bed, washed, dressed, and dug out my journal. As I reread my daily entries starting six months before Gracie's disappearance, and I wrote notes, I was shocked at the number of people who could be suspect in taking my sister. I wrote every detail I could glean from my musings about these couples, all of whom were childless for one reason or another. I laughed bitterly as I read about the way they adored Gracie because of her charm. Remembering Gracie made me sad again and I cried. I beat my fist against my mattress; I was getting sick and tired of this.

I angrily stood up, found my shoes, snatched up my journal and ran downstairs. It was almost noon, so I ended up helping set the table. Mom had fried chicken and made mashed potatoes and gravy, baked biscuits, sliced tomatoes and cucumbers from our garden, and then presented her first apple pie of the season. Everyone ate with gusto, even after our mealtime prayer which always remembered Ian and included a plea to bring Gracie back. As I slathered my biscuit with fresh honey, the courage to go and see if my bear had remembered me sprang up, and my heart began to beat wildly.

Since they had always been early risers, Mom and Dad had developed the custom of napping almost every day after the noon meal. We would have dinner on the table by 11:30 and be finished with the dishes by 12:30, unless we had company. During this time, we children, whether we wanted to sleep or not, were expected to stay in the house where our parents knew we were safe, allowing them a refreshing, worry-free hour of rest. My older siblings would make wry faces and lewd winks at one another during those times when we heard the bedsprings squeak in a constant sing-song rhythm. Later, as I grew less innocent, I knew what caused their embarrassment, and I would cover my head with my pillow when hearing the same thing in the dark of the night.

Even though the atmosphere in our home was warming, I needed to see my bear. Pushing my fear aside, I tiptoed down the stairs, made four peanut butter and honey sandwiches, grabbed my journal, and ran up the hill. I looked all around before I sat down on the boulder, and then I laid my kitchen towel-wrapped parcel beside me, my senses going wild. My breathing was shallow, and my heart beat like a drum roll. I felt dizzy, and yet, I could see, smell, and hear everything. The taste in my mouth was full of both fear and excitement. I looked out over the landscape, taking in the intense green of our watered lawn, willow trees along the creek, and the deeper green of pine trees. The meadows, now golden, lay before me, basking in the sun which had graced their grasses over the summer with a warm, flaxen hue.

I could smell those grasses curing in the heat along with the just-mowed, final hay crop of the year. I could hear bees frantically going from the last clover blooms of summer and back to their hives in the quiet of a breezeless afternoon. One landed on my offerings, and I chased it away. "You've already made that and have eaten some. This is for me and my spirit bear."

I cringed inwardly when I heard a rustle in the grasses growing between the aspen and turned just in time to see my white bear emerge. I took a deep breath and waited. He came slowly, and becoming frightened, I reached into my knapsack and pulled out a sandwich. He stopped for a moment, listening intently, watching my movements. I held out my offering. "Hi! You hungry?"

He walked toward me, still cautious, and when he reached my side, he stood on his back legs and let out a half growl, and then almost a purr. I gasped, and without thinking, whispered, "Shhhhh, they'll hear you down below." He dropped down onto all fours and began that soft moaning he had done before. He turned to me and shaking his head, sat back on his haunches, staring at me while making that same low sound. He hadn't reached for his sandwich yet, so I laid it down behind me. He made another *m-m-r-r* . . . sound and getting back on all fours, came closer, gently licking off the salty trail of my tears from the morning's cry.

When he seemed pleased that he had done a proper job of cleaning my face, he reached for the sandwich, picked it up, and sat in his teddy-bear position happily eating his peanut butter and honey treat. When he finished, he nuzzled me under my arm a bit, and I carefully, in slow motion, reached for another sandwich. After he had eaten his second gooey morsel, he worked and worked to rid his mouth of that pasty, sweet stickiness. I couldn't help but giggle at that, and he looked at me a moment, turned, and ran back into the woods.

I sat there, stunned. Was that all for today? But just as I accepted that our meetings would be short, he came running back. This time he only scared me a tiny bit. His mouth was wet, and he seemed very pleased with himself. He had run to the little creek up above to quench his thirst and clean his mouth with that cool, refreshing water. He sat for a while, teddy-bear-like, and then nosed under my arm again. I took out the two remaining sandwiches and offered him one while I bit into the other. His sandwich was gone much sooner than mine, but he had eaten it so carefully and with such delicacy, I decided to give him the rest of mine. When he finished that, he plopped down on his rear haunches and seemed to meditate for a while, and then, in an instant, was up on his feet running for the woods. He stopped, let out a little growl as if to say goodbye, and was gone.

I sat on the boulder, reveling in my experience. I hadn't yet written about my bear, worrying that if someone would find my journal and read it, they would discover my secret. I sat there for almost an hour reflecting on this and realized that if I ever told any of my siblings or friends at school about my bear they would never believe it. After talking to Ian for a time, assuring him that no one had forgotten him, but that things felt a little more normal, I ran back down the hill. Seeing my bear once again had given me the courage to tell Mom and Dad about the suspects I had found in my writing, and I said a little prayer thanking God for my bear.

Autumn and New Suspects

. . . .

The private investigators came back with disappointing news concerning Jessie. They followed her for several weeks—heeling her so closely that she eventually confronted them. She had cleverly steered them into a police station where they were forced to disclose their mission. Before that, she had led the men on numerous false trails, never staying in one place until she finally moved into a new apartment near the munitions factory. She had stayed with different friends or in hotels for several weeks before settling into her own place. She had also frequently visited someone at a small modest home in the suburbs. It took some time before Dad's men could gain entrance, but when they did there was no sign of a baby in residence. Jessie broke down and cried when they explained their investigation to her. Mom and Dad received a letter from her a few days after, but they didn't tell us what she had written, and we never saw her again until years later.

I had given Mom and Dad a list of my suspects. At first, they were hesitant, but after a time they decided to turn the list over to our private eyes. First on the list was a young couple named Jean and Don Allen. Dad knew Don because of the Civilian Conservation Corps. Don lived and worked at the Philipsburg F-75 Flint Creek camp which had been set up seven miles from town to facilitate tasks necessary to satisfy FDR's plans to improve natural resources and to conserve them as well.

The young CCC men fenced off government lands and developed parks and the roads needed to get to them. They constructed lookout towers to help prevent forest fires from getting a start that couldn't be stopped. They developed springs in the newly set aside government-owned forest land that was leased to local ranchers for grazing. They built and paved roads all over Montana, making going from town to town much easier. And, best of all, they made electricity and telephones available to rural communities in our state.

Montana and its people were special to FDR because of the strong support our U.S. Senators, Burton K. Wheeler, a progressive Democrat, and Thomas J. Walsh had given him when he ran for office. He rewarded them, and thus Montanans, with important projects such as the Fort Peck Dam and others bringing modernity to Montana, even to those living in remote areas—the boonies, as we still call those it-takes-hours-to-get-to-town places.

Dad had taken a liking to Don, and when his fiancée came to join him, Dad hired her as a housemaid when Mom was bedridden in her last months of pregnancy. Jean was there for us in every way. The only time she left us was the weekend she and Don went to Butte to marry and have a one-night honeymoon. They kept their marriage secret, with Don still living at the camp and Jean staying with us. Jean had a way with us children, settling Blair whenever she began to cause trouble, which was usually picking on Cameron who was just as difficult.

Mom had christened us with special Gaelic names, and we all seemed to fit them. Aileen, second mother to Colin, Ian, the twins, and me, means "little Eve." Craig means "rock." Everyone could rely on him, and what he said he would do, he did. Colin means "victory of the people." Years later, Colin would serve as an advocate for Native Americans when they decided to stand up and fight for more equal rights. Ian's name meant "God is gracious," and we had all, as well as our livestock, benefited from his amiable disposition and kindness. Blair is the Gaelic name for "battlefield" while Cameron's name means "crooked," and Callum means "dove." Callum lived up to his name as peacemaker between his ever-ornery twin and the world. My name means "father's joy," which I was, especially after Ian died. Grace is a virtue name that means "full of grace and charm."

We missed Jean when she left with Don to move to Bozeman where he would work for the forest service. Jean's final farewell was painful since she broke down after handing Gracie over to Mom. Blair told me once that Jean had confessed to her that she had been married before and couldn't become pregnant. She believed she would never have her own child, and she longed for a baby just like Gracie. I had watched as she, just like Jessie, followed my pregnant mother with sad, envious eyes, and after Grace was born, Jean showed a possessiveness that made me nervous, despite my affection for her. Mom wept after the two men left to check out the Allen couple. "Before this is over, we won't have any friends."

Our men came back with news that Jean Allen was pregnant, and that they were planning to move to Michigan where Don would earn his Forestry degree at the university there. They, too, were shocked at the news of Ian's death and that someone stole Gracie during that time. Fortunately, since our guys had been more circumspect this time, the Allens never knew they were suspects. Mom received a letter along with a sympathy card, saying that they wanted to keep in touch and that they hoped we would find Gracie.

The next couple on my list was David and Adeline Breckenridge. They were wealthy, and I secretly hoped that if any of these couples had taken Gracie, it would be them. She would have a good life with them. They had been very pleasant guests when they stayed at the ranch. Mom and Dad put them up in the bunkhouse, which now had indoor plumbing and electricity. Before they arrived, Mom spent days fixing it up, cleaning it, and supplying it with fresh linens. Mr. Breckenridge was a cattle breeder of circumstance from Nebraska, and he and Dad talked about cattle that entire week. The Breckenridge couple were both handsome people, and I wished that someday I could be as beautiful as Adeline.

One day I heard her saying that the doctors said they could never have babies of their own, something about sperm count. I was getting tired of hearing about that because the men's obsession for cattle breeding brought that subject up constantly. I asked Ian what sperm count was and why they were so concerned with scrotum size, and he just blushed. But then he explained things to me, making me promise not to tell Mom. "I would never," I said, my face feeling as hot as his was red.

"You know, Abi, I am surprised that you didn't figure it out on your own. You are so old and wise for your age."

"Is that what my English teacher means when she says I'm the youngest, but oldest soul she has ever known?"

Ian chuckled. "Yes, Abi. You have quite the relationship with the lady, don't you?"

I smiled. "In school, she's my best friend after Rosie."

Rosie, or Rosella, was my good friend, and after a long summer of separation, I was anxious to be with her again. Her father sent her to Eastern Montana every summer to stay with her mom. The entire community still hadn't gotten over the valley's first divorce. When the Ryans divorced, everyone had something to say about it. It was talked about even more than when Andrea Mueller became pregnant out-of-wedlock and kept her baby. The party lines constantly buzzed.

I thought I might tell Rosie about my bear. But then again, I probably wouldn't because it felt so special to me. My bear and I had developed a pattern of meeting at Ian's grave. I had taken up some almost-gone salt blocks for him to lick, and I always brought him peanut butter and honey sandwiches. I didn't go every day, and kept it sporadic, reasoning that then I would never disappoint him if I couldn't get up there for some reason. When school started, I would have to go up later in the day. But I knew he would leave to hibernate when winter came, and then I would be the lonely one.

It was strange how he always seemed to sense my being there. He would come, greet me with that *m-m-r-r* . . . sound, and hold out his claw to accept his first sandwich. I struggled to keep from laughing when Mom accused the twins of eating too many peanut butter and honey sandwiches. The dumbfounded looks on their faces made it even more difficult to remain sober.

"I'm going to have to start buying bread if this keeps up, boys." Mom said, furrowing her delicate brow.

We children thought Mom was the best bread baker around, and I think Bear would agree with us on that. He continued to be so mannerly when eating his treats, and I couldn't get over that, just like I still could not comprehend our friendship. Now I could understand how strangely special the Virgin Mary must have felt when God's angel, Gabriel, came to tell her that she would have the honor of giving birth to Jesus, who, as an adult, would save sinners throughout the ages. Mary's experience, like mine, must have been incredibly awe-inspiring and frightening at the same time. I've always felt sorry for Mary. She had her little baby only to have to sacrifice him for humanity. Watching the agony Mom went through after Ian died and Gracie disappeared has always made me think of her.

Our men came back to tell us they couldn't find any sign of Mr. and Mrs. Breckenridge. The people in their community said that they had just picked up and left one day, after quickly selling their land, their cattle, and all that they owned shortly before leaving. Dad told our guys to keep trying to find their trail, that there had to be some evidence left behind to give them a lead. Meanwhile they had one more couple to investigate, and Dad hired two more detectives to check them out.

Dad had brought a couple home one night after finding them stranded on the highway. They stayed in the bunkhouse for five days until their auto was repaired. They were very down-and-out, and he was hoping that his job as an engineer at the Fort Peck Dam construction site would work out and give them a new start. Duff and Laura Davis seemed to be decent, religious people who would never dream of stealing someone else's child. They helped around the ranch, with Duff and Dad becoming great friends. Duff was a giant of a man and helped Dad a great deal, such as repairing and changing the tires on our brand new International Harvester tractor's enormous back wheels. Dad constantly warned us to be very cautious when using that modern machine.

When Dad was a youngster, Grandpa MacDougal accidentally ran over him with a manure spreader. He spent the summer in bed with everyone thinking he would never walk again or father children. The back tire of the spreader had run over his middle, and they counted him lucky to be alive. He recovered, walked again, and by fathering as many children that he did, proved everyone wrong.

Both my mother and father came from the same little town in Ohio. Culloden had been settled shortly before the Revolutionary War after the English had brutally crushed the Scottish Highlanders in 1746. The

Highland Scots had revolted against the British, attempting to reinstate Bonnie Prince Charlie as king of Scotland and England.

After defeating them, the English stripped the Scots of all they could to demoralize them and make them suffer. They could no longer speak their own language, and the right to wear the traditional Highland plaid, representing each different clan, was taken away from them. Their traditional class structure of Scottish lairds and their clans was banned, as were their rights to assemble and to bear arms. The English robbed them of everything—gold, jewels, land, even their food. A flood of Scots emigrated to America at the same time thousands of Irish fled Ireland because of their country's potato famine.

Our father was Scottish, and our mother, Irish, third-generation offspring of these immigrants, and they both came from well-to-do families. Mom talked about how she knew, the minute she set eyes on Dad, that they would marry. James MacDougal, our grandfather, out of guilt and worry that Dad could not pursue an agricultural livelihood, sent him east to be educated. Our father could have been a lawyer, but chose farming instead. He returned home, courting and eventually marrying Mom while helping on his father's farm. They came west for a honeymoon, fell in love with the mountains, and decided to move here and ranch. Despite that Dad had proved he could do almost anything except lift very heavy objects, Grandfather sent him on his way with a large sum of money, just in case things didn't work out.

Mom and Dad started ranching and a family at the same time after moving here, just four miles from the small mining town of Philipsburg. They had their operation up and running by the time Aileen was born. They had built a new house and a bunkhouse while living in an old miner's cabin. This humble abode sat up above their new buildings in woods that fringed their entire ranch property.

I was proud of my parents. Mom, Nora Katherine Callaghan, fit her name because she was, indeed, a person of "honor and valor." She, like Craig and Colin, always delivered on everything she promised. Her strength and stoic acceptance of the many injustices and losses life laid on her amazed me.

Angus Colin MacDougal completely lived his life true to the meaning of his name: "a helper of his people who does so with wisdom and intelligence—a singularly strong man." He had been a kind, caring person before our tragedies, but now, he had become particularly compassionate to those in need. He never laid a hand on us children again in punishment, forever suffering guilt because of the harsh discipline he had meted out to Ian the evening before his death. He now found consolation in doing civic work, devoting his spare time and energy helping young boys left fatherless by men killed accidentally in the mines. He became many a young boy's hero and surrogate father.

Naturally, when he found the Davis couple in need, he helped them. But, Laura, like all the other women, fell in love with Gracie, and when they left us, she too, cried when parting from such a loving child. Mom and Dad decided to have them investigated, despite their obvious goodness and decency. Duff had told Dad that he doubted they would ever have children since Laura had suffered a miscarriage each time she became pregnant.

War

The Friday before school began, the Germans invaded Poland, and by Sunday, September 3, Britain, France, Australia, and New Zealand had declared war on Germany. World War II had begun. I knew our family life had nearly returned to normalcy since Dad began to lecture us with history and geography lessons concerning the war at the supper table. The memory of his beginning lecture about World War II is still as clear today as it was that night, and remarkably prophetic.

He explained that this new war began because of leftover issues from World War I. Germany, especially, had felt cheated after the peace conference. He told us about what they called the Polish Question, an international political issue that had plagued Europe for centuries.

The Polish Question had been a major topic at the Congress of Vienna in 1815 and at the Versailles Conference of 1919. Dad told us that Poland had been an independent state called the Polish-Lithuanian Commonwealth, which had been established in the second half of the 17th Century. After a time, Poland's more powerful neighbors, the Austrian Empire, the Kingdom of Prussia, and the Russian Empire, invaded their country and partitioned its territories with each of them taking a parcel of Polish land.

He shook his head. "From 1795 until 1918, no independent Polish state existed. The Poles staged several uprisings, but each time they were unsuccessful. World War I weakened their powerful neighbors and their power declined. The Austro-Hungarian Empire was divided into multiple new states based on ethnic lines. When President Woodrow Wilson presented his peace plan, the Fourteen Points, to the Versailles

Conference in 1919, he proposed that Poland should be declared an independent state because of its indisputably Polish population. He also insisted that Poland have access to the Baltic Sea."

Dad finished his lecture with a sad shake of his head. "Now, I suspect, Germany wants the Poles' corridor to the sea, as well as their land."

When we heard of the Pied Piper evacuation in England on a radio broadcast, I closed my eyes and envisioned columns of children following a pipe-playing, impish elf dressed in multi-colored clothing and boots with curled tips, leading millions of youngsters out of London and other British cities to the countryside. At first I found that image amusing. But then I realized that to keep their children safe from German bombing, British parents had to give them up to distant relatives or even strangers and remain separated from them for the duration of the war. I felt sad for them and guilty about my own, relatively happy, situation. Ian was dead, and Gracie missing, but we remaining MacDougals still had each other.

I had just read *Heidi*, a novel about a young German girl who had to go live with her estranged, grumpy grandfather in the mountains. Her Aunt Detie, who had become ill and had been taking care of her since her parents' deaths, was the only family she had known until then. It took some time before she could win over and become loved by that bitter, old man who had lost his faith in God. I thought of the millions of British children experiencing that same, unhappy experience while I was here in America, safe with my family. Then I thought of Gracie, who was now with strangers. I asked Mom if she thought Gracie missed us and was sad. She explained that Gracie most likely wasn't lonesome for us or sad because little children, babies especially, forget people easily and love those who are taking care of them. She wept after that, and I vowed never to ask such questions again.

The war in Europe continued to seem far away despite Dad's nightly discourse on the subject. My nine-year-old mind swam with vivid images of German and British bomber planes shooting at one another in the skies and at cities full of people, and their warships and U-boats doing the same at sea. Dad did not shy away from telling us that the

European children suffered just as much as their parents in this all-out German Blitzkrieg.

One night, I decided to ask Dad about some things that had puzzled me ever since he began talking about the war.

"Who are the Nazis? Are all Germans Nazis? And, if they are, why are they called that?"

Dad laughed. "Well, first, the name comes from what the German socialist party call themselves—Nationalsozialistische Deutsche Arbeitparte or NSDAP. But their enemies changed it to *Nazi* as an insult. *Nazi* comes from a term used for a backwards peasant who is considered awkward and clumsy. I find it extremely amusing that this vicious German political party has inadvertently accepted such a name."

Blair spoke up. "That name sounds like a word for bugs. Nasty pests."

Dad shook his head. "Wish that were true, but, no, they are people. Dangerous people with much power, with enough strength to think, I'm afraid, that they are capable of taking over all of Europe."

I raised my hand. "Is that why they have so many weapons? They must have been planning for a long time. Because to have those bomber planes—those Stukas that carry those heavy bombs, cannons, and machine guns—they must have known they would go to war sometime. Don't you think?"

We had been gathering in the parlor every night since the war had begun, listening intently to the news. We heard that the Germans called their war a Blitzkrieg, which in German means lightning war, and that they wanted to invade Poland and take that country as quickly as possible. We listened as they talked about the bomber planes, the Stukas, armed not only with deadly weapons but also with terror sirens, and how these German planes swept over the big cities in Poland, killing thousands of Polish citizens and intimidating the survivors with those awful sounds. The news people played them on the radio, frightening me even though I sat safe, nestled between Mom and Dad.

"Yes, and now the Germans, unfortunately, have come out with a new plane—the Messerschmitt, a fighter plane with two engines that can carry more weight in arms and fly longer distances than the Stukas.

That's why the British are preparing to defend themselves from heavy bombing and moving their precious children out of the large cities. The Brits are also working night and day to develop their own bomber planes with which to fight back. What they have now are not doing well against German war planes."

Dad released a heavy sigh. "Well, should we go listen to the latest?"

That night, we were sent to bed early after listening to the nightly broadcast. Dad had come home from town this afternoon, armed with fresh newspapers and the newest *Time* magazines, and I knew he would sit up late, immersing himself in information. Tomorrow's lecture should be interesting.

Cruel Kindness

....

Dad never delivered his lecture that next evening, but we did listen to the nightly news about the war because we didn't know what else to do after the day's startling events. We children arrived home from school and found Mom sitting at our little wooden kitchen table, staring off into space with blank eyes. When we spoke to her, she looked at us vacantly and handed me a picture from the mess of mail that lay before her. It was a picture of Gracie but of an older Gracie. I calculated the time in my head. Gracie had been gone nearly four months and had changed. She still had her striking auburn curls and big, blue eyes, but she had become more of a toddler than a baby.

"Oh, Mom. Oh, Mom. Oh, God." I couldn't find any other words to say to her, so I just hugged her, hard. She handed me a note that simply said in an unidentifiable scribble, "Gracie-okay."

I knelt before her and wrapped my arms around her waist. I nestled my face deep into the folds of her apron, inhaling her comforting scent of soap and perfume, and cried. She began to cry, too. Blair began to wail, and the twins just stood there snuffling, trying to be manly, rubbing at the traitorous tears that spilled from their eyes. Dad walked in just then, stood for a moment, and then warily went to Mom. I stood up to get out of his way.

"What's this?"

Callum handed the picture to Dad. He stood up and stared at it, drinking in the image of our missing Gracie. He shook his head and stooped to Mom, getting on his knees, embracing her.

"Oh, Nora, Nora. How incredibly cruel and yet kind."

He shook his head, silent for a time. "She looks like she's doing well. That's all we need to concentrate on. She's okay, and we will get her back. What's the postmark on the envelope?"

Callum looked through the pile of mail, found the envelope, and handed it to Dad.

"West Virginia. Some town in West Virginia." Dad read aloud in an almost whisper.

The reverence in his voice broke my heart. Realizing that he felt so emotional about some town in West Virginia just because Gracie was there, made me feel like crying again. But Mom had stood up, with lips tightly pursed and her shoulders showing that stiffness again, just like they were right after Ian's death. She picked up Gracie's picture, and rummaging through our catch-all drawer, found the tape, and attached the picture to the refrigerator door. Then she picked up the note and did the same with that. Every time we would go to the ice box, we would be able to see Gracie and know she was fine.

Mom turned to Dad. "Well, Angus, you had better contact your detectives."

Dad nodded. "Come on boys, let's get the chores done before it gets dark."

Mom stopped in the doorway going out to the porch. "Girls, I want you to start supper. I don't have any meat thawed, so we'll just have grilled cheese sandwiches. Oh, and heat up a couple tins of tomato soup. I'm going up the hill for a while. I want to be alone."

Blair and I worked silently as we followed Mom's instructions and then set the table. Blair couldn't stop crying. When I didn't think I could take it any longer, she stooped over, and clutching at her stomach, howled in pain. I stopped and just looked at her.

"Just cut that out. It's not gonna do any good to carry on like that. We need to just be happy that Gracie's doing fine. Now stop it! You're driving me nuts."

"No-o-o!" Blair screeched. "I'm not crying about Gracie. My stomach hurts bad! Bad. I don't know what's wrong. I gotta go to the bathroom."

When Blair came back into the kitchen, her face was the color of Ian's skin when he lay in his casket. Her eyes were wide with fright. "I must be dying. There's blood everywhere down there."

"I'll go get Mom."

As I ran up the hill, all I could think of was that Blair would be the third. Oh, my God, what kind of disease must she have? I prayed the same little plea all the way up the hill. "Please, God, don't let her be sick and die."

When I told Mom, she just laughed and acted like some apple-headed person.

"What? What, Mom?" I got up into her face, and sternly said, "Why are you laughing about this? Are you okay?"

Mom grabbed me and gave me a long and crushing hug, and then shook her head. "What a day! Your sister became a woman today, that's all, honey. Let's go down and put her mind at ease. And you might just as well hear it, too—after all, you are almost ten. You should know about these things. I feel bad that I haven't talked to Blair about this before. Come on, Abi, let's go take care of your sister."

I stumbled down the hill after Mom, bewildered and worried. What in the Sam heck was going on?

When Mom had her talk with us, she became completely serious. It was no longer a laughing matter when she explained what being a woman was truly about, and I felt betrayed, and angry. I understood that as a woman, you menstruated continuously until you were pregnant, and that was the only break a woman would get from the whole messy affair. Uck! I thought. Now, I really don't want to grow up.

After that night, I went around feeling disgusted with life. God, how awful it must be to have your period, or Grandma visiting, or have the curse all the time. When I thought about Mom telling us about these crazy terms used to name this bodily function, I became angry. I was a black cloud, trudging stormily through each day. Rosie, my teachers, and even the twins kept asking me *what is wrong*. When Mom confronted me, I went into a rage and told her everything I thought about what had happened to Blair, what would happen to me—and what happens to every living female, and then the bad things that had happened to our family.

She chastised me for my angry words such as *pissed off*, *God-damned*, *shitty crap*, and *being mad*. "And don't say *mad*, Abi. You're not a dog. Only dogs get mad."

I rolled my eyes at her "I'm angry. I'm angry about everything. Losing Ian, not having Gracie any more, about this woman stuff, and about you, Mom." After she finished rolling her eyes, I said, "Yes, Mom. I am angry that you don't take us to church any more. I know you're *mad*, angry at God, but if we don't go to church again soon, I'm afraid of what will happen. The *third* horrible thing will come about if we don't obey God, and if we don't honor him by going to church. You'll probably become like Heidi's grandfather, all bitter and estranged from God and people. I understand that it's hard to not be angry, but it doesn't help anything! I have been so miserable since Blair got her period. But now she says it stopped and I'm worried she's pregnant."

Mom looked at me in shock. "First, Abi, Blair is certainly not pregnant. Women and girls menstruate only five days out of each month. You thought you would be bleeding the rest of your adult life?" She came to me and gave me a hug. "Oh, my poor little Abi. I'm so sorry that you misunderstood and were worried about it. And about church, yes, we should go this Sunday. You know what day Sunday is, don't you?"

I shook my head. I hadn't been thinking clearly for days.

"Sunday is October 22—Ian's birthday."

"Oh."

"Let's go to church, because I know now that we both need it. You are a faithful little thing, aren't you? And, what is this *third* you keep talking about. I've even heard you yelling about it in the middle of the night."

"After Gracie was stolen, I heard people saying, 'You know everything comes in threes. Wonder what the third tragedy will be for the MacDougals'."

We went to church on Sunday, and I wept silently the entire time. The looks people gave us when we walked in made me sad but grateful.

My raw emotions made me shake as I tried to get a grip on them. I could feel the intense feeling of good will and sympathy surrounding my family. I felt like we were in the Ascension picture, where Jesus is rising into the heavens amidst swirling shafts of warm, golden light and misty clouds.

Outside, my mother repeatedly received hugs and invitations to coffee or lunch. "We have to get together. It's been so long."

Men walked up to Dad, shaking his hand, and speaking gruffly. "Glad to see ya, Gus."

I still feel that good will when I remember that day, being Ian's birthday and all, and how our family returned to the comforting arms of friends, neighbors, and our faith. I laugh at my thinking then, about the *third* happening if we didn't turn back to God and keep the Sabbath. Yes, and I still suffer from my Catholic guilt, and whether it's a good thing or not, it has kept me in line and made me a better person.

On Wednesday, October 25, we joyfully celebrated Cameron's and Callum's birthday, and three months later, on Christmas morning, Mom and Dad announced that there would be another baby in the family.

1940

Small Blessings

After months of investigating, Dad's private eyes came back with no leads as to where David and Adeline Breckenridge could have gone. They had also combed through every city, town, and tiny burg in West Virginia, armed with pamphlets and posters featuring the new photo that Gracie's abductors had sent us, but they found nothing. The two men assigned to check out the Duffs at Fort Peck came back saying that they had found them living in a tiny shack which had been so poorly built that the wind virtually howled through it. A young child could never have survived such lodgings.

The Duffs planned to move into a better place come spring, when several engineers would leave since they had completed their part in constructing the dam. Housing was always short at the Fort Peck dam site, and what was there had been built hurriedly. Most homes were meant to be temporary; people had come to build a dam, not homes. They had come from all over the nation, looking forward to having steady work, not anticipating the delays in completing the project or the hard, cold, windy winters nature would deal them. Then it was the opposite in summer, when temperatures would soar into the one-hundred-degree range accompanied by a harsh, hot wind. Fort Peck had become the newest boom town in Montana, and just like in the past, when mining camps had sprung up to accommodate a new and disparate population, it was a rough and tumble town—not a place to raise a child.

That winter, when I saw Bear for the last time, I sensed it was our final meeting for the season. It was nearly the middle of December, and it seemed as if he had put off his hibernation for me. Bear *m-m-r-r . . . ed* more than ever before he left. He seemed so human, and thinking of the Velveteen Rabbit story, where a stuffed bunny becomes a real live rabbit because he had been loved so much, I asked him before he left, "If I were a fairy and I kissed you, would you become human? Perhaps Ian?" Bear leaned over when I finished talking and nuzzled me with his nose, bringing tears to my eyes. I nuzzled him back. "I love you, Bear." After he licked each salty path running down my cheeks, he turned and left. I felt guilty watching him go because he had gotten so fat and round on my peanut butter and honey sandwiches.

With Bear gone, and the fall projects finished—the sorting and then the weaning of our calves, pregnancy testing the cows, and finally, shipping the calves to market—I had time to read. My books became my saving grace because their stories took my mind off Mom's up-and-down moods; Mom, being pregnant, had become extremely emotional. Every day without any news about Gracie took its toll.

I talked her into reading some of my books. She liked *Little Women* and *National Velvet,* and we would talk about them while baking bread and other goodies. I felt such guilt about feeding Bear bread, I decided I should, at least, learn how to make it. When the baby first began kicking, Mom let me feel it, and we laughed and then cried. I had decided never to have children, but now I realized that if I didn't, I would miss out on a whole lot of wondrous experiences like this one.

In December Mom and Dad took Blair and me to Butte to Christmas shop. Craig came out from Missoula to supervise Colin and the twins and help with the chores. Mom and Dad took us to see the movies *Heidi* and *Little Women.* I felt disappointed in the first movie. Shirley Temple's whiny voice and her performance seemed unreal to me. But I loved the actresses in *Little Women*—Katherine Hepburn as Jo and Joan Bennett as Amy, Jean Parker as the tragic character Beth, and Frances Dee as Meg. I fell in love with Douglass Montgomery who played Laurie. For months, I would lie awake, waiting for sleep, fantasizing about Laurie, and I could never decide if I would rather have been Jo or Amy.

I received new novels in December because of Christmas and my birthday. I was born on the thirty-first of December, just one day before Gracie's birthday on the first of January. I appreciated my new books since I had read the newest ones in the school library and the bookmobile. I loved the bookmobile because it had books that were not just for school-aged people. Once in a while I would luck out and find an interesting novel with some sex in it. I had become especially interested in that subject after Blair had "become a woman." I thought if we females must go through suffering and bleeding because of our sex, there must be something good about it, too. I had seen animals on the ranch breeding, and to me, it had looked like they were fighting. But I had also seen my parents' lovesick looks at one another, their love for each other in general, and I had heard their sounds during the night.

One day, Mom dropped me off at Aileen's so I could help with her new baby, and I questioned her about things that puzzled me, hoping she could enlighten me about being grown-up, married, and having babies. I knew her life had greatly changed when she brought my first niece into the world on November 19, just before Thanksgiving.

She, like Gracie, had auburn hair, but it was straight-as-a-stick like mine, and they named her Ianna Grace. While her name was certainly unique, I knew that people who didn't know our family and its history would want to say *I*-anna, instead of *E*-anna, and that bothered me. But then, each time one of us or Ianna would correct people about the pronunciation of her name, it would remind us and her of Ian. That way, he would never be forgotten, and that comforted me.

"Did you and Kendall have a romantic courtship? Was he a romantic person? Is he still?"

Aileen smiled. "Well, yes to the first two questions, but now that we're married and have a baby, everything has changed. I still find him romantic, not for his offerings of flowers and trinkets, or for taking me to the movies or for drives, but for the things he does to help me with Ianna. When I first came home from the Baby Factory, he not only surprised me with a new washing machine, but he also did the laundry until I was strong enough to safely use that wonderful, new-fangled but dangerous thing, and that was romantic to me."

The Baby Factory's actual name was the Maternity Home, but the people of Philipsburg had nicknamed it since birthing babies and all that was involved, including pregnancy, was never openly discussed. Before Aileen told me the facts about those events, it looked like a mysterious place where women went in fat and sassy and came out skinnier and with a baby. The nurses would wrap their middles as tightly as possible with long, soft cloths, which the new mothers would wear the entire time at the Baby Factory so they could get their waistlines back; Aileen said that when they were in there, they were pampered and treated like fragile invalids.

"What else does Kendall do that makes you happy?"

"Kendall takes Ianna when I finish nursing her and sends me to bed for a nap while he burps her and puts her down to sleep. Then he'll do whatever chores I haven't gotten to yet, such as wash the dishes, sweep the floor, and tidy up the house; he will even cook our next meal if I sleep long enough. And then when he comes to wake me up, the way he does it, well, now that's romantic."

Sex Education

B ecause Aileen's face glowed with rapture, and her eyes had become dreamy, I couldn't help but ask, "Does he wake you up with sex?"

Aileen looked at me, startled. Her eyes became serious, narrowing while she made the decision to tell me more or not. Then she took a deep breath. "First, Abi, don't just call it, or think of it as sex, not for people like Kendall and me. I prefer using the term *making love.* That sounds better."

I nodded. "So, he wakes you up with sex, I mean, making love?"

Aileen blushed. "Yes, if we have time before Ianna wakes up."

"Does it. . . does it feel nice?"

Aileen's cheeks reddened. "Yes, more than nice. Now Abi, don't you say a word of what I've told you to anyone, not your friends, Blair, and especially not Mom. She would wring my neck."

"Oh! I promise I won't. But Rosie told me that her cousin said that it hurts and that you bleed."

"Only the first time, Abi."

"Why do you bleed the first time?"

Aileen rolled her eyes, and I sensed that she thought this talk had gone too far.

"Please, Aileen. I've just got to know. Please?"

"Okay, I'll tell you, and that's it! All girls are born with a little barrier down there—a little piece of skin that must be torn through the first time. It bleeds just a little, and hardly hurts." Aileen gave me a final, stern look and said, "That's all for now, Abi.

Senseless Worries

While my new books had some romance in them, they were basically benign regarding sex. But I became worried about other issues, and fretted fearfully about what the future might have in store for me. Because Polly almost loses her eyesight in *Five Little Peppers* from the measles, and Mary Ingalls, in *Little House on the Prairie,* does lose hers, I worried about becoming blind. Oh, God! I wouldn't be able read any longer, or write, or see the beautiful people in films. I wouldn't be able to see the wondrous change of seasons, or watch our babies develop into little people. The most terrible thing would be not being able to see the changes in Gracie as her stealers (that's how I thought of them) sent new pictures of her.

I worried that I might be kidnapped after reading about the organ grinder taking Phronsie in *Five Little Peppers,* and the gypsies, in Kate Seredy's novel, *The Good Master,* stealing Kate. After reading *The Singing Tree,* Seredy's second book about Jancsi and his family, I worried that if my brothers fought in the war they would come home changed and bitter like Jancsi's father, who had been a kind, wise, and happy man before he fought in World War I.

Mom and Dad had also given me *The Bobbsey Twins* series, which I only read when I had nothing else since those stories did not seem true-to-life. Their lives often seemed too wonderful. But after reading *Caddie Woodlawn,* I vowed to become adventuresome and daring like her. In remembrance of Ian, I was even more determined to finish training Jewel and many more colts after reading about Caddie, who was a tomboy like me.

Prejudice and A Troublesome Brother

The Germans continued their deadly stomp through Europe. There were several families in town of Germanic descent, and I felt bad for them because some of the children at school tormented them simply because they were German. I had never seen prejudice first-hand before. I had heard about that sort of thing—about people wrongly judging and treating others badly only because of their skin color. We didn't have many Native Americans around Philipsburg, but whenever we ventured away from Granite County, especially when driving to eastern Montana, we saw numerous native people from different tribes. I thought it was awful that they could not go to restrooms, bars, or restaurants and because of the color of their skin. During my growing-up years, there were signs everywhere in Montana blatantly saying, *NO INDIANS ALLOWED.*

One day I saw Cameron teasing one of the German boys in the school yard. He was shoving him around and calling him names. "You're nothing but a Kraut—a nasty little Nazi. Go back to Germany where you belong. You and your entire, rotten family."

Cameron was nothing but a bully. When I observed him push other kids around at school, taking advantage of his much larger size and strength to intimidate and harass others, I found myself grinding my teeth and clenching my fists. The truth is, I nearly always found

Cameron loathsome. I wasn't only angry and disgusted with him, but also with myself because I, like Callum, let him push me around and dominate me at home because I was afraid of him.

After Ian was gone, Callum and I did the bulk of the work when Dad assigned us to various projects. One day, Dad sent the three of us up into the government grazing lands to walk the fence line and fix whatever had become loose or untidy. Barbed wire isn't very efficient if there is a floppy strand or a fence post coming loose. Those clever, inquisitive beasts always find those weak spots. Even now, as a grownup, I can imagine our cattle walking the fence, looking for a break.

And who is responsible for these compromised stretches of fencing in the first place? Other bovines that came before. It's as if there's a constant conspiracy among these animals to slowly break fences down. I knew, deep down, that they only wanted to scratch an irritating itch, rubbing their behinds and backs however and wherever they can to give them relief. But I still resented them for making so much never-ending work.

When we went fencing, Cameron would boss Callum and me, not lifting a finger until it was obvious the two of us didn't have the strength to stretch the wire tight enough. Then Cameron would step in with his brawniness and help. But it was Callum and me who did all the grunt work. The only time Cameron would pick up a shovel or pitchfork when we mucked out the barns was when he saw Dad coming to check on us.

Soon after I had seen Cameron tormenting that little German boy, we three were sent out to clean up some grass hay that had loosened from the stacks, load it onto a wagon, haul it into the barnyard, and restack it there. Then we were to go out to the straw pile and haul in a wagonload of bales to be stacked near the barn so they were handy for bedding down stalls during calving. While doing chores with my twin brothers, I often worked silently, my head down, avoiding any interaction with Cameron.

That day, I kept busy picking up pitchforks full of hay and tossing them onto the wagon without paying any attention to the twins. Suddenly, I heard a terrible howling. I knew it to be human, but it sounded like an animal screaming just after it had stepped into a trap.

The pain in those shrieks gave me goose bumps. Cameron had thrust his pitchfork into Callum's thigh. I watched in horror as Cameron pulled it out and then heaved it down again; this time two tines went through Callum's left foot, pinning him to the partially frozen ground.

Cameron then stepped back, admiring his evil work, and stood laughing. I ran to them and gave Cameron the biggest shove possible, and he went flying, landing on his sorry ass. While he lay there stunned, I turned to Callum and pulled the fork out of his foot. Callum fell backwards. By then, Cameron was up and coming at me. When he reached me, he slugged me in the belly as hard as he could with his fist.

I lay gasping for air, doubled up in pain. Dad came running. He must have seen Cameron's attack because as I struggled to breathe and escape the agony, I heard a guttural grunt of pain. Dad had slugged Cameron with the same violent punch he had dealt me.

"Don't you ever belly-punch your sister again! If I ever see such a thing, I will take my belt off and use it on you until you won't want to sit for a week! What in the hell are you thinking, stabbing your brother like that with a pitchfork? Are you crazy? What ails you, son?"

"But Dad, I asked him a question, and he wouldn't answer me! The little bastard's always ignoring me!"

"You call that good reason to do such a heinous thing—to your own flesh-and-blood. Your twin?! To anyone? And don't ever let me hear you call someone a bastard again. Do you hear me?"

Dad picked up Callum, cradling him in his arms, and turned to Cameron. "You finish this project alone, while I take your brother to the doctor. And for the greater part of this winter, until calving season, you will be outside doing everything alone. And when you are in the house, you are to be banished to your bedroom for two weeks. I will assign you passages from the Bible to read that will, hopefully, teach you lessons in what it takes to be a decent human being. What you have done to your brother and sister today is very damaging to them, not only physically, but also spiritually. Why you act so hatefully, I will never know. But it must stop. Understand?"

Dad had given Cameron some of his own medicine, which was tonic to my tortured soul. Cameron had been mean before, but never this violent and hateful. Maybe he would change after this, and I wouldn't have to feel so much guilt for carrying this heavy load of revulsion for someone I should love.

While Mom and Dad prepared for their trip into the hospital, warming up our car and giving Callum and me each an aspirin tablet, I thought of how vulnerable I would be, and I begged to go along. Blair was spending the night with friends, and I would be alone in the house. I had seen the spiteful look in Cameron's eyes as I struggled to my feet, still doubled over in pain. He didn't even blink at that, just stood and gave me menacing looks. When it came time to go, I gladly crawled into the front seat of the car alongside Dad. Mom sat in the back with Callum, talking softly to him, seeking to soothe his pain.

I felt bad for Callum when he was forced to bear more discomfort while having his wounds disinfected and then given a painful injection of tetanus vaccine. But he took it like a man, with never as much as a whimper coming from his clenched lips. His hospital experience probably was nothing in comparison to the pitchfork going into his tender flesh twice, and then being pulled out again. The best thing about the incident was that after it happened, a great divide emerged between the twins. Callum's independence from his domineering twin allowed him to know himself better, and I especially liked that we became good friends—not like Ian and I had been, but we became close.

In the evenings while Cameron did the chores, Callum and I would sit in the parlor, doing our homework and discussing the books I had talked him into reading. He became almost as ardent a reader as I was, and was even more fun to be with. Because Cameron had become so bitterly bent against us, shooting us hateful looks, we talked Dad into taking us into town once a week for a strength-building class. There, in the gym, Callum observed older boys, football players, working out with weights, and while we waited for Dad to come take us home, we both began using them.

Nazis

W hen Dad talked of the war and we listened to the news, I came
to see Germans as a pack of bullies made up of a bunch of
Cameron-type individuals. I felt the same aversion for them as I did
my brother. Last September, the Germans had taken the western half
of Poland and the Union of Soviet Socialist Republic had taken the
eastern half, and since then, the USSR had begun the Russo-Finnish
War, invading Finland at the end of November. By the time calving
had begun in March, the USSR had become almost as aggressive as
Germany. Dad told us that their leader, Joseph Stalin, had made plans
to turn Finland into a Communist state, and that Hitler was forced
to allow this since he could not wage war in both western and eastern
Europe. Hitler detested Socialists but would have to suffer Stalin's
aggression and deal with it later.

As we listened to the war broadcasts each evening, we realized—even
a young girl like me—how frightening and threatening the Nazis were
as they moved from country to country, invading them and taking them
over. It truly was a "lightning war." In April, Denmark surrendered to
Germany, and in May, the Nazis had attacked France. By the fifteenth
of May, German armies had invaded and taken the Netherlands, who
surrendered to them by May 28. The Germans entered Paris June 18,
and France surrendered June 22. Italy had joined the Germans that
month, declaring war on Britain and France. And by July, the Battle
of Britain had begun, with the entire non-Nazi world cheering on the
Brits.

The Germans had invaded Norway April 9, and by the end of May had secured their victory there. The Nazi leaders, who advocated taking Norway, wanted to do so to ensure several things: They wanted to out-flank the British at sea, challenging their control of the seas. Secondly, if Germany controlled Norway, the Royal British Navy would need to patrol the immense Norwegian coastline which contained many ports and fjords, perfect for basing German U-boats and hiding German Kriegsmarine warships. Also, the Germans would have a much shorter route to Atlantic shipping lanes. Finally, the Germans knew that the port at Narvik, Norway was free of ice in winter, guaranteeing them access to the high-quality iron ore coming from Sweden, which they desperately needed for their war machine.

Dad explained this to us one night after reading the newest *Time* magazine. The next evening, he told us of the concentration camps he had read about. Recently, Germany had begun deporting people to work camps, starting with Polish Jews. Nazis had built their first labor camp at Dachau, Germany in 1933 to hold political opponents and criminals, referring to these incarcerations as "protective custody." Now they began hunting Jews and gypsies, placing them in the camps as well.

Dad shook his head. "The idea behind these work camps is to force the prisoners to work themselves to death. Between working over twelve hours a day, corporal punishment, poor diets and clothing, their plan works efficiently, for the most part. Many people die, and they kill those that become too weak to work, or are too sick and old, using lethal injections, gas, or a bullet to the head."

We had listened to stories on the radio of people being forced to dig their own graves, and of the deprivation and starvation in those camps, as well as in the ghettos where people had been herded to await their fate. Jews in the Netherlands were made to wear yellow arm bands to identify them once Germany fully controlled their country. As we listened in horror to these stories and to Dad's lectures, we also knew that the United States still held to their Neutrality Act, despite the constant and sometimes deadly German attacks on our merchant ships hauling goods to Britain. But with these atrocities occurring in Nazi-conquered countries, we knew, too, that many Americans wanted to go to war against Germany, if only for decency's sake, believing it was the moral and honorable thing to do.

All these stories terrified me, and one night I had an awful nightmare. I was in one of those camps, all alone. The rest of my family had already disappeared, and I feared they were all dead. The female camp guards had me peeling potatoes (my most hated kitchen chore) all day long until my hands wouldn't work any longer. They were stiff and sore, with little cuts all over them. I was horribly cold, and my teeth chattered. The awful woman in charge saw that I was no longer doing my assigned task and slapped my face hard, several times, and then she walked out of the kitchen to report my insolence.

The week before, they had taken me to this room, examined me, and pulled three gold-filled teeth from my mouth. The pain was excruciating, and my gums were still swollen. My cheeks stung, and my mouth ached. Soon the woman came back with two men, who each grabbed an arm and drug me from the room as I screamed and screamed. . .

I woke up, terrified, with Mom hugging me while Dad stood in the doorway, looking worried. His eyebrows were so knit together that he looked like he had a moustache hanging over his eyes. I had been clenching my teeth, so my mouth ached. My hands had fallen asleep, so they tingled and burned, and I had kicked my covers off, so I was freezing cold. Later that night, I heard Mom telling Dad, "Perhaps you should stop being so graphic with your stories of war."

"No. They need to know, Nora. War is terrible, and it's necessary that they know that. Everyone should be terrified of war—then maybe it wouldn't happen."

Months before, the British had begun rationing gasoline, while the Germans rationed their bread and flour. Mom and Dad began a program of stockpiling things they knew would be rationed should the United States join the war. We saved everything—old rubber tires, tins from canned goods, our old work clothes—which we boxed up and put in the attic, and Mom laid in a huge store of foods that she thought could become scarce. We had bags and bags of sugar and flour. Despite our beehives on the ranch, Mom wanted that sugar. We purchased boxes and boxes of ball jars and lids, waiting to be filled with bounty from our garden, boxes of pectin for making jam, rubber boots for working the ranch, rubber rain gear, vaccines for the cattle and horses, medicines, such as our always-go-to aspirin tablets, bandages, and numerous other items.

Mom and Dad took us to Butte to lay in supplies of clothing, some much too big for us, but things that would eventually work for someone in the family. We all chose boots and shoes that we could grow into later. Dad bought supplies of oil, nuts and bolts, everything he could think of for maintaining our new farming equipment, such as our tractor and baler, and for our car and ranch truck. He butchered one of our old work horses, and Mom canned the meat for stews and such. He bought a young, strong work horse, and made sure that the wagons we had formerly used to haul things and feed the cattle with were in good working order. If need be, we would use horses and wagons again to save on gasoline.

America joining the war seemed inevitable, and with that hanging over us like a black, threatening thundercloud, we became jittery, despite our parents' plan to take care of us.

A True Blessing

....

When we woke up the morning of July 19, and found Mom in the parlor nursing our new baby brother, we forgot about war. During the early morning hours, Matthew Rory MacDougal decided to join us in this earthly realm. Dad said he came fast and easy, in a hurry to be born. He would be that way all his life—rushing through each day wanting things done yesterday.

Mom named him Matthew, which means "a gift from our Lord—a true blessing," and gave him the middle name Rory for his brilliant red hair. It wasn't auburn like Gracie's—it was as red as the Indian paint flowers that would grace the mountainsides come autumn, and his wisps of hair stuck up like the red comb on our recently purchased rooster, who was also a new addition, along with two dozen laying hens that pecked me as I took eggs from their nests.

Hurricanes and Spitfires

By August, the Brits were fighting the Germans in the air. They had improved their fighter planes to the point that they eventually made the Nazi attack on Britain an impossible task. The British didn't have many planes, but what they had recently developed were indomitable. They named their redesigned fighter planes Hurricanes and Spitfires.

One night we listened to Churchill's speech about the few fighter pilots protecting Britain with these new planes. His words made chills go up and down my spine, giving me visions of courageous young men climbing into their planes, waving farewell, with crowds of people cheering them on. I imagined them returning to adoring crowds, victorious, after eliminating dozens of German Messerschmitts. "Never in the field of human conflict was so much owed by so many to so few."

Italy, now on the side of the Germans, invaded British Somaliland, starting the war in Africa. By September 13, the Italians had the nerve to invade Egypt. In September, Germany, Italy, and Japan joined together, signing the Tripartite Pact, binding their Axis alliance.

Despite our family's pleasure in having a new baby, the war was difficult to ignore. In October, the German army had invaded Romania, but by October 31, finally, the Battle of Britain had ended with the Brits fending off German air attacks to the point that the Nazis finally gave up. The night we heard that broadcast, Mom and Dad gave each of us just a sip of wine, while they toasted the British and their stubborn resistance with full glasses. Things were looking up. But by the end of November, Hungary and Romania, two countries previously conquered by the Germans, signed into the Tripartite Pact, bringing them totally under the control of Nazi aggression. But on December 11, we took heart as the British took back the Egyptian cities of Sidi Barroni and Sollum. Perhaps we Americans wouldn't have to join the war effort after all.

We enjoyed our two newest family members, little Ianna Grace and Rory. They each were, in their own way, a wonderful balm for our sore hearts. Concerning our baby brother, the name Matthew would not stick to him like the obvious label, Rory. While being a very amiable soul, he had a fiery temper fed by his extremely persistent nature—all seeming to match his bright red hair. He truly became our little "Red King" as his Gaelic name suggested. He out-did his older niece, who was his senior by eight months, with his feistiness. We enjoyed seeing them staring at one another, and, as they later developed mobility, their engaging escapades. While Ianna was an only child, and coddled, we older siblings challenged Rory constantly.

Can you do this, we would say, as we coaxed him into further accomplishments. He watched us with the same intensity with which we observed him. By Christmas, he could sit up by himself, and began to reach for things. When he couldn't immediately attain his object, he would continue to go for it for a long time before he finally gave up in outrage. We never forgot Gracie, of course, but Rory helped fill that empty spot she had left, while we knew we were missing her, by-now, toddling attempts at becoming an independent human being. We weren't there to see her first steps. We would not be the ones to teach her how to use a spoon, or to introduce her to the wonder of baby kittens. We would miss another birthday soon. Sometimes it was just too much for me to think about, so I didn't.

After Rory's birth, Mom did much better. She did not fall apart when we received our second Christmas photo of Gracie. She appeared happy as she looked up into Santa's face—seemingly fearless—and she was so beautiful with cheeks glowing and a smile showing her dimples. As a little girl approaching her second birthday, she appeared well-cared for, and that night as we gathered around the supper table, we gave thanks that whoever had her, loved her and did their best in caring for her.

Bear and Another Year Older

E arly in summer, Bear had come back to me. He looked thin, and I worried about him. I began taking him even more sandwiches than the year before. Then one day he came with two cubs. He was a she! I was cautious, at first, knowing how protective and fierce a mother bear could be. But she just came up to me, gave me her usual *m-m-r-r* . . . greeting, and feasted on her sandwiches, handing one to each of her cubs.

I still called her Ian—she would always be my Ian. And then I wondered, if we died and were reborn (I had just read about reincarnation), would we come back in our same sex, our same body— would we be human again, or possibly animal? I was intrigued but happy to be reunited with my bear, and I enjoyed her and her fast-growing cubs all summer and fall.

I loved her, and felt that she loved me. I became the best bread-baker in Granite County, next to my Mom, and my pilfering food for my bears was never discovered. I took them salt blocks, and the broken, used-up honeycombs from the hives, and scraps from our meals, but I never fed them any meat. That fall, as we said goodbye for another season, I cried. Bear just licked my face free of salt, and left with a *m-m-r-r* . . . Her cubs had accepted me as their friend, and I knew I would miss the three of them greatly.

I told Bear that Dad had finished training Jewel, and that I knew I would be big and strong enough to start training colts next spring. She just nodded her head, and then gave me a small tap on my back, as if to say, *Yes, just do it, Abi. Just do it.* She was still my Spirit Bear, giving me solace and the confidence to do the best I could in every situation. I wondered how long could I love and enjoy her now that she had babies.

On December 31, I became an eleven-year-old girl, but I felt much older. I knew this worrisome mind of mine had done that to me, and I determined to have more fun in 1941. I would make my dream of becoming a great horse woman, training horses, and perhaps even breeding them, come true. It could probably be profitable to train and sell horses if we entered the war. But then, it would be difficult to sell a horse since we hardly ever did that. Old age and maternity leaves were usually the only reasons we didn't use a horse. Dad almost never sold an older horse because they were perfect for beginning riders, and so far, there always seemed to be one of those. As I drifted off to sleep, I closed my eyes and imagined Rory and Ianna up on our old mares, excited and feeling big to have such an experience. I thanked God for them, and prayed that Gracie was happy, like she seemed in her pictures.

1941

Conflict Spreads

The new year started with the war escalating at an alarming rate, not only in Europe but also in Africa and the Middle East. The Germans continued to move quickly and decisively, and now had allies with which to wreak even more havoc. There were thousands of casualties due to bombing. World War I, the war that was to end all wars, had not satisfied the urges of nationalism and had only sown the seeds for yet another world conflict. Even as far away as we were, it had reached out with its greedy grip and affected our lives. It was all everyone talked about, and now, because of the tales of atrocities happening in the German work camps, Americans argued.

They wrangled with one another over whether we should join the Allied countries in the shooting war. Most people did not want to enter the war, hoping that, somehow, the Germans would eventually be worn down and overcome. And now there were reports that the Soviets would fare no better than the rest of the world. Rumor insisted that Germany appeared to be planning to invade its former ally, a friend with whom they had partitioned between them the lands of Poland, Lithuania, Romania, Finland, Estonia, and Latvia. People against entering the war contended that when fighting broke out between the Soviets and Germans, the Nazis would become vulnerable enough to be stopped because they would be fighting a two-front war in Europe. Those who didn't want to fight the Germans still considered it because of the horrific accounts of Nazi treatment of Jewish people and others. Many did not believe these stories; they were too brutal and inhuman.

But we MacDougals knew of the heartless and inhuman acts that people can commit against others; we were still struggling to survive one of the worst of them. Our hearts still ached for Gracie, and despite the pictures periodically sent, we still worried about her. Our men would investigate huge parts of the surrounding area where the last envelope had been postmarked, but had no luck.

Gone with the Wind

Our family, day by day and event by event, went on with our lives. On February 14, my parents traveled to Butte to celebrate their wedding anniversary with a dinner and a movie. They went to see *Gone with the Wind* with Vivian Leigh as Scarlett and Clark Gable who played Rhett Butler. Mom and Dad jokingly role-played their characters for days after. We younger MacDougals just rolled our eyes. Dad carried Mom into their bedroom one night with much giggling. They assumed we children were all in bed, but I had been sitting in the parlor in the dark, thinking about how to approach Dad with my horse-training plans. Their sexual tension had been so thick that I did not want to hear or see anything that might be happening in their bed. I stayed there for a while before I went up to bed.

The next morning when I announced the next book I wanted to read was *Gone with the Wind* by Margaret Mitchell, Mom gave me a look. "You will not be reading that book until you are at least fifteen, Abi. Understood?"

"Why in the Sam heck can't I?"

"It has too much sexual innuendos for an eleven-year-old girl." I rolled my eyes and stood to gather up the dirty breakfast dishes.

Dad was in a good mood that morning. After helping Blair with the dishes, I brought him a fresh mug of coffee and sat down across from him and cleared my suddenly-gone-dry throat.

"Dad? May I talk to you about something?"

He looked up from his *Time*, dated December 25, 1939; its cover was graced with a gorgeous picture of Vivien Leigh.

"Well, sure. What's up, Abi?"

I took a deep breath. "Come spring, I want to start training Babe and Lucy. I've watched Ian enough to know I can do it. And they are such sweet fillies; I know it will be easy. I already have them eating out of my hand. Since Christmas, I have been going out on the warmer afternoons, catching them, putting them in the horse barn, just like Ian did, and feeding them treats while brushing them. I leave them standing in their stalls so they get used to the barn. That's a good start, right?"

Dad laughed, and I could see he was proud of me. "Well, I'll be damned. You want to take up Ian's job? Good for you. But you must promise me that when it comes to the tough stuff—getting them accustomed to the saddle and getting on them for the first time—you'll do it in my presence."

I leapt up and ran to him, stooping to kiss his cheek.

"Yes! Yes! Thanks, Dad, for letting me try, and for your confidence." I began walking away, and then, I couldn't help it. I stopped, turned, and laughingly teased, "So you didn't get enough of Scarlett the other night, huh?"

He blushed a bit. "Well, she is a spunky character—reminds me of you and your mother."

"Really?"

The next school day, I noticed the novel on my English teacher's desk. After class I stayed behind and asked her if she liked the book.

"Oh, yes. It's difficult to put down. I keep hoping the protagonist, Scarlett, will finally end up with the man who really loves her. It's frustrating, though, because she's so silly and stupid. She thinks she loves another man who is married. But the novel is so much more than a love story. It's about the Civil War and its aftermath and how it affected the South. Would you like to read it when I'm finished?"

My eyes widened. "Why, yes. I would love to read it, and then we can talk more about it. Have you seen the movie? My parents went to a showing and they loved it. But they said the movie is quite long."

She shook her head. "It will most likely be years until I see it. But I did hear the other day that someone is thinking about opening a movie theater here in Philipsburg, and that would be nice. It's difficult for a single woman like me to drive to Butte or even Anaconda to see a movie. Oh, and did you hear? We may be getting a drive-in restaurant soon—just like in the bigger towns and cities. You just drive up, stay in your car, order from a waitress, and they bring the food right to your car. You don't even need to get out and go in to eat. Funny how much automobiles have changed our lives." I left her shaking her head over the amazing auto and its revolutionary effect on life.

Later that afternoon, while doing chores and playing with my new projects, Babe and Lucy, I thought of the way my sister Blair had changed, almost overnight, into a fetching young woman. Mom had said that she could start wearing a little makeup and lipstick when she turned fifteen in March. I had witnessed her in the bathroom at school with the other girls putting on cosmetics and lipstick. When she was made up, she reminded me of Vivien Leigh's photo on the cover of *Time*.

I also watched as she played the boys. They could not ignore her looks and considered her a "babe." She would tease and flirt with them shamelessly, stringing along several of them at a time. She had signed up for pep club, which meant she could stay after school, and we all believed that was the case. But one afternoon when I went to Aileen's house and she sent me down to the drugstore, I watched in amazement as Billy Gustafson drove by in his brand-new, fancy, bright blue Pontiac with Blair in his passenger seat. Later, when my teacher loaned me her copy of *Gone with the Wind*, I made a bargain with Blair.

I knew she sneaked out at night to meet Billy at the end of our drive and rode around with him for hours. Sometimes she would come home smelling of alcohol. After begging her to not drink anymore, because it would lead to trouble—our parents' constant warning—I told her I wouldn't tell on her if she wouldn't tell Mom I was reading *Gone with the Wind*. We made the deal with sticky, spit-covered hands.

After that, Blair and I would sit, antsy, waiting for the nightly radio broadcast to end. We would give Dad his good-night kiss, rush up to our room, put our pajamas on, and wait for Mom's nightly tucking-in. After she left, I would put a rolled blanket next to our door to keep the light from giving me away and re-tuck myself into bed for a long night's read. Blair would dress, make up her face, do her hair, and crawl down the ladder attached to the house just below our window, which Dad had installed there in case of fire. When she came back later, I would reluctantly close my book, hide it, turn out the light, and settle into bed, my head spinning with the vivid images from Margaret Mitchell's novel.

Blair turned fifteen that month, and when she came downstairs for school the next day, Mom took one look at her and gasped.

"Go to the bathroom and scrub your face. You look like a hussy! I'll come in after a minute and show you how to apply your cosmetics and lipstick so you look like a proper young lady."

When they emerged, Blair looked gorgeous in a sweet, but attractive way. I hadn't realized that too much make-up could take away beauty. I made a note to myself about that. I couldn't wait to be fifteen, after seeing how lovely Blair had become.

Her hair was black, like Mom's, and her eyes a luscious green that would turn golden when she was mellow, which wasn't that often. It was as though she had an aura about her full of invisible, mischievous fairies constantly flitting around her. When we were small children and rode in the car, or were gathered in the parlor, Blair would always do something to make a disturbance. When we were much younger, she would pinch the nearest person—usually Cameron, since he was always the closest. They were drawn to one another, and yet mixed like oil and water, fighting constantly over nothing. If no one was nearby to pester, she would hum or sing loudly until Dad would tell her to "Cut that out!" Blair would become quiet but her eyes would still snap with energy.

I, on the other hand, was much less striking. My eyes were a soft, honey brown like Ian's had been, and my golden hair was streaked with blond because I was in the sun so much. I wore it long and straight—I had so much of it that I found it difficult to manage in any style. Often, I wore it in a thick braid that hung down my back and swung back and forth as I moved. Also, I was the quiet one of the family and mostly, I liked to keep my thoughts to myself, except when Dad gave his nightly supper-time lectures. After the older boys moved out, I was the only one, besides Mom, to question Dad. Mom commented once, "Abi, I wish I knew what was going on in that head of yours; you are so quiet compared to the rest. You never chatter like Blair, or tease around like the twins. Especially ever since . . ."

My chest tightened as Mom struggled to rein in her emotions. I went to her and hugged her. "Yes, ever since Ian died, I *have* become really quiet. We talked so much that I sometimes feel like I have forgotten how to carry on a cozy conversation." I smiled, thinking of all the one-sided talks I had with Bear and Ian in his grave. "I'll try to do better, Mom. I promise. Blair and I have nothing in common, so she's hard to talk to. And now, with the twins becoming older, we seem at odds. It's just not the same as when we were little."

Mom nodded, looking like she was swallowing the lump in her throat. She wiped her eyes with a careless swipe of the back of her hand and went back to kneading her bread dough.

Blair and I were completely different creatures. She was small and petite and loved feminine clothing and nice, up-to-date hairdos. Her figure was a perfect hourglass and well-rounded in all the right places. I had a tall, boyish figure, and at home I had taken to wearing Ian's shirts and pants now that I had grown into them. I wore simple clothes with straight lines to school. My home-economics teacher once told me I looked elegant, not plain like I felt. I was going to be tall and willowy, like Mom and Dad, and at the ripe age of eleven, my breasts showed no promise. Blair's, on the other hand, were full and lush, and I watched the boys at school licking their lips over her bosom, talking and joking about it. Blair and I were just plain secretive with one another. She had her girlfriends to confide in, and I had Ian and Bear.

One Awful Night

In February, we listened to Winston Churchill speak during a nightly broadcast. That evening, it was heard worldwide. He asked the United States to help by sending arms to the British: "Give us the tools, and we will finish the job." Now, in March, after much terse discussion, the Lend-Lease Act had been passed, allowing the United States to send money, equipment, and supplies to the Allies. We were no longer considered a neutral country. By the end of the month, all German, Italian, and Danish ships anchored in U.S. waters were taken into "protective custody." Less than two weeks later, the U.S. acquired full military defense rights in Greenland, and would do the same later in Iceland. Then a few days later one of our destroyers dropped depth charges on a German U-boat. In nearly every aspect, we were in the war except for sending troops.

When May arrived, we fought about what we would listen to each night. To entice people to see his new movie, *Citizen Kane*, Orson Welles allowed radio stations to replay his hit broadcast, *The War of the Worlds*. It had first been broadcast October 30, 1938. Since it played like an actual news broadcast, many people had taken it seriously and as an actual, unfolding event, and there had been a panic on the East coast. I could understand why, because the show frightened me. If I hadn't known better, I could have sworn we were under Martian attack.

Another evening, Bob Hope's first entertainment for the United Service Organization, commonly known as the USO, was aired from California's March Field where he wowed the troops with his dry humor and his team of talented performers. Then, during a game against the

Chicago White Sox, Joe DiMaggio set off his 56-game hitting streak as he went up against their pitcher, Eddie Smith, going one for four. We managed to keep up with the war news, and listen to everything else.

Billy Gustafson escorted Blair to the spring dance. She looked beautiful that night in an off-white satin gown. I helped her dress by fastening the long row of buttons that ran up the back of a gown that conformed wonderfully to her exquisite figure. Off-the-shoulder straps completed the lace-overlaid bodice with a plain, satin skirt falling in a flirty swirl. Her hair was in an up-sweep, setting off her neck, adorned by a creamy pearl choker. I fastened her necklace and then helped her pull on long, past-the-elbow gloves. She looked like a model on the front of a magazine.

Mom was downstairs fussing with her new camera and took many pictures of Blair that night. When Billy came to collect Blair, he received a lukewarm reception from Dad, who did not approve of him. He'd often comment on how spoiled-rotten that boy was, and that he would turn out to be worthless in the end. But Mom obligingly took a picture of them together, and they left to see his parents.

That evening, as we listened to the war news, we heard President Roosevelt proclaim an "unlimited national emergency." The week before, a German U-boat had sunk an American freighter nearly a thousand miles off the coast of Brazil. But since then, the British had sunk Germany's newest battleship, the *Bismarck,* as she made her maiden voyage. We all cheered at that news. The United States had recently increased their production of military equipment because the government had begun selling the first Series E war bonds and Defense Savings Stamps to raise money. Dad had dutifully gone into town and purchased some of each.

That night, I slept uneasily, worrying about the war and Blair. Each time I woke up, Blair's bed was still empty. The last time I woke, the sun had just made its brilliant appearance. I woke up later to a ruckus in the kitchen. Mom was trying to comfort Blair with soft-spoken words while Dad yelled, "I'm gonna go punch that son-of-a-bitch myself. He should not have taken you to a wild drinking party, and that idiot should not have gotten into a fight. But since he did, you should've just let that guy go at him! Jesus, Mary, and Joseph! What were you thinking, trying to break up a fight between two nearly grown men?"

I heard Blair whimper and say something in a whispery voice. I threw on my housecoat and slowly crept down the stairs, avoiding the one that creaked, and then hovered on the second-to-last step.

"You will never be allowed to be with that Gustafson boy ever again! You understand?"

I could tell by the intensity of Dad's voice that he was nearly insane with anger. Then I heard Blair say the strangest thing: "Don't worry, I never want to see him again. I wish he would dry up and die." And then she began crying uncontrollably; her sobs made shivers go up and down my spine. Blair hardly ever wept—I was the weepy one—she rarely showed her emotions. Even when Ian died and Gracie disappeared. I saw her cry only once, and that was just after the initial shock of realizing what had happened to them.

I couldn't stand it any longer, and I finished my way downstairs, stopping short when I saw my sister. Her dress was torn, her hair mussed, and her right eye swollen shut. Her mouth was an angry-looking, bright circle, with her lips and the skin around them bruised a purplish-red. I turned and ran up the stairs, not wanting to see her like this, and plopped down on the bed. By the look of her face, she not only had been hit once, but twice, maybe more.

Finally, I grabbed her housecoat and ran back downstairs. Blair had been shivering so hard I heard her teeth chattering. Dad turned his back on us, as Mom and I guided her out of what was left of her dress and helped her into her robe. I ran into the parlor, taking one of our wool throws, and made my way back to the kitchen. She looked up at me then, and as our eyes met, I saw guilt in them. I smiled a little, but she turned away and buried her head in Mom's bosom. I draped the blanket over her shoulders, and stooped to pick up her dress.

Shaking it out, I assessed the damage. It was ruined, never to be worn again. One shoulder strap had been completely ripped off, the bodice nearly torn off the skirt, and many of those tiny, pearly buttons down the back had popped off. Then I saw the ultimate damage, a brownish-red stain on the back of the skirt. My mind in a whirl, I hurried upstairs with it. In our bedroom, I saw that the stain was in just the right place to catch virgin blood. My sister had been raped, or worse, she had consented. Oh, God! If Dad found out . . .

My mind tore through several scenarios, and I remembered him shooting Ian's horse. Images of him going to the Gustafson place and confronting Billy and his family, gun in hand, flashed before me. At the very least, I imagined Dad punching Billy out, or worse, Billy's father entering the brawl, and the two of them beating the heck out of Dad. I ran into the bathroom, dress in hand, and cranked the cold water on to fill the bathtub. I raced downstairs and ran out to the side porch where we did laundry and grabbed the box of detergent. I took the stairs two-at-a-time and shut the bathroom door, working feverishly to remove the stain. When I felt satisfied that most of it was gone, I left the dress soaking in the tub. If the dress was a sodden, wet mess it wouldn't be examined for a time and perhaps never.

By the time they got Blair settled down and tucked into bed, Mom and Dad never bothered with the dress, though they looked at me with a sliver of doubt when I told them that I had laundered it. I'm sure they thought me a bit apple-headed about that, but in the end, it was worth it to seem a bit nutty. No contentious incidents with the Gustafson men occurred, and a month later, Billy was dead. He and a friend had been doing the "drive around" while drinking, and when Billy hit Deadman's curve a few miles down the valley, he rolled his car and both young men died. Billy took his time doing that—rumors abounded that it was a long and painful dying.

Secrets

It seemed to take forever for Blair's injuries to heal, and she wouldn't tell me a thing, even after I told her about the bloodstain, and that I knew what it meant. I had recently read a book with a rape scene in it where a virginal girl had been violated and I knew that Blair had experienced the same sort of trauma.

She would lie in bed all day and hardly ate anything when she would listlessly come down to join us at mealtime. When I tried to talk to her, she just turned her head into her pillow and wept. After a while, I left her alone. I still worried about her, as did Mom and Dad. When her bruises finally healed, we could see that her spirit hadn't, and I wondered whether she was heartbroken because she had truly loved Billy and he was gone forever, or if she was upset over being assaulted and forced to have sex?

I was also troubled because Bear hadn't yet appeared. I took to reading while waiting for her up at our graveyard. I wanted to finish *Gone with the Wind* before I became completely involved in training Babe and Lucy. I told Ian about Scarlett's and Rhett's unrequited love and how frustrating that was. In talking to him, I discovered that I now had a great distrust for the opposite sex. I still couldn't believe Billy had violated Blair like that—the violence of it and it being such a special night in a young girl's life. I vowed to never go to the prom, or allow just any boy to court me until I knew what he was like.

Bear finally came to me at the very end of May. I was so relieved that I kissed her on her nose and gave her a big hug. She hugged me back, and I must say, that when people refer to a bear hug—it is quite a hug. She nearly squeezed the breath out of me. I fed her a sandwich, and laughed when I told her how many times I had to go back to the house and talk the twins into having peanut butter and honey sandwiches. Then it dawned on me—she was alone.

"Where are your babies?"

She *m-m-r-r . . . ed* and hung her head, and I swear I heard her snuffling tears. I watched as one slid out of the corner of her eye. I wiped it away. "I guess it was time to let them go out into the big world and make it on their own. Right?"

Bear *m-m-r-r-ed* and then held out her paw for another sandwich. We sat in a compatible silence for a long time, and then she turned and left. I ran back down the hill, ready to begin the touchiest part of training a horse.

Some people call it breaking a horse, but we certainly would never want to "break" them in any way, especially their spirits. They are highly intelligent, regimented animals with long memories. They have, over the years, been bred to please their human masters and to work with them. They enjoy herding cows as much as people do and are always willing to carry their weight on a ranch. Some, over enthusiastic, will almost work themselves to death. Also, the mountains can be hard on cow horses of any breed; thus, having an ample working-horse herd is necessary so each horse isn't over-exerted or worse, injured. I was anxious to add two more ready-to-perform horses to our ranching operation.

I ran upstairs, hid my book, and changed into an old shirt and a pair of Ian's trousers. Blair lay prostrate on her bed. I couldn't stand that any longer, so I decided to invite her to come down to the barn with me. She could brush down Babe while I worked with Lucy. I planned to put saddles on Lucy and Babe while they were still in the barn. I had to beg for a bit, but surprisingly, Blair agreed to join me.

We went out to the pasture where we kept the young, green colts. She watched me put a halter on Lucy, and then she followed suit with Babe. We took our eager girls into the barn. They came willingly, knowing they would receive treats and a good brushing. Blair hummed a little when currying Babe, and that made me happy. As Lucy munched on her treats, I slowly placed my saddle on her back. She turned and gave me a look of indignation mixed with curiosity. I would come to know that look well over the next two months. She turned back to her grain, and I finished saddling her.

Next, after finding Blair's barely-used saddle, I gently placed it on Babe's back. That didn't faze her one bit; she kept on eating. I finished saddling her with not a look or a reaction from her. I told Blair to rub her neck, talk soft baby talk to her, and kiss around on her. After that, I explained, we would lead them out into the horse corral and fasten their lead ropes onto the fence. They needed to learn to stand and wait patiently for their rider once they were saddled.

I cozied up to and loved on Lucy. Soon Blair began talking. She told me she had done a lot of thinking, and had decided that she needed something to occupy her spare time—something meaningful. Up until her disastrous dance date, she had been nothing but a social bug—on the phone all the time, chatting and gossiping, and going into town and hanging out with friends whenever she wasn't needed by Mom for housework or babysitting.

"I don't want to be looking for entertainment all the time, like I've been doing, and I don't want housework and child care to be my only contribution. I want to do something to make Mom and Dad, my entire family, proud of me. I'm thinking about becoming a nurse. You know, when Betty's mom almost died after having her last baby, I helped Betty take care of her. She was so weak we had to help her walk to the bathroom. She had to be bathed in bed, and during the first few days at home, even spoon-fed. And all that icky, personal woman stuff—we did that for her, too. I know that sounds disgusting to you, but it made me feel like I was doing something worthwhile. And for once, I felt like I was in charge."

I laughed. "Yes, we know who is in charge at our house, don't we?"

Blair laughed. It sounded so good to hear her laugh again that I couldn't help myself. I gathered her into my arms and gave her a big squeeze—a Bear bear-hug.

"It's good to hear you talk and laugh again, Blair."

"I'm sorry about how I've been. I have felt so weak and depressed. It's been hard to even move. I know you know what happened, and I appreciate you not telling Mom and Dad. But I can't talk about it. Don't know if I ever can. And I feel so guilty about Billy dying after I had wished that upon him."

"It's all right, Blair. I think I understand. Just a little, at least. And know this—Billy made his own early death when he drank and drove so fast on Deadman's Curve. He should've known better." I let go of Blair. "Can I make you something to eat? You're getting very boney, you know."

"Sure, Abi, let's go find something. I'm hungry for once. Is it okay to leave the horses out here?"

"Yes. They can stand in the barn, saddled. Tomorrow we'll take them out to the corral. You in?"

Blair nodded, and my heart soared.

Blair and I worked together with the horses and became close, just like I had always hoped. Little by little, she smiled more, laughed more, ate more, and she even began reading some of my books. She had pulled away from most of her friends, and began volunteering at the old-folks' home.

Weeks later, Dad, Mom, Blair, little Rory, and Callum cheered for me and Lucy as I set my butt down into the saddle on her for the first time. All she did was stiffen a bit and then she began following the few signals I had taught her before mounting her. She would be considered a green-broke horse for some time, but we had a good start.

Babe, on the other hand, surprised me—all of us—with her reaction to being ridden. She stiffened, and then threw a fit, whinnying, bucking, running sideways, trying to rub me off on the fence. My sweet, sweet favorite wasn't so agreeable after all. I thought she would be the colt most likely to be the easiest to be gentled and taught, but instead, she was a challenge. The second time I got on her, she managed to buck me off. After Dad made sure I was fine, he made me get back on her. That time, I astonished her, because even though she worked and worked to rid herself of me, I stayed on, and finally, she calmed down and began following my signals.

The day after that was the anniversary of Ian's death, Summer Solstice. We were all subdued and quiet. I was in the horse corral working with Lucy under Dad's supervision, with Blair looking on. An old, rickety, wheezing truck pulled into the yard. I didn't pay much attention as a man made his way to us. I had my back to him but I heard him say, "Heard in town that Bonney Creek Ranch's lookin' for some help." He whistled through his teeth. "Nice horseflesh. Real nice. I know horses, that's for sure."

Something about that voice made my skin crawl, and chills went up and down my spine. I rode to where Dad and Blair were standing. The man had an old hat pulled low over his face, but I still recognized him. He was the horse trainer from the circus—the one whose wife had wanted Gracie so bad. I dismounted and led Lucy into her stall and fed her some grain. I came out of the barn, so I was on the same side of the fence as Dad.

"Well, I'm telling you again, you heard wrong, sir." Dad was saying. "Don't need more help. Got all I need."

The man began scowling, and then he argued with a wheedling voice, "Well, I heard ya did." He spat, and then grumbled, "Make up your mind."

Dad took his hat off, running his hand through his still-black hair, "I said we don't need any help. Now leave."

I sidled up to Dad and stood on my tiptoes, whispering in his ear. "Dad! He's the one from the circus. His wife is the drunk lady that came after Gracie." I turned and examined the man. He looked rough, like he wasn't well, and he smelled of alcohol. I turned back to Dad and said aloud this time, "He's been drinking. Be careful."

Suddenly, I was flying through the air. The intruder had picked me up and thrown me out of his way as he stepped over to Dad and punched him in the face. Dad shook his head to clear it and before the man could land another punch, my father walloped him a good one in the belly. I heard the man go *woof,* and then he went flying and lay where he landed. I almost felt bad for him because I knew what it felt like to have the wind knocked out of you. Dad followed him to where he had landed, picked him up, and hit him again, this time right on the nose. I heard it crack, and I was sure Dad had broken his ugly snoot.

Blair stood nearby, wringing her hands and crying.

"Go in the house, Blair, and call the sheriff. Tell him to come out as soon as he can!"

When I heard those words, I remembered Dad saying those very same ones to me when Ian died, and I started to cry. The tension of the past few weeks, the challenge Babe had given me, and now this awful man bothering us, made me lose control. When I finally stopped, I saw Dad was still landing punches on the about-to-pass-out man.

"Dad! Stop! Stop. He's not going to hurt you anymore. Stop. Please."

Dad came to his senses just as Mom came running out with Blair. He stood, huffing and puffing, wiping blood off his hands and face with his handkerchief.

The man lay still with his eyes closed, then he slowly sat up, pointing his finger at my parents.

"You! You two . . . and your God-damned private eyes. Ruined my marriage. I don't have no job or a wife, now, thanks to you. We didn't take your little girl. We would never do that. But, no! Those men of yours had to keep hounding us 'til my wife couldn't take it anymore. She left me. I lost my wife and partner for the act, so now I've been kicked out of the circus."

He stood up. His knees wobbled, and I feared he would go down again. Dad handed him his tattered hat. "Go. Just go. Before the sheriff gets here. I'm sorry about your bad luck. We're only doing what we can to find our daughter. That's all. You didn't do yourself any good coming out here, all vengeful like. Just go."

Dad turned to go into the house, and the man stumbled to his truck, spitting out blood and shaking his head. His old rig groaned as it came to life and then clattered its way out of the yard, meeting the sheriff coming up the driveway. Dad explained the entire event to the sheriff while Mom cleaned up his face. Blair and I sat out on the porch swing, feeling empty.

After the sheriff left, we went inside. Mom and Dad were arguing. He wanted to go into town to find the man. He wanted to help him and set things right. Knowing my Dad, I knew he felt guilty—any time he lost his temper and went overboard to whatever, he always got this look on his face. He had it now, and I knew Mom would lose the argument.

Dad came out of their bedroom dressed in clean clothes. Mom just turned her back to him as he picked up the car keys and headed out the door.

"Good luck, Dad," I thought he was doing the right thing. Mom shot me a look, and I tried to defend myself.

"That man has had a bad life. Maybe Dad can help him. I don't see what it could hurt."

Mom sniffed. "Didn't anyone ever tell you that children are to be seen and not heard?"

"Not in this house. You and Dad have always been fair that way, and now I think it's just that Dad's trying to find him to see if he can help him."

Dad came home as Blair and I were setting the supper table. I saw his whistling, as he walked in the door, as a sign of success. Dad spent the entire time during supper making up to Mom. Blair and I gave each other a look when she finally showed signs of forgiveness. That night, we eavesdropped as our parents sat on the porch and Dad related the events of the afternoon to our mother.

Dad had gone into town, straight to the Corner Bar. The man, who went by the name Larry Pierson, had just started "tying one on" and despite the way he looked, was being served. Dad coaxed him out of there, telling him he had thought of a job for him if he wished to stay in the area. He took him to a motel, and after Larry had showered, they went to the J.C. Penney store where Dad bought him some decent clothes and a hat. Then they went out to the Bar D Ranch, a horse-breeding operation, to see its owner Dennis Leary, who had been needing more help. Upon meeting, the two men seemed to have an immediate connection, and Dennis hired Larry on sight. Dad sighed with satisfaction when he finished, and then Mom sighed in acceptance, and then we heard deep kissing. Blair and I rolled our eyes at one another and crept up the stairs and crawled into bed.

I finished reading *Gone with the Wind* and had found an article about it in *Time* disappointing because I wanted to hear more about the author of this captivating story. The critics had mocked the novel, claiming the story to be a "*bore* and its writing—*drab*." But then the article said ordinary people liked it because it was a "first-rate piece of Americana." I liked it because now I could imagine what the South had been like before the war, and I loved the romance.

I wished I could have attended the grand premiere of *Gone with the Wind* held in Atlanta. The governor of Georgia declared a three-day statewide holiday, while the mayor encouraged women and men to attend, not only the grand ball, but the premiere itself, in period clothing. People got to meet Vivien Leigh and Clark Gable and all the other actors in person. The only puzzling thing was that Margaret Mitchell didn't attend.

On July 19, we celebrated Rory's first birthday. That will always be a bittersweet day because that is the day Blair and I realized she was pregnant.

Life's Consequences

The morning of Rory's first birthday, I woke up with stomach cramps, and Blair ran to the bathroom, nauseous. The night before, we had decided to take Babe and Lucy for an early ride so we could help Mom bake a cake and get ready for the party. After vomiting, Blair declared she felt much better, and we quietly dressed and tiptoed downstairs. My belly pains persisted, and I waited with dread for my stomach to heave up what I had eaten the night before.

It was fresh and cool outside, and we both began to feel better. The sun had begun its climb and would soon be beating down on us. We hurriedly caught, grained, brushed, and saddled our horses, and hit the trail. The beauty of the morning made us feel cheerful. I forgot my cramps, especially when Blair's laughter burst out each time Lucy stopped to rid herself of gas. We had never heard a horse fart so much before, and we wondered what in the Sam heck she had eaten.

We finally had to rein in our girls since Lucy's flatulent state made us both come down with fits of giggles, rendering us senseless. I laughed so hard, it felt like I had wet my pants, Ian's old ones. We dismounted and let our horses drift on their own. They were becoming increasingly accomplished as cow horses, not green any longer, and we could trust them not to run off. When we eventually sobered, I told Blair that I thought I had had an accident in my britches. I stooped over while pulling up Ian's favorite flannel shirt and asked Blair, "Does it show?"

"Oh, my gosh, Abs. It shows and it's not pee; you just got your period!"

I stilled. I unbuckled my belt and pulled my pants down. Sure enough. Now it all made sense—the cramps and feeling poorly that morning. I sat down abruptly. I wanted to cry but only laughter came out. Rosie had written to me about getting hers, and I had been a bit jealous. But now, I wasn't so sure I should be happy; the cramps had not been pleasant and I had just become saddled with every woman's curse; my days on earth would be dictated by my cycles. Also, I knew from all my reading that my body's need to reproduce could be disastrous if I weren't careful, that passionate love and the human need to populate the earth were responsible for many unplanned births.

"Oh, gosh, Blair. I'm a woman now, if I look at this like Mom does. Oh, God."

Blair stood silent with her face awash in a sickly white.

"What? What's wrong. I'll be okay; I just need get used to it, that's all. When we get back to the house, will you help me with the necessities?"

Blair didn't answer. "Blair, what's wrong with you?"

She looked at me, her face as ashen as the sky above us. The sun had suddenly hidden behind a cloud, and the heavens had become a sullen gray.

Blair plopped down beside me. "I haven't had a period since. Since . . . since Billy raped me."

There—she finally said those words. She had been forcibly taken by Billy, and I was happy to hear that she hadn't consented after all. She was still, basically, a good girl, and she had not lost her virginity willingly. But as the implications of her revelation settled in on me, I became frantic, wondering if she could be pregnant. We sat there, quiet in our thoughts.

"No, Blair, you couldn't be pregnant. Life can't be that cruel. It just can't be."

Blair began to cry, and in between sobs, she declared, "No, Abi, I feel it in my bones. It's clear to me. Mom had to buy me a new bra two sizes bigger at Penney's the other day. Aileen told me that your breasts grow when you are expecting. And I've been sick every morning. Today, you just happened to be up to see it since we were riding early. I have morning sickness."

"No, it can't be. No, Blair. It wouldn't be fair. You can't be."

"You're wrong, Abi. I'm pregnant," she finished with a wail.

The only thing I could do was to turn to her and clasp her into a tight hug. We clung to one another and cried. Then we gathered our horses and rode home without saying another word. Finally, when we were in the barn and brushing our horses, I spoke up. "Blair, we've got to tell Mom and Dad. They'll know what to do."

"What to do?" Blair shrieked. "I'm going to have a baby. A baby created in a horrible way by a boy now dead!"

I swallowed hard to rid myself of what I wanted to say. I sensed she would need time— time to figure things out and to accept this terrible fate. We were Catholic and Presbyterian. There would be no getting rid of the baby. Blair would go to hell if she did that. I cursed myself for my obsession about reading those novels that had educated me to the possibilities, and I prayed for forgiveness for having thought such a thing as a way out for Blair.

When we returned to the house, Blair went into the bathroom to gather things I needed. We met in our room, and she showed me how to attach the Modess pads to a sanitary belt. Mom had several boxes on hand along with several Silent purchase coupons which coyly stated: *To Sales Person—one box of Modess, please.* I had seen these things before but now I suddenly understood them. I wasn't the only one ashamed of and wanting to hide this womanly condition, and those coupons meant women didn't have to say anything when purchasing their protection. No, we had these discreet notes to hand over to the clerks stating our need for *the new sanitary napkins made by Johnson+Johnson.*

I stifled my giggles over the word—*napkins.* I would never look at a dinner napkin the same way. Blair had been gathering everything together when Mom walked in. She stopped short. "Oh, Blair! I was wondering when you'd finally get your period. Oh! I'm so glad, I thought . . ." Then, she simply cleared her throat. "Never mind! I'm happy to see things becoming normal again. That's all."

As Mom left our room with a light-hearted wave of her hand, we looked at each other with wide eyes. Blair begged me to not say anything to anyone.

"Blair, I won't say a thing. Just let Mom think you have finally gotten your period, because I don't want a big fuss about me getting mine. But in time, we'll have to talk to Mom and Dad. You can't hide this forever."

Blair breathed a heavy sigh. "I cannot believe my bad luck. I'm only fifteen. What am I going to do? I don't want a baby!" I held her as she cried again, and when she was finished, she ran cold water over her face and eyes. We went downstairs to help Mom get ready for Rory's birthday party, and that's when I realized that a year from now, we would have another person in our family. Blair's and Billy Gustafson's child would join us in life, created in violence not love. Would that baby be any different than those made in love?

I felt ill the entire time we celebrated. All our family was gathered to recognize Rory's first year of life and were so happy, except Blair with her weighty secret, and me holding it inside my burdened heart. I could not escape the cloud of gloom that loomed over me, and I thought of how life's events would, again, test our family and our strength. Blair would be having a baby out-of-wedlock, and there would be much talk. I desperately hoped premature motherhood wouldn't change her.

I had begun reading my father's magazines, curious about and often puzzled by the things he said concerning the war. The United States' actions against the Axis had so far been only to send arms, and every other good it could to help the Allies. Our country, too—just like the countries involved in the actual shooting war—faced many shortages, such as aluminum, steel, gas, and even silk. News articles warned women to be aware that the days of silk stockings were over, and that every day, another stocking factory was being closed, as were glass container factories needing fuel oil for their product.

Our country had not only stopped producing luxury items but practical ones, too. Tool factories shut down due to lack of available steel. On the east coast, gasoline stations closed early every day to curb people's insatiable appetite for leisure driving. Iowa's largest manufacturer of window blinds, Pella, closed because aluminum and zinc were not available. The list of shortages went on and on, and the saddest thing was that many people faced poverty despite our country's boom. Jobs were lost each time a factory shut down.

Blair and I were relieved once the party had begun. Mom had asked us continuously that day, "What's wrong with you girls? You look as if you've lost your best friends."

We would just smile. "Nothing. Guess it's just the gloomy day."

Blair smiled bitterly, "Actually, Mom, I have lost my best friend. She's too wild and crazy for me now. She has no time for me since I have settled down. Guess I'll have to find new girls, proper ones, to chum with when school starts."

I couldn't help but stare at her, and she only gave me a watery smile and then turned her back on me. I sighed at the obvious precursor of what was to come. We MacDougals were in for another hard time. And, when I thought of the information I had gleaned from the *Time* articles, I knew that our country's involvement in the "shooting war" was only a matter of time. I prayed that none of my brothers would have to cross the seas to fight.

That night, with a melancholy heart, I took picture after picture of our family. I hated how my curiosity and the answers I had found had given me the doldrums, and I tried to smile before I choked down the piece of cake Rory offered me. We had baked him his own special cake (and one for Ianna), following the tradition of allowing a child to dig into and fully enjoy their first cake without the good manners that would be required on future birthdays. Rory, always bossy, insisted on feeding each one of us our own little chunk of his cake.

I fought off tears as he held his chubby little hand out to me, thinking of how innocently happy he was, unaware of what life might bring him, his bliss symbolizing the MacDougal family's joy and complacency of that night. My family's unawareness of the consequences of life that Blair and I faced—she now carried a baby, and I simply was growing up—made my throat close tight, and I struggled to swallow Rory's offering.

Cameron

J ust before school began, Callum and Cameron began football practice. Ever since that terrible day when Cameron had attacked Callum and me, Callum had continued with his weight-strengthening program. Mom made him keep his weights out in the horse barn, where he would faithfully do his workouts while the weather was mild. He even had a mirror to work in front of—an object that had to be turned around when he finished since it created a ruckus with the horses when they saw their reflections. During the cold months, he would go into the high school gym to do his conditioning. Callum took a lot of guff for his passion, but always with a grin.

Cameron, on the other hand, had become a silent, bitter young man, who always seemed intent on dampening our family's well-earned times of contentment. His surliness and evil looks weren't lost on any of us. I heard Mom and Dad fretting over him often before they slept. Whereas Callum had become strong, with sinewy muscles, Cameron seemed to be overeating his way through life. Surprisingly, he hadn't become obese, but he certainly was not in good shape. We tried our best to overcome his moods and silent aggressiveness, hoping he would snap out of his obvious contempt and loathing toward others. But every time he seemed to be coming around and trying to fit in, he would inadvertently do something odd or even worse, menacing to one of us.

He would *accidentally* let go of a calf's legs when he and Callum were wrestling it down to be branded or doctored. The last time he did that, Callum almost lost his right eye, causing him a trip to the hospital again. Once he *accidentally* roped me around my neck, giving me a horrific, painful rope burn that took forever to heal. He would trip Rory, making him fall face-forward onto the floor. Blair, having outgrown their competitive, combative sibling rivalry, completely ignored his taunts and so he let her be.

After those incidents, when aid and attention were lavished onto the victim, he could be heard cursing under his breath. We never heard what he said, but we could well imagine what his words were. When Dad stood up to that, ordering him to speak out loud, he simply turned his back on him and left the house. He was grounded for a long time until Dad gave in and allowed him to attend football practice with Callum, even though Cameron had never caved in his defiance. No one was surprised when the boys came home announcing their luck at tryouts. Callum would play quarterback, halfback, or running back for the offense since he was so quick and such a fast thinker. Callum had honed his running skills throughout the years—running in fear from his twin brother. On the defense, Callum would be the safety.

Cameron didn't respond when asked what position he would play. He simply picked up his small hunting rifle and went out to kill whatever he could find. Usually, he would go after squirrels, birds, rabbits, raccoons, and skunks. He would leave for hours at a time, relieving his pent-up frustrations in killing, for the most part, harmless creatures. During hunting season, he would leave with his more powerful hunting rifle, and often came back with a kill. Despite our raising beef, we MacDougals ate a lot of venison and elk. After he left that day, Callum told us Cameron hadn't made the team and had only been offered the position of manager, which he refused.

Promotion and Jake

Monday, the second week of school, Principal Jeffries took me out of class. When we reached his office, Mom and Dad were there. They looked at me with pride mixed with apprehension and doubt, and I knew that something unusual was happening. I sat down, my heart pounding and palms sweating, trying to think of what I could have done to deserve a dressing-down.

Principal Jeffries cleared his throat. "Abi, I'm not sure how aware you are of your wonderful, exquisite mind or how you have excelled in scholastics far beyond your peers, but last spring's test results show that you have the capability of doing tenth-grade level work at the very least, and in most subjects, you actually test higher. We don't want to get too far ahead of ourselves in promoting you due to your tender age of eleven. But for now, I suggest we take you out of the seventh grade and start you out at freshman level, at least until you mature a little, and then we will address the issue again."

Silence filled the room while my parents and I absorbed this new development.

Mr. Jeffries cleared his throat again. "Well, I imagine you and your parents will need to think about this and discuss it. Give it some thought and let me know what you decide."

He stood up and came around to us, shaking each of my parent's hands and then mine. Outside his office, Mom and then Dad gave me a big hug. They told me how proud they were of me, but that this was a very serious decision to make, and that it would be mostly up to me to determine whether to accept this promotion.

"You would be just one grade behind Blair, and one ahead of the twins. How does that strike you?" Mom said this in such a noncommittal voice that I knew my parents were truly leaving this decision to me. I shook my head, still befuddled.

Dad just winked at me and gave me a peck on the cheek. "You can talk this out with us tonight, but I know you will make the right choice."

I walked back to my classroom and sat in a blurry state of mind. The only positive thought I had regarding this change was that I would be in high school and thus, closer to Jake. I had seen Jake in the hallways ever since school began. Now as seventh graders in Junior High, our classes were held in the high school building, which was streets away from the elementary school. I sorely missed the coziness of our elementary school where everything was a warm, rich wood—the floors, the stairs, the walls, even the outside was all wood including the magnificent bell tower that sat proud and high above the entrance.

Since I was already adjusting to that change, and Rosie had gone to live with her mother in eastern Montana, I didn't feel that more change in my life would make much difference. The longer I thought about my opportunity, the more enthusiastic I became. Jake always winked at me when we passed in the hallway, making my young heart race. Would he see me differently if I became a Freshman, just three years behind him in school?

He had been Ian's best friend, so I knew of his kind and generous ways. And he was nearly as good-looking as Ian had been. Since my family did not attend the circus and carnival any longer, he would hand-deliver his yearly-won stuffed animal to me at our house. This last summer he brought me a small black-and-white kitten, and we stood on the porch and talked for over an hour. I was in a state of nervous excitement just being near him.

I remember talking about horses and training them, and my telling him about my experiences with Babe and Lucy. He told me about his job with Baird Construction and how he had saved up enough money to put a few cattle and horses on the small piece of land his family owned just six miles on the other side of town. When he graduated, he planned to start a small ranching operation but would remain working for Baird's.

His family was Italian, and I found that fascinating. He was blessed with a thick crop of auburn hair, more brown than red, intense, almost black eyes, and swarthy skin. Jake's one flaw was a small gap between his upper front teeth, which made him even more endearing to me. As we stood together on the porch that day, I noticed that we stood almost eye to eye, and I hoped that I wouldn't grow much more. I wanted my man to be taller than me.

The Murano family owned the second largest hotel in town, which boasted a billiard room, a restaurant, a bar, and a beautiful, spacious lobby, all decorated with lovely, rich wood and marble floors. Their restaurant was well known for its wonderful T-bone steaks and pasta dishes. They also ran a boarding house, and once, when a boarder owed them months of rent and was leaving town, he deeded his small ranch to them as payment. Now Jake would own that, and I was excited for him, as well as for the fact that we were of the same mind in knowing what we wanted to do with our futures.

I arrived home that afternoon having decided to accept the promotion. Luckily, Bear appeared to me that day, and I saw her coming to me as a sign, assuring me that I had made the right decision. She was becoming quite round again, and I knew she would come next spring with one or two new babies. I laughed at that thought, and when she stood up to stretch, I shook her clawed paw and congratulated her on her coming offspring. She gave me one of her fierce bear hugs and went running back into the woods, and I marveled at how sometimes we humans can enjoy such a connection with animals.

The supper table discussion that night was raucous and undisciplined, just like it had been before we lost Ian and Gracie, and before our older siblings left the nest. My parents were joyous over my decision, and it made Blair happy, too. I knew she was thinking that she would need all the support she could receive after having a baby out-of-wedlock, and now, I would graduate just one year after her, which would benefit our new sisterly bond. Callum literally cheered for me and came and gave me a big hug. Cameron just sat and glared. Little Rory, enthused by all the excitement, burst out with his third spoken word, *Abi, Abi, Abi*. He had already learned to say Mum and Dat. We clapped to congratulate him and my heart swelled. But then I remembered clapping for Gracie at the same words and tears welled. That night when I said my bedtime prayers, I pled even harder for the grace of God to bring our Gracie back to us.

The next day at school, the principal escorted me to my new class. My new curriculum included Geometry, American Literature, and World History. I also had the choice of either Earth Science, Physical Science, or Biology. I chose Biology because it had the most to do with animals. At first it was a little unnerving to be my brother-in-law's student. But we soon got over that.

The class that made me the most uncomfortable was Physical Education, where we girls had our own locker room in which to change. Our classes were not co-ed, and our instructor seemed to believe she was some sort of drill sergeant. She worked us hard in calisthenics and made us run around the football field three times a class period when the weather permitted. We were forced to wear ugly uniforms which consisted of bloomers and tight shirts. The boys would stare and make comments about us from their side of the field.

I did like the fact that I was still the tallest girl in my new class and that my breasts weren't that far behind my older classmates, and I thanked the heavens for my great genes. I had just read an article in *Newsweek* written by the Danish botanist Wilhelm Johannsen about genetics, which he simply called genes. I found it fascinating that scientists all over the world worked together to understand the many mysteries of life and that they shared their discoveries. Once a month I would proudly hand my *I'm having my period* slip to mean Miss Brookes, just like the rest of the girls. On those days, we didn't have to do calisthenics; we only ran laps. Also, on those days, if Jake stopped to speak to me in the hall, my body would do strange things, making me feel more womanly, and I wouldn't mind menstruating so much.

Blair and I counted out the months to calculate when her baby would be born. We decided it would arrive around the last week of February. Blair still suffered from morning sickness but it seemed to be subsiding, and oddly, instead of getting bigger, Blair became almost thin. She had always had a weakness for sweets, preferring cinnamon rolls or pancakes for breakfast. She loved to bake peanut butter cookies, luscious bars, cakes and pies. But now she rarely baked anything and chose to eat boiled eggs for breakfast, and mostly meat, fruit, and vegetables for dinner and supper.

When I asked her about this change, she shrugged her shoulders. "I don't really know why. One thing is certain, and that is that sweets make my stomach churn, and now I crave meat. I suppose it's because of my pregnancy. I also like things salty. But you know what, Abi? I want to stay as slim as possible so I don't show so soon. I dread the day when people can easily see that I am expecting a baby. I suppose I'll get used to being stared at and talked about, but I am certainly not looking forward to it."

Blair looked good. The boys at school took notice, and it took a while until they realized that Blair was not the same person she had been last May. She turned everyone who showed interest in her down and shunned her old girl friends as well. Her change in personality did not escape gossip, but she seemed oblivious to it. She became good friends with several girls who weren't considered popular or "babes." Blair's new friends' steady and down-to-earth natures seemed to please her. She told me that she hoped they would still be her friends after they knew about the baby.

We talked about whether to rat Billy out, or to just remain quiet. When I asked if she wanted the Gustafson family to know, she said she hadn't come to a decision about that. They were good people whom everyone respected and even admired. They were a nice-looking family, and they attended church as often as we did. Their ranch was kept up as immaculately as their home. They appeared to have high standards in everything they did apart from raising Billy.

But then, when I thought of how he could be so spoiled and get away with being wild, I thought of Cameron. Everyone in our family, especially Mom and Dad, treated him differently simply because of his penchant for being disagreeable and nasty. His constant pouting made us try to please him. We gave him attention and praise for any little positive act or attitude, trying to pull him out of his depressed orneriness.

All of us children feared him; we never knew what unkind or violent act he would do since he had already done many despicable things. Since school began and Callum had become a football star, Cameron spent most afternoons out in the woods shooting things. The fact that a MacDougal was allowed such a depraved activity proved that even Mom and Dad didn't know what to do with him. Callum and I preferred he stay away from us as we did the afternoon chores, so he wasn't even held accountable for doing his part any longer.

But unlike Billy Gustafson, Cameron had no charm. Blair told me how, in the beginning, she thought of Billy as the most wonderful, gentlemanly boy she knew. But the more time she spent with him, the more she saw the real him. When they hung out at the Gustafson house, the family treated Billy like a prince. Blair said he would be sweet and lovable to his family in their presence, but had a disrespectful attitude toward them when they weren't around, especially for his mother since he usually talked her into allowing him to do nearly anything he wanted. Blair said Denise Gustafson was even nicer and kinder than Mom, which I found difficult to believe. She also told me that Dan, Billy's father, seemed so good and decent that he most likely would never accept the fact that Billy had done what he had done to her.

The first girl in my new freshman class to welcome me and treat me nicely was Billy's sister, Gail, who seemed the opposite of her dandyish, out-going brother. She was quiet and reserved. She dressed plainly and wore no makeup and kept her hair short like older women did in those days. She wore glasses with lenses so thick that her eyes appeared enormous. But they were kind, wise eyes, and at first, that was what I liked most about her. She studied hard and took everything seriously like me, and we quickly became close. When I asked Blair if it would bother her if I became good friends with Gail, she looked at me like I was loony. "Why of course not, she and I are already good friends."

Suspicions and War

Suspicion seemed to invade everyone's life those days. As I read articles from my Dad's magazines that fall, I realized that some people in the United States didn't trust their own president. There were articles discussing FDR's New Deal policies accusing him of being too much of a Socialist and that he was trying to "pull the wool over his fellow Americans' eyes and replace democracy with socialism."

Most articles were about the war. We weren't in the shooting war yet, but we were, as a nation, getting ready to enter it. Our relationship with Japan was exceedingly tenuous and fragile. In July, FDR had frozen every Japanese asset in our country, and now a new naval station had been built on Midway Island as the first line of defense in a 5,860-mile water bridge between Pearl Harbor and the Philippines.

A new rifle had been designed for the Army which could be used as either a semi-automatic or a full automatic with rapid firing,. They hadn't decided which yet, but every officer, infantryman, paratrooper, cavalryman, tanker, machine gunner, and even noncombatants would carry this new Garand rifle.

Using Virginia's roughest and most congested countryside, an area near Fredericksburg, a sergeant jump-master had his men do their first practice jump, which was considered a success despite several chutes being ripped when jumpers hung up in trees. My heart went out to those young boys in the belly of that plane. To keep their minds off the coming trial, they began the strains of a song but couldn't finish it because they were so scared— "I'm a ramblin' wreck from Georgia

Tech . . ." My eyes teared up when the implications of that sank home, and I said a little prayer for all the men who would fight in this war.

Pages of articles in *Time* were dedicated to the Battle of Russia in August, and by September, articles now claimed that the Germans were about to sever the last route into Leningrad, and after that, this German aggression went by the name, *The Siege of Leningrad.* In October, we began to send supplies to the USSR, hoping to help them push the Germans back, and shortly after, Americans suffered the first casualties at the hands of the Nazis when a German U-boat torpedoed one of our destroyers, the USS Reuben James, near Iceland, killing 100 U.S. Navy sailors.

Time and *Life* also contained gossip pages about high society and Hollywood celebrities, and there was a humorous side to them. I loved the ones about Hollywood's stars and their lives—about their marriages, their separations and divorces. They revealed the amount of allowance the young socialite, Gloria Vanderbilt, received, who "now 17 and quite grown up, has been doing Hollywood so hard that most of her $25,750-a-year allowance is reported spent within six months." That was a lot of money to spend in such a short time, and for a while, I fantasized about what I would do if I had that kind of money. I dreamed of going to New York and used that scenario to imagine my life as a wealthy socialite, but then I remembered Jake and shoved that idea out of my mind.

Dad, thinking that new car production would be terminated, bought a beautiful 1942 Lincoln Zephyr V12 for $1,250. It was luxurious to the point that I felt a little like Gloria Vanderbilt when riding in it. It was called the Zephyr because it was so streamlined and had a smooth ride due to its newly-invented automatic gear shift, which meant Dad didn't have to mess with a clutch anymore. We were awestruck over its sleek look, its ride, and its power. One afternoon after church, Dad took us out to a straight stretch of highway and demonstrated how fast and powerful his auto was with its V-type 12-cylinder engine.

After that, I could easily believe that Americans were turning out fighter planes by the thousands, and were also producing one new railroad car every four and one-half minutes. The Goodrich Tire

Company had created a new synthetic material called Koroseal for the manufacture of gas masks that proved to be resistant to any gas or acid the Germans could come up with. The ads also bragged that the goggles were guaranteed to be fog-free. Men were signing up by the thousands in anticipation of the United States entering the "shooting war." But despite our country's patriotism, many were rejected because of "defective or deficient teeth."

Ian's birthday, October 22, was another sad, dreary day of remembrance. This year a bitter cold front swept in from Canada, dumping several feet of snow on our still-green grasslands, and we were snowed in for two days. We felt like caged animals and worried about our creatures outside. Luckily, we had just shipped the last of our calves, so our concern was only for the adult cattle and horses. Dad and the boys went out after it quit snowing, turning the old feed wagon into a sleigh by putting its runners on. It was still quite a job to feed hay, and we were relieved when on the third day the sun came out and quickly melted the snow. We grieved for the victims and their families that were on airplanes that iced up and crashed during that storm. Of the two crashes, only one pilot survived, saying that he just couldn't keep the plane up because of the weight of the ice.

By November, Blair was beginning to show a small baby bump. We became creative in concealing her condition. We would sit up late at night in our room shortening several of my skirts. She wore heavy sweaters over those. But we knew that this ploy would only work for so long. I begged her to tell Mom and Dad, but she emphatically shook her head. When I asked why she kept putting it off, she became tearful. "I know they will send me away once they know, and I just can't leave yet."

Thanksgiving & Christmas

On Thanksgiving Day, Mom accidentally walked in on Blair as she stepped out of the bathtub. Blair was nearly six months along, and her pregnant state was undeniable. After Mom's discovery, our household became a convoluted, emotional mess. Dad began shouting, and despite Mom's attempts to hush him, Dad swore like I have never heard before. He kept yelling about what that "dead boy" had done to Blair.

Mom told me to dress Rory, who kept asking, "Wut rong? Wut rong?" and take him outside. Callum, Cameron, and Colin were out feeding, and the rest of the family had not yet arrived. It was obvious that Mom and Dad would be secretive about Blair's pregnancy, and a wave of sickness clutched me as I realized Blair's fear of being sent away would probably come true. But I supported Mom and Dad's need for privacy by talking my brothers into taking us for a sleigh ride since we had just the right amount of snow. I grabbed a handful of cookies on my way out so hunger wouldn't be a motive to return to the house early.

When we returned home, all was quiet. Mom worked in the kitchen, and Dad sat in the living room, listening to the radio and reading a magazine. Blair was nowhere in sight. Before I offered to help Mom, I took the stairs two-at-a-time to check on her. She lay with her back to me on her bed, and I could tell by her snuffling and hiccupping that she had just finished a long session of weeping.

"Blair?" No answer.

"Blair, talk to me. What did Mom and Dad decide to do?"

Silence.

"Do you want me to leave you alone?"

More silence.

"I'll just go then. I'll ask Mom."

"No. No, Abi. Don't go."

I heard her take a deep breath. "They want me to live with Grandma and Grandpa MacDougal until the baby is born. That will give them time to think of what we should do."

"Oh."

I plopped down on my bed, thinking. Blair had been right. Oh, God! What would I do without her now that we had become so close? Ohio was so far away. How horrible, despite how lovely our MacDougal grandparents were, to have to go live with them and leave us. What were our parents thinking? Sending her away would not fix anything. Blair would still have been raped and would still give birth to a baby she didn't want. Well, perhaps in time she would want it, especially after feeling it moving inside her and giving birth to it. Mom, when discovering she was going to have Gracie, hadn't been too keen on the idea of another child until she felt her first kicks, and then she was fine, and after she gave birth to Gracie, Mom couldn't have loved her more. And then, with Matthew Rory, his christened name said it all—"a blessing from God."

I sighed, and crept slowly to Blair's bed, carefully lying down beside her, cautiously spooning my body around hers. I threw my arm over her and found a hand to clasp.

"Blair, don't you worry. Everything will work out for the best. The Lord has his ways." As I mimicked Grandma Callaghan's favorite comforting phrase, I thanked the Fates that Grandma Fi—that's what we called our Grandma Fiona—would be there, too, to help Blair through this difficult time.

Blair sighed—sort of an acceptance-mixed-with-sorrow breath— and sat up, pulling her hand from mine. "Yes, I guess I need to start looking at things differently now that Mom and Dad know. They wanted to know who knew, and I told them just you and Father Timothy."

I sat up. "You told Father Boyle?"

"Yes. One day I thought about taking Babe or Lucy and riding hard and fast through the boulder pasture, hoping I would have an accident and die, or at least miscarry the baby, just like Aileen lost hers."

"Oh, Blair! No!"

"Yes! I have felt desperate and crazy. And, then, just as I dressed to go out, the baby kicked, and I realized that I couldn't do such a thing, and images of Gracie, Rory, and Ianna flashed through my mind. Later that week, I went in along with Mom to the church and when she finished her confession, I had my own session with Father."

"What did he say?"

"He blessed me and my child and then told me almost exactly what you just said—about the Lord having his ways. He reassured me that once people knew how this baby had been started, they would forgive me and accept me for who I am—a good and decent person—and that they would commend me for having this baby. I told him I didn't know if I wanted the world to know about what happened, and that I thought my own behavior, at the time, had led to Billy's awful deed."

"What did he say then?"

"He said that no one ever deserves such treatment, such a betrayal of trust."

Blair began weeping again. Shaking her head, she pounded the bed with her fist and burst out, "Mom and Dad want this kept secret, just between them, you, Father Doyle, now our grandparents, and me."

I stood, silent, clenching my fists in anger. How could they send her away? Both Blair and her baby? That wouldn't fix anything; it would only buy them time to figure out how to handle this. But still.

"What did they say about the Gustafson family knowing?"

"That's just it, they don't know how to handle that. They told me to keep it quiet until they have more time to think."

"What do you think? About Billy's family knowing, I mean."

"I don't know. I think we don't have to worry about that if I do what Dad wants me to do."

"Really? What is Dad wanting you to do?"

"Go live with Grandma and Grandpa MacDougal, have the baby, and give it up for adoption."

"Give it up?" The thought had never occurred to me. Give it up? All I could think of was how we had already given up one baby. How could he think that? I stomped my foot and ran out of our room, planning to have a talk with Dad. But when I reached the kitchen, Mom and Dad were there making over Ianna, who had just arrived with Aileen and Kendall.

I could not believe how that Thanksgiving dinner seemed like the ones before with no hint of Blair's terrible trouble. When she came down to join us, she was composed and beautiful. Mom and Dad cheerfully carried out our family traditions, never showing their state of upset over Blair's predicament. They prayerfully gave thanks for their blessings, remembering Ian and Gracie in their prayers, and then proceeded to carve the turkey and present a feast of our family's favorite holiday foods.

Our youngest made this happy atmosphere joyful. While waiting for dinner to be served, they engaged in some aggressive fighting, but at the same time showed their affection to one another, which made us laugh. Ianna, now able to express herself, hit Rory over the head and declared, "Wary, a beefer and stumblebum!" She had been trying to put together a wooden puzzle of the map of the United States, with Rory screaming, "No. No. No. Rong!" and pulling out the pieces as fast as she placed them.

We knew how Kendall, the sometimes-frustrated science teacher, sometimes referred to a few of his students as "beefers"—complainers, and "stumblebums"—lazy people, with Aileen constantly warning him, "Watch yourself, Ianna will mimic you!" After Rory interfered with Ianna's puzzle piecing and was reprimanded for doing *rong*, Ianna went to him and gave him a big hug, and then swept her chubby little arm across the partially put-together puzzle to show her commiseration. Then Rory gave Ianna a bigger hug, tumbling them to the floor on which they contentedly rolled around, trying to outdo one another, again.

After the dinner dishes were finished, Dad made a big announcement. "Since we all love our radio broadcasts and sometimes they become a bit static, and our old phonograph has died on us, I bought an early

Christmas present for us. Boys, will you help me take out the old and move in the new?"

Dad had purchased a state-of-the-art Magnavox International radio which guaranteed static-free FM broadcasting and played records. We listened to the news for a while, and then he pulled out a stash of new recordings for our listening enjoyment. We heard Glenn Miller and his new song "Chattanooga Choo Choo," and many of his other hits. Bing Crosby had a new album out, featuring many of his old songs as well as his new. We listened to Spike Jones and "Der Fuehrer's Face" which made us laugh, not just at the lyrics but also at the performance our toddlers put on with their awkward dance moves.

We burst into laughter when the song got to the part where the horn was played to sound like a big, messy fart, and Rory stopped his dancing at just the right moment to fill his diaper. Soon the twins were up and dancing to the lyrics and doing what boys do best, making sloshy wind sounds underneath their armpits. For days after, when depression about losing another sister clutched at me, I would maniacally sing, "When der fuehrer says we is de master race, we heil heil heil right in der fuehrer's face, not to love der fuehrer is a great disgrace." And then I would burst into tears.

When Dad played Sammy Kaye's new hit, "Daddy," Blair became very quiet. Next, he played Jimmy Dorsey's "Green Eyes," and she burst into tears and ran from the room. I jumped up to go after her, but Mom stopped me and said she would see to her.

Dad stood up and stopped the music as everyone began talking, "What's wrong with her?" "What got into her?"

"It must be because of losing Billy," Aileen speculated.

Dad cleared his throat, and began speaking. "Your Grandmother MacDougal appears to be losing her mind. She wanders many nights, all night long, muttering to herself, and becomes frantic about something she's simply imagining. That's what your grandfather guesses, anyway. He's having a difficult time managing her, and the other night she fell down the stairs. She broke her leg and will be in a wheelchair until it heals. Since she's been volunteering at the old folks' home, Blair is willing to go for a time to help. She just has mixed emotions about leaving."

Cameron laughed aloud, and said with a twitter, "Ha-ha-ha. Gram's losing her marbles." Everyone turned to him and gave him a look. Dad ordered him to stop making fun of his grandmother. "This is not a laughing matter." I knew he wasn't referring only to Grandma's situation.

I could only stare at my father with my mouth hanging open. What a damned lie! I could feel my face heat as the anger swept over me. I stood up and left the parlor and went into the kitchen and began pulling out leftovers for our traditional finish-everything-up Thanksgiving supper. I banged pots and pans and bowls—anything to wear off my fury. I dropped the lid of the turkey roaster onto the floor, and it bounced and made an obnoxious twanging rhythm as it attempted to right itself, bringing Aileen to the kitchen.

"What's going on in this family?"

I shrugged my shoulders.

"Abi? What is happening here?"

"Go ask Dad," I muttered.

Then, suddenly, I felt bad. I felt guilty about my anger and resentment toward my parents; I knew they only wanted the best for every one of us. I turned, and reaching out for Aileen, I overdid it, and we both went down. I started to laugh when I saw her startled face, and then began crying. We lay on the floor, arms around each other, and cried. She had no idea why she cried, but I knew why I did. I guessed she most likely cried about having just lost another baby to a miscarriage.

Finally, I could say the words. "Oh, Aileen, Blair and I have become so close, good friends, actually, and now she will be leaving. We've lost two sisters. I know Blair will return, but still."

Aileen smoothed the wisps of new baby hair escaping my braid that fell over my forehead like bangs. That sprouting growth of hair was the only thing that drove me crazy concerning my hair. "Don't worry, hon. I'll never leave. You may, but I won't." She put her voice into a whisper, "We planned on telling everyone tonight that we just bought a house in town."

"Oh, good!" was all I could breathe out. Aileen held me so tight, I could hardly catch a breath, let alone move. And then I knew that, yes, I would become close to yet another sister, and that this one also grieved for the loss of Gracie and the soon-to-happen leaving of another.

Mom and Blair returned to the kitchen, looking as if nothing was bothering them. We finished putting the leftover food on the table and went into the parlor to announce that supper was ready. After we took our seats, Kendall stood up, fetched a bottle of wine from the porch, and poured us all a little in our glasses. Ianna and Rory had apple juice. He announced his and Aileen's new purchase, and we toasted.

We ate our heavy Thanksgiving desserts after devouring much of the noon leftovers. Aileen, Kendall, and Ianna returned to town, along with Colin, who had a small apartment there. Mom, after much trouble, finally got Rory settled down for the night. Blair, worn out by the day's emotions, had gone to bed. The twins never stayed up past ten o'clock.

Dad and Craig stayed up late, sitting in the parlor with barely audible music playing on the radio and a bottle of Dad's favorite Old Angus Scotch. He always joked about that being his special brew, named after him. "Well, you're not old," we always assured him. But tonight, as we sat around the supper table, I saw new, silvered hair around his temples and in the sprout of the baby hair on his forehead. Then I felt awful about my rash of anger toward him.

I went up to bed, and when I said my nighttime prayers, I prayed hard that we could continue to have all of us together for holidays, and that any one of us who would need to leave for some reason or other, would always return. I said my special prayer for Gracie, and then lay there sleepless.

After I heard Dad come up the stairs to go to bed, I threw on my housecoat and tiptoed downstairs. The lights were off in the parlor, and I assumed everyone was in bed. Craig, when home for a visit, usually slept on a cot in the heated laundry porch. But he had stayed up and was listening to soft music flowing from Dad's new phonograph. I knew that Dad would often stay up late now, listening to recordings that he loved when thinking hard about something, like he had when he grieved over the loss of Ian and Gracie. He had, virtually, worn out the old player then.

Craig greeted me with a sad but resigned voice that told me he knew about Blair. "Hi! Little Abs, how ya dealing with all of this?" My anger flared, again, realizing that I had been ordered to keep quiet, but then my father had told Craig. I stalked into the kitchen for a glass of water, rudely ignoring my oldest brother. But by the time I returned to him, my resentment had begun to dissolve. Of course, Dad would confide in Craig. Craig was wise, and I knew my father considered him to be a man now that he had earned his Forestry degree. Because of his high honors, he had been chosen to stay on at the university to study forest fires and the nature of them as a graduate student.

I sat down across from him and sighed. "I'm not looking forward to losing another sister. Nothing is the same around here, and it all started when you and Aileen moved out, and then Colin, and then we lost Ian and Gracie. What the Sam heck am I supposed to think?"

"Well, Abi, that's life. Things constantly change, sometimes for the good, sometimes for the bad." His glib statement threw me into another fit of anger, and I couldn't trust myself to speak because I knew I would say something I would regret. I sat and sipped my water. Craig refilled his glass with scotch, not even bothering with soda. Oh, yes, I thought to myself, you adults can deaden your feelings with booze. Not fair. What in the Sam heck was a nearly twelve-year-old, now physically a woman, supposed to do?

Craig sat quiet, cool and collected, waiting for me to speak. He and Dad had had their talk along with how much scotch, I wondered. I stood up, picked up the bottle, and studied it. I had been the one sent to fetch it, after which Dad ordered, "After this, it's time for bed, Abi. You've had a big day." He had treated me like a child. I was certain he and Mom hadn't put things together yet, that I was the one having periods instead of Blair. For some reason, I now resented going through the throes of womanhood without them knowing.

I held the bottle higher—yes, they had put a sizable dent in it. I don't know what possessed me, but suddenly I felt extremely rebellious and put-off. I wrenched the cap off and stood chugging scotch until first my throat and then my stomach rebelled. Craig grabbed the bottle from me as I stood coughing and gagging. Tears ran free as I reflexively gulped down that God-awful stuff, and then I began to cry. I tried to tell him how terrible I thought it was of Dad to send Blair away, and then insist she give her baby away to strangers. Only bits and pieces came out, but Craig understood me.

When I was very small, and Craig still lived at home, he had become my second father for a while. Mom and Dad had their hands full caring for my twin brothers. Cameron had been delivered with forceps and his development was slow. His soft spot took nearly two years to grow together, and he required a lot of attention in the beginning, only seeming to catch up to his brother by the time they turned three.

I felt like that little toddler again as Craig picked me up and cradled me in his arms, whispering soft words of comfort. When I finished crying, I jumped out of his lap, embarrassed. But my weeping had washed out all the anger and frustration, leaving me feeling empty.

When he finally spoke, I could tell by his voice that he was just as upset as I. "Abi, I know this sounds a bit uncaring, but just know—it could be worse. We MacDougals will get through this, too."

I hung my head in shame. "Yes, we have been through worse. I forgot."

I hugged him goodnight and went to bed.

Christmas was subdued with many forced smiles and much false laughter. Mom and Dad did their best to provide a happy occasion; we all received fine gifts, expensive ones, with the little ones receiving a bounty of toys and games. Dad had refused to allow Rory to have any of the very popular miniature replicas of planes, tanks, jeeps, guns, or anything to do with war. Both Craig and Colin had signed up to serve in the U.S. Army. They wanted to jump out of planes in Europe, one of the newest but most dangerous of combat duties. They had volunteered to train with the Parachute Infantry division of the U.S. Army at Camp Toccoa, Georgia, and would leave soon.

After the Japanese had surprise-attacked our naval base at Pearl Harbor, our country went completely war-obsessed, including my brothers, which broke my heart, as well as Dad's and Mom's. I had thought the United States war-crazed before, but now it had completely taken over people's lives. I quit reading Dad's magazines for a while because I didn't see the necessity because war news and propaganda was everywhere—in the air waves, in advertisements, on posters all over town—encouraging our young men to be patriotic and sign up to fight. I grew sick of hearing about patriotism, and that we should all be stoic.

Our family made a mess out of stoicism when seeing Blair off for her time at Grandma and Grandpa MacDougal's. Everyone cried but Dad, who remained strangely silent. Blair left on my birthday, which made it even worse, with a belly now showing her pregnancy. She wore one of Mom's old, loose swing coats, but it still revealed her condition. That night, I refused to cut my birthday cake and went upstairs to bed to a cold and empty room. Dad, Mom told me later, stayed up all night, drinking his scotch and listening to his new records.

1942

War Comes a Little Closer

As I looked at Gracie's newest photo taped on the refrigerator door, I thought she looked as happy and contented as a little girl could be. She would turn three years old at five p.m. this evening, and I remembered the afternoon when she began to work her way into this world. Mom had been energetically cleaning house after the holidays, and she'd told us the baby would be coming soon because her nesting instinct had her in its grips. "It's nature's way so that when the wee babe comes everything will be clean and ready."

Dad didn't have time to take Mom into town because she doubled up in agony with her first pain at four o'clock, and Gracie was born a mere hour later. After giving life to eight previous children, Mom had finally been granted an easy birth. Later, Rory, too, had come as easily as Gracie. Maybe that was God's reward to her for being a good Irish-Catholic woman who had done her duty. But our family was shrinking. Ian and Gracie were gone, and Blair, with Craig and Colin who would be leaving soon for training.

To a young girl living in the mountains of Montana, the war still seemed far away, despite that it would now have a greater impact on us with our two oldest joining the fight. The people most affected were those on the coasts and in larger cities, enduring blackouts every night, while shortages reared their ugly heads in all aspects of life, especially in manufacturing.

Entrepreneurs and scientists all over America worked day and night to develop replacements for every good now dedicated to the war effort. Women no longer could buy new girdles, due to rubber shortages. But someone did discover how to turn coal into synthetic rubber since Japan now controlled the world's largest rubber supplies. Stockings, even the cotton and nylon ones that were to replace silk stockings, were in short supply, making some women desperate enough to use leg paints, which came in the form of a large crayon. After coloring their legs, they would draw seams up the backs of their legs with eyeliner, to replicate the look of silk hosiery. Corn sucrose replaced the sugar needed for Coca-Cola, which was advertised as a necessary source of vigor and energy in everyday life.

"The damn Japanese!" was an utterance Dad made often those days. They had achieved many military victories since their deadly attack on Pearl Harbor, which, for a time, stunted our strength in the Pacific. They had taken Guam and Wake Island in December, and then the Philippines, the Dutch East Indies, Hong Kong, Malaya, Singapore, the Solomon Islands, and Burma in the first part of the year. They ran wild for six months, conquering East Asian countries. I prayed that neither of my brothers would have to join the forces fighting Japs. In the newspapers and magazines, they seemed evil, cold-hearted, and were known for their tenacity in battle.

Rumors and Speculation

In school, there was much speculation about Blair's disappearance. Everyone wondered why a beautiful young fifteen-year-old would want to take care of an old, ailing grandmother. So many kids asked questions, I finally decided to lie, explaining that Blair was still upset over Billy's early death, and that Mom and Dad had decided that perhaps a change would help her.

It worked, and soon I could concentrate on school work. Our principal called me to his office one day and told me that if I kept progressing as I was, they would move me into junior-level classes next year, and after that, I immersed myself in my schoolwork even more.

Since we were now involved in a shooting war, our country, confident in its citizens' strength and ingenuity, more and more often spoke of an imminent end to the conflict. All of Dad's magazines addressed issues as if the war would soon be over. I felt this attitude matched my family's mistaken perception after losing Gracie—that getting her back would happen soon and at any time, though we knew better now. Our private eyes had resigned to become investigators for FBI Director J. Edgar Hoover. Apparently, the U.S. needed thousands more agents trained in counter-espionage and surveillance of citizens suspected to be foreign spies.

We were devastated when they abandoned us, but we realized that there seemed to be no new clues to bring us any closer to finding Gracie. All leads had gone cold, and unfortunately, it had become obvious that Gracie's location would never be found by searching areas near and around each new postmark. Whoever her kidnappers were, they were clever.

In January, we received our first letters from Blair. Mom and Dad received one, and I had an envelope addressed only to me. Our parents raised their eyebrows at that, but they gave a mutual shake of the head saying, *Well, okay.* They knew that if Blair told me something alarming, I would tell them. I hadn't received much scolding for keeping her secret before, but they had me promise that I would share any knowledge of such astronomical personal matters with them in the future.

Blair's letter relieved my worry about my dear sister. She said that Grandma hadn't shown any signs of craziness or dementia. The doctor gave her pills that calmed her so she didn't get distraught and ruin the healing of her leg. He was pleased with her progress, especially considering that she had just turned seventy. He attributed her rapid recovery to her craving for protein and calcium. She couldn't seem to get enough milk or milk products. Our uncle, who still had dairy cows, brought her gallons of it, and Grandpa learned how to make cheese and cottage cheese for her, since dairy products were on our nation's shortage list.

The young doctor, Henry Badt, was a resident at the hospital and had trained in a specialty called physical therapy. He had Grandma doing small exercises with her leg as it healed. Blair told me that he was teaching her how to help Grandma through these exercises, and that they talked a lot. *I was so embarrassed, one day, when he asked me when my baby was due. I blushed and asked, "How did you know?" "Well, I am a doctor. I know."* She also told me how he had made an appointment for her to be examined by another doctor, who pronounced her to be healthy and that the baby was doing well, despite that he seemed small.

You know, Abi, how I wanted to be free of this baby. But now, I want it so bad. He kicks and wriggles around in me and then I feel this surge of love that I can't explain. Grandpa, like Mom, wants me to keep him. By the way, I'm sure it's a boy. But like Dad, Grandma keeps urging me to give him up for adoption. She keeps telling me that she knows of a couple that would be happy to take him. I'm so confused, Abi, I don't know what to think, except that Henry doesn't see me as a horrible person for finding myself in this predicament, and I haven't even told him about being raped.

I wrote back to her and said that she, and only she, should make this important decision. *Maybe it's the good Lord's plan that you have this baby and keep it for some reason. Or, maybe not.* I told her that she would know how to make the best choice.

Her next letter was all about the baby's movements—how it felt like he was doing somersaults—as if he, too, was doing physical therapy. I knew that she wanted to keep him, despite Dad's letters telling her that she should give it up to someone who wants and needs a baby. I knew she understood that, too—after all, someone had been desperate enough to steal Gracie at the risk of being a criminal. The rest of Blair's letter was about Henry, and I knew she was falling for him.

She told me that he was pure German and came from a family that had, a century ago, left Germany to farm in the Volga River valley in southern Russia. Needing a better agricultural system, Catherine the Great had invited these competent German farmers to come work her land, giving Russians a good example and some lessons in successful farming practices. Since their farmers were merely serfs, and had no rights or freedom, I didn't find it surprising that Henry told her that these virtual Russian slaves were still poor farmers despite the German influence.

His family emigrated from Russia to the United States to escape the Russian Civil War. Despite that these people had been assured they could forever keep their German citizenship while in Russia, they had become hapless victims at the mercy of both the Red and the White armies. One day the Reds would come and steal much of their harvest and forcibly take men to fight for them, and a few days later, the White Army would do the same.

Blair went on and on about Henry, how good-looking he was, how kind he was, and how when she finally told him about the rape, he only embraced her and told her she was brave. She said he worried that when he finished his residency the government would force him to become an Army surgeon and send him to war. I had just read in a magazine that the government was recruiting doctors by the thousands to send overseas, so I knew his concern to be valid.

Blair said that Henry planned to wean Grandma from the sedatives, and that Grandpa was worried about her becoming agitated again. Grandma's broken leg had completely healed, but she still used a cane to get around. Blair added that her doctor expected her to deliver sometime between late February and early March.

On Our Own

Mom and Dad purchased train tickets for February 26, hoping to arrive in time for the birth. They knew now that Blair planned on keeping the baby, but Dad still hoped to persuade her to give it up for adoption.

We had just finished calving most of our cows, with just a small number of mostly heifers still waiting to give birth. Just like humans, first time bovine mothers tend to be late. Mom and Dad left on a cold, bitter day, leaving Callum, Cameron, and me to finish the calving under the supervision of Larry Pierson. He and Dad had become close friends, though Mom still refused to invite him for supper. But Dad figured he would do just fine since, in his words, *any man that can help a mare birth her colt will do fine with a cow.* The first few days and nights went well. Larry watched the cows during the day while we were in school, and at night we took turns doing four-hour checks as Dad had ordered.

But on the fifth night, there was trouble. When we returned home from school, it was snowing hard, with a pouty wind blowing us about as we did our chores. I was to do the last night check since it was up to me to cook supper. Mom and Dad had taken Rory with them, and it was just me and the twins on the ranch at night, with the plan that we would call Larry if we needed help.

I went out after doing supper clean-up and my homework, relieving Cameron. He told me that he had brought in an itchy heifer, who looked like she was thinking about calving but with no immediate signs of strong labor. He had left her in a stall, and when I checked on her she seemed fine. She was kicking at her side and occasionally her tail would go straight up, the first signs of labor.

I settled down on a straw bale to write to Craig. We had been closer again after our late night on Thanksgiving and had decided to write to one another while he was gone. It had taken a while for his first letter to arrive, and I was excited to respond to it. I reached into my coat pocket and pulled his letter out. He and Colin had been latecomers to the camp and to the newly forming E Company, 506th Regiment for the Parachute Infantry, which constantly sought to replace the "washouts" with new, more capable men.

Craig first told me that it had been easy for him and Colin to catch up because of their background. Dad had worked Craig and Colin just like he worked us younger kids. All my older siblings still helped with the big projects at the ranch such as calving, branding, gathering, herding, and haying. Craig and Colin, when in town, ran and worked out with weights and sometimes, even challenged one another to miles-long races. Their competitive spirit and the need to better one another kept them working hard to keep strong, flexible physiques.

Consequently, they both excelled in the physical training exercises at camp. Craig went on by telling about their routine each day and everything they were learning, and about the men at camp. *We start the day early in the morning doing calisthenics and then we move on to the obstacle course. After that, we have some down-time—listening to lectures and learning map and compass reading, signaling, codes, infantry tactics, and how to use radio equipment and switchboards, field telephones, and how to do wire stringing. Then after lunch, we run up Mount Currahee, more a hill than mountain, but here, since it's 1,000 feet high, it's considered a mountain.*

Now the distance up Currahee is a three-mile run up and three miles down. They call it the "wash-out" run since many new volunteers never make it the first time and then are "washed-out" from the program. So many have not made it, Abi. They try and usually end up puking their guts out and then they're finished. They are sent to the "wash-out" section of camp and are gone the next day. I guess the point is that we only have one chance here, just like the only one we will have when we fight, except that one chance wasted when fighting means death or injury, not merely being demoted to the regular infantry.

Some of these men break my heart. They come here after growing up during the Depression, having always been hungry and surviving—never having shoes or if they did, ones with holey soles. They wore ragged, worn-out hand-me-downs, and had none of the niceties we grew up with— educations and parents to instruct them in the ways of the world, watching carefully over every stage of development. Those days of deprivation still cling to them, and they often don't have any concept of the world besides where they and their families have lived, with only survival from day to day having been the order of business for each of those days. They had no extra money with which to travel, buy radios to listen to, or even autos to drive.

They've volunteered for this outfit, not only for the bonus pay, but to prove, mostly to themselves, that they can be better, even the best. But many of them don't make it through the first day, no, the hardships they have suffered have made them physically weak or with deficiencies, and have left them with low opinions of themselves and with emotional bitterness. Sometimes, that acrimoniousness and caustic attitude is all they have to give them the strength and determination to get through our tough training, but unfortunately, many feel defeated before they enter camp.

We were lucky, Abi, to have all the food we could eat, and parents that had the time and energy to provide all we needed to grow and excel. Remember when we older kids came home from school upset and feeling bad for our poorer and down-and-out school chums? That is how I feel now. I can see that Colin feels the same, but you know him, he won't say anything aloud—he'll need to put it all down in writing.

But those of us that make it here, both the better-off and the ones I just wrote about, we all know that we're in this together, jumping into enemy territory at some point, and that is what glues us together despite our different backgrounds.

I sat for a long time, thinking about Craig's words. He sounded positive and confidently enthusiastic, and for that, I was glad. Then I heard the splattering torrent of the heifer's water breaking. I smelt the odor of it and saw steam rising when the cold air of the barn met that hot wetness. I went back to starting my letter to Craig, but soon, the heifer began a soft moaning, and I could see that she had a bubble out. Good, I thought—she's progressing nicely. But as the night went on, it became clear that she wasn't getting anywhere. Her obvious pain with each contraction unnerved me, and I guessed it was time to get help. I zipped up the front of my coat and put my hat and gloves on, preparing to run out into the wild, raging wind to wake up the twins and to call Larry.

I couldn't believe it; Cameron had accidentally latched the door on the outside. We had that latch on the outside to keep the door from blowing open during high winds. I wiggled the door. I slid a knife between the frame and the door, hoping to move the wooden block on the outside. But it remained in a horizontal position. I stood there, shaking my head, and then I had an awful revelation: Cameron had purposely locked me into the barn. There was no other explanation. Now I heard the heifer, bellowing in her pain and frustration. I was furious and wanted to scream out loud, too.

I stood thinking—no use to yell or scream, no one would hear me inside the house even on a quiet night. I ran and opened the gate to the pulling stall after seeing the heifer push helplessly with each contraction. She would need help. I opened the gate to her roomy sixteen-by-sixteen-foot stall to move her into the much narrower one called a squeeze chute, where we secured the cows before helping them birth their calves. She threatened to chase me at first, but finally went waddling in the right direction. She obligingly walked into the wooden chute, and I hurriedly pulled the rope and tied it tight around a beam so the panel held her tight. But then she fought going into the head catch, shaking her head around, beating it against the wall. Finally, after I stood back and let her be, she unconsciously thrust her head into the catch at the onset of her next contraction, and I pulled that rope, securing it tightly.

I washed my hands in the bucket of cold water, and then gathered the pulling chains and tossed them in. After a bit, I took them out and hung them on the hook next to the backside of the pulling stall. I took a deep breath and slowly reached inside her. She bellered in indignation and pain, but I was happy to feel that the calf was coming head first. I skirted my hands around her cervix, gently stretching it like I had seen

Dad do before. I panicked when she threatened to go down with the next pain. "Oh, please, girl, don't do that!"

I thanked the Lord when she remained standing, and I reached inside to fasten a chain on each front leg, and feeling how large the hooves were, I understood why she was having trouble. The calf's nose emerged with the next contraction and the mother threatened to go down again. I broke the water sack away from her baby's nose so it wouldn't suffocate, pulled its chained legs out as far as I could, and sat on the floor of the barn, bracing my feet on the squeeze gate and the wall next to it. When she contracted again, I stiffened my legs as tight as I could to get some leverage and began pulling on the chains. And then, I became angry and screamed curses, mostly at Cameron, and when the next pain came, I pulled hard.

As the calf slid out, I cried for joy. He lay there gasping, struggling to catch his first real breath. I found a straw and tickled the inside of his nostrils, making him cough and sputter fluid from his lungs. But, unfortunately, the heifer had gone down. I pulled the calf out into the open area between stalls, took off the chains, and went to get the mother up. She just sat there while her baby lay shivering. I found some old towels and dried him off and then worked again on getting the cow up.

She finally stood, and I unleashed the ropes that held her tight, holding my breath until she slowly backed out of the stall. She sniffed her baby, and then suddenly, she began butting him with her head. He gave a little *moo*, but that didn't deter her from hurting that little thing that had caused her so much discomfort. I attempted to shoo her off, but then she tried to take me. I climbed the nearest stall gate and kicked at her head, which she was using against me like a battering ram. I kicked again and swore at her. She turned and ran back to the stall where she had been penned before. I hurried to latch the gate, and then turned my attention to the calf.

He was shivering and bawling, wanting his first sucks of sustenance. I had brought out water, and I made him a bottle of colostrum, an artificially-made substance to replace the mother's first milk, which is so essential to a newborn calf's well-being. And, despite its chill, he drank gustily. I finished drying him off and opened a fresh bale of straw, and then I spooned my body around his shiny, little black body and covered us both with straw. He finally slept, and I sobbed myself to sleep.

I woke up from a deep slumber, responding to Larry's soft murmurings. "Wake up, girl. Abi, what are you doing out here? It's as cold as a witch's tit."

I moaned, feeling chills overtake me and a funny, painful stiffness in the back of my right thigh. When I struggled to get to my feet, Larry grasped my right hand and pulled me up.

"Why in God's name are you locked in the barn?" I hadn't known until then that he even knew or thought about God.

"Dear Abi, your hand is as icy as the North wind." He began rubbing both my hands between his big warm ones, and chills went shivering up and down my spine.

I shook my head, trying to remember everything as I climbed out of my troubled sleep. I had dreamed all night, and while I couldn't remember what they were about, I knew my dreams had been unpleasant. I stood for a moment, wavering on my frozen feet, and as I looked down I realized the calf had slept a healing sleep. But now, because of our voices, he raised his little head and gave a weak *moo*.

Still puzzled, Larry looked down at him and instantly realized the events of the night.

"So, he and his momma had a bad night, yes?"

I nodded. "Cameron accidentally turned the wooden latch outside when I took over. She"—I waved my arm toward the ornery cow—"had a difficult time birthing him, and I had to pull the calf. Then she went crazy, beat on her baby, and tried to take me. When she finally stalked off to the stall Cameron had left her in, I locked her in and took care of the calf. But I'm sure he needs to eat again soon."

Larry took his hat off and ran his hand through his hair. "Well, I'll be damned." He kept shaking his head, and then said, "How old are you, girl?"

"Twelve, sir."

Noticing my teeth clacking, he again began rubbing his hands up and down my arms. Then he opened his jacket, and pulled me into his warmth. I began crying and he just stood there, still working on my arms to bring hot blood to them.

When I could speak again, I blubbered, "I'm so sorry, Larry—so sorry."

"Sorry about what?"

"I was the one who put the suspicion on you and your wife because of that night at the circus. What I wrote in my journal made you first on the list of suspects in Gracie's disappearance. Can you forgive me?"

"There, there, there . . .," he kept repeating. And then he said, "Abi there is absolutely nothing to forgive. What else could you and your family think?" I began hiccupping in my attempt to quit crying.

"There, there ..." Larry repeated, patting my back like I was a little baby. Soon the soothing sound of his soft murmurs and the feel of his big, rough hand calmed me, and I stepped out of his warm-jacketed embrace.

"Let's get you to the house, Abi. Don't worry about things here." Larry jerked his head in the direction of the cow. "I'm sure she'll soon be a good mama. They get confused sometimes, these girls, they say it has something to do with hormones, which I don't know anything about. But since she went back to the place where she last was before calving, drawn by the smell of her baby where her water broke, she'll be a good mother. I just can't believe that you, a twelve-year-old-child, managed to pull a calf all by herself—the courage and strength it took."

I giggled, now a bit rummy, "Well, look at me—I am almost as tall as you, and I'm not exactly a child."

He laughed. "Taller than me in many ways, kiddo. Let's get you into the house before you catch pneumonia."

I began limping along beside him.

"You're not walking too well—is your leg still asleep?"

"No, sir. It feels like I pulled a muscle in the back of my thigh."

"Oh, Abi," was all he said.

We made our way slowly to the house, trudging through two feet of fresh snow.

"Should I call the school and tell them you won't be there today?"

"Yes—that would be great."

I ran a bath and gratefully sank into the hot, steaming water, remembering the steam put out by my scary heifer's amniotic fluids, and I began to feel a sense of pride. Yes, in many ways I had out done my brother's cruelty and had survived to be a heroic young rancher-girl. The truth would come out later. He would suffer embarrassment over his feigned mistake, and perhaps some punishment, too, and I would be praised. My plan to become a great cattle breeder, horse breeder and trainer now seemed more possible than ever—and with Jake, of course.

I collapsed, warmed but exhausted, into my bed about five in the morning. Later I heard Larry yelling at the twins to wake them up, and then much stern talk as Larry berated Cameron for his "mistake." My revenge had already begun.

That night, I invited Larry to stay for supper since he planned to do my calving shift. Cameron could only glower at me the entire evening, though nothing was said about his behavior the night before. Our conversation was light and mostly about horses, training them, and their incredible personalities—so varied like people. But I was nervous about Cameron when Larry went out to relieve Callum.

The next afternoon, Larry changed the calving schedule, making Cameron the last to do the checks. I sensed animosity between him and Cameron, and wondered what exactly had been said. But I felt safer that night when Cameron went up to his and Callum's room to immerse himself in his comic books after Callum started his shift, and Larry went home to rest a bit. While Callum and I loved more literate and serious reads, Cameron chose comics such as *Captain America, Superman,* and the *Justice Society of America.*

His favorite, though, was *Captain Marvel.* We all knew this since he loved to come up flashing his fist in front of one's face saying, "Shazam!" When you made the mistake of blinking and ducking, he would get a big charge. I'd read one of his *Marvel* books and discovered Shazam was an ancient, three-thousand-year-old wizard. Yes, I thought, it will take you three thousand years to become a wise wizard, dear brother.

Mom and Dad called the evening after they reached Culloden. Blair had delivered her baby the night they arrived—a perfect baby boy whom she named James Joshua MacDougal. We were glad to hear they were both healthy, and that he didn't have many features proclaiming him a Gustafson—they were all blonde and had blue eyes, except for Gail with her gorgeous brown orbs. James was dark-haired with our signature strong jaw line. Mom told me that Blair loved him completely and unconditionally to the point that Dad had decided to keep quiet, accepting her decision to keep him.

I felt happy and relieved, I went up to my room, buried my head in my pillow, and cried a deluge of joyful tears. The next morning when I awoke, I felt free and floaty. The gripping pain I had carried around on my shoulders was gone. Ever since I had learned of Blair's pregnancy, I had had these awful headaches and when my head didn't hurt, my shoulders ached. But now, that had all disappeared. I got up that morning and made us a nice breakfast and invited Larry to join us. He winked at me and announced that he planned to keep the new calving schedule and would stay in the bunkhouse each night. I knew he had seen the looks of spite Cameron cast my way, and I would forever hold Larry close to my heart.

In February, President Roosevelt had put in place an energy-and-light saving policy called Daylight Saving Time. We complained about it at first, but soon everyone all over our nation began to see its benefits. The blackout cities had one more hour of light, and we who made our livings in agriculture appreciated the extra daylight for our labors. Mornings were now darker again, but we knew that they would brighten up soon as spring came fully upon us.

I continued to have Larry in for meals, and we grew to be great friends. There was an easiness about him that even Cameron came around to liking and respecting. In fact, I noticed one day how Cameron had come to imitate some of Larry's mannerisms, and when he did that, he was likable.

Larry would not have conversations about the war, and that was refreshing. He said he didn't need to worry about going to fight since he had severely damaged his spleen when very young. At night, Larry would allow Cameron to stay in a little later to join us in listening to his favorite radio shows.

Larry was addicted to comedy. He loved to laugh. We had to catch *Duffy's Tavern,* his favorite. I loved it too, because it felt good to laugh after all we had been through. The show would open with "When Irish Eyes Are Smiling," which became my favorite song to hum or sing when doing chores or housework. When training horses, I noticed they loved my crooning that tune. During the song, a telephone would ring and a man would answer with "Hello, Duffy's Tavern, where the elite meet to eat. Archie the manager speakin'. Duffy ain't here—oh, hello, Duffy." Duffy was never there nor did he ever speak. When I asked why the owner was never there, Larry only shrugged his shoulders and said something about dry humor. Then I wondered—was there such a thing as "wet humor?—and soon found there was. The characters were so funny and did such odd things that soon we were all laughing with tears running down our faces and hands slapping our legs.

Another show I especially liked was *Fibber McGee and Molly* because of his hilarious and nonsensical stories and his wife's short, succinct responses to his silly talk. The show called *Inner Sanctum Mystery* thrilled me to the point of making shivers run up and down my neck. I loved the squeaky door, the spooky music, the host's sarcastic jokes, and his closing which was— "Pleasant dreeeeeaams, hmmmmmmm."

Henry, the War, & Psyche Therapy

Mom and Dad came home mid-March without Blair and her baby. I was bitterly disappointed. Blair turned sixteen March 9, and they didn't think that exposing her to gossip at her tender age would do her any good. They claimed she was happy to stay and take care of her baby and Grandma and Grandpa. James was a good baby and slept much of the time. Mom said Blair was a natural mother. Dad told me that there was no way she could have ever given up her child, and then he just smiled at me and gave me a hard, quick hug. "I don't know how you do it, Abi, but you always seem to know what is in a person's heart."

What I didn't know was what was in Cameron's heart. He went back to his old, pouty, black moods when Mom and Dad returned. We talked Dad into letting us listen to some of the funny and lighthearted radio shows that Larry had shared with us, and that made life a little happier for all of us, especially Cameron. I loved to hear his laughter and wished he could find some peace and joy in life instead of stalking around in such misery.

Mom excitedly came home one day with the pictures she had taken of Blair and the baby. They were in color! She had found the newly developed Kodacolor film for making color prints in Ohio. James was beautiful, with dark, slightly curly hair and deep, dark eyes—so bright. He looked alert and healthy, with the chubbiest cheeks I had ever seen.

And Blair was thin again, with glowing skin and dimpled smiles. She looked happy, and I knew why.

I had received a letter from her shortly before Mom and Dad returned in which she told me that Henry had declared his love for her. They planned to become engaged as soon as he finished his residency. They would take their time in marrying since Blair was still so young. But if Henry had to go to war, they would marry before he left.

But she had disturbing news about Grandma. She had begun her nightly wandering through the house again, wringing her hands and repeating, "Should have not done it. Should have not let her. Can't live with myself. Can't. Shouldn't. Oh, why? Why?" Blair said she would go on like that all night, and each time Blair finished nursing James, she would try to settle Grandma down, who then became even more agitated. "Don't give up your baby, Blair. Don't. Don't let them take him . . ." Blair wrote that she would try to calm Grandma, saying, "No, Grandma. No one is going to take him. I would never let anyone take him. Never."

Blair went on to say that Grandma would then embrace her in a hard, bone-breaking hug. Then she would let go and say, "But they took Gracie. They took Gracie. You gotta be vigilant, always. They're out there. Ready to strike. Be careful."

Blair told me in a later letter that in the mornings when Grandma saw her nursing James, she would sigh a long, huffy sigh of relief. "Thank God, he's still here. They didn't come. I'm going to bed." After that, Grandma would sleep away the day and then be up to wander all night again. Despite her appetite for dairy products, she had begun wasting away. *She's as thin as a rail, and I don't know what to do, Abi.* I wrote back to her and simply said, "Just love her, and when James is old enough and strong enough, let her tend to him a little. Babies always make things better, don't you think?"

Havoc reigned worldwide. War reared its ugly head everywhere. After calving season, I had more time for Dad's *Time* magazines. The first of the year, President Roosevelt, Prime Minister Churchill, Maxim Litvinov from the U.S.S.R., and T V Soong from China, had signed a United Nations Declaration in which they agreed "not to make any separate peace with any Axis national powers." In time, 22 additional nations also signed this declaration. Our country and Britain also made an agreement to establish a combined Chiefs of Staff and to make defeating Germany their priority, a policy later called Europe First. On January 26, our first U.S. troops had arrived in Britain and later in the year, British and American forces began their push to defeat General Rommel and his forces in North Africa.

In March, FDR signed executive orders authorizing the internment of American Japanese, German Americans, and Italian Americans. Thank God no one came and took Jake and his family away. I thought these orders cruel and unjust, but what was happening in Hitler's conquered countries was far more disturbing and monstrous.

Also in March, the Germans finished building the Nazi Belzec extermination camp; in April, they completed a camp at Sobibor; and in July, a second camp at Treblinka. Hundreds of thousands of people were murdered, causing the Allies to issue a Joint Declaration by members of the United Nations to publicly acknowledge these horrible doings as the *Holocaust*.

The Japanese proved to be just as depraved and brutish. When they defeated the Filipinos and Americans on Bataan Peninsula, they summarily executed over 350 Filipino officers, and then began marching the remaining 110,000 troops sixty miles to the capital of Bataan. They beat, bayoneted, and starved their prisoners to death, causing this horror to be called the Bataan Death March. The Japanese also dropped germ bombs on China, killing hundreds who died of bubonic plague.

I was mesmerized by what was going on in the world. But after a while, the war news was not all bad. In May, our U.S. Navy repelled the Japs at the Battle of the Coral Sea, and by June our Navy had stopped the Japanese naval advance in the Pacific, defeating them in the Battle of Midway. In November, our naval forces were close to recovering control of Guadalcanal. In August, the first raid had been carried out by heavy bombers of the U.S. Eighth Air Force against occupied France. It was deemed a success, with twelve Boeing B-17 Flying Fortresses going out and all twelve returning. By Thanksgiving, the Soviet counter-attack,

Operation Uranus under the command of Georgy Zhukov, had the German Sixth Army surrounded at Stalingrad.

The progress the Allies were making made our holidays more cheerful. Craig and Colin came home for a week at Thanksgiving after having completed their training and first jump school at Camp Toccoa. They each wore their coveted and hard-worked-for wings. They stood taller and even more handsome in their uniforms which now sported those wings on the left pockets on their jackets, on a patch on their left shoulders, and one on their hats. They had earned the right to wear paratrooper boots with their trouser legs tucked into them. Despite that we hoped and prayed they would not have to go overseas since the war effort seemed to be more and more successful on all fronts, saying our goodbyes to them left us empty and heartbroken.

Then ten days before Christmas, our spirits were dampened. Blair's latest letter contained awful news. Blair first wrote about Grandma's rapid mental deterioration during Crazy Aunt Peggy's visit in the second week of December. Blair said they argued constantly with a bitterness she had never seen. *It was just terrible. Peggy would bundle Grandma up and take her out onto the porch. They would yell and scream at one another until I came close. I could never hear what was being said; every time I came near or walked out there, they would finish the current argument with hissing, hateful whispers and then turn and smile at me. Grandma never seemed demented when arguing with Peggy. By the way, Peggy's still the same. Wears old mannish clothes, her same ancient fedora, and all the rest. Peggy would sit out there yelling, almost seeming to threaten Grandma, with her silly pipe hanging out of her mouth half the time.*

At night, they would stay up and keep fighting when Grandma would usually wander. I gave up trying to hear what the argument was about—I needed to sleep when I could because James, my little man, is a hungry boy right now, and I need to nurse him more and more often. You wouldn't believe how much he has grown.

Anyway, I got up the third morning after Peggy arrived and all was quiet. I nursed James and then went in search of them. No one was in their bed but Grandpa. I looked outside and saw that Peggy's car was gone. When I went into the kitchen, I found the note Peggy had written. 'Have taken

Mom to a hospital back East for psyche therapy. Will have her back home before Christmas.'

This is the awful part. You had better sit down when reading this. Dad stopped reading aloud, and I watched, horrified, as the color left his face and then came back a roaring red. He sat silent for a bit and then stood up, put on his coat, hat, and gloves, grabbed the car keys, and went out the door. Soon we heard our car sputter to a start, and we watched as Dad drove down the driveway.

As soon as she finished the letter, Mom handed it to me and told us kids to go into the parlor. As we walked out of the kitchen, I heard Mom pick up the phone, asking the operator to connect her to Grandma and Grandpa's number. I sat down to finish reading the letter to my three silent brothers; even Rory was quiet, sensing something major was wrong, and he nestled into my lap.

Peggy brought Grandma home last night, leading her into the house as if she were a little child. Grandma's hair had been shaved from her ears up, and down to her forehead, with an ugly scar rising over the top of the highest part of her forehead. Grandpa went into a rage. I never thought I would see him behave like that. 'What in the hell did you do, Peggy?' Peggy answered him with not a blink of an eye, 'I had her go through a procedure called psyche surgery. Now, Mom won't be so troubled. She'll sleep like a baby and won't be upset all the time.'

Grandpa roared in response. 'How the hell did you do this without my authority?'

Peggy got up close to him and said, 'I signed the paperwork after telling them you were too old and feeble to bring her yourself.'

Then, Grandpa slapped Peggy so hard, she fell. He kicked her repeatedly, telling her to get the hell out of there and to never, ever come back. Grandma just sat at the table, smiling and humming. After Peggy left, Grandpa sat down and cried, saying repeatedly, 'That bitch. That bitch. I always knew she was nothing but trouble.' He looked up at me and asked, "What has she done to my Aileen?' It was so sad, I just sat down on another chair and cried, too, which made James cry.

When I finished nursing him, Grandma held out her hands, saying 'Baby. Baby.' I took James to her after I burped him and set him in her lap.

I had to help her position her hands around him so she could safely hold him. She began rocking back and forth, humming the lullaby she has always sung to us, all the time shaking her head and interrupting her humming with, 'Can't remember the words. Can't remember the words.' When she began to cry, I took James and said, 'It's all right Grandma. Let's have a little sleep and then you'll feel better,' and then I put them both down for a nap, and they fell asleep like babies.

Grandma is just a child now, and I miss her so much. I hate Peggy for what she did. But Grandpa says he doesn't expect to ever see her again. This visit was the first one in years, and he doesn't even know where she lives or what her address is. He said he knew that she and Grandma had written letters back, and, forth, but that Grandma had either hidden them or burned them in the fireplace, because he could never find any evidence of them in the house.

It's so sad around here. It just as if Grandma has died, leaving only a ghostly shell of herself with us. Grandpa grieves so. He just sits and stares, and when I try to cheer him, he shakes his head as if my gesture is useless. I wish you, Dad and Mom, and everyone, could come and spend Christmas with us, though I'm sure that is out of the question.

But please call me when you get this. Please?

By the time I finished, we were all crying, even Rory, who turned and buried his face into my shoulder. The weight and the warmth of him soothed me some, and as I comforted him, I realized that this, too, we MacDougals would bear with dignity and strength, and that we would get past this like always.

Christmas

Dad came home that night with train tickets for all of us, including Aileen, Kendall, and Ianna. Aileen had managed to carry her latest baby to full term. But like Dad said, "Well, if she delivers her child in Ohio, that'll be fine—it appears they have good doctors there, too." He finished this declaration with a wink, so I knew he was aware of Blair's romance with Dr. Henry Badt, and that gave me a spark of happiness.

Train travel, I decided, had its good aspects and some bad. But all things considered, Callum, Cameron, and I found it thrilling. The littlest ones, Ianna and Rory, must have found the rhythm of the ride soothing, because they both slept most of the time. We older children could go to the observation car, climb the stairs, and see the different landscapes passing by like a picture show. I tried to read. My English teacher had assigned me several Sinclair Lewis novels, and I had *Main Street* with me but I found it difficult to concentrate because of the many different scenes passing by—little towns, bigger towns, cities, and the beautiful landscapes. Besides, I knew that with each mile eaten up by our speeding train, I was getting closer to my sister and her new baby, and I became nearly as antsy as the little ones when they were awake.

When we arrived at Grandma's and Grandpa's, we found a very happy Blair holding her baby with a pride and possessiveness I'd never imagined, but then, beaming, she let us pass him around. Grandpa hugged each one of us with misty eyes while Grandma chattered like a small child, looking at us like we were strangers. It was very hard to accept the fact that we didn't mean anything to her, but as the days went by, she recalled little things about us. And when that look of recognition surfaced in her eyes, we praised her and accepted those crumbs with enthusiasm, making her clap her hands with joy.

Just before our trip to Ohio, I had found *Time* magazine's horrifying article on this new psyche therapy Peggy had put Grandma through. I wept the entire time as I read the description of each step of the procedure. What bothered me most was the fact that the patient is given only a local anesthetic at the temples and only that area. They claim the brain itself is insensitive so they keep the patient awake during the entire operation while cutting only into the brain. They do not remove anything—they only cut into the prefrontal lobe on each side of the brain, separating it from the thalamus, which is the area of the brain that controls emotions and intellect, including memories. The article said that the patient is encouraged to talk, sing, pray, or recite poems, and when it appears their patient had become sleepy, confused, and disoriented, then the doctors know they have cut enough.

With this procedure, they fully intend to strip people's minds of intellect and emotion—the very things that caused the psychotic behavior in the first place. In about a year, they believe the patient's brain will form new, internal pathways of thinking, enough so that they can once again lead a "useful" life. When I saw the results of this therapy in Grandma, it was obvious that whoever performed the surgery had gone too far with their cuts. My anger made my blood feel as hot and furious as my churning mind, and my heart beat wildly.

But we had a nice Christmas, after all, counting our blessings and moving on from our sorrows a bit. James, our newest, and Aileen with her engorged, wiggling womb, gave us promise and hope for the future, as did Ianna and Rory, our two, always-entertaining, little hams. They uprooted one of Grandma's favorite plants, and Grandma only giggled. After Mom and Aileen had the mess cleaned up, Grandma, communicating with her strange, childish voice, had the two toddlers help her replant it. That, too, gave us some hope that she would regain something of her old self.

That Christmas Eve, Blair and Henry announced they were engaged. He would leave for training at the end of January. As I watched them with arms wrapped around one another's waists, facing our crazy world as one unit, I was happy for her. Blair had been through hell and had found joy again, and our family continued to grow.

1943

Birthday Party

Before we left Ohio, my family and all my aunts, uncles, cousins, Grandma and Grandpa Callaghan, and Grandpa MacDougal held a grand birthday party for me. No one had forgotten Gracie on her birthday, but they thought that when a girl turned thirteen it should be a memorable event. They prepared my favorite foods and Aunt Violet, my mother's sister, baked a cake adorned with candy roses with real ones in the middle.

Mom and Dad gave me a pearl necklace and a beautiful pair of high-heeled, black leather pumps. Everyone teased me about them since high-heeled shoes had recently made the shortage list. "Ye'll be the only one struttin' around in a new set o' heels, me lass. Ohhhh, you'll be the envy of all the bonnie lasses, both young and old, wearin' those beauts." Grandpa Callaghan slapped his knee, chortling, and I knew he had already had a few too many Irish whiskeys.

I loved my Grandpa Callaghan because he was what he was—he never put on airs or pretentions. He and Grandma gave me a gift I have always treasured—a leather-bound scrapbook with pictures from their life in Ireland and photos of their new life and family in America. Before opening my next gift, I peeked at a few pages. The last page I took in had a picture of Gracie, sitting bolstered by pillows, beaming her dimpled, heart-warming smile. I slammed the book shut and thanked them with tears in my eyes and a lump in my throat. My emotional response pleased them greatly, and I was rewarded with a hard squeeze and a kiss on the cheek from each of them.

Grandpa MacDougal, not a sentimentalist, gave me a thousand-dollar check. "For your college fund," he whispered to me as I went to hug him and kiss his cheek. "I know you will need to go on with your studies—the way you read and such." Grandpa could not get up and come to me because Grandma had taken to clinging to him whenever there was a crowd, so there he sat with Grandma's hands tightly clasping his, and her fragile body tucked inside every curve of him. I took Grandpa MacDougal's loving look and wink as a message not just from him, but from Grandma as well, though for most of my party, she sat staring blankly into space. Grandma had always been a winker, and I knew Grandpa's was on her behalf.

I received mostly feminine items; some made me blush—silk stockings, another item on the shortage list, from Blair, who had been saving them for over a year, along with a lovely lace garter belt. My aunts and uncles showered me with perfume, talcum powders, hair combs, jewelry, and a hat, which I secretly swore I would never wear. Aunt Vi had knit a gorgeous shawl for me. It seemed to me that everyone saw me as a young lady now, a notion I had not yet embraced. I felt like a long-legged, skinny, flat-chested, lumbering daddy long-legs spider.

My most interesting gift was from my cousin Tim. He was my age and, like me, loved to read. We sat in the corner of the dining room on the window seat the first night we were there and talked books the entire time. He scoffed at my choices, and I explained that my teacher, being a proper person, had made it clear I should only study the authors she suggested. I told him that I doubted she had read many of Sinclair Lewis' books because I had found *Elmer Gantry* sensual and risqué, and *Main Street* had seemed a much-too-harsh criticism of people living in small towns.

"Actually, Lewis made me feel that there are hardly any redeeming qualities in people anywhere in America in any class of people. In his novel, the citizens of Gopher Prairie were vicious toward anyone different than them, and they especially felt superior to the Swedish immigrant farmers and their families. I did get the sense that Lewis approved of that hard-working, start-over class of people. When I think of the kindness extended to our family in Philipsburg during all our troubles, I must disagree with him about small-towns-people. Yes, they can be two-faced, gossipy, deeply prejudiced, and cool to newcomers, but then again, I know how good-hearted they are at the same time."

Tim told me about his favorite author, a man from Russia.

"Have you read any of Leo Tolstoy's works? *War and Peace?*"

I shook my head, hoping to ask him about the author, but he rushed on in his excitement.

"*Anna Karenina?*"

"No."

"Oh! You must read those two books."

Tim's gift to me was a beautiful, leather-bound edition of *Anna Karenina*, which I gobbled up immediately after I finished reading *It Can't Happen Here*, another one of Sinclair Lewis' social-commentary reads. That novel not only criticized American society's tendency to be wishy-washy and easily led, but also fictionally depicted how one man, craving total and complete authoritarian dictatorship, could take over America and ruin democracy.

Anna Karenina made me cry; despite that, though, I preferred Tolstoy's way of putting things. But when I read *War and Peace*, I felt that he was just as harsh and critical of the Russian upper class as Lewis had been of America's middle class in *Main Street*. Both writers had a way of emphasizing the silliness in human nature, especially homing in on the beliefs and practices that portrayed the inanity of the societies from which they came. Why and how, I wondered, do we humans manage to create such pointless, foolish, and illogical standards with which to judge ourselves and others, and then go on to create ridiculous rules of conduct and propriety accordingly?

I reflected on our sparsely-populated society in Granite County. We had our own set of standards when trying to do the right thing, and in saving face when we didn't, we just hid terrible truths. For instance, I worried if what we were doing about Blair and her baby, James, was right, even honorable. Was it wrong to keep his existence secret and not let the Gustafson family know a part of Billy still lived? Shouldn't they be told they have a beautiful grandbaby? Shouldn't they be allowed to love and enjoy him? And, really, shouldn't his surname be Gustafson—he was as much Gustafson as he was MacDougal. But unfortunately, American society and its standards dealt harshly with young, unmarried mothers, no matter the circumstances.

Christmas in January

I t wasn't until we returned home that we opened our Christmas presents. It was a bittersweet event. We were still missing much of our family, all with futures dramatically unpredictable. We hadn't found Gracie, but had received our annual Christmas gift from her abductors like always. Gracie's picture depicted a four-year-old beauty with auburn hair, falling in ringlets that would put Shirley Temple's to shame, and big, wide-open-to-the-world eyes. Mom and Dad exclaimed at how much she resembled me, and that made me proud, despite that I realized I had nothing to do with it.

I received a bounty of much-needed clothing since I had outgrown most of my wardrobe. I loved the new austere lines in women's clothing. They suited me well. The fashion magazines tagged this modern, wartime look as the "duration" silhouette or the "utility" design. Designers had taken the fluff out of fashion to save on material goods—no more ruffles, turn-back cuffs, pleats, or longer skirts. Skirts had become knee-length, and bodices were collarless with short or three-quarter-length sleeves. I noticed when trying them on that I was growing a noticeable bosom, especially when wearing my new brassieres. I had grown taller, forcing me to take down the mirror in our bedroom and hang it higher.

American designers were having a heyday since war-torn Europe no longer influenced the fashion scene. American women wore white-rimmed sunglasses and daring bathing suits on the beaches, and most factory-working-women wore pants, which I thought were ridiculous since they were high-waisted and wide-legged. I preferred wearing Ian's old trousers. Mom had gift-wrapped Ian's leather chinks for me. I choked up when I ripped that gift open, and then when Dad made a ceremony of presenting Ian's spurs to me, warning me to not become too reliant on them, I held them close to my burgeoning breasts, my eyes misting.

These gifts did not stop Mom from insisting I wear my hair in a more ladylike style. I tried putting my hair up in the pompadour hairstyle which Betty Grable and Bette Davis had made so popular. I gave that up because it made me appear too old for my age and taller. My five foot ten-inch frame didn't need more inches. The working girls at the munitions and war machine factories had taken to wearing snoods—fancy hairnets to keep their hair from being caught in the machines. Women had been scalped when wearing their hair down and loose. Snoods had become a fashion statement, and I preferred them, along with berets. I liked how berets suited me, and I gladly wore them since they allowed me to wear my hair down. I also learned to put my braided hair up in an attractive way that passed Mom's inspection.

We had celebrated the holidays in a sober mood, but when Aileen gave birth to John Jacob O'Leary on January ninth, we all toasted to this wonderful addition to our lives. This time Dad even gave me and the boys the same amount of wine as the adults received. I babysat Aileen's children often, which helped me since I still missed Blair and her baby. We wrote back and forth frequently, and I hoped to go see her in the spring between calving and branding seasons. True to their nature and awful experiences, Mom and Dad took forever to decide if I should go or not. They thought I was too young to travel on my own, though I didn't. I felt old—like an aging mother who worried about everything and everyone.

I vowed to stop reading my father's *Time* magazines, which always contained alarming news. I once heard someone say, "News should make you uncomfortable and if it doesn't, then it really isn't news." How cynical—if the story is a happy one, it should be shouted to the world and celebrated.

Bear

L ast summer Bear and I found it difficult to spend time together. Cameron had begun shadowing me as I walked up the hill to visit Ian and wait for Bear. He always had his gun and often shot at some animal, causing an uproar in the otherwise peaceful fauna. Blackbirds and crows would fly up in black clouds, screeching their fear and indignation. Squirrels would jump from branch to branch until they were high up, calling out their alarm. Their urgent warnings sounded exactly like the hens when I took their eggs out from beneath them— an obnoxious, loud *balk, balk, balk.* I would feel my own body going into an alarm state since along with the hens' outbursts of rage would come the pecking. This instantly put me into a bad mood, and I would angrily shoo my brother away. "It's none of your business!" I retorted when he asked me why I went up there all the time.

But even when Cameron left me to myself, Bear rarely appeared on those days and I began to go to our meeting place at odd times. It took her a while to sense this change but when she did, we enjoyed some quiet, companionable times together. She had come alone this summer and seemed older and more tired, and I wondered for the first time how old she was. I looked up black bears in an encyclopedia which reported that they live 18-23 years. The article also stated that bears don't have any predators except humans, and when I thought of what Cameron would do if he ever saw me with Bear, chills went up and down my spine.

One day I coaxed Bear into following me to our beehives. Once she understood where we were heading, she willingly followed. Our hives were surrounded by wild plum trees and chokecherry bushes. Sometimes our honey had the flavor of plums along with the tang of chokecherry. I would feed Bear honey and peanut butter sandwiches, and then she would graze the fruit-bearing vegetation surrounding us. I followed her or sat cross-legged in the grass, either silent or constantly chatting about nothing or complaining about what was bothering me that day. When she had had her fill, she would join me in the grass, and I felt as if my presence made up for the emptiness she felt from not having any offspring.

I knew we were perfectly safe since Cameron was the only one of us that refused to help Dad harvest honey. He had gone with Dad once and, not heeding Dad's precautions, had been severely stung by dozens of bees and was sick for days. But Bear was cautious and any little human sound from below would send her crashing through our protective boundary, and then I would worry about how soon we could be together again and if we would have a good summer.

Cameron's Idea of Horse Training

The summer before, Cameron had become leaner and well-muscled and more even tempered, perhaps because Dad punished him for his meanness by assigning him hard, tedious tasks. When Mom and Dad heard about his locking me into the barn, he had to do all the evening chores on his own for two months, and then again last summer, he was punished again with hard labor.

Last May, I had been working with a sweet-natured and very wanting-to-please gelding named Larry. I had named him so because we appreciated our friend Larry's kindness, and most of all, his positive effect on Cameron. Mom often invited Larry to join us for dinner, and we would get a break from Cameron's bad attitude and behavior for days after.

I never understood what made Cameron respond like that to this one person, but whatever it was, I liked it. Unfortunately, we still had encounters with Cameron's disruptive disposition. One day, I noticed that Larry wasn't responding to me with his usual easy-going nature. He acted nervous and distracted, and when I tried putting him through his paces, he was skittish and balked at learning new signals. The next morning, I decided to get up early to beat the heat and work with Larry in the cool of the day. When I went into the barn to gather his halter, it was gone, and then I heard the ragged cry of a horse in pain.

I ran out to the corral to find Cameron holding the end of the halter rope in one hand and beating Larry, using a cow whip, with the other.

"Stop that!! For the love of God! What the Sam heck do you think you're doing?"

Cameron kept his back to me and continued whipping Larry, yelling the usual prompts but not getting anywhere. I ran to him and tried to wrest the whip from his right hand. I couldn't do it, and he continued slashing at Larry. I grabbed his left hand and wrested the rope out of it. Cameron turned on me and began using the whip on me. I cowered down into the dust of the corral, screaming, trying to hedge off the blows with my arms and hands until Dad came to my rescue.

For the rest of the summer, Dad made Cameron fork hay onto the stacks, the most dreaded job on the ranch, on his own. After working and sweating all day, Cameron didn't have the stamina to listen to the evening radio shows and news, and he went to bed just after supper. But amazingly, the harder Cameron worked, the more he seemed to enjoy life, as if he'd found the self-esteem he had been lacking for so long.

Peace and War

Remembering the bittersweet days of last summer, I decided to walk up the hill simply to be close to Ian. I didn't have much to say. I had already told him about Crazy Peggy rendering Grandma childlike and emotionless with new-fangled psyche therapy, about Blair and Henry, about John Jacob joining us, and how our older brothers insisted in volunteering for one of the most dangerous duties of the war. As I looked out into the peaceful March landscape, becoming white again as snow fell languidly to the earth, I realized how lucky I was to have this tranquility when most of the world was in turmoil.

But the Allies had become more aggressive in their plans and their fighting, and had enjoyed more victories. By the end of January, over 90,000 German troops had surrendered to the Soviets, and our troops had completely recaptured Guadalcanal from the Japanese. And per Craig's letters, the 101ˢᵗ Airborne was close to filling it ranks with a tough bunch of men willing to literally jump into battle from planes, recklessly relying on the integrity of their silk parachutes to get them safely to the ground.

Craig and Colin

Craig's tales made Cameron's harsh punishments of the summer seem inconsequential. When my brothers came home in November, they entertained us with many stories from Camp Toccoa. Colin chimed in occasionally to set Craig's version straight or to add something, but most of the time he would just sit and nod in agreement.

One of Craig's accounts attested to how much my brothers wanted to be part of this specialized, elite branch of the army. Just before they left Camp Toccoa, Colonel Sink decided to break a well-publicized endurance marching record made by a Japanese Army battalion. They had covered 100 miles in seventy-two hours. Sink had his men march out with each man carrying whatever gear and weapon came with their specialty. Craig said he felt sorry for the mortar squad which carried heavy machine guns. It was to be a 118-mile march through rough country with no roads. The first day they marched in freezing rain and snow, and when that stopped, a cold, harsh wind came up to finish off their misery.

When they stopped marching late that night, their commander chose a bare hill on which to camp, so open and exposed their camp stoves wouldn't stay lit. Craig figured it must have been below freezing because when they moved out again, their boots were stiff with frost and their weapons were frozen to the ground. They covered another 40 miles the second day, and had 38 miles to go until they reached Atlanta. The last 20 miles of the march was on a cement highway, which they found even worse than the muddy, slippery route they had covered thus far.

We gasped when Craig told how on that third night, some of the men crawled to get their rations. The next morning, they marched into Atlanta led by a band, with crowds cheering along the route. They received praise all over Georgia via newspapers and radios. Only a dozen men could not complete the task but Colonel Sink still felt victorious. The parade through Atlanta to Five Points at mid-city and the public's response were the men's only rewards, but Colonel Sink had bragging rights to claim his men had broken the Japanese endurance record by marching his men 118 miles in only 75 hours.

Dad was proud, but Mom was aghast at such treatment of her boys. I felt a little of each, and when they left the day after Thanksgiving, I begged Craig to write letters not only to Mom and Dad, but also to me. I told him not to hold anything back, that I could take whatever he had to tell me, and that I would always think of them and pray for them. But Craig's next letter, which was very slow in coming, was disappointing because he basically just told me the same things he had told Mom and Dad. The only difference was that he told me about his and Colin's drunken brawl.

Camp Benning

Craig told me of the crummy little huts built on sandy, treeless ground and how awful the food was at Camp Benning. But luckily, their time there was shortened because their 506th regiment was in such great physical shape that they ended up skipping the first stage of paratrooper training. I could hear him chuckling as he wrote how he and his fellow men embarrassed the jump school sergeants by "beating the pants off them" when they attempted to fulfill Stage A—physical training. Their commanders gave up and immediately put the 506th into Stage B.

Craig went on to explain their training stages. *In Stage B, we double-time march every morning to packing sheds where we learn to fold and pack our parachutes. Then we march double-time back to what they call the Frying Pan area, we eat lunch, and then practice jumping from fake doors set on pretend sides of planes that are just 4 feet from the ground into mounds of sawdust. After that, we jump from 30 foot towers in parachute harnesses suspended from a steel cable.*

This last week, we began Stage C, after warming up with our Stage B exercises, and then we made free jumps from 250-foot towers. Sometimes they use a wind machine so we have a realistic feel of controlling and collapsing our parachute canopies when landing in stormy weather. They say next week, we will go to Stage D when we will make actual jumps from C-47 transport planes.

I've got to go now, but first, I want to tell you about an embarrassment involving Colin and me. You know how extremely competitive we always have been, well, the first night here, we were allowed to go to a local tavern.

I'm sorry to say that both of us over-drank, and somehow, when our buddies started praising us as the "tough MacDougal brothers," it led to their urging us to engage in a fisty-fight to see who was the strongest.

We fell for it, with bets heavily made as to who would win, and I still can't believe it—we beat the hell out of one another with no one winning. Colin and I sheepishly made peace the next morning while doing latrine duty as our punishment, and decided from here on out to 'Stand Alone Together,' the motto of the 101ˢᵗ based on the Indian word 'Currahee.' Remember, Currahee is the name of the lone mountain next to Camp Toccoa, and it means 'standing alone.' Colonel Sink had just come up with this motto, instructing us to also use it as our battle cry. As brothers, Colin and I will stand together as well as with our fellow paratroopers and whatever allied troops we encounter when we jump into battle. Until later, all my love . . .

The next letter from Craig took months to arrive, and it was to all of us. Craig began: *Two weeks ago, we did our first jump out of a plane. Oh, my God, it was fantastic once we did it. But before we jumped, we were all so nervous. We told stupid jokes, laughed crazy over nothing, and smoked cigarettes while waiting to be called to the plane. We packed our chutes repeatedly. We would put them away and then someone would get worried about whether his was done correctly, and then we would all recheck our chutes and have to repack them. We hardly slept until reveille at 5:30, and no one could eat breakfast. I swear, each of us ran to the latrine a dozen times before we boarded the plane. Then we loaded up. The plane took off and circled. When a red light signaled to the jumpmaster that we were high enough, he yelled, 'Stand up and hook up.' We hooked the backpack cover of our main chute to the anchor line that ran down the middle of the top of the fuselage. We were told to do an equipment check and after doing so, we sounded off our numbers. After our jumpmaster ordered us to 'close up and stand in the door,' we all jumped, one at a time, except for one fellow who froze and couldn't jump, but finally did after everyone was out.*

Colin went ahead of me and asked me to give him a nudge since he felt he was freezing up and wouldn't be able to do it on his own. 'Are you sure?' I asked. He nodded. I did what he asked, hoping I wouldn't be seen by anyone. It was my turn, and what could I do? My little brother had gone before me, so I jumped, and it was wonderful!! It felt weird at first but after this thing called the static line attached to the hook on the anchor line in the plane pulled the back cover from my main chute (I know much of this is only mumble-jumble to you), pulling my canopy out of my pack, and the prop blast inflated my chute, I began drifting down slowly, gently swinging back and forth. The sky looked beautiful and the air felt good. I let out a 'Yippee!!' And then realized I wasn't alone in feeling this free and wonderful feeling. We were all yelling and cheering, happy in the realization that all that time spent training had been worth it.

Even our silent Colin yipped and yelled. We had a celebratory regimental parade after which we were given a speech by Colonel Sink, who, surprisingly, bragged us up tremendously. 'You are a member of one of the finest regiments in the United States Army, and consequently in the world,' he told us 'Walk with pride and military bearing, take care of your personal appearance, and remember Currahee, the 506th's motto and battle cry.'

I know my letters are coming slow. But it takes a while for whoever censors our letters to read them all. They told us to warn our families that there will be times we can't send any letters home due to keeping our whereabouts secret, especially when they ship us out—we won't be able to let anyone know where and when that will be. I expect to be able to write to you for a while, though. I've got to go now, but we're moving out soon to a place where they say they have nicer, more comfortable barracks, better food, a great PX, and even a movie theater.

There we will start jumping with rifles. And best of all, we'll have more down time and get to go to town to socialize. The men are all anxious to see some girls, dance with them, and perhaps steal a kiss or two. Don't worry, Mom and Dad, Colin and I certainly are not looking to get attached or hitched, but it will be nice to dance with a sweet-smelling, soft-talking gal . . .

Craig ended his letter with a hand-drawn wink before he signed off. I will never forget that crazy wink, nor will my family, because that one little wink instilled the optimism in us that Craig wanted us to have while waiting for them to come home safe and whole.

Coming Clean

· ·

In April, just after Colin's 22nd birthday, Blair called us, announcing that Henry would be leaving soon to train as an army surgeon, and that they planned to marry before he shipped out. She also told us that they had decided to tell the Gustafson family about James. They wanted to start by doing everything right.

Dad felt this revelation wasn't necessary. He stormed around, grousing about it for days while Mom patiently listened to his negative remarks. One day when we were alone in the house, I asked her how she truly felt.

She shook her head. "I'm not sure, Abi. I think it's the right thing to do, I always have felt the Gustafsons should know about James. But I agree with Dad—it will cause a scandal with many people wanting to believe the worse about Blair. And it would be rotten to let the valley in on the fact that Billy had raped her. It would only be right to leave it up to them whether or not to expose Billy's sin to the world. James turned one in February, and one thing's for sure, when they do find out they have a grandson who's already a year old, they'll feel cheated, having already missed the babyhood of his life."

Later that night after everyone had gone to bed, I went downstairs to talk to Dad. He sat reading in the parlor, listening to music from the radio. I sat across from him and tentatively spoke up. "Dad, can I talk to you about Blair and Henry wanting to tell the Gustafsons about James?"

He sighed and put his book aside. "Yes, Abi, I don't see why not. What's on your mind?"

"Well, I know how awkward this situation is for everyone. But the way I see it is that the Gustafson family has lost a boy just like we lost Ian. They have had a hard time, too, losing a son, but unlike us, they only had Billy, Gail, and their little brother, Raymond. We have so many more in our family—not that anyone could ever replace Ian, or Gracie. But we have loved ones to fill those empty spots, at least just a little bit."

I saw a hard look cross Dad's face when I brought up Gracie, but I took a deep breath and went on. "I know we will get Gracie back someday, I haven't given up hope, and I don't think anybody else has either. My point is that we have that hope and we also have such good memories of Ian. They don't have as much as we do; no one has come into their lives to fill that emptiness. Denise hasn't had any more babies like you and Mom, and she and Dan don't have any grandchildren except for James, who they don't know anything about. I think Blair is right in needing to tell them they have a grandson, something in this world that Billy left behind. I know that Billy died because he made a big mistake, but in a way, so did Ian."

Dad sat up in his chair, and I could see that his ire was up. I had made him angry by comparing Ian to Billy. His face was now deep red, and he took a big swill of his whiskey. I stood up, walked to him and knelt before him. "Please don't get angry. But Dad, they should know. I think they should know everything that happened. It doesn't need to be announced to the world, but they should know about James and how he came to be born. He's Blair's child, and she is the one who has suffered the most in all of this." I sighed and went on. "I believe she is doing the right thing, Dad. If there is one decent outcome in this whole thing, it's to let Denise and Dan know about their grandson."

I had placed a hand on each of his knees. He slowly pushed them off, and I could see that I was about to receive a barrage of arguments and perhaps a dressing-down. He cleared his throat, but I rushed on.

"Dad, please listen to me. What if, and I'm not saying Ian would ever have done what Billy did to Blair—he never ever would. But what if, under different circumstances, Ian had left a child behind in this world. Wouldn't you want to know and love that one, too, like all the rest of your grandchildren?"

Dad stood up, and I scrambled to get out of his way. He began pacing and cleared his throat again. But I wasn't ready to let him talk. I stepped in front of him and clasped his arms, continuing my petition.

"Please let me finish, and then you can yell at me and tell me how wrong I am. I just want to say that I know Blair, and all of us are—what have you Scots always said—*caught between the devil and the deep blue sea?* We are in a tough spot, a horrible quandary. If Blair tells them about the rape, Billy's memory will be tainted for them. But what's the trade-off? They'll have a grandson to love and a living legacy of Billy in James."

I plopped into my chair, exhausted and nervous. Dad paced for a few minutes, and I began to sweat, worrying that I had gone too far. Dad stopped in his tracks and turned to me.

"I understand your thinking, Abi. But have you thought of what it would do to Blair if the Gustafsons don't believe her story, and then were indiscreet about it? Blair would suffer again if this got out and either way, it would make great gossip whether people believed she was raped or worse yet, would think she had been loose and was just as responsible for her pregnancy."

"But, Dad, the Gustafsons are good people. Gail is my friend, she's the nicest girl I know. And Blair has told me how lovely and decent Denise and Dan are. Don't you think you and Mom could talk to them and make some sort of deal so no one else ever knows about this?"

"It's too risky, Abi. I can't honestly say that I can trust that they would do that. You're being naïve. It's just safer to keep things the way they are. James will have a wonderful life with us, and Henry will be a good father to him. Now go to bed. It's late. Good night, Abi."

I stood up to go, and Dad grabbed me by the arm. He gave me a big hug and kissed me on the top of my head.

"Sometimes I think you are too good for this world, just like Ian was, and that scares me. Don't worry so much, hon. We'll get this figured out."

Wounded Heart

When school started again after Christmas, I wore my new lingerie and clothes and abandoned my simple braid, and saw a spark of surprise in Jake's eyes when we met in the hall. He didn't give me that wink that he had formerly reserved for me as Ian's little sister. Instead, he swallowed hard. "Man, Abi, you're turning into a killer diller. You had better be careful, or you'll break every heart in the school."

I knew his using the term—*killer diller*—was his way of telling me he thought I was a looker. It seemed to me that the war, somehow, was making society loosen up. Terms such as *a loose woman, smooching around, messing around,* and *knocked up* had become common, and when my twin brothers used them at home, they were chastised and told to never use them around family.

We older children went to the movies often. A ticket cost 35 cents, and for some reason, the war hadn't interfered with the production of great movies, many of which were based on war stories. *Casablanca* won the Academy Award for the best movie, and another favorite was *For Whom the Bell Tolls*, based on Earnest Hemingway's novel about the Spanish Civil War. Mom and Dad went often, too, leaving us older children to babysit Rory.

They always went when the theater played newsreels that showed actual war scenes, but Dad wouldn't let us view those since he didn't want us to be exposed to such brutality. He also didn't want to risk having his impressionable teenage sons become enamored with the idea that fighting in the war was commonplace and heroic.

When Jake came to the movies, he always came in with a pack of his friends. Despite that we rarely spoke then, I often caught him eyeing me, and I began to put as much time into dressing and fixing up for the movies as Blair had done before her bad night. His attention was just enough to give me hope that someday my dream of marrying him would come true.

But that fantasy was crushed when Jake came in one night with the most beautiful girl in high school, Charlotte Dingall. Jake, in his final year of high school, had finally begun to date someone, and it wasn't me. I knew if I told my parents that someone had asked me for a date, they would never have allowed it, even if it had been Jake. But this turn of events completely broke my heart, leaving me sick to my stomach and feeling hopeless.

That hopeless, helpless feeling turned into bitterness when the Spring dance came around, and I had to listen to everyone talking about Charlotte and her beauty, and how it matched Jake's good looks. Though she was only a Junior, everyone would vote for her to be Queen because we all knew that Jake would be King. I was not only jealous, but I felt bad for the Senior girls who didn't have this last chance to be honored.

Charlotte was a beauty. I couldn't deny her that. She had long, thick, shiny dark brown hair with streaks of gold that she wore in a pompadour. Even though she was shorter than me, she was tall for a girl and had the most exquisite curves that showed well in her style of dressing. Her eyes were almost violet, and her skin glowed like gold, with just the right amount of high color across her cheekbones.

Worst, she came from a wealthy, established ranch family and was known for her horsemanship. She didn't train them, but competed in every major rodeo and did well. During the first week in July, she and her family would travel to the ten-day event in Alberta, Canada—the Calgary Stampede—and then at the end of July, they would travel to Cheyenne Frontier Days in Wyoming. She always missed the first days of school to compete in the Pendleton Round-up in Oregon.

My anger and frustration made me ignore Jake now, and that hurt the most. I knew he knew I was jealous, which embarrassed me and made me even more resentful. He and Charlotte were King and Queen of the dance, but that didn't keep the government from claiming him and sending him off to war once he graduated.

Since he wasn't the only young man in the valley leaving to be processed and then trained, I knew of his departure date and time. I had Callum drive me to the train station, and despite that I witnessed an emotional farewell between him and Charlotte, I ran to him just as he was about to board the train. He stopped and turned to me, surprised, and then he broke into a huge, happy grin, which made me cry, rendering me speechless. He grabbed me into a hard hug, and I managed to squeak out, "Take care of yourself, please. I'll pray for you." He kissed me in the middle of my forehead and blessed me with his endearing, crooked smile showing the space between his two front teeth. His auburn hair had been tousled by the wind; I smelled that windblown freshness on him, and that's how I remembered him for the next two years.

Craig and Colin Join the 101st Airborne

Craig only had time to write to Mom and Dad, who he knew would share his news with us all. I had stopped writing to him because I hate one-sided conversations. As I had told no one else about my heartache, it would have been good for me to tell my older, wiser brother who had suffered many a broken heart. In the meantime, Colin stopped writing to us since he knew Craig was faithfully doing so. He had been hired by an Atlanta newspaper to write about the intense training of the paratroopers and their camps. Later, he would become one of their war correspondents when fighting somewhere in our war-torn world.

Craig's letters were now short and no longer chatty. They had been moved from Camp Benning to Camp Mackall, North Carolina, where each man began jumping with at least 100 pounds' extra weight. This additional weight consisted of small arms, pieces of larger arms which could be taken apart and then reassembled on the ground, hand grenades, other explosives, maps, and food.

At the end of May, Craig and Colin's regiment met up with others at Sturgis, Kentucky, doing maneuvers there and in Tennessee and Indiana, marching to each new place. They were there a little over a month, living in pup tents, using latrine trenches, and eating creamed chipped beef on toast. Craig drew a smile when he told us what they called that dish—shit on a shingle. But while marching around in the country doing their maneuvers, the locals treated them to fried chicken, making life a little more bearable. Craig said they all felt extremely tired, filthy, and itchy, and I could see his wry grin when he wrote, *I didn't think I would ever yearn for clean underwear. We have all gotten to the point of laundering them in the streams, which helps, and when it isn't raining they dry overnight.*

Craig gave a short explanation of their maneuvers. They were divided into a Red Army who tried to outmaneuver the Blue Army. He had been assigned to the Red Army and Colin, the Blue. That had initially made him uncomfortable, but it never became a problem. The maneuvers consisted of long night marches, wading through streams, climbing muddy banks and stumbling over slippery rocks, tree roots and stumps, and then when at base camp, they would do more jumps.

He told of one time when the heat inside the plane was unbearable and each one of them, including their jump master, vomited, covering the entire floor of the plane. The smell of their mess kept them spewing until everyone had emptied their stomachs or jumped. He ended that letter announcing that they had attached to the 101st Airborne Division, and their regiment, the 506th, had been declared the best and toughest unit to do so.

A June Bride and Lilacs

April is the cruelest month, breeding
Lilacs out of the dead land, mixing
Memory and desire, stirring
Dull roots with spring rain.
T.S. Eliot

Blair, Henry, and James arrived by train the first of June. My sister and her fiancé would marry Sunday, June 6. James had turned into a precocious eighteen-month-old boy. He spoke a small number of words, including Mommy and Daddy, which he called Henry. He spent much of his time doing somersaults, and he constantly attempted to stand on his head. He loved being read to, and I accommodated him in that as much as I could.

Shortly after arriving, Blair announced that they had scheduled a meeting with the Gustafson family at their home, making Dad angry, though he knew there was nothing he could do to stop it. Blair invited our parents to go with them, Dad said, "No! You made your bed, now sleep in it—alone." But none of us were surprised when he relented and said he and Mom would accompany them.

I wanted to be there in the worst way, but I had to be satisfied with making Blair promise to share everything with me later. She said that on the way to the Gustafson ranch, she told Dad that she wanted to introduce the reason for their visit herself. But then he said, as her father, he had a few things to impart to them. They were greeted cordially by

Dan and Denise. Denise had made a fresh pot of coffee and offered them a cup. Blair said all she could do is say, "Perhaps later." She smiled wryly at me then, telling me how upset her stomach had felt and how with each quick heartbeat, her head pounded in pain.

She told me how after they had all been seated, and she had introduced Henry as her fiancé, there was a deadening silence in the room, with only James jabbering as he entertained them with his antics, somersaulting and laughing at his own efforts.

"What a lovely child you have there," Denise finally said.

Blair told me that all she did was look directly into Denise's eyes and say, "He's your grandson." Then she laughed, telling me there was another long stretch of absolute quiet.

She had hoped Dad wouldn't say anything for a bit until she had had her say. But, of course, she said, laughing a bit sarcastically, he couldn't contain himself.

"Yes, that's your grandson. His name is James, and this young man," he said waving his arm toward Henry, "plans to adopt him and give him his name even though James is your son Billy's child. The night Billy escorted our daughter to the dance, he drank too much and forced himself on her."

Blair told me she felt sorry for Denise and Dan as they sat in stunned silence, trying to digest this wonderful, yet painful news. She said she couldn't remember any of what she had planned to say about the harsh fact that James existed because of Billy's violent act.

"I had it all planned out, Abs. I really did. But it slipped away when I watched their reaction. And then Dad just kept on talking while Denise broke into tears and fell to her knees in front of James, hugging him and crying."

"What did Dad say then?'

"'Blair and Henry insisted they tell you about your grandson, even though I was against it. I'm hoping I can convince you to keep quiet about the rape. We don't need to sully Blair's or Billy's reputations; this situation doesn't need to be common knowledge in the valley or anywhere. James' existence is not Blair's doing—all she could do was to give birth to him. I had hoped she would give him up for adoption, solving the problem. But she fell in love with James and couldn't give him away to strangers.'"

Blair went on. "Dad sat silent for a bit. Both Denise and Dan were on the floor, embracing James, crying and taking in his entire little being like they couldn't get enough of him. Then James began to cry, frightened by their overwhelming emotion. They stood up, sat down, and tried to pull themselves together. I'll never forget that scene, Abi. It was touching, making me feel emotional as well, but also angry with myself for having been so nervous and uncertain about telling them. The relief I felt washed over me with such force that I wept happy tears and became giggly."

"What did Dad say then?"

"Well, he started to speak, but Dan interrupted him." "'Angus, Blair's secret will be kept by us. No one else will ever know—not even family. I just ask one thing. Can we see James often? Be at his birthday parties and other major events in his life? It will just seem as if our families have developed a close friendship. People will never know.'"

Blair chuckled. "Dad did his usual deep-thinking routine, rubbing his chin and then running his hand through his hair. When he stood up and walked toward Dan to shake his hand, that shock of hair sticking straight up made me laugh like I was a crocked fat-head. James saw me laughing and he quit crying. He sat still for a few minutes and then came to me, picked up his bag, and said, 'Book.' I helped him find it, and then he went to Denise, handed it to her, and crawled into her lap to be read to."

That meeting was the beginning of a wonderful relationship between our two families, and Dad, being the fair-minded person he could be when not in a fit of anger, told me once again that I had good judgment, and that he would try to listen to me more. I swelled with pride, and the frustration of not being included in that remarkable meeting subsided.

The Gustafson family came to Blair's wedding. She looked every bit a sweet, innocent, and virginal bride in her wedding dress, which was demure, and yet showed off her beautiful figure. I was her bridesmaid and wore a soft blue, almost lilac-colored dress made of chiffon, matching the fabric of her dress. Her elbow-length veil was made of net with an embroidered floral design, falling from a simple but sequined crown. Ianna was her flower girl and wore a dress similar in design to mine and in the same color. Rory, of course, was their ring bearer.

Blair carried a small bouquet of red and white roses on top of our family Bible—red for passion and white for a lasting, sacred union. My bouquet was made of shooting stars—rosy purplish flowers with red and yellow rings that I had gathered from the hillside up above our house. Ianna dropped rose petals from her little basket. Blair had wanted to use lilacs for everything. When she began practicing tying sprigs of the fragrant blooms together for our bouquets, I became cold as winter inside, remembering Faith's lilac offering near Ian's grave.

I did not want her to use lilacs, and I tried to bite my tongue and remain silent. But then I thought of the poems by T.S. Eliot. In *The Waste Land,* he used lilacs in the section he named, *The Burial of the Dead,* reminding me of Ian's untimely death and burial, and in *Portrait of a Lady,* he mentioned them again in a stanza about a "buried life."

I talked Blair into using roses for nearly everything, but she insisted on placing lilac bouquets in vases on the tables. She believed a June bride should honor the tradition of using lilacs in her wedding, but I couldn't help remembering Faith's final offering to Ian, lying so beautiful and fragrant beside his open grave.

Blair's wedding was small with only our family and the Gustafson family as witnesses. Grandpa and Grandma Callaghan came, as did Grandpa and Grandma MacDougal with Aunt Peggy in tow. When they arrived, there was a big brouhaha between Dad and Peggy. Despite his ferocious anger, Dad was a forgiving man, and when Peggy got down on her knees, begging his forgiveness, explaining she had no idea that the therapy would be so invasive, he melted as Grandpa had done.

The MacDougals do not believe in lingering feuds. As Scots, they had seen too much of the awful stubbornness that can ruin families. Scottish history was wrought with an obstinacy which my father and his father, and his father before that, believed to have contributed to the Scots' downfall when dealing with the English.

Peggy brought her friend Mary to the wedding, and she was as feminine as Peggy was manly. When I talked about how strange that was, Aileen rolled her eyes again.

"What? Why do you always do that about Aunt Peggy?"

"Well, Abi, I guess you're old enough to know that just because you're born a certain sex, it doesn't mean you're going to behave like that gender. Do you understand?"

"Well, no, not really." Aileen just rolled her eyes again and went back to making fancy sandwiches for Blair's wedding luncheon.

Grandma Callaghan and Grandma MacDougal cried happy tears as Blair and Henry said their vows. I was so happy to see some emotion again in Grandma MacDougal, it made me tear up. It was a beautiful day. Dad and the boys had made an arbor under which everyone but the wedding party could sit comfortably in the partial shade. We painted it white, and it took a while for us to find enough newly-grown vines to cover it, but it was worth the effort.

I liked Peggy's friend, Mary. She was a sweet, kind-hearted woman who appeared to love everyone. She enjoyed holding the smaller children and laughed at them when they entertained her with their tricks and toddler talk. Sometimes she looked at them with such yearning it made me feel sorry for her. Mary was thin and mousy and coughed a lot—like she really wasn't all that healthy. Surprisingly, Peggy, unlike the tough character she usually was, constantly followed her around with a throw or shawl when there was just a hint of cool in the air.

I had enjoyed seeing the handful of relatives who came for the wedding. But I was relieved when everyone, except for Tim, and Blair and her family, left for home. I wished they could have stayed, but Blair felt she needed to be at Grandma and Grandpa MacDougals' to look after them. I had to agree since both had aged since Grandma's therapy. Grandpa had become as thin as Grandma, and they were both slow and cautious in their movements. Grandpa, just like Aunt Peggy with Mary, took care of Grandma and rarely let her out of his sight. He still needed to coax her to eat, and he dressed her every morning like you would a child.

Human Predator

B ear returned in the spring without cubs and seemed more depressed than last year. I didn't know how to help her except do what I had done the year before—wander through the woods with her as if I were one of her babies. There were two colts to train this summer—a beautiful buckskin filly we named Lily and a lively paint called Sebastian. Sebastian wasn't a ranch-born colt. Dad bought him and his mother, May, to replace our palomino brood mare, Liz, who died last summer.

Having a paint on the ranch was new to us, and comparatively unique in horse-breeding. An American paint is a breed of horse that combines both the conformational characteristics of a western stock horse with a pinto spotting pattern of white and dark coat colors. Western stock horses, also called American quarter horses, make good ranch stock because of their body type. They carry a refined head, and a strong, well-muscled body smaller in stature than many horses, with a broad chest and powerful, rounded hindquarters, and have been bred to have a great amount of cow smarts. They are quick and agile, perfect for working cattle.

A good ranch horse will almost work on their own without the rider's signals. They cut cattle instinctively—peeling off just one pair, a cow and her calf, either from the edge of the gathered herd or from deep inside the bunched cattle. They will stand still while you rope an animal and then back up to create tension to hold them while you either put on an identification tag, brand them, inoculate them, or doctor them.

Quarter horses come in many earthy colors, the most common being sorrel or chestnut, a brownish red. When you breed a pinto with a quarter horse, you never know what you're going to get; the coloring comes out different every time. Sometimes the colt will come out only a solid, dark color, but most often the colt is a paint.

Sebastian's mother was a sorrel so he turned out to be a beautiful paint with white coloring contrasting with the dark red with perfect white stockings on each leg. Dad and I decided not to cut him so we could use him as a stud horse, adding new blood to our breeding stock. Sebastian's mother was ultra-protective of him. I had to wait until we had earned the mother's trust and for that tight bond—so strong between a mare and her colt—to ease up, and then wait for Sebastian to get over his weaning woes before starting him. When a colt is weaned from its mother, it is inconsolable for a long time. I have always disliked weaning a baby of any kind, and every time we weaned the calves or colts, it made me wonder if Gracie had missed nursing Mom when she was stolen.

One day Bear and I traveled to new territory. It was within our property line, and was full of boulders, rocks, and obnoxious weeds hardy enough to grow in a dry terrain. Besides occasional rain, the only water there ran deep in the same creek that ran shallower down near our ranch yard. Since our cattle never grazed there much, we rarely rode there, and then it was only to gather a few stray pairs that had wandered away from the main herd.

That day, Bear seemed different, leading me up there at a pace that made me run, making me think, God, I hope I never need to outrun a bear. I was awed by my relationship with this wild animal. She was so full of what I thought of as the human spirit that I still could not escape the notion that she was truly a Spirit bear.

This did not fit any other beliefs I held about animals. Sometimes I would look at our ranch dogs and play with the thought that they had souls of some sort. If they sensed you were sad, or if they saw you crying, they would come and gently put their paw on you as if to say, *It's okay. Everything will be all right.* Not so with cats, which I considered to be haughty and selfish. They whined if they didn't get their share of milk in the mornings, and fought with one another over table scraps.

As children, if we managed to tame a batch of kittens, they would want special favors as adults, trying to sneak into the house, and mewing at our doorstep.

Mom would not have any animals living in the house. "We have plenty animals outside, and I don't see the need to be caring for or cleaning up after any more creatures. I have all of you, along with your father, to take care of."

When I finally caught up with Bear, she stood in front of an old shack that had been there for as long as I could remember. Part of the roof sagged, and because of that our parents told us constantly to never go in there. I had never had any desire to go in, but now Bear, slow and cautious, walked up to the door. I remembered it as always hanging open, looking like a gaping mouth, making the building seem appalled at its own sad condition. But now it had been repaired, closed, and padlocked. Bear turned to me and *m-m-r-r . . . ed* sadly, her head drooping to the side.

She stood on her hind legs and used her right claw to work the padlock loose. I stepped up close and shook it. It was a strong and heavy-duty padlock, which would be difficult to cut with even our largest cutter. Someone didn't want anyone in there, and I assumed it was my parents' doing. I felt bad for Bear because her sadness was so great it virtually dripped off her, making me sad, too. I coaxed her away and took her to the beehives for a special treat.

Two days later, it was my turn to ride up to the forest service pastures to check on the herd. The Forest Service had a system which we had to obey. Every other spring, we would be told to take our cattle as far up as possible into the government land. On the off years, we were instructed to take them just a bit farther from the fence that partitioned our land from government land.

This summer, the cattle would start out close to our ranch, but then in September, we would spend many more hours on the other side, finding them and then herding them home—that is, if we had a long, beautiful Indian summer. But in autumns when an early winter seemed sure, the cattle would graze their way closer and closer to our ranch, and we would simply open the gate and most of them would wander home on their own. Colder temperatures and freezing rain and snow was their signal to return to the place where they knew they would be well taken care of when snow covered the earth.

Our spring and early summer checks on the herd would take much less time with the pairs so close to home, and that year, Dad sent us out individually to do these early checks. I decided to take Larry that day, since he was my favorite. With him, I always felt that I wasn't alone—we seemed of the same mind. I could relax and enjoy the scenery, fresh mountain air, birdsong, and other creature-sounds of the forest. I considered Larry my best, most successful product in horse training thus far.

I decided to go up the long way, following the creek to where Bear and I had recently gone. That route would get me to the herd just fine. I forsook the well-worn path we usually took on the other side of the creek, but starting out early, I had all the time in the world. As we came close to the old shack, I decided that I would ride back down the same way so I could snoop around at my leisure. I hadn't been able to stop wondering why now, when most of us children were older and more responsible, our parents had fixed the door and locked it shut.

I allowed Larry to mosey and find his own way. He seemed to be drawn to water, which was the opposite of most horses. It usually takes time and patience to train a horse to cross a creek, or any water for that matter, since most have an aversion to going through water or even across bridges. Not Larry, the silly boy; today he made his way as close to the creek as possible, only moving away to dodge the willows growing on the bank. Suddenly, I heard a loud snapping sound, and Larry went down. I was able jump off before he landed and began screaming.

I walked around him and saw that he had stepped into a huge trap, which had severed his lower leg. He lay there thrashing his head, screeching, mad with fear and pain, and I sobbed as I pulled out the .44 Colt Dad insisted we carry when we rode alone.

Dad had taught us that when putting a horse down, you need to shoot them right into their tiny brain, the size of a walnut, so they die instantly. The rule of thumb in locating their brain is to mentally make an imaginary X, drawing a line from the left ear to the right eye and another line going from the right ear to the left eye, and aiming at the point where those lines intersect. There you can take close aim and have the bullet enter directly into the brain, and the horse is gone in milliseconds. Dad had trained all of us to shoot any weapon on the ranch and had also insisted we watch the procedure of putting a horse down. He hadn't had to do this often, but such a monumental act is easy to remember.

I waited until Larry wore himself out fighting his pain so I would have a better chance to aim the gun accurately, sending the bullet straight into his brain, which was agonizing, making me vomit several times. When he stopped throwing his head around, I took aim, and luckily, my shot was right on and he was gone in an instant. I threw myself over him and cried until there were no tears left. I don't remember my walk to the ranch yard—I didn't see, hear, or smell anything except for the hideous scent of gun powder.

I stumbled into the house just before dinner time, falling into Dad's arms, babbling my story. Everyone else was washing up for our noontime meal. Dad consoled me a bit and then turned me over to Mom. He and the boys left to take care of Larry's carcass, and Mom held me until I settled down. Then she gave me an aspirin and some chamomile tea with a few drops of laudanum in it and put me to bed.

I refused to leave my bedroom until the next day at dinner when everyone quietly and in their own way gave me words of condolence, except for Cameron, who asked me what the hell I was doing up there off the trail and on the wrong side of the creek.

I gave him a withering look and said, "There is no wrong side of the creek."

After I recovered and had let a few days pass, Bear and I went up there to place wildflowers on Larry's grave. Bear m-m-r-r . . . ed again, like she understood my grief. And then we did our usual haunting around the old shack. I was determined to get inside, as was Bear. Since it had no windows, I couldn't think of any way to get in but with the key to the padlock. I wanted in because I thought it had some connection to that huge fifty-pound bear trap Dad reported that Larry had stepped into. I knew that whoever set that trap was a cruel and hard-hearted man. Dad speculated that it could have been there for years, and then I felt guilty for riding that side of the creek with Larry.

Closer to the Front

Craig's next letter came from Fort Bragg, North Carolina. They had been treated to decent barracks with comfortable cots, hot showers, and good food at Breckinridge, Kentucky, for a week before moving on to Fort Bragg. There too, they had good quarters and received new clothing, gear, and weapons. They spent their days at the firing range. Again, the MacDougals earned a great deal of respect because of their excellent shooting—their hunting background had served them well.

Craig told us they knew they would be shipped out soon. Where, no one could guess, and if they did know, it was a secret. His letter came to us the first week in August. After that, we didn't hear a word from him until we received his first V-Mail from Camp Shanks, which was 30 miles up the Hudson River from New York City.

V-mail, short for victory letters, consisted of small pages, almost the size of the 5 by 7 pictures we received from Gracie's abductors. Craig explained that their letters would first be censored, then copied to thumb-sized images on negative film. Upon reaching their destination, each letter would be blown up to 60% of their size and printed back to paper. This would deter acts of espionage by foiling the use of invisible ink, microdots, and microprinting, as well as reduce the many pounds of heavy mail that occurred when thousands of servicemen corresponded with their family and friends back home.

He told us about the medical check-ups they underwent along with their receiving so many inoculations; they joked about feeling like their Grandmother's pincushions. He also told us about the division between the paratroopers and the regular enlisted men—some of that difference declared itself in benign joking, but most of it ended in brawls. The subject of the difference in pay a paratrooper received in comparison to the lesser amount paid to regular soldiers was the meatiest bone of contention.

Later, Mom received a letter from Craig and Colin's Captain Sobel. Both my brothers, along with the rest of their company, despised him. They considered him a weak puss who had somehow acquired this position of authority. He was a city boy and had been a Jewish clothing vendor before joining the Army. He, despite that he was not tough or athletic, demanded those qualities from his men. They said he was a mean, cruel bully, who treated the men he did not like unfairly.

Now Mom had received a letter from him: *Dear Madam, Soon, your sons, Privates Craig and Colin MacDougal, will drop from the sky to engage and defeat the enemy. They will have the best of weapons and equipment, and have had months of hard and strenuous training to prepare them for success on the battlefield.*

Your frequent letters of love and encouragement will arm them with a fighting heart. With that, they cannot fail, but will win glory for themselves, make you proud of them, and their country ever grateful for their service in its hour of need."

He had used a form letter, so in Mom's, he had to cross out the singular pronouns and make them plural. He had signed it with a fancy signature, full of curlicues—*Herbert M. Sobel, Capt., Commanding.* Mom wept after reading this and then raged at his nerve in telling her and the other mothers to write to their fighting sons.

"As if we wouldn't do that. What a horrible, stupid man!"

Mom became more resentful when we didn't receive a letter from either Craig or Colin for two months after that, and we were left to conclude they had been shipped out. Mom checked the mail faithfully and was disheartened each time there was nothing from her boys.

She ranted, "How are we supposed to send encouraging letters to them when we don't know where they are?" Every time we prayed for them, we also prayed to hear from them. During that time, we thought it was a terrible thing to undergo, but little did we know that by the war's end, sometimes many months would pass without hearing a word. My mother aged much while they were gone. Her smile lines didn't deepen around her eyes, but the grim pursing of her mouth etched deep grooves of bitterness that were a testimony to our mother's worry.

Shocking Revelations

I t was late October and we had been blessed with a long, beautiful Indian summer. Bear hadn't left yet. We had finally had our first heavy frost during the week, and now, walking up to the shack, I enjoyed the soft rustling of brightly colored leaves as I walked through them. Leaves gently drifted down as I stepped through the trees, making me think of old people gracefully dying in their sleep. The leaves seemed to detach from the branches without resignation, but were in no hurry. They slowly floated through the air down to the ground, making me think of what Craig had described about their first parachute drop.

The floor of the forest would soon be as colorful as the trees. The orange red of the Rocky Mountain maples contrasted with the golden yellow of the poplar and cottonwood leaves. The quaking aspen leaves had turned their usual yellow, boasting veins of red. The Boulder raspberry bushes were nearly purple, and the Western mountain ash leaves had turned a blazing scarlet, almost as deep red as the trees' clumps of berries. Soon the willow bushes along the creeks would lose their leaves to show off their winter branches. Some branches would turn brick red while others became deep purple.

It was Saturday, and I didn't have much time to spend in this autumn beauty. I hoped to see Bear, and I quickened my steps. The twins had left for town to warm up and dress for their final football game. Cameron made the team this year, and having become tall and husky, he made a perfect defensive end. Our entire family was expected to attend this last game of the year, ending a season in which the MacDougal twins had excelled. I was ready to go into town but wanted to escape the hustle and bustle. Rory loved going to the games but hated being readied for them. He reveled in his bath in the evenings, but a morning bath was too much for him to accept, especially a hurried one. Mom and Dad were nervous since the burden of winning or losing this championship game lay largely on the shoulders of their sons.

Callum had sat outside the house, blaring the horn because Cameron had taken his good-ole-time in getting ready. I believe he was the most nervous of our football heroes since he had refused to eat breakfast with the rest of us. He left before the table was even set to "walk off his nerves" and returned just as I finished cleaning up the kitchen.

The air today was fresh but heavy with the smell of changing leaves and pine. I looked around, taking in the fleeting majesty of fall colors and saw that Dad had separated the bulls from the cows and had put them in their winter pasture. I stopped short, watching as one bull rode another one as if trying to breed him. I knew the cows that hadn't become pregnant over the summer were easy to find and identify as *open,* not pregnant, simply because they, too, rode one another in desperation, and we would think, yes, they're in heat. Now after observing the bulls doing the same thing, I continued up the hill deep in thought about this new phenomenon.

Suddenly it dawned on me: this same-sex breeding was what Aileen had tried to tell me about Aunt Peggy. Animals of one sex don't always need to do it with the opposite sex. *Do it* was our ranch term for breeding, and now I had applied it to humans. Holy, gosh! Aunt Peggy was one of those.

One of those was what Gail had called a boy at school who seemed too frail and timid to be a boy. His voice sounded like a girl's, and when the other boys constantly picked on him, I felt bad for him. When I brought that up with Gail, she had simply said, "Oh, he's one of those." I had been too proud to say I didn't know what that meant. I had always felt sympathy for those people who didn't seem to fit their gender but hadn't ever allowed myself to think much about why.

Now it was clear to me. There was no strict rule in nature to just *do it* with the opposite sex; if animals did it with their same sex, then perhaps people did, too. I continued my trek to the shack, thinking hard. Oh, my gosh! I did it to myself sometimes—I couldn't help it. I worried it could be the same, but then, no. I couldn't imagine kissing another girl like men and women kissed in the movies—I just could not. Never.

I reasoned that I only did it to myself to ease the build-up inside me, just as Gail had explained to me about boys. When I did it to myself, I only fantasized about boys or men who didn't have faces or names. Sometimes Jake came to mind but I stayed away from that because I wanted to save him for the real thing—whatever that involved. Blair told me she couldn't really remember much of when Billy took her and made her pregnant, and that all she recalled about the event was feeling pain and humiliation. She didn't remember coming home, or much of what had happened until Mom and Dad began questioning her that morning after, and then she had had to think of a story to tell them so Dad wouldn't go after Billy.

Gail told me about what boys do, and said it was all right because they couldn't live with too much of the build-up that happened inside them. When I asked her how she knew, she said she had caught Billy doing it to himself once, and when they cleaned out his room after he died, she had found magazines with dirty pictures, and one of them had had his built-up stuff smeared on a page. She also told me how her mother had a fit about her looking at them and had later sat her down to explain it all. It was too much to think about that day, but I decided to quiz Gail about it the next time we had a stay-over.

As I came closer to the old shack, I began calling softly for Bear. When I walked around the corner, I knew she was there—I could smell her scent. The door stood open, and she was inside. "Bear, what you doing? Wow! I can't believe it's open." I stood inside the doorway, allowing my eyes to become accustomed to the dark. When I could finally see, I gasped. There were piles upon piles of furs—beaver, raccoon, muskrat, mink, fox, coyote, and—bear.

Bear stood holding what I identified as small bear skins, m-m-r-r . . . ing sadly. I understood immediately what her obsession with this old building had been—she could smell the scent of her babies inside. I was relieved to know that she could still have babies, but at the same time appalled that someone would kill them for their small hides. I wandered around inside, seeing traps of all kinds and the instruments used to make the furs ready for sale. Tiny, thin-bladed knives, big knives, scrapers, and wooden racks, which I figured were needed to stretch the hides so they didn't curl when curing.

"Oh, Bear! I am sorry. I regret that there are people in this world that do this. Dad will be furious when I tell him. He doesn't believe trapping is okay or humane. Oh, Bear . . ." My voice trailed off when thinking of the enormous bear rug in our bunkhouse. Dad was very proud of it. No. He would never say one thing and do another. Not Dad.

I went to Bear and hugged her goodbye; I had to get back to the yard so no one would come looking for me. I planned to remain quiet until I thought this all out. I coaxed her out of the shack, her baby's furs clutched in her front legs, and sent her on her way, promising her I would do something about this so her babies would be safe next spring. I watched her rumble away on three legs, clutching what was left of her offspring between her leg and her breast, and I ran all the way home, my mind in a whirl.

Harvest of Souls

Granite High School won the game, and my brothers and their team enjoyed a short spell of being worshipped and held in high esteem until basketball season was under way. Callum, always an understated athletic star, even allowed his head to swell a bit. But the one who really benefited was Cameron. For nearly two weeks, we MacDougals basked in Cameron's haloed state. He went around whistling happy tunes. He sat down and played juvenile board games with Rory, and taught him how to play Go Fish. He even offered to help Mom and me with the dishes one night.

One evening I was struggling to finish a paper on Henry James and his writing. It was due in the morning. I will never forget how Cameron came to me, put his arm around my shoulders, and offered to do my share of the evening chores so I could finish my assignment. That memory has often haunted me, and I have often wished my strange brother could have always enjoyed the state of mind he was in then.

But life events put a quick end to my family's short time of calm and replaced it with calamity. A strange but deadly influenza swept through Culloden, Ohio, ending many lives: two of them were Grandma and Grandpa Callaghan. Aunt Vi had been nursing them, and found them both dead, clasping hands in their bed of fifty-three years. They had fallen in love on the ship bringing them to America and married at the age of seventeen, never having been apart for even one night. The Callaghan clan had a double casket built, and they buried them while Aunt Vi, now stricken with the ailment, struggled to survive.

Because of the danger of getting and spreading the deadly disease, we could not go to Ohio, making Mom's grief more intense. The regret of not being able to properly say her goodbyes to her parents tortured her. Dad did the best he could to comfort her but she was inconsolable, and we all discovered the best thing to do was to tiptoe around her and not say a word. That was an awful, frustrating time. Watching someone grieve so deeply and not being able to do a thing is agonizing. I took over preparing the meals and doing all the housework, but no one really had much of an appetite. Mom lost even more weight than she had when Ian died and Gracie was stolen, and she seemed like a ghost herself.

Cameron became his old self. Out of our entire, extended families, he had liked Grandma Callaghan the most. Mom said they had bonded deeply because Grandma was there when he, as a tiny baby, had suffered from one of his horrible, high fevers, and Mom credited her for saving his life.

Cameron never did deal well with the emotional ups and downs in life—always retreating into his own world—and he, now again, took up his old habit of leaving for hours at a time with gun in hand, wandering around in the woods. One Saturday afternoon, I tried following him, but when he realized I was there, he turned and cursed, telling me to get the hell home. But I could tell he had been crying—his eyes were swollen and red.

Grandma Callaghan had a way about her. The more reclusive and unpleasantly antisocial a person was, the more Grandma was attracted to them. She, for some reason, could always connect with the loners of the world. She had befriended many difficult people in Culloden, and the family told us later that they had attended the funeral in full force in tribute to her and her kindness. That day in the woods, hoping to replace Grandma somehow, I ran to Cameron instead of leaving. I truly wanted to comfort him, but when I reached out to hug him, he pushed me so hard I fell on my butt, and then he aimed his gun at me, yelling at me to get the hell home and leave him alone.

Dad had retreated to his workshop in the garage. I didn't blame him—the silence in our house was oppressive, and Dad, always a doer, had to get out. Sometimes I could hear his electric wood saw and sanders going and wondered what in the Sam heck he was building. One day he came inside, triumphant, telling us to put on our coats. Mom resisted. "Come on Nora. I have, and I think everyone else has had enough of this. This miserable grieving you are insisting on won't bring them back. Now go get your coat on. The fresh air will do you good."

We followed Dad up the hill to our graveyard. He was like a little kid about to give someone his first hand-made greeting card or drawing to be displayed on the refrigerator until the edges curled. He opened the gate and ushered us in, as if we were about to see one of the Seven Wonders of the world. He threw his arm around Mom's shoulders and led her to a covered object close to Ian's grave, and with great aplomb, pulled an old quilt off a beautiful, handmade, wooden cross with our grandparents' names and dates carved into it.

Mom wept while hugging and kissing him, sobbing out her thanks. We stood reverently while Dad said a prayer and eulogy for our dearly departed. After that, we wandered the woods, bringing back what flowers still lived in the long Indian summer to adorn their faux gravesite. Rory proudly brought piles of nuts and pine cones and a cow skull, which we placed below the cross.

Mom came back to life, and I have always been amazed how our father, who can be so obstinate and ornery at times, also knew just the right thing to do to bring people back down to earth. I guess with our family history, he had plenty of practice doing so.

Two weeks later, early in the morning before we left for school, we received a phone call from the MacDougals of Culloden, telling us that Grandma and Grandpa MacDougal had perished in a house fire. They had found their two bodies together. It looked as if Grandpa had tried to carry Grandma out of the blaze but didn't make it. Again, we wouldn't be able to attend their funeral services because influenza still plagued the town.

Later, we would learn that Grandma MacDougal, having regained some of her memory, had insisted that Gracie would be coming home soon and that she had to have treats for her as well as a carved, lit pumpkin for Halloween. Grandpa had indulged her in her fantasy and had lit a candle in the pumpkin each evening. The authorities reasoned that the candle was the cause of the fire. No one knew if Grandpa had forgotten to extinguish it or if Grandma had lit it again as he slept.

We were thankful that as soon as the deadly influenza strain began taking lives, Henry had Blair and James join him at Fort Bragg, where he was in training. But since we had not yet received a letter, we still worried about our boys and wondered if they had joined the front lines in Europe. We clung to the idea that no word was a good word. Mom and I had reluctantly hung an American flag in our parlor window, as was the practice to show you had men fighting in the war. Every day I would touch the two gold stars we had sewed onto it and pray for my brothers to make it home alive.

Dad dealt with his grief very differently from Mom and allowed us to hug him and say how sad it all was. Each night, he could be found in our parlor listening to music and drinking his favorite Old Angus scotch. One night when I could not sleep, I went downstairs and found Dad and Mom listening to soft music wafting from the radio. They each had a glass of scotch in hand. I wedged myself between them and grasped their free hands, and we sat there, not saying a word. The next morning, Dad left right after breakfast, and I could hear the saw and the sander going again like before.

A week later, we gathered around a new cross in our graveyard, embellished with the names of our Grandma and Grandpa MacDougal and their dates. We honored them too with prayer and a eulogy, but this time the first flakes of winter snow swirled around us in a soft, seemingly benevolent wind. Aileen and Kendall had brought out hothouse flowers, which would lie underneath each cross, often covered with snow until spring winds scattered their petals across the countryside.

1944

New Year's Resolutions

....

We experienced one of the most depressing and miserable Christmas seasons ever, and I was glad to have it over and done. I had turned fourteen on the last day of the year, and Gracie turned five the next day. Her picture came late this year, making us even sadder. But, finally it came, the day before Christmas Eve, which helped make us a bit happier, as did our little ones. Ianna proved to be every bit a match to our precocious and overbearing Rory, and I wished we could have extracted some of his moxie to send to our fighting men. He and Ianna fought over who would dominate overseeing the antics of John Jacob, who would turn one in January, and their competitiveness was fun to watch.

Our Christmas prayers centered on our two boys in the 101st, whom we had not heard from since early fall. They didn't know that both sets of grandparents were not of this world any longer, and we still clung to the idea that no news was good news. I felt overwhelmed by the darkness, the heaviness weighing down on us. The realism in the stories and novels my English teacher assigned oppressed me, and I still remembered our times of silly, happy-go-luckiness, and how we had embraced the simple joys of life. But now I wondered if life was all that wonderful.

When I gazed into the mirror, I didn't recognize the person who was supposed to be me. I was tall— every bit of the 5'10" inches that I measured—and thin, only 120 pounds, and I also saw the womanly figure I now made, but I knew that my mindset had not yet caught up to my body.

I was also alarmed to see early signs of crow's feet etching the outside corners of my eyes, and I decided then that my New Year's resolution was to find as much joy and decentness I could in life and then celebrate it. I decided to take a walk up the hill to the graveyard and then wander through the woods to clear my head and to take in as much fresh, healing mountain air as possible.

Being outside had always helped me feel better and never failed to connect me to my memories of Ian, and I needed him that day—him and his eternal optimism. He would not have let the burdens of life bring him down; he never had. But then, I reasoned, if he were alive, he would be right there, in the fight, along with my brothers. Ian would have turned twenty last October—a perfect age, as far as our government was concerned, to draft men and send them off to war.

They wanted brave, young warriors, preferably unattached to a woman or wife, who hadn't yet taken on life's inhibitions and still thought of themselves as immortal. *No, I won't catch a bullet, perhaps the guy next to me, but no, not me.* Our country and our two strongest allies, Britain and Russia or the Soviet Union as they now called it, had made their New Year's resolution, which was to invade Europe and take back what the Germans had stolen, and I knew that this would certainly involve my brothers. I stopped at our little graveyard before going home, asking Ian to please be a guardian angel to Craig and Colin. Then I fell on my knees between my Grandparents' crosses and asked the same of them.

The Samaria

At last, we received a letter from Craig. It had taken nearly three months to reach us, but we still felt relieved and grateful to know, at least, where they had been for a while. Craig told us that he expected they would be training in England for some time.

He told us how excited they were to finally ship out, but that there had been no big parade or send-off since German submarines, lurking in the waters between the United States and England, would have blown them out of the water had they known the ship carried the highly trained and touted 101st Airborne. Since it was suspected that there were many enemy spies circulating on the East coast, shipping an airborne division such as theirs was very secretive.

We had to remove our 101st patch off our shoulders and weren't allowed to wear our jump boots. We were to appear as regular army. We marched quietly but with dignity out to our ship. And once on board, we silently lined the rails to see the Statue of Liberty, which made us all realize what we were leaving behind and what unknown dangers we would face. My heart was in my throat. I felt like I did when I boarded the train, leaving all of you behind. But then, at least I knew where we were heading. Now I have no idea.

The ship they put us on was a nightmare. I guess that was part of their strategy—who, in their right mind, would ship out valuable soldiers on such an old mess? The Samaria was a wreck of a thing. It was crowded as hell, 5,000 of us on a 1,000- passenger ship. The decks were packed full of men, and since we were ordered to constantly wear a life jacket along with our cartridge belts with canteens attached, we kept running into one another. Tempers flared as we stumbled around, pressed together with all our bulk. We had to sleep in our clothes and could only sleep on a bunk every other night. On nights we didn't have a bunk, we stayed up, walking the deck or gambling. Some of us tried to read if we had something to read. There was just a handful of us that had thought to bring a book. Colin and I took turns reading the same two books—The Great Gatsby and A Tree Grows in Brooklyn. Abi, you should read them if you haven't.

Everywhere we went, there was an awful smell, and it was almost unbearable down in the mess hall where we were fed boiled fish and tomatoes. That's all those sloppy, filthy cooks, who were just as unappetizing as the food, put together—just fish and tomatoes. Nothing else, no salt, pepper, or spices. But we ate because we were hungry. Oh! And they only fed us twice a day, I guess because it took so long for us to all go through the mess lines. We could shower, now and then, in ice cold salt water. But that, too, was better than not showering.

Finally, our ship docked at Liverpool, but we had to stay one more night on board. The next morning, we took a train to Ogbourne St. George where we boarded trucks, which stopped about a mile and half from Aldbourne, which would be our home for some time. We marched the rest of the way to our barracks in total darkness, except for our flashlights, because of the blackout. Our barracks were huts warmed by pot-bellied stoves. They gave us mattresses, which we had to stuff ourselves with straw, and crummy, itchy wool blankets. We all crashed, exhausted, looking forward to being in one place for a while.

I know I sound like I'm miserable and complaining too much, and yes, Dad, I need to buck up. I do realize that wherever and whenever we're in the combat zone, conditions will be much worse than they were on the Samaria. But while I'm homesick for home and all of you, I miss our good food the most. Colin and I were talking about how much we would give to eat a plate of Mom's Salisbury steak and mushroom gravy and Blair's biscuits. I've got to go now. Our leaders plan to indoctrinate us on British ways and customs. It's pretty here in the village, and Colin and I can't wait to see the countryside. I'll write soon when I have more time. Colin sends his love, too. Love again, Craig.

Feeding the World

T he next evening, we sat glumly around our supper table, realizing that we still had no idea where the boys were since Craig's letter had been written months ago. Dad tried to cheer us up by telling us how well the Allies were doing.

"The Axis powers are losing the war. It will still take time and effort, but we're gaining on those bastards."

Mom gasped. "Gus! Not that language, please?"

Dad smiled sheepishly. "Sorry, Nora, but you know how I feel."

Mom shook her head, and Dad continued: "Last year, the largest combined naval operation ever, which they called Operation Torch, invaded French North Africa, defeating the Axis forces there. Now the word is that another operation is being planned to invade Europe and force the Nazis out of every country they have conquered, and then fight them on their own turf."

Dad stood up, pacing around the dining table. He stopped to gather his thoughts, running his hand through his hair.

"Getting back to North Africa, the main thing that made that invasion a success was that FDR and Prime Minister Churchill teamed up to plan a strategy. What they discussed was kept very secret, but since they combined their forces, both land and naval, the Allies have been successful."

Rory began fussing so Mom stopped Dad's lecture and insisted we eat. We ate hungrily, having taken heart from Dad's lecture. After Rory finished eating, I sat on the floor and played "Go Fish" with him, while listening to Dad finish his talk.

"Mussolini has become weak, losing support, and Hitler has made plans to invade Italy to keep the Allies from gaining any foothold where they could gain access to German-occupied Balkan states. That's why the Germans still cling to control of the northern part of Italy. The man replacing Mussolini set up a new antifascist government in southern Italy which is cooperating with the Allies."

"It all sounds so complicated," Callum said, "but interesting."

"Yes, war is complicated. While our army and naval and marine forces are taking back territory from the Japanese, and the Soviet troops are doing the same on the Eastern front, we—the United States—are feeding the world. The price of beef is sky high, as well as pork and mutton. Every agricultural commodity is in demand and making things profitable for those who supply them."

"Does that mean we're rich now?" Cameron queried, his eyes brightening.

Dad laughed. "Yes, the ranch is making good money—we all are. But since most people struggled through the depression and their memory is long, we're not spending it. Who knows what will happen when the rest of the world's economies recover. Besides, our government urges us to save. We're paying income taxes now, and the government still wants us to buy as many war bonds as possible."

"Is that why we still have rationing?"

"Yes, Abi, we are sending food all over the world and to our troops, as well as clothing, medical supplies, war machines, airplanes and bombers, munitions—you name it. We're manufacturing it or growing it and sending all we can overseas. Our Merchant Marines should be thanked for their heroic action in making sure these cargoes get to where they are needed, they are fulfilling their duty, despite that they lose many more men than our regular navy as well as ships. The Germans' most effective ploy against the Allies is having their submarines attack and blow up as many cargo ships as possible."

"Ugh! No wonder Craig and Colin's ship was so gross. The damn Germans got fooled that time!" Callum commented with a big grin.

Cameron screwed up his face. "Well, I think it's stupid to give away so much and short ourselves."

Dad sighed, his enthusiasm dampened by Cameron's negative remarks. "Let's all help with the dishes so we can go catch the news and a show or two."

On a Wing and a Prayer

They say that curiosity kills the cat, and that was me after we knew the boys were in England, which everyone guessed would be the push off point when the Allies invaded Europe. Knowing my brothers would surely be involved, I began reading Dad's magazines with more fervor. Sometimes he would bring home a *Life* magazine, which I loved because its pages were larger than those of *Time* and full of pictures.

Previously, my interest had centered mostly on articles featuring things about here at home and how the war was impacting us. I would scan the news on specific battles, but found it confusing because they were everywhere and mostly in places I had never heard of before. These stories concentrated on telling what officers and units had fought in the battle, how many ships or planes had been destroyed, and how many men had been killed. I would give up, knowing that my understanding that element of the war would make no difference.

Now when I looked at these periodicals, I searched for comforting information that would lead me to believe my brothers were not alone. I wanted to be assured that they went into battle with the best possible defenses and equipment.

I noticed the ads, while bragging with much explanation about the quality and usefulness of their goods, all advertised the sale of war bonds. A Studebaker ad in a February edition of *Time* ended their full-page ad by insisting we buy more bonds to expedite the return of our fighting men. The page exhibited a stamp saying *4ᵗʰ war loan. Buy More Bonds*. When I asked Dad what that meant, he told me that each time we purchased a war bond, we were loaning money to the U.S. government to fund the war.

He explained that it took a lot of money to fight the war and manufacture things necessary for fighting. He said that these bonds were sold at 75 percent of the face value and would mature in ten years. "Just think of it this way, Abi. If you spend $18.75 on a bond, it's face value is $25, and that is what the government will pay you when the bond matures."

"Well, why don't we just lend the government the $25 in the first place?"

Dad smiled. "Putting cash into bonds helps prevent inflation, they say. They're like a savings account. Right now, our nation's economy is as healthy as it will ever be, but no matter our circumstances, the economists always worry about inflation."

I wanted to ask him about inflation but Dad, as usual, settled into a long lecture. He explained that bond sales were conducted in the context of rallies. "We have had three, and are now starting the fourth. I believe there will be more before the war's end." He reminded me how we had listened to rallies where Betty Grable had auctioned off her stockings, Hedy Lamarr, a kiss, and Jack Benny, his violin, and how Carole Lombard had lost her life flying home from a bond rally, along with her mother and a press agent.

I was relieved when Dad left to feed the cattle so I could reread the story accompanying Studebaker Corporation's push to sell war bonds. Its story was written like a novel: *Somewhere in England a limping plane was attempting to land safely, sending out a flare to indicate she had wounded men on board. She was full of bullet and cannon holes, losing her tail, with motors destroyed, and one of her wings barely hanging on.* I'll never forget the words they used to finish the story—*she came home, literally, on a wing and a prayer.* That afternoon after dinner, I begged Dad to take me into town so I could buy more war bonds.

One article cheered me, and I told this funny story at supper time. Women were in trouble across America, and Army postal officers were angry because lipstick kisses on V-mail made it impossible to reproduce those letters because the sticky stuff had ruined the page they were on and the ones following them. They would have to stop the automatic feeder and clean it before they could process more letters. We laughed, and Mom said, "We'd better warn Blair about that before Henry ships out."

That night before going to sleep, I prayed that my brothers' planes would make it through each mission and that the Germans would give up the fight soon. Then I thought of the last article I had read. It was about a man named Charles McGonegal, who was a veteran of World War I. This veteran visited convalescent hospitals on the East coast showing young men who had lost an arm or both how many things he could do with his steel claws. He had lost both his arms just below the elbow, but could light a cigarette, use a telephone, write, and play cards. When one boy asked him how he danced with a girl, Charles did a few turns with a nurse, and said, *warmth comes from the heart, not the hands.* But I still prayed that neither of my brothers or Jake would have to learn his skills.

We received a letter from Craig just weeks after his first letter from England had come, and he was in a much better state of mind. He said he and Colin were adjusting to life in Aldbourne, and after their indoctrination on English life and customs, they were reminded that they were guests in that country and needed to heed all social rules and norms and to be respectful in all ways.

They hadn't had much time to spend with the local people or in public houses, but when they did, lots of girls were there, but not one young man. He said the beer was either very bitter or extremely mild and that he hadn't decided which he preferred, but that their homes were quaint—made of stone with thatched roofs and rose vines growing over them. Church bells rang out on the hour, which were at times annoying but other times were nice to hear, especially toward the end of the day.

They trained six days a week, eight to ten hours a day. They went on fifteen- to twenty-five-mile marches into the countryside, through rolling hills full of sheep grazing enclosed in mostly picket fences. Company E had already angered a local farmer because some of the men, to get Captain Sobel in trouble, had cut a wire fence, insisting that had been their commander's orders. "So, we were back to fencing for a day," Craig wrote, and I easily imagined his chuckles when he told of how frustrated and angry Sobel became when confronted by the sheep farmer.

The food is awful here, but when you're hungry, you'll even eat horse meat. Yes, horsemeat is pretty much our only source of protein except for powdered eggs. Yes, that too, and powdered milk, along with dried apricots and dehydrated potatoes. We eat a lot of cabbage, turnips, and Brussels sprouts. We get three candy bars a week, which we guard diligently because they have a way of disappearing.

We still march out on night ops, and at the barracks, attend classes on map reading, the Germans' weapons and their uses, chemical warfare, combat and street fighting, first aid, booby traps and mines—how to detect them and detonate them— and how to use all the different communication devices.

Last week, we went out on a three-day exercise where we were ordered to dig foxholes and sleep in them. By the way, the English soil here is just as rocky as at home, unfortunately, and my arms are still sore from the hard digging. We barely got the things dug when they came at us with Sherman tanks. They roared toward us, and we all ducked down into our holes just in time, as the damn things drove right over us. This week, we will go again but without rations, so we'll have to live off the land. We're allowed to hunt deer and any other wildlife we see, so Colin and I aren't a bit worried about that exercise.

Our Company still leads all the other ones when competing within the regiment, out in the field, in the barracks, or in athletic contests.

Take care, my dear family. I'm sorry about losing our grandparents but now, at least, they won't suffer from the pain and misery of old age and the worry of war. Colin sends his love, as I do. Love again, Craig.

Planes, Trains, Trucks, and Ships

No spot on earth is more than sixty hours' flying time away . . .

In a March *Time* edition, I came across a two-page ad sponsored by an aircraft manufacturing corporation with factories in San Diego, Fort Worth, Louisville, and Allentown. Their two largest boasts were about the miracle of airplanes in the war and then about what we civilians could expect when the war was over.

The first vaunt was about a mission executed by 1,000 Allied bombers, in which they destroyed an entire German city where factories built fighter planes and machine guns. It took a mere forty minutes to wipe out this city, and I wondered how many people—men, women, and children—had died during that attack. The article went on to explain, in graphic detail, what it took to supply such an endeavor: millions of gallons of gasoline, thousands of gallons of oil, millions of rounds of machine gun ammunition, tons of bombs, tons of food, bombers and bomber engine replacements, and tons of other supplies.

The ad went on to explain how the U.S. got all this material overseas. It displayed a picture of eight cargo ships with one fighter plane hovering over them, protecting them like a mother hen as they crossed the Atlantic. Another photo showed a plane, train, truck, and a ship. The ad finished with pictures of the different types of aircraft this one manufacturer produced, along with a promise that after the war, *No spot on earth is more than 60 hours' flying time from any local airport.*

Battling the Luftwaffe, the German Air Force, took much material and many men. Another article reported that during a six-day aerial battle between the Nazis and American and British bombers, 20,000 tons of bombs were dropped on Nazi targets, bringing out the Luftwaffe fighter planes in full force. After the fight was over, the Nazis had lost 440 planes while the Allies lost only 195, but, unfortunately, the Allied forces lost more men.

That explained another short article reporting that U.S. Generals and Admirals wanted 1,160,000 more men drafted into the armed forces. The article discussed the choices the Selective Service had in filling that wish. They considered drafting 250,000 fathers, but, no, the Generals and Admirals didn't want them because they thought that having families back home would distract them. They wanted more 18- to 25-year-old men without families. Steel companies didn't like that because many of these men were pulled out of their workforce, which had already lost 42,000 workers to the draft. As the Selective Service tallied up the possible draftees, they included 250,000 new 18-year-olds. Callum and Cameron would turn sixteen in October, and I began to look at them in a different light, praying that the war would end before they could be taken.

Missoula

....

Dad had business in Missoula and decided to take Mom, Rory, and me along, leaving the ranch under the care of Callum and Cameron, with Larry checking on them. We would be gone three days. Craig owned a house near downtown, and close enough to campus to walk there. We planned to stay in his home and make sure everything was in good working order. We boarded the train in Philipsburg and, in no time, arrived in that seemingly quiet and yet bustling college town. Dad told us that many people who came to attend school there never wanted to leave and that was the reason it had grown like it had.

After Dad finished his business, we took one of the spanking new city buses that had replaced street cars to tour the internment camp at Fort Missoula. The men were friendly and seemed content. Except for the handfuls of Germans and Japanese, who were U.S. citizens, but with questionable loyalty, most of the camp consisted of Italian sailors who had the misfortune to be on Italian ships taken by the government when we entered the war. They were merchant seamen, World's Fair employees, and crew members of an Italian luxury liner. They had nicknamed the camp Bella Vista— beautiful view—and worked as laborers on local farms or for the Forest Service, fighting fires in the hot, dry summer months.

Some of them worked at the camp, doing laundry, cooking meals and baking. Dad said they were happy because they knew they had escaped the terrible fighting in their homelands. The food smelled delicious, and the steam coming from the wash house gave off clean, fragrant odors, reminding me of wash-day at home. That night we had supper at an Italian restaurant so I knew the wonderful scent of their food had tweaked my parents' taste buds as well.

Craig's house was pleasant and sat on East Pine Street. The street was lined with maple trees and was wide with a nearly-as-wide median full of newly-planted flowers. He had purchased a Craftsman-style house. It had a lot of heavy woodwork and built-ins in the same wood. It was cozy and had a small backyard where I played tag with Rory, running off his three-year-old energy so he would sleep well at night. We walked everywhere, which helped too, since Mom and Dad made Rory do his own walking most of the time. Pacing ourselves to his small steps didn't bother me, because Missoula seemed like a large city compared to Philipsburg, and there was a lot to see and take in.

The day before we returned home, we toured the college campus. It was beautiful with acres of green grass with many trees and bushes. The main hall was an elegant building with a tall bell tower holding a clock, which chimed with each passing hour. Mom and Dad wanted me to finish my education there, just as Craig had done. They, along with my principal, wanted me to graduate this spring, but I had dug my heels in and refused. I would not leave home until my brothers returned home from the war, and besides, I wasn't even fifteen yet.

I wanted to be home when the boys and Jake came back, and I wasn't sure I needed more education to become a rancher and a horsewoman. I begged them to allow me to do more independent studies like I had been doing. My parents made me promise that if Craig came home soon and returned to Missoula, I would consider attending the university because he would be there for me.

We went shopping after viewing the campus and that night, we went to supper at the Florence Hotel, which was the fanciest place in town. I had fried shrimp for the first time along with the best French fries I had ever eaten. Then we enjoyed live theatre in the tallest building in Missoula, the Wilma. The play was a comedy and made us laugh like we hadn't for a long time. Rory giggled along with us. I think he thought we were funny because of our belly laughing. Perhaps living in Missoula wouldn't be so bad after all.

The Shack

The morning after we returned home, I went for an early morning walk, hoping that the exercise and cool, fresh air would chase my migraine away. As I left our little graveyard and veered off to the left, following the little trail I had made with my constant treks up to the shack, I noticed truck tracks going up the hill as far as a vehicle could safely travel. Then, when I reached the forlorn building, I could see that the newly-greened grass had been trampled down near the door, and that someone had forged their own fresh trail back to where they had parked the truck. The padlock was in place. Out of habit, I gave it a shake, but it just rattled unyieldingly.

I knew then that the secrecy of this place was not Dad's doing; he had been with us in Missoula, and the day before we left, I had visited, and there had been no sign of anyone. I'd decided I had better reveal my findings to Dad—I couldn't put it off any longer, and went reluctantly home to help Mom with the laundry.

It was my job to collect the dirty clothes, sort them, and mix up Mom's miracle solution for whites. She still didn't trust me to use the washing machine but allowed me to hang everything out on the line after she ran them through the final rinse and pulled them through the wringer. I loved that job, except when it was windy; then, it was a battle to keep things pinned to the clothesline and off the ground. Mom did most of the ironing apart from the sheets, pillowcases, handkerchiefs, and my clothes. I guess she thought I would be more careful while learning the art if I pressed my own items. I may have been a tomboy, but my appearance was still important to me.

That day, I hummed a strange tune repeatedly, which I tended to do when perturbed. I hated that about myself, and so did everyone else, and I was glad Mom had not yet made it out to the wash room. I absentmindedly fished through everyone's pockets, making sure they were empty before laundering. The last item I picked up was a pair of Cameron's jeans.

I found a piece of Dubble Bubble chewing gum, which I happily unwrapped and stuffed into my mouth. Next, I pulled out a bank receipt. It was for a very large deposit, and I found that to be puzzling until I pulled out a key—a key designed for a large padlock. What the Sam heck? Cameron? He was the secretive, intrepid trapper?

Mom came in just then and found me standing there, speechless, choking on a flood of sweet saliva made from the gum. I sputtered and coughed, and the more I tried to speak, the more I choked. Finally, I was able to stop, and I began wiping the tears from my eyes while making up a story for her. But Mom took matters into her own hands. "Oh! Honey, I know you have your period. Why don't you go lie down for a while until you feel better?" I shook my head and ran, grateful for the chance to go to the shack and see if the key worked, but angry about Mom's keeping track of my menstrual cycles, though I understood she did so because of what had happened with Blair.

I crept out the front entrance, hanging onto the screen door so it wouldn't close with its usual bang. When it finally latched shut, I tiptoed down the steps and headed for the hill as fast as I could. But Dad happened to be coming toward the house, swearing as he usually did when exasperated. I stopped, not daring to leave in front of him. "What's wrong?"

"One of your brothers ran the truck out of gas, and now I have to go see if your mother has some gas coupons or we won't be driving this week. I hope to God we have some left."

He stormed past me, and I ran up the hill like a horse just let out of a racetrack line up. By the time I reached the shack, I had a stitch in my side, and I leaned over to stop the cramping and catch my breath. My hands shook as I tried the key. It worked beautifully, and I stepped inside. The furs were gone—not one pile or bundle was left. But the traps were still there, many of them hanging on the wall and several lying on the floor—hard, steel traps with wicked teeth.

Suddenly, I heard voices. I crept out the door and saw Callum and Cameron on the other side of the creek. It was their turn to check on the pairs. I hurriedly walked back to the door, shut it quietly, snapped the padlock shut, and turned the key. I put the key into the pocket of Ian's old jeans, and after the boys had moved on up the trail, I ran down the hill, my mind about to explode.

I needed to figure out how to handle this. I had to do something, before Cameron discovered he no longer had the key. I knew I should tell Dad, but I didn't want Cameron to hate me any more than he did. But I also wanted to get rid of those traps before any more animals suffered, and especially before Bear came out of hibernation with a cub or two. I knew there were still two bear traps. I had seen them among the wide assortment of awful devices my brother kept in the shack.

I tiptoed up the stairs to my room, trying to think clearly. I had to get rid of those traps, and I knew I had time, since trapping season had ended for most animals, if not for bears. I thought about digging a large hole and burying them. No, it would be nearly impossible to dig a hole up there in that sandy, gravelly, rocky soil. Also, they could just as easily be dug up. I thought about burning the old heap down, but steel traps would survive the heat of the blaze. That might put an end to the illicit—under Dad's law—activities of my brother since he wouldn't have a place to carry out his cruel deeds in secret. But those damned traps would still exist, and I wanted to be rid of them.

My head swam, and I experienced the weird dizziness, which I sometimes did on the first day of my period. I laid on my bed, hoping it would soon pass, thinking about all the things I had to do. I chided myself for committing to help with the scrap drive on Saturday. Today was Thursday, and how could I get anything done before then? I had to do something quickly before Cameron discovered he'd lost his key. I knew I could go to Dad, but Cameron would be in dire straits with Dad—big, big trouble. And I didn't want to start anything like that.

Mom came and asked me how I felt, and I went down to help her with dinner. But I couldn't eat and just moved my food around on my plate. I didn't pay much attention to the dinner-table talk until I heard them talking about football camp and the empty gas tank on the truck. Dad kept repeating that if someone didn't own up to driving needlessly and using the remaining gas, no one would be attending football camp in Missoula.

Callum came up with a story about going into town for more vaccine for branding. But I knew different. Thinking of the bank receipt, I knew damned well Cameron had taken his furs into town and sold them. I wondered what he had told the buyers. We knew that Callum would, most likely, earn a full-ride football scholarship to college because of his prowess, and he needed to be seen by the scouts at camp. I understood his deception, but still felt bad for Callum because he was innocent and had had to plead guilty.

Mom and Dad found enough gas coupons to fill both the car and the truck for the next few days. Camp began the next afternoon, so the boys would leave early in the morning to catch the train. Perfect, I thought, I would have a day and a half without Cameron around to get those traps down the hill and into town to the scrap drive, an idea that had come to me in the middle of the night. That would take care of them forever, and I would be doing my duty for my country. If Dad caught me, well, so be it.

The next day, I was blessed with even more time of my own when Mom and Dad decided to spend some time in town doing errands and treating themselves to lunch after seeing the twins off. I worked feverishly, riding one of our workhorses up to the shack, filling several gunny sacks with the bulky traps, and loading them onto an old, miniature wagon hitched to the horse. I was grateful that the remaining bear traps were only thirty-pounders or I never could've handled them.

As I led the horse down the hill, I wondered what to do with those heavy bags until the next day. We kept our truck parked next to a straw stack that we hadn't completely used last winter. I threw the bags into the stack and covered them. I made two more trips to the shack, and finally, it was empty. The next morning when Gail came to pick me up, I convinced her to not tell a soul what was in those gunny sacks and that we wouldn't unload them until the drive was nearly over and most people had left.

She wouldn't leave me be until I told her what was in them, and when I explained, she gasped. "Oh! Gosh! Abi. Your brother will go nuts if he ever finds out! Are you sure you want to give all those traps to the drive? It's not against the law or a sin. Trapping got many families through the Depression, right?"

"Yes, Gail, but this is Cameron. He doesn't need the money. He needlessly kills animals for their fur, and I don't think it's right. One of his traps—a bear trap, mind you—put an end to Larry's life. What if one of us would have walked into that huge contraption? We would have been maimed for life. I just hope he has all the traps pulled in for the season."

"Well, I think you should let your father know about this so he can have a talk with Cameron about why it is dangerous for the rest of your family. *Please* talk to your dad, Abi—when I think of the things Cameron has done to you, I have a terrible fear of what he would do if he ever found out. He would be so angry, he wouldn't be able to think straight."

"Okay, I'll talk to Dad because I want to burn that damn shack down as well."

Gail rolled her eyes. "Where is Cameron right now?"

"He and Callum rode the train to Missoula for football camp."

We didn't talk the rest of the way into town. I knew Gail was right—about everything. I felt sick to my stomach and a headache starting. I wouldn't have done any of this if I hadn't believed Cameron would never know. I would tell Dad, who I hoped would help me keep my secret and burn that damn place down to the ground.

The piles of donated materials at the scrap drive were impressive. The school parking lot was filled with donations. Three tremendous piles of tires and old rubber dwarfed the mounds of tin and metal. Containers of engine grease stood heating in the hot sun and fouled the air, and they had run out of gunny sacks and boxes to hold the used paper products. Clothes lay on the lunchroom tables for exchanging. People could trade item for item so families with growing children could upsize their wardrobes. People stopped coming in around noon, and soon high school boys and their fathers began loading the trucks that would take the bounty to train cars which would then take the goods to the appropriate manufacturing centers.

When we had finished packing boxes full of leftover clothing, Gail drove her pickup next to a truck full of scrap metal. My principal was there and helped me throw my offering onto the truck bed. I begged him to not tell anyone about what I had brought, and he swore he wouldn't, but not before he demanded to know where I acquired so many traps. I told him I had found them in an old shack on our place, and that I wanted things kept secret because I suspected one of my brothers of using them after our father had forbidden them to trap. He nodded his head and told me to leave the rest of the bags on the ground and he would take care of them. As we drove away, I turned to see men swarm toward him as he emptied another bag. But he waved them away, shaking his head without speaking, and they helped pitch the torturous objects onto the truck.

I thanked the Fates that my principal had kept his word, and suddenly I was ravenous. We went to the corner drive-in and ordered chocolate malts, fries, and hamburgers. We laughed about some of the scenes at the drive, especially the ones where either a wife or a husband had brought some object that the other one wanted to keep. Gail imitated old Mrs. Filler cursing at her husband in German while attempting to pull a cast iron skillet from his hands, and I nearly choked on a fry, giggling.

We talked about Blair, who instead of coming home to stay with us as we'd hoped, was staying at Fort Bragg to work as a volunteer at the U.S. station hospitals there, getting a free, government-funded education in nursing. I told Gail how Dad was upset because he worried about who would be taking care of James when she was gone, and Gail told me how her parents had hoped to spend more time with James, too.

Gail shook her head. "I don't know why they dote on your little nephew so much, but they sure do like him. Maybe it's because Raymond is becoming so big and grown up and they miss that. It seems like it was just yesterday when they told Billy and me there would be a new baby in the family, and now he's already twelve and hates it when Mom and Dad smother him with too much attention. Now that Billy's gone, and Ray is growing up, I guess it's good that they have another little boy to love. It's strange, but sometimes I see something of Billy in the photo of James they have taped to the fridge. I guess I see that just 'cause, even though Billy was a brat, I still miss him."

I took a big bite of my hamburger, stuffing my mouth to keep me from spilling the truth, and then remembering how much I appreciated my principal keeping my big, fat secret, I reminded myself that the truth about James was not my story to tell. After I had finished swallowing, I reached over and gave Gail a half-hug and a peck on the cheek. "Well, you and your family can borrow James, when he is here, or any one of our sweet little babies any time they want. I love that our families have become such good friends, don't you?"

Shocking News

I came home that afternoon in a sunny mood, relieved that Bear would no longer lose babies to Cameron's fetish. Thinking of Dad's ample bear rug in the bunkhouse, I still wondered why Cameron would want such small ones, and I worried that he knew about me and my relationship with Bear. I shook my head at such a wild thought. How could he?

I walked into our house, glad to be in its coolness. Mom had cleaned and opened the windows and had pulled the venetian blinds closed to keep out the red-hot heat of the sun. She had baked gingerbread and set it on the countertop to cool, and I inhaled wafts of sweet, earthy molasses and tangy ginger, making my mouth water. I could already taste the heavenly mixture of sweet whipped cream and soft, spicy, moist bread.

Suddenly, Dad's booming curses shattered the sweet-smelling peace. My parents were in the living room, and Rory must have been napping. I heard Mom attempt to quiet Dad with hushed murmurs, and I stopped and stood still, barely breathing, to hear what they were discussing. Then I heard Dad speak Craig's name in a softer tone, and I heard him utter, *"Married. Married?"* I heard the way he said the word and envisioned it in five-foot lettering on a theater marquee.

"Why in the hell did he have to go and get married? To an *English* girl of all people. *English?*"

When he said English in that way, I again envisioned it spelled out in large, garish, flashing red letters. Then it struck me, Craig had married an English girl. Holy gosh! My big brother had married, and in no time at all, just months perhaps even weeks after meeting this English girl. I believed in love at first sight because I truly was a romantic. But still, after all these years of girlfriends and dating, Craig had married a person he could only have known a short while. I understood why my father couldn't accept that his oldest son had married an English girl. Despite that Dad and Mom were second-generation Americans, they still held a distinct dislike and distrust of Brits, as they often called them.

I took a deep breath and walked into the parlor. Dad had turned to a dose of whiskey even though it was early. I rarely saw my father drunk or even tipsy, but he did imbibe when things got, as he labeled them, "out of hand, incomprehensible, or unbearably tragic." That was my father, constantly struggling to be in control, to understand, and to be stoic.

"Hi! What's going on?"

Mom gave me an eye roll. "We finally received a short V-letter from Craig. The boys are both fine, but he couldn't say anything pertaining to their fighting status or where they are exactly, or what the plans are for the 101st. But he did send a picture of a lovely-looking English girl who he, since his last letter, has married."

Mom turned to give her full attention to Dad. "Your father is having a fit, now, over something he can't do anything about or change. What's done is done." She turned back to me. "Here, Abi, take a look at the newest member of the family. She's quite pretty, don't you think?"

I took the photo and went to the window to examine it in better light. I pushed a couple slats up, and peered at the girl my brother had married. Her smile was infectious and made me smile as I took in her looks. A dimple accentuated one side of her turned-up mouth, which looked generous and lush with sensuous lips, the bottom one appearing a bit pouty. Her eyes were wide-set, giving her a look of innocence until you noticed her high cheekbones, which made her appear more aristocratic as did her straight but ample nose. Her eyes looked as if they were dark as well as her hair, which fell in abundant waves onto her shoulders. Her jaw was as strong as any MacDougal chin. I turned the picture over. She had signed it—Ruth Anne Pritchard, 1944, London, 20 years old.

I handed the picture to Mom. "Gosh, I think she's gorgeous. Her face suggests she's a happy, honest, and open person who would be fun to get to know."

"Well, that's good, because she'll be coming here to live with us until Craig returns." Dad finished off his dour-sounding statement with a hand brush through his hair, and said, "I'm going to saddle Buck and take a long ride to think and hopefully, cool down a bit."

Mom and I both giggled after Dad left. I felt excited about it all, and I think Mom did, too. We stood close and perused the photo of our new relative, a person that my brother must have fallen for instantly.

"Well, she looks good. I hope she is as good inside as she appears outside," Mom said with a wistful sigh.

"Yes," I said with a shrug of the shoulders. "I don't think it would be right to think negatively of her, like Dad's doing, without us knowing her. Plus, I don't think Craig would choose someone with a difficult personality. No, not him. I bet she's as peachy as she looks."

Mom laughed and patted me on the cheek. "Yes, Abi, all we can do is hope for the best and give her an unbiased chance to become one of us when she arrives."

"When will that be?"

"Christmas."

"What an interesting Christmas present she will be to us."

An Uneasy May

If you need wisdom, ask our generous God, and he will give it to you.
He will not rebuke you for asking.
James 1:5

All morning long, I tried to find a good time to tell Dad about Cameron and the shack, but I kept playing with the idea of just going up there and burning the place down myself. Every time I began mentally running through how I would open the conversation, my mind would play tricks on me with images of the blaze I hoped would engulf and destroy that old heap. Bear, typically, didn't appear until sometime in June, and time was running out since Monday would be May Day, and that was the day the boys would return from camp.

Dad's long ride yesterday hadn't seemed to do him any good, and his antsy state today nearly drove Mom and me nutty. Every time I woke last night, I could hear his music, so I knew he had been up late, therefore he was not only still agitated, but he was also tired and cranky. Rory had recently recovered from a runny nose, and now had an earache, which put him in the same state as Dad. Mom and I left our two miserables to take care of each other and went to Mass.

The opening Bible verse spoke of asking God for help in all things, and I prayed hard during the service for guidance in dealing with my desire to burn down a place which I knew was precious to my disturbed brother. It didn't feel right to add to his distress just for my own satisfaction. But when I thought of Bear and the other animals' suffering at his hands, I knew I would be doing the right thing. I went home determined to tell Dad about what I had found, what I had done yesterday, and what I wanted to do now.

A long nap and a dozen stories read and ditties shared had done wonders for our guys. Dad was back to whistling, and Rory had quit pulling at his ear and was singing his newly-learned verses.

> *Dan, Dan, the funny wee man,*
> *Washed his face with a frying pan.*
> *He combed his hair with the leg of a chair,*
> *Dan, Dan, the funny wee man.*

Rory continued to play with his cars and trucks with intermittent putt, putt, putts, and switched to another song.

> *Mrs. McGuire peed on the fire*
> *The fire was too hot so she peed in the pot,*
> *The pot was too round so she peed on the ground*
> *The ground was too flat so she peed on the cat,*
> *And the cat ran away with a pee on his back.*

Mom had gone out to the root cellar to gather parsnips for dinner and came in just as Rory proudly finished his song.

"Angus MacDougal, how dare you teach our son that silly rhyme? Will you ever outgrow your boyish obsession with peeing? I swear you men have too much fun with that thing. Humph, humph, humph—some things never change." The boys had once told Mom and me how Dad had taught them to write their initials in the dirt with their pee, which we found quite amusing.

Rory, Dad, and I had been laughing. But when Mom subconsciously used her mother's opening humphs, telling us that we were about to receive a lecture, I sobered. Oh, Grandma, how we have missed you—how we have missed all four of you. Not that we had seen one another much in the recent years since we children were growing up into our own lives, no, it wasn't that kind of missing, it was the kind of missing that comes from knowing we can no longer visit you like in the old days when we were young, knowing that you were available to love and to be with. We miss a past that will never be repeated except in our memories.

Despite my melancholy thoughts, I couldn't get the *Mrs. McGuire* ditty out of my head. I looked at it as a sign that I should tell Dad everything, and plead with him to help me burn down the shack. My nervous stomach made it impossible to do justice to Mom's wonderful roast beef dinner, and it wasn't lost on her.

"Abigail, what is your problem? You have been playing with your food for three days now. Is everything all right? Is there something you need to get off your chest?"

I nodded. "May I talk with you and Dad after we do the dishes, and Rory is down for his nap?"

My parents looked at one another with that "oh, no" look, and the lovely dinner was wasted on us, except for Rory, who wanted more catsup to dip his beef in. We decided to save the gingerbread until everyone had more of an appetite.

After dinner dishes were done and Rory had been put to bed with promises of a treat if he took a nice nap, Mom, Dad, and I sat down at the dining table. It was just the three of us, and that gave me lonely thoughts. I remembered when we filled every inch of our table with us children lining each side, and Mom and Dad at each end. It took me a bit to get to the task at hand, but finally I collected my thoughts and began.

My parents were both shocked and angered by Cameron's deception and disobedience. When I reached the part about deciding how to get rid of the traps, they lightened up a bit. Then when I told them about my principal keeping my secret, and how he waved away those men anxious to reclaim my contribution, and wouldn't tell them where the traps came from, they both began giggling. Dad slapped his knee with gusto, his laughter becoming louder and louder, turning into a belly laugh, making his eyes water. He kept shaking his head and pointing at me since he couldn't speak.

Mom kept saying, "Angus, quiet down. I think Rory finally fell asleep."

Rory had gone down like a good little boy, wanting to earn his after-nap snack. But we had heard him singing his newly-learned ditties for a while before he fell silent. Each time he sang the line about the fire being too hot, I became a little braver about asking for my fire. I sat quiet for a bit, trying to think of how I had planned to request Dad's permission and help to burn away that creepy place forever.

"Abi! Abi! Hey, Abi, come back to us."

I stopped my pondering and pulled my attention back to my parents. "Dad, Mom . . ." Dad had just finished slapping his knee again, but this time it was one of those slaps he made when he had come to a decision. "Well, Abi, it rained just enough last night I think we can safely have ourselves a little bonfire. What do you think?"

I sat up straight and smiled big. "Let's do it. I was just going to ask you if we could burn it down, but you know, that old shack must be special to Cameron, so I don't know if it is the right thing to do. He'll be upset when he finds it gone."

Dad smiled one of his rare, soft-hearted smiles steeped in understanding. "Yes, Abi. But he was disobedient, cruel, and devious. I told all my boys there would never be trapping on this place, and he ignored that rule, disobeying me, and he stole from the ranch. He made a lot of money, and what he wants to do with it, I have no idea, but the fact remains that what he did was defiant, selfish, and dangerous. Think of poor Larry. Think of those bear cubs losing their lives for what, tiny bearskin rugs—I'll never fathom that. I guess I'll never understand that boy."

After glancing at Mom with guilt and sadness, he turned to me and chucked me under my chin. "Come on, Abi—time's a wasting, and don't you worry, Mom and I will never tell anyone about this, got it? I know how hard Cameron can be with you, and that's a whole 'nother story."

Before we started the fire, Dad put the key into the padlock and turned it, keeping the door locked. "This will make it a mystery as to how this fire got started. Cameron will come here snooping and will see that the padlock hadn't been unlocked." He finished with a pat on my cheek. "No, I don't want you worrying about Cameron ever finding out about your involvement, and if he ever does know or suspect what you did with his traps, I will deal with him."

"I just hope he doesn't go mad with anger. I've been praying that he did well at camp this weekend, and maybe then he won't care so much."

Dad grinned. "Yes, we can only hope."

We had taken straw and lined both the inside and outside walls with it. Now Dad brought out some bottles of oil left over from our days without electricity; he gave me one and showed me how to squirt it on the straw. After we emptied our bottles, he brought out the box of big wooden matches and handed it to me.

"Here, Abi, you do the honors."

I took the box and lit a match on its side. I threw it into the straw, and then repeated that a dozen times as I walked around the building. Soon it was ablaze. It was a good fire with much smoke plummeting high into the sky. Dad and I sat cross-legged on the ground a small distance from the blaze, just out of the heat, and watched.

Dad shook his head, and picked up a straw to chew on. "I'm not going to say a word to Cameron. Burning down his secret place is punishment enough. I just don't know why that boy is such a difficult egg. Just don't know."

I nestled closer to Dad and looked up at him. "I just don't understand why he dislikes me so much, even hates me—he always has it out for me no matter what I do or say."

Dad let out a bitter laugh. "Well that, little Abi, is something I do understand and can explain to you. When the twins were born, Cameron came first, and it was a difficult birth. They had to cut the umbilical cord that was wrapped around his neck, but even after that, it was still hard for him to take his first breath. They no sooner got him breathing than Callum was born, fast and easy.

Until they turned two, there was a big difference in how they progressed. Cameron was always behind in development, and sickly. They both went through the usual baby and childhood ailments, but while Callum easily overcame them, Cameron would struggle and usually scared us with his high fevers, which required cool baths and always set him back physically and mentally. Callum learned to walk first, talk first—he did everything before his brother and at times it would be months until Cameron caught up to him. Your mother doted on Cameron, spoiling him, always working with him to bring him up to par with Callum.

Then you came along, and your mother turned her attention to you. Pure and simple, Abi, your brother has always been jealous of you. You were beautiful and precocious, turning everyone's head. Cameron resented that even as a little boy, and now he's nearly a man and still has those grievances. Mom and I have always hoped he would outgrow his animosity."

I began to cry, and Dad put his arm around me, pulling me close, not saying a word, just holding me until the fire died out.

The next morning, I woke with my stomach in knots—I dreaded what might happen when Cameron saw that his shack had been burned down. I couldn't eat breakfast, and Mom sent me up to my room to lie down. I took the latest *Life* magazine with me, hoping to get my mind off my brothers' homecoming. The entire edition reported the tension building throughout the world and especially in Europe since everyone knew the Allied invasion of Europe was imminent. One article said there are more fit, young American men in England than there are in the United States and Canada. They quoted one young British woman as saying, "I keep expecting our country to sink, it is so heavy with men and weapons."

There were pages and pages of pictures taken in England of our men along with an entire page dedicated to the Allies' Supreme Commander of The Allied Expeditionary Force, Dwight Eisenhower. I turned the pages, fascinated with the pictures, wondering about my brothers' whereabouts and activities. A full-page picture of 100 paratroopers swinging through the air captured my attention. The next page's title, *Invasion by Air will be the Biggest in History,* really caught my eye. The pictures on that page showed individual paratroopers and then one larger one of Churchill and Eisenhower inspecting *maneuver-hardened U.S. paratroopers.* I took a close look at every photo, discovering I didn't have to imagine where my brothers were or what they were doing. I jumped up, stomachache forgotten, and ran downstairs, screaming, "Dad! Mom! *Life* has pictures of our boys in it!"

They huddled around me as I pointed to an individual picture of Colin. He was sitting and writing, of course, but with a helmet on, leading us to believe they had just finished a maneuver. The picture with Churchill and General Eisenhower partially showed the front line of paratroopers as these leaders inspected them. Out of the six men pictured, Craig stood out, tall and proud. Mom cried, and Dad just kept repeating, "Boy isn't this a honey of a deal. Our boys made the *Life.* Man! What a honey of a deal. Can't wait to hear what they have to say about Eisenhower and Churchill. I've read that Eisenhower is known for his friendliness and interest in his men—that he stops and asks where they're from and about their hometowns."

I went through the rest of the day happy, completely distracted from worries about Cameron. We knew our boys were alive and fine, and that changed the pensive mood in our house to optimistic. Mom made a special supper, steak and mushrooms, along with mashed potatoes and gravy, and when the boys came home and smelled the food and were shown the pictures, they whooped and hollered. We had a great night, and our football heroes talked about nothing but camp after they settled down. It appeared that Cameron had as good a time and as successful a performance at camp as Callum. The next day after he returned from his usual walk in the woods, he never said one word about the shack and wouldn't for months.

Five Bells

"Ladies and gentlemen, we may be approaching a fateful hour."
Robert St. John, 1 a.m. June 6

*A*ll night long bulletins have been pouring in from Berlin claiming that D-Day is here. One—unconfirmed by Allied sources, of course—says that heavy fighting is taking place between the Germans and invasion forces on the Normandy Peninsula, about 31 miles southwest of Le Havre. After hearing those words from National Broadcasting Company announcer Robert St. John, Dad came upstairs and woke me as he had promised. We, like the rest of the world, had been anticipating the Allied invasion of Europe for days. I made Dad swear he would come and get me when it began. I had been sleeping a mere two hours before he woke me, and I came downstairs in my housecoat, still blurry-eyed.

"I was dozing, myself, when I heard five bells," Dad commented as I settled underneath my favorite woolen throw, blowing on the hot chocolate Dad had fixed for us. The Associated Press wire service teletype machine used bell-tone signals to indicate if the coming news was an important story—five bells—or ten bells if the news was considered of *transcendental importance*. We usually went to NBC radio station to hear the day's news, and Robert St. John's familiar voice nearly always comforted me even when stating bad news. Today it filled me with relief as he continued his broadcast.

We interrupt our program with a special broadcast. German news agency, DNB, has just sent a trans-ocean bulletin saying that the Allied invasion of Europe has begun. They report that Airborne troops have landed at the mouth of the Seine River and are a real threat to German operations. This may be an enemy trick. Nazis may be fishing for information, and I repeat, we have no confirmation from Allied sources. Nazi sources also say this may be a fake dress rehearsal or false alarm, another ploy for better information. Perplexed, the Germans are hoping to gain information on which they can rely. We will be in news transmission all night.

Dad and I stayed up all night, as well, but as time went on and the same information was repeated and the different news announcers continued to say that Allied sources had not yet confirmed that the invasion had started, I curled up in my chair and slept. After we had breakfasted, listening to the news in the parlor while eating, a first ever, Dad sent the boys out to do the chores and the health checks on the calves, who become more susceptible to their childhood ailments during late spring and early summer. The ultra-rich green grass, which my father claims one can watch growing, gives all bovines very loose bowels. The cows can handle this powerful food, but the baby calves get what we call the scours, and if not doctored for it, will often die.

Mom and I cleaned up the kitchen and put our dishes away as quietly as possible to hear the news coming from the parlor. I showered and dressed for the day, and returned to sit in front of the radio with my parents' blessing. Rory had received a large set of Lincoln logs for Christmas, and we built things until his attention span had been exhausted.

The first of the latest and newest news they announced came again from the German news agency DNB saying they had sent out an alert to all of Holland's coastal citizens, ordering them to leave their homes and move at least 18 miles inland, preferably to the woods, staying away from all roadways, railroad lines, and crowds. London news claimed that many British had reported hearing the roar of planes early in the morning. Dad explained that these planes, most likely, were the ones taking the Airborne troops across the channel to be dropped into German territory. What they were ordered to do was anyone's guess. A bit later, they announced that the German DNB reported that Allied planes had been flying over Germany. At dinner that day, we prayed for the safety of our brothers and all the brave men landing on the European continent.

We hovered around the radio for most of the afternoon. The news broadcasts were repetitive except for men of all different religions coming on every two to three hours to pray for the Allied cause and the *divine protection* of Allied troops.

Announcers spoke of how the beaches of northern France were now full of men and weapons, with many planes flying over, most of them Allied and hardly any German, and how there were acres and acres of ships out at sea with many more convoys coming that way. They talked of the thin first line of German defenses at the beach and assumed the Airborne forces had been able to disable several of their large guns since the Allied landing had been deemed successful. They went on to reveal and elaborate on the meetings between Roosevelt, Churchill, and Stalin, prior to this momentous event in which, it was assumed, the major policies and plans to rid Europe and the world of our Fascist enemies, once and for all, and how to defeat them were agreed upon.

They also predicted that the Allies would move fast to take Cherbourg as well as Le Havre since they were both strategically situated ports. They reported a drop of dummy paratroopers up the coast to the north intended to confuse the Germans, which it did. The news proclaimed that landed paratroopers were only under a light and scattered small arms fire, with only light casualties. We clapped and cheered, and Mom cried with joy, hoping that her sons were okay. We ate a late supper then, going to bed early after saying our own prayers for all the Allied soldiers.

The next day we ate breakfast in the parlor, and hurried through our chores of the day. Dad stayed near the radio. When news announcements were interspersed with regular programming, such as *Mirth and Madness*, and *Adelaide Hawley*, whose daily household tip was to *do your regular housework to get your mind off invasion worries but do send pictures to your soldiers as soon as possible*, I knew things were getting back to normal. The intense drama of the invasion had returned to the slow grind of fighting that had occurred prior to the invasion. It was understood that our Allied forces would now attempt to make their way across Europe, taking back the countries the Germans had conquered and oppressed. The only programs taken over by invasion news that next day were *Fibber McGee and Molly* and *The Bob Hope Show*, in which he interviewed flyboys from California, who were all *anxious to get into the fight before it ended*. When the soap operas were aired like always, I knew the progress of the invasion had slowed and D-Day excitement was over.

Summer

. . . .

Despite that waiting for the war to end was difficult, making each day seem endless, our summer days flew by fast and furious. Bear came to me one beautiful morning near the end of June, on the anniversary of Ian's death, with two chubby, good-natured cubs. They accepted me as if I were just another cub and wanted to tumble around with me. After Bear interfered, saving me from getting too roughed up, I pacified them with peanut butter and honey sandwiches. Bear had gained all her weight back and her pearly coat shone once again.

My meeting with Bear made me feel happy and justified in my destruction of Cameron's shack of shame. I no longer felt the same guilt about being human and Biblically considered superior to all the creatures of the Earth, and the idea that we humans often misuse this God-given dominance. I still felt bad for having to burn brands on our stock animals, cut the testicles off most of the males, for having to separate and wean babies from their mamas, and eventually sell them as food or eat them ourselves. I had been raised on a ranch and had been fed meat as soon as I could chew, so I loved eating almost any form of protein—I just couldn't allow myself to remember them as babies or think of them as grown living beings.

I began working with two fine male colts in July. One was a paint we named Seb's Son since poor, pubescent Sebastian had been given the job of breeding one of our top brood mares. The idea of perpetual male dominance in mating went down the tubes the day Sebastian and his much older, experienced mate created Sonny, our nickname for this new colt. It's a wonder Sebastian could even get the job done, since he received many more bites and kicks than he returned. The results were worth it, though, since Sonny turned out to be much like his sire in coloring, beauty, and temperament. He had his father's tobiano looks with the pure, white stockings along with a perfect star on his forehead, a gift from his mother.

Lefty's coloring, on the other hand, was subtler, but he was still considered a good-looking horse. Dad bought him from Larry's boss and didn't know if he would cut him since he thought his mating with Sebastian's future, female offspring would be interesting. Lefty was a red dun with a reddish-golden body set off by his deeper red mane and tail. His back legs carried two white socks. We named him Lefty because he had this tendency to carry his head to the left, which at times made his training a bit of a challenge.

Outside of doing their chores and helping with major projects on the ranch, my twin brothers spent their free time training for football season. It would be their second-to-last year in high school, and they wanted to, again, enjoy being athletic heroes. They attended two more camps, jogged into town three times a week to build endurance, and then lifted weights for strength. They played basketball to improve their flexibility in movement while on the run. The shack was never mentioned, and I felt more worry-free than I had in a long time when meeting Bear and her babies.

My brothers also engaged in target practice with other boys after their time in the gym. They had gotten together to plan and set up their spot, which was out of town far enough away and adequately isolated to ensure the safety of others. But Dad still worried about their safety and felt that a dozen sixteen-year-old boys shooting guns should have supervision. Kendall took on that responsibility and reported that, for once, Cameron outdid his twin in sharp shooting.

Blair came to visit to ensure James kept a deep connection to his extended family. We had numerous barbecues with the Gustafsons and when it came time for Blair and James to leave, the goodbyes were tearful. Blair reported that when the war was over they planned to move to Montana, and we all took heart at that news.

I received a short letter from Jake, addressing me and speaking to me as Ian's little sister, like always, but the fact remained, he had written to me, and since Charlotte Dingall had begun dating a fellow high school boy, hope blossomed in my heart once more.

The United States government had begun a program to teach English to many immigrants who were naturalized but had not yet learned our language and wished to join the military. Surprisingly, Philipsburg had families who did not yet speak English. I volunteered for that program and found it to be rewarding and a good way to make the time pass. Because of my anxiety over the fate of my brothers, Jake, and all the other men I knew fighting overseas, I couldn't concentrate enough to read much and this was a good alternative. Not only was my volunteering rewarding, but the fervor these men had, wanting to fight for their new country, for the freedom of all people, made me more sympathetic of my brothers' patriotism and their sacrifice.

After D-Day, the tide turned in favor of the Allies. Just two days before June 6, they had captured Rome. Later that month, they liberated Cherbourg, and in July, USSR troops took back Minsk, while the Allies freed Caen. In August, the Allies liberated Florence and Paris after bringing many more troops into the south of France. Meanwhile, Soviet troops captured German- occupied Romania, which surrendered to them. In the Pacific, the United States forces made many successful amphibious assaults on the Japanese, regaining much territory, rendering the Japanese Navy virtually powerless by the end of October.

In September, we received word from Craig, telling us that the 101st was recouping in England until they would be sent back to Europe. Due to security reasons, his letter didn't say much, but he did ask us to be good to Ruth Anne—*she has had a rough time of it since the war began.* Because of Craig's information and the recent speculation of an airborne military operation in the Netherlands, Dad was sure our boys would be involved. Later it was reported that the operation was unsuccessful. German troops having knowledge of Allied plans to secure and control important bridges near the Rhine river, had enough time in advance to destroy most of the bridges prior to the paratroopers' landings. It was reported that many Allied troops were killed or taken prisoner by German forces.

Nora

While we all worried about our boys, Mom stewed the most about what condition her sons might be in—despair etched lines into her beautiful face almost overnight. She couldn't sleep and when she did, nightmares chased her thoughts around like demons. Sometimes I could hear her crying out in the night, babbling nonsensically, or worst of all, sobbing in her sleep. I would jump out of bed, but then I would hear Dad talking softly to her, waking her out of her torturous slumber.

She began going to see Father Boyle with regularity like she had after Gracie had been taken. That seemed to help, but when sleep completely eluded her, Dad took her to the doctor, who prescribed a sedative and sleeping aid, which helped her to escape her angst at least at night. During the daytime hours she kept busy, seeming to follow Adelaide Hawley's advice to *do household chores to get your mind off invasion worries.* Our home sparkled like never before. She polished the furniture and floors until they gleamed. She either washed a wall or painted it with leftover paint kept in the root cellar. She either washed every curtain or replaced them with her own home-sewn creations. She expanded our garden, sowing seeds of vegetables we hadn't had before. That fall we put away broccoli, cauliflower, purple cabbages, and Brussels sprouts, everyone's least favorite.

Dad, seeing how this flurry of activity helped her, decided to begin planning an addition to the house. He wanted to add a two-story extension that would contain three bedrooms and a bath on the second floor, and one bedroom, a bath, and another parlor on the main floor.

"Nora, our family keeps growing and I know, I sense that both our boys will return, so, as I see it, we need more space. What do you think of . . ."

His voice had lowered to the point I couldn't hear exactly what he had said to Mom. All I know is that it did the trick in distracting her from her intense worries. They would sit up at night, almost whispering their ideas to one another. Over morning coffee, they would sit at our little kitchen table, drawing plans. Mom began humming while doing her household chores again, only stopping when her mind went to that dark place where she conjured horrid scenarios that her boys could be in, struggling with an injury, hoping to escape imprisonment, or worse, fighting for their lives and losing them in some unknown place across the sea where their bodies would remain.

Despite the debacle in the Netherlands, September was a big month for the Allies, who were slowly sweeping across Europe, taking back city after city, aiming to enter Germany where they hoped to end the conflict. Near the end of August, they had liberated Paris, a victory *Time* magazine fully covered. It made my heart swell with happiness and pride to see the people lining the streets, cheering, waving flags, almost worshipping their liberators, and I wondered if the boys were there. The Soviet forces were doing the same coming from the east. They had ended the German siege of Leningrad that had begun three years ago. After that, they were unstoppable, liberating cities and countries one after another.

Dire Consequence of Meddling Gossips

S hortly before the twins' October birthday, their team once again won the football championship. This final victory and their role in it assured Callum's securing one of Granite County's loveliest girls. They started spending most of their free time together. Sandra Kennedy, though only a Sophomore, seemed to be the most self-assured girl I knew. Callum told me he was attracted to her because she and her self-confident air reminded him of me. I spoofed at that. "Well, if you only knew all my insecurities, dear brother, then you wouldn't feel that way."

Sandra wasn't a snob despite her high self-esteem. She wasn't beautiful in the conventional way of the times. She was so blonde her hair was almost white. She didn't tolerate the sun all that well, and a day outside usually gave her skin a ruddy look and brought out a new splash of freckles, which looked adorable across her nose and cheeks. She blushed easily, which also brought a scarlet flush to her cheeks. She was sweet and good-natured, except for her dealings with Cameron. Cameron's jealous nature once again plagued him and affected his relationship with Callum and his new girl.

Cameron returned to his old ways, refusing to socialize. His withdrawal from our family life began gradually, but the more he disengaged, the more remote he became. He took up his old habit of leaving the house early, coming home in time for breakfast, doing his chores, and disappearing out into the woods as soon as he was granted free time. The only time he spoke during mealtime discussions was when the subject of Japanese kamikazes came up. "Damn, I wish the Allies would have such a policy, I'd go volunteer for that."

Dad sighed. "Well, you know that would mean instant and sure death, don't you?"

Cameron only nodded.

Dad shook his head, but I could tell he didn't take Cameron seriously. He began lecturing us about what brought about the kamikaze raids. "The Japanese have become desperate." Dad explained that since the Japanese had failed to stop the American offensive, they had decided that the only way they might overcome their enemy was to deploy kamikaze suicide bombers against the more powerful American warships. "Kamikaze means divine wind, which makes the idea of crash-diving your plane into American war and escort ships, blowing them up, attractive to young Japanese pilots. Supposedly, accepting a kamikaze mission gives them an opportunity to attend their own funeral and enjoy treatment as a sacred entity."

Two days later, the twins came home on bad terms. As they walked in the door, I heard Callum say, "Just forget about it, Cameron. This is as wild and crazy a story I've heard in a long time. Where in the hell would Abi find dozens of animal traps to donate to the scrap drive? The entire story is a bunch of crap. Now, just forget it."

I had been in the kitchen making peanut butter and honey sandwiches for Bear and her cubs for the season. I hoped they hadn't gone into hibernation, but since we were well into November, I sensed that they would be leaving soon. I must have walked into the dining room with a downright look of guilt. Cameron stood glaring at me, accusative. "Did you?"

I don't know why, but defiance took over reason, and I said, "Yes."

In a moment, Cameron had me on the floor with his hands around my neck. I never realized until then how quickly strangulation can happen, making it feel as if death is just seconds away. I remember thrashing my legs, trying to free myself. All I could think of was to get a breath and I felt as if my head would pop, spilling out my brains, but instead I peed myself. As fast as Cameron had me down and under his deadly control, he was gone just that quick.

I struggled to sit up. My throat burned and my brain still felt under pressure. I began to breathe in deep gulps of air but the urge to vomit took over. When I finally caught a decent breath, I became aware of my surroundings again. My brothers were already bloodied beyond recognition, blood was on the floor, all over their faces and shirts, and smeared across the upturned dining table. I pulled my body through my mess, and took refuge in the kitchen doorway, trying to get enough strength to get up and call for Dad, whose whereabouts were completely unknown. He could have been anywhere on the ranch, or in town, or over at Larry's.

Cameron was now on top of Callum with that same stranglehold on him as he had had on me. Callum had reached his hands up and around his brother's neck as well. I started to sob but the more I cried, the clearer things became. I had to help Callum. I weakly took hold of the kitchen counter and pulled myself up. I walked over to where Mom hung her prized cast iron frying pan. It was heavy, and I shook my head as I realized that it had never registered in my mind how weighty it was. I crept to my struggling brothers and lifted the skillet. My first hit seemed to just bounce off Cameron's head, but the next one put him out cold.

I knelt beside Callum, who was still fighting mad, and after I helped him to his feet, hugging him, he gave me a vicious shove. "God, Abi, you smell."

I started to laugh crazily between my declarations, "Yeah! I peed myself and puked. So there. I thought he was going to kill me."

Callum turned from me and went to our catch-all drawer, pulling out the roll of duct tape. He handed it to me, and I stopped my crazed cackling and cautiously approached Cameron's still body. Callum rolled him over. My hands shook as I pulled off a long strip of tape, chewing it on an edge to start a rip so I could tear it into strips. I handed him one. The thought of treating my difficult and strange brother like a prisoner made bile boil up in my throat, and I ran to the bathroom.

When I returned to the dining room, Dad had just come in, and I slid to the floor, still a shaking mess but relieved.

"What in the Sam hell is going on here? I could hear you clear out in the meadow." Dad stood in the doorway, taking in the bloody battle scene—blood stains drying on the floor and dining room table, the table and three chairs in disarray, pictures hanging lopsided on the walls, me on the floor looking like a half-dead mouse the cat dragged in, Callum with his bloody face and clothing, holding a roll of duct tape, and Cameron lying on his side on the floor with his hands bound behind him.

Dad came to me first, squatting beside me, examining my neck. My voice was hoarse when I spoke. "Cameron found out about the traps at school and . . ." I had to stop since my voice quit working.

Callum picked up the story. "Yeah, Cameron went crazy on Abi, threw her on the floor, and tried strangling her. I think he would have killed her if I hadn't been here to stop him. And then, after we fought for a while, he got me down and was choking me. Abi came with the frying pan and knocked him out. Dad, I didn't know what else to do; he was insane with anger. So, we bound him with duct tape. He was really upset when he heard about Abi bringing those traps to the scrap drive. Then, all the way home, he kept mumbling about some shack being burned down, and kept repeating, 'at least I got the money before she could ruin that. At least I got the money.'"

Callum finished by taking a swipe at his bloody nose. Dad rose, his knees creaking as he unfolded his long frame and just stood there, for once not having anything to say. But not for long because soon he stomped into the kitchen and came back out with a pitcher full of water, which he threw into Cameron's unconscious face. Cameron came to, sputtering, looking bewildered, but when he remembered, his face contorted with an angry look I will never forget. It was mean and threatening to the point that Dad even stepped back.

But in the next moment, Dad grabbed Cameron by his shirt and hauled him onto a still-standing chair. He stood back and stared at his wayward son, not saying a word. Cameron kept looking down, refusing to meet Dad's eyes or speak. Finally, Dad told me to get upstairs and clean myself up. "Don't want your mother seeing you like this, Abi."

I went obediently, anxious to get away from that awful scene and to get rid of my stench that bothered even me. Dad must have told Cameron the same thing, because soon I could hear him on the stairs, and after my quick shower when I was in my room dressing, I could hear him showering.

I sat on my bed, exhausted and mindless. I couldn't let myself think of what had happened this afternoon. I felt guilty for my brother's even more hateful attitude toward me, yet I knew I had done the right thing. He shouldn't have been doing what he had done, and he shouldn't be allowed to go through life not obeying or abiding the rules Dad or any authority had defined without consequences or being punished. I was reminded of my earlier conjecture that Mom and Dad also feared him to a certain degree. At the very least, they were afraid of the incomprehensible, mean, and destructive acts he was capable of. I sighed; here I was thinking about it when I had forbidden myself to do just that.

I was about to stand up and go downstairs, my curiosity getting the better of me, when Mom stepped into my room. She had been crying, and she came to me and hugged me hard, and pulling away, she examined me. She gasped when her eyes lit upon the red ring around my neck. "Oh, Abi, I'm so sorry." "Mom, it's not your fault. It's not anyone's fault. Not Dad's. Not mine. Not the world's. He's just that way." My voice broke, but I managed to squeak out, "And I'm afraid he'll never change." We sat on the edge of my bed, silent, finding strength in our closeness.

I'll never know what Dad said to Cameron, but my brother, in a very gracious manner, apologized that evening, saying the right things but with the usual emotionless, dead eyes he has when frustrated and angry. The next morning, he was gone.

The Search

Cameron had run off during the night, and Mom and Dad combed through the boys' room, looking for some clue as to where he may have gone. They found a full-page ad under his mattress about the Merchant Marines needing sailors to ensure that food, weapons, and medical supplies continued to reach the battlefields overseas. I told Mom and Dad that I remembered reading that ad in *Time* about three months ago but that I hadn't seen one since.

I couldn't stop feeling guilty about my part in this tragedy, and knowing that everyone felt some degree of culpability didn't help. They say misery loves company, but that wasn't making things any better; now Mom and Dad had three sons in harm's way. We had no idea where he could have gone but to join the Merchant Marines. And yet, we knew that sixteen-year-old boys weren't old enough to join any armed division.

The old pickup Dad allowed the boys to drive was gone, and Dad found it at the depot. He took the receipt I had found in Cameron's pocket into the bank to check out the account. Cameron had started one on his own, but since he was a minor he had added Dad's name to it, forging his signature as co-signer. When Dad checked the balance, he discovered nearly half the funds had been withdrawn two days before the twins' October birthday, six weeks ago.

When Dad came home with this bit of news, we felt some of our guilt lifting, at least about when Cameron had attacked me and Callum, feeling betrayed by my getting rid of his traps and most likely, realizing that Dad and I had burned the old shack. He had been planning to leave for weeks. Because of the war, there were no other available sources that would assist us in our hunt for him. There were shortages in every aspect of civilian life, especially police departments. No one really cared about a sixteen-year-old runaway. It had become common for boys his age to leave home and join the military, using fake birth certificates—they were that eager to join up.

The silence in our house was again deafening. We would soon enter the Christmas season with one more chick out of the nest. Not even the antics of the grandchildren brought Mom and Dad relief. We went through each day, going through the motions of living but with the burden of guilt and worry. It was a bleak time, and we hoped the war would end soon.

It looked as if the Japanese would soon be defeated. In late October, American, Australian, and Filipino forces had landed in the Leyte Gulf, eventually liberating the Philippines and cutting off Japanese supply routes in Southeast Asia. Now, U.S. B-29 bombers were heavily bombing the mainland of Japan. But we didn't talk much about the war. Silence had invaded our mealtime talk, with only Rory chatting away in his blissful innocence.

We received a short V-letter from Craig, saying they were in Europe somewhere enjoying a three-week break from combat, and that Ruth Anne would be arriving two weeks early. She had completed her indoctrination about American society and all the things a foreign-born wife should know before entering the United States. The atmosphere in our home changed drastically. We knew two of our strays were okay, and a new member of the family would be here shortly. Mom and I went into high gear, doing our usual holiday preparations. Mom and Dad finalized their plans for the addition, and I received a job offer from the school.

Teachers in the Granite school system had been quitting by the handfuls—civilian jobs paying much more than teachers' salaries had tempted them to leave. The school district was desperate to fill these positions and offered me my high school diploma and a job teaching first grade, starting after Christmas break. I knew that since I had refused to graduate last spring, I had become a problem. My teacher who had been tutoring me in my independent studies had left, and I was feeling lost.

I had finally finished my study of Henry James. After reading *The Portrait of a Lady, Daisy Miller, What Maisie Knew,* and *Washington Square,* I was tired of reading stories written by 19th Century novelists who wrote only to criticize the social norms of their times. But perhaps their work did help to change society in that women had become much more independent and not so restricted by earlier social codes demanding they give up their freedom and their money when they married.

I was thankful to be growing up during the 20th century, and looked forward to marrying a man I could share my life with on an equal basis, like Mom and Dad. Since James' novels were all about character, his tomes also helped me realize that it's normal to have abnormal individuals in one's family, and I made a vow to try to be more understanding when it came to Cameron and Aunt Peggy.

The Call

∙∙

The first Saturday in December, we were getting ready to go into town to pick up Craig's Ruth Anne, who was expected to arrive on the 10 A.M. train. I was ready as was Rory, who had balked at a morning bath, but despite that, I had managed to get him bathed and dressed. I kept him busy by allowing him to make a train, which went all the way through the dining room and into the kitchen. He had used every dining room chair and the ones in the kitchen to make the longest train possible.

The phone rang, and I answered it, thinking perhaps it might be Blair. But it was a man's voice, asking for Mr. Angus MacDougal. I yelled for Dad to come take his call, but not hearing me, he didn't answer.

"Sir, may I tell him who's calling? I think he is still dressing for an early engagement in town."

The man cleared his voice. "Um, humph, yes, this is Captain MacGruger returning his call. I have news about his son, Cameron."

"Oh, just a minute, sir! I'll get him right away."

I ran to my parents' bedroom, pounding on their door. "Dad! It's Captain MacGruger on the phone, wanting to talk to you about Cameron!"

Dad burst from their bedroom, still pulling up a sock, and running into the kitchen, he fell over one of Rory's train cars, and crashed into the kitchen table. He stood, rubbing his knee, and grabbed the receiver from my hand. "Hello! You have information about our son?"

I tried to make sense out of the one-sided conversation and was soon joined by Mom, who did the same.

Dad's end of the call wasn't exactly enlightening. "Oh. Okay. Yes. What? He's out to sea? Already? What does that mean? What?"

Dad stood listening, running his hand through his hair, shaking his head. "Oh, all right then, I guess you can't tell me much more than that. You will call if you hear any more? If something . . . happens?" He became silent then, listening, and then nodding his head he hung up.

He turned to us, his face ashen. "The good Captain has just informed me that Cameron was able to join the Merchant Marines. He came to the U.S. Merchant Marine Academy at Kings Point, Long Island, in New York City, where he was to train for a time before boarding a ship. He managed to get in despite his age, looking much older and able, and now he has snuck aboard a ship leaving with the latest convoy. He's out at sea; God only knows where. The Captain told me that the recruiters aren't too fussy about who they accept since they've suffered such a high rate of casualties."

Mom and Dad came together over one of Rory's train chairs, clinging to one another, hoping to find some sort of solace for an inconsolable situation. We all knew from Dad's information-gleaning concerning the Merchant Marines how high the casualty rate was for that division of our military. It was higher than for the Marines, almost twice as high as for the Army, and over four times higher than for the Navy. Cameron couldn't have chosen a more dangerous place to be in the war with only one exception—the 101st Airborne.

When my parents broke their embrace, Dad chucked Mom under the chin. "Nora, it's going to be all right—it just has to be." She nodded. "Yes, and we better go and retrieve our newest. Perhaps she'll distract us from our worries."

Callum had the car warmed up and in front of the house. We all piled in, and Dad gave him the news. Callum only nodded, not saying anything, but I watched as he swallowed hard, making his Adam's apple bob.

The English Girl and Bess

We were a bit late by the time we arrived at the train station. Most of the passengers had dispersed, and we didn't see any sign of Ruth Anne, causing Dad to become disgruntled and begin grousing about his boy marrying an English girl. We went inside, and there she was just coming out of the restroom. She had the same dark hair as in her picture, but didn't look at all like I remembered her from her photo. She was short and quietly pretty with a round face that made her look much younger than the frozen image Craig had sent us. Her carriage wasn't exceptional, no getting around that, and I felt pangs of disappointment.

Mom stepped forward, holding her arms out to her. "You must be Ruth Anne."

She shook her head. "No. No, I am not Ruth Anne. I'm Bess Murano, Jake's wife. Are you the Murano family?"

I realized she was just as confused as we were, despite that I felt light-headed and sick to my stomach.

"No, dear, we are the MacDougals here to take Ruth Anne home— our son's wife from England."

Just then another girl came out of the restroom, patting her hat and then sliding on a pair of white gloves that had seen better days. She was tall and strikingly beautiful with her near-black hair falling in shiny waves. She was rail-thin and looked older than her twenty years—her eyes were rimmed with that purple smudge that comes from lack of sleep and stress. When she approached us, I could see streaks of white in her hair, while noting her graceful elegance.

Mom stepped forward and took her in her arms. "You must be Ruth Ann, our new daughter-in-law. You look even lovelier than your picture, dear." Mom stepped back after their embrace, pointing to first herself, and then Dad, saying, "I'm Nora, and this is my husband, Angus, just call him Gus."

If I hadn't been in such a state of shock, denial, and anger over Jake's marriage to this Bess, I would have burst into giggles when seeing Dad's look of pleasant surprise over the appearance of Craig's English girl. I could see that he was instantly smitten with her, her engaging mien at least.

He stepped forward and awkwardly took a small, fine-boned hand between his ample paws, shaking it for a bit too long, lost in those eyes of hers. "Welcome, Ruth Anne."

Just then the Murano family burst in, all nine of them—Marie and Antonio and all of Jake's younger brothers and sisters. Gusts of fresh, cold air accompanied them inside, bringing me to my senses, fine tuning them to green envy—I had hoped they would be my family someday.

Dad and Callum loaded Ruth Anne's small trunk into the back of the car, and then we drove downtown to Muranos' restaurant for lunch. It was my unlucky day since they, too, had decided to do the same thing. As they all crowded around their table, there was much laughter and chatter, and I became even more envious of that English girl that Jake had married. It had only been six months since he graduated and more likely, only two or three months since he had been in England. And during that time, he had written me a letter. I didn't know what to think except that I was miserable, feeling foolish for ever having any thoughts of marrying him.

Our group was more subdued, with Mom and Dad asking Ruth Anne simple and benign questions about her and her life. We had awkward silences with only Rory to break up the tension with his enthusiasm for this new adventure in eating out, making him a bubbly little fountain of joy. Ruth Anne couldn't keep her eyes off him when Mom and Dad weren't engaging her in conversation. Her looks certainly were enchanting. Though tired-looking and ringed with dark circles, her eyes were lovely—all bright and soft at the same time. They were kind eyes that didn't miss much, and they just pulled you in, and her smile was genuine and infectious just like in her picture.

Mom and Dad ordered a bottle of champagne with which to toast to our newest family member. Everyone but Rory received a small glass, but Ruth Anne only sipped at hers, looking a little green. Rory had his glass of apple juice and raised it to her. "Here's to my new sista. Thanks for being here, Rute Anne." She smiled at him, raised her glass to his, and took a small sip. She sighed and threw up her hands in apology. "Oh, blimey, I'm just going to come out with it. I've been hoping for a good cup of tae, dying for one ever since leaving England. Would you mind if I ordered tae?"

Dad looked quizzically at Mom, who asked Ruth Anne, after a pause, "And what is tae, Ruth Anne."

"Tae? Well, you know, it's tae, I prefer that over coffee."

Mom chuckled and turned a bit pink in the face. "Oh, my dear, you mean tea. I'm so sorry, it may take a while to get accustomed to your accent."

Ruth Anne blushed. "I'm sorry, I guess I must have a horribly strong British accent—I've had the most awful time communicating here in the States, and on board the ship." She defensively sat up straighter as if trying to overcome this perceived shortcoming.

Mom patted her arm. "No. No, it's not bad at all. It's quite lovely and charming. I'm sure we sound different to you, as well. Don't worry, dear, we'll get along just fine."

Our meal was served just after that, and everyone was satisfied with the excellent food, except for me—I had lost my appetite. Rory's four-year-old entertainment loosened up the tension, though. He had ordered fries and made grandiose gestures as he flew each individual fry into his pile of catsup, pretending that each one was a B-29 bomber. I noticed that Ruth Anne carefully cut each one of hers into three sections, picking up each of those one at a time with her fork, and then daintily dipping it into her catsup. When eating her hamburger, she did the same thing. The only thing she picked up with her hands was her cup of tea, but when we had banana splits, she became lost in her enjoyment, closing her eyes with delight after each bite.

When leaving the restaurant, my parents stopped to visit with the Murano family. Their English girl continued eating her pasta dish with enthusiasm while we visited, and she had a spot of red sauce on the bosom of her jacket. When she emptied her plate, she picked up a slice of bread and sopped up the remaining sauce with it. Oh, Jake, why would you marry someone like her?

When we drove home, Ruth—she had insisted we lose the Anne—praised the beauty of our mountains. It had snowed lightly while we were in town, and now the sun shone bright on the glistening white snow. The evergreen trees looked frosted like the ones on Christmas cards. As we drove up the lane, Ruth exclaimed, "Oh, blimey! You have a lovely place! You are a toff family. I knew you would be because Craig is first rate. He's certainly not a bugger or ponce like so many of those Yanks I met. He's the real thing, a real gentleman, and now I can see why. Thank you for having me and opening your home to me."

"You are very welcome, Ruth. Any friend, I mean, a wife of Craig's is welcome, and I hope you like it here with us." Mom told her this after giving herself time to digest and figure out exactly what Ruth had just said.

Ruth must have thought the long pause before Mom's welcoming meant we were not that enthused about her coming to live with us, and she remained quiet as we slowly crept up our lane. But when Dad pulled in front of our house, Ruth exclaimed, "Oh blimey, what a lovely place. I've never seen anything like it. No wonder Craig gets gutted from time to time about missing his family and home. He would become homesick, and I would let him talk and talk about his home and family, and all the bits and bobs about your life here, and soon he was right as rain."

Ruth stepped out of the car, and stood quiet, looking all around. Dad and Callum unloaded her trunk and started up the stairs. Mom turned to Ruth. "I hope it's all right, but we thought Abi could share her room with you since her sister is now married and gone."

Ruth stopped taking it all in and turned to me. "Abi? It won't bother you to have me invade your privacy? Your Mom and you have it sorted?"

I just nodded and smiled, thinking, oh, yes, I don't mind at all, and when we are alone, I am going to have fun quizzing you about Craig and how he was when you last saw him, and all about these alien terms you use, and about Bess. I smiled at her again, relishing the idea of teaching her some good American English. I grabbed her hand and led her up the steps to the house, listening to her latest puzzling exclamation. "Blimey, it's bloody freezing out here. It's just plain monkeys outside!"

After Dad and Callum had taken Ruth's trunk up to my room, Mom asked Ruth if she would care to take a nap. "After your long journey, I bet you would like to rest and then freshen up. And after you come back downstairs, perhaps you will teach me how to make a proper cup of tea. I noticed you didn't exactly care for yours at the restaurant. I need to learn how to make a nice cup that will please you."

Ruth smiled, sheepish. "I didn't care much for the tea in town. I'm sorry it was so obvious, and I am quite knackered and a kip, I mean nap, sounds wonderful."

Having delivered Ruth's trunk, the guys came downstairs, and we stood around the dining table in clumsy silence. Dad ran his hand through his hair. "Yes. Well, Callum, let's go and make sure the water tanks are still running out in the barns and corrals. It's as cold as a witch's tit out there, and they could be freezing up on us." After realizing his very American, rancher-like phrase probably made Ruth uncomfortable, Dad blushed and apologized to her. "Sorry, my dear, just our way of saying it's really cold out."

Ruth just grinned at him, taking another piece of his heart with that enchanting smile of hers. I grabbed her hand. "Come on, Ruth, I'll help you get situated and into bed for a well-deserved nap . . . kip." Everyone chuckled, and we went our separate ways, I'm sure with each of us wondering how long we would be uncomfortable with one another.

I opened Blair's bed while Ruth used the bathroom and changed into an old flannel nightgown, which was so faded and worn, the flowers appeared ethereal. Her trunk was open, making me want to dig into it and look for more clues to her former life as an English girl.

I resisted the urge, knowing that by all appearances, Ruth, her life thus far, and her entire belief system was an open book, offered honestly and sincerely to anyone who cared. But she needed rest and sleep, that was obvious. She returned, and I asked her if she would like me to close the shades.

"Oh, please do."

I closed them, and on my way out, she asked, "Does your family really want me here? I feel lost and a bit unwanted. Your Mum and your Dad seem angry and tense, and I don't want to be here if they don't really want me."

I shook my head. "Don't worry about their unpleasant attitude; it's not directed at you. They are worried about something else that just came up this morning before we met you at the train station. You know Craig and Colin are in one of the most dangerous divisions in the army, well now, my brother and Callum's twin, Cameron, has run off and joined the Merchant Marines, probably the second most dangerous division of the United States military. He's very different and odd acting at times, he likes violence and doing mean things to people—mostly to us, his own family, but we still love him and hope he's safe."

Ruth had nestled deep into the bed and stifled a long, drawn-out yawn, and said, smothering another yawn. "Yes, Craig has told me about him, his difficult demeanor, and about some of the things he has done. He told me that Cameron has always worried your Mum and Dad."

Ruth yawned again, and I told her, "You need to sleep now. We'll talk later. Okay?"

"Right-o, Abi. I hope we can be frank with one another as we become acquainted. If I'm going to be in this family, I had better know what you are going through and the past, too, so I better understand everyone, and I expect you want the same of me."

I nodded, thinking that I was going to like her and end up loving her, too. "Just get some sleep now; you deserve a nice nap—well kip, I guess."

She laughed. "Yes, nap. And please will you help me learn your kind of English here in the States? I think that would make everything easier." I nodded and closed the door.

When Ruth woke up from her nap, she came downstairs fully dressed in the same clothes she had worn before. Mom and Dad had planned an outing—our annual trip out in the woods to find a Christmas tree and evergreen boughs and pine cones for decorating. Since Ruth's dress was worn thin and her shoes unworthy of a hike in the woods, they sent her upstairs to change into something warmer and more practical. She seemed nervous, so I offered to help her unpack her modest trunk.

When we reached my room, Ruth turned to me in a panic. "Abi, I don't have anything better to wear on my feet, and my wardrobe has hardly anything in it." She pointed to her coat lying on my bed. "And that's the only coat I own."

"Well, let's just see what you have, and we'll go from there. Okay?"

"Right-o."

Poor Ruth hardly had a wardrobe; her trunk was full of mostly mementos—lots of pictures and photo albums and little things that women keep as treasured items from happier days. Her stockings had been darned so many times over that they looked more like torture implements than the smooth, comfort items they were supposed to be. She had one woolen skirt and sweater which would have to do for today. Her feet were larger than mine, and appeared to be smaller than Mom's. We would need to work on that. I found woolen mittens, a hat, and some heavy cotton long johns that would suffice for today, and we clomped downstairs—me with my winter boots on and Ruth in the same shoes as before. When Mom noticed that Ruth wore the same flimsy coat, she went hunting and found one of her warmer ones for her to wear.

We set out on foot, which was our normal routine. It had begun to snow again, and our moods lifted with the freshness and the promise of a white Christmas. Ruth remained quiet, but I could see that she admired our countryside. She would stop every so often and just breathe in the cool, crisp, unsullied air, look around in awe, and then smile, her lips curved into a lovely semicircle, her eyes sparkling.

We found our tree a short distance from our farmyard and harvested boughs there, too, until Mom was satisfied we had enough. Then we made our way back home, singing Christmas carols. Dad and Callum took turns dragging the tree, and we women walked home, arms loaded with fragrant pine branches. Dad set the tree in a large bucket of water on our front porch, while Mom and I laid the branches in an old water trough out back. We always thoroughly soaked our boughs and tree before taking them in the house, but the house fire that took our MacDougal grandparents made this practice even more essential to us than before.

Mom and I made hot chocolate after we had stripped out of our outdoor clothes. Ruth stood in front of the fireplace, rubbing her hands together, and gratefully wrapped her hands around the hot cup of cocoa I handed her. I noticed again how worn her stockings were, and it appeared that our outing had created fresh holes in them that needed darning. I went into the kitchen and told Mom that Ruth hardly had any clothes at all. "What do mean, she has almost no clothes?"

"Mom, I helped her go through her trunk, and she virtually has no clothes."

"Ummm, well, we better do something about that."

When we returned to the parlor, Ruth was sitting in our big comfy chair closest to the fire with my favorite throw tucked in around her. Dad must have noticed the state of her stockings, too, since he looked up at Mom, asking, "Nora, could you find some heavy wool socks for Ruth so she can get her feet warmed up? The poor girl can't stop shivering. I guess our trek into the woods today was a bad idea for someone who has traveled all the way from England."

He turned to Ruth. "I suppose you must be worn out, and our cold seems much different than what you are accustomed to."

She smiled. "Yes, but it's much damper there, making it bone-chilling, and I'm sure I got chilled today because I'm over-tired; I had a difficult time settling in this afternoon so I didn't sleep much. But I'm used to being cold. In England, they ration our utilities by making them so high-priced we can barely afford to heat our homes. There have been times that I thought I would never be warm again. But don't worry, I'll rally once I catch up on sleep. Train travel isn't very conducive for sleeping; that's a fact." And then she nodded to her cup.

"This tastes wonderful, and it's warming me up. Thanks. Thank you for everything."

Ruth looked as if she could cry, and Dad made a big production out of turning on the radio and finding his favorite program. We sat in cozy silence for a bit, drinking our hot chocolate and listening to the Abbott and Costello show. Ruth loosened up and began giggling at their antics, making us laugh because she even laughed with an accent.

That night after we ate, Mom, Ruth, and I congregated in my bedroom. Mom had found several dresses she had never really liked so they were hardly worn. When Ruth tried them on, they fit her like a glove, and I have never seen anyone so pleased with their new clothes. Ruth twirled in front of my full-length mirror, tickled. Mom also found a pair of winter boots lined with sheepskin that fit her and would make life out here more bearable. Next, she presented Ruth with a pair of pumps—ones I knew she treasured and had hoarded for some time before wearing them. They fit Ruth, who said they were the most comfortable shoes she had ever worn.

Soon Ruth was in tears. "I've never had it so good. I had nothing, really, but now I have so much—a caring husband and his family, decent clothing, and beautiful food. Blimey, I have never eaten such delicious food. You are a wonderful cook, Nora. Thank you so much."

Mom and I looked at one another with understanding. That night at the supper table, Ruth had eaten her food as if she had not eaten for months. Mom had roasted a fine rib roast with all the trimmings, and Ruth had eaten her entire plate, relishing every bite, but still using the same polite manners she had exhibited at the restaurant. She refused a glass of wine, but other than that, our newest family member had thoroughly enjoyed the bounty of our table. Mom gave Ruth a housecoat of hers that fit her perfectly, and after Ruth hung her dresses in the closet, we talked her into taking a warm bath and urged her to either put on her nightclothes and join us in the parlor, or to just crawl into bed for a nice long sleep.

After we left Ruth to her bath, showing her our amenities there, we went downstairs to join Dad and Callum in front of the radio. They were nearly asleep, and Rory had been down since shortly after supper.

Our outing, along with the novelty of having an English girl, a foreigner in our house had, indeed, distracted us from our worries, and soon everyone was in bed sleeping peacefully while the first winter winds howled around the corners of our house, lulling us into deep sleep. I hadn't thought of Cameron all day until I was in bed, and I ended my prayers with a special one for him and his well-being.

When I woke up the next morning, Ruth was still sleeping. I donned my housecoat and tiptoed as quietly as possible out of the room, closing the door without making a sound. I hoped she would sleep all day if that's what it took for her to rally, or "rawly," as she pronounced it. I shook my head as I brushed my teeth and thought of how attentively we all listened to Ruth when she spoke; her accent was so strong I was sure we would all be speaking like the British in no time. There had been times yesterday that I found myself wondering exactly what she was saying. I'm sure she wondered if we were all daft since we would just nod our heads when that probably wasn't the correct response at all. *Daft*. There, I was already adapting my language after hearing her say *daft* many times in response to things, especially when listening to the comedy shows on the radio. "Oh, thot's daft!" and then she would giggle her special British laugh.

It was amazing how much she knew about Americans and our politics. She knew that President Roosevelt had been reelected, sweeping the electoral college and beating Tom Dewey soundly. She had watched many of our newest movies. She knew that the United States had dealt with an epidemic of rabies cases this year, as well as tuberculosis, and about all the small children being stricken with polio, making it the worst epidemic since 1916. But she didn't know about Sal Hepatica and its purpose.

When Ruth woke up from her long, deep sleep, she ate the breakfast food that Mom had saved for her, but then suffered from heartburn. She asked if we had anything for that, and Mom said, "Oh, yes. There's Alka-Seltzer in the downstairs bathroom in the medicine cabinet. Just help yourself, dear." We eventually discovered that we were out of Alka-Seltzer after Ruth became almost instantly ill, spending the rest of the day in the bathroom. After she recovered and joined us later in the parlor, she explained that as soon as she had taken the medicine, her stomach began to cramp. Mom asked if she had used Alka-Seltzer, and then Ruth explained that the box was empty so she had taken a dose from a bottle next to the empty box. The bottle's label was worn off, but she assumed it was the heartburn medication.

We all began to laugh, even Rory, and Ruth burst into tears and ran upstairs to our room. I followed her and found her lying across her bed. I cautiously approached her. "Ruth, it's me, Abi. We didn't laugh out of cruelty or anything like that, it's just that we have all experienced the speed in which Sal Hepatica makes a person run to the bathroom. Sal Hepatica is a laxative, and we are very sorry about the mix up. Will you please forgive us?"

Ruth just nodded. I slowly sat down on the bed next to her and began to rub her back like I did with Rory or Aileen's kids when they were having a crying jag. Ruth didn't resist my sympathy, and soon I found myself pushing hair away from her face and gathering it up to lie on her neck and back. "You have gorgeous hair. You're beautiful in every way, Ruth. You really are, and you're so elegant and stately with such a lovely figure. Craig is lucky."

Ruth sat up and pulled her legs to her chest, wiping away the tears wetting her face. "Oh, Abi, I miss him so much. I love him and miss him and worry he won't come back to me."

"Well, join us in that misery. We have three, no, actually, four gone from home to worry and fret about."

"Four?" Ruth shook her head, and then nodded. "Oh, yes, counting Gracie, and now with Cameron gone . . ."

"Yes, and it's almost Christmas and we haven't received Gracie's annual photo yet."

"What do you mean?'

"Craig didn't tell you about that?" I shook my head, I would have thought he'd tell her about such a strange thing. Gracie's kidnappers sending us one picture of her at Christmas time every year, to me, was odd, if not a little insane.

I told Ruth about us receiving a new picture of Gracie around Christmas time every year, and then we talked until after midnight. I told her all I could about our family and our past—about losing Ian, about Cameron and his odd and cruel nature, and what Dad said about that, connecting it to his troubled birth. I told her about our grandparents, our aunts, uncles, and cousins. She was touched by the story about Crazy Aunt Peggy and her sickly girlfriend. "That's what they are, you know, girlfriends, lovers." I gasped, "Oh, Ruth, I can't think of them that way."

I fell silent then, shaking my head over the idea. Ruth laughed, her laughter becoming more endearing by the minute. "You know, Abi, we British are not prudes like you Americans. England is full of all kinds of people. We have huge populations of Indians from India, Black people from all over the globe, especially Africa, Australians and Asians from the Southeast, and we have come to accept them as fellow countrymen and we, for the most part, do not judge their ways.

"I think people with the preference for a sexual relationship with their own sex are not scrutinized and persecuted like they are here. But on the other hand, we have enjoyed our Yankee soldiers stationed in England; they've been a breath of fresh air in our sometimes-stilted society and our stubborn clinging to aristocratic labeling and social distinctions. That's what I like most about Craig, he's polite and fun at the same time. And he never shows the same carelessness and disregard about our things, our public houses, like many of the other Yanks. The 101st Airborne Division nearly sacked London the last time they were there on leave. Craig wasn't like that."

"Tell me about how you met. Please?"

Ruth smiled big. "I was standing in a long rations line. I had hoped to get some sugar and Spam. I love sweets, and it had been a long time since I had anything like that or any sugar. I also love meat, if you haven't already noticed. My family had been taking care of my Uncle George, who had been sick with consumption even before the war began. Mom and Dad had sent me out to the countryside to stay with distant relatives so I would be safe from the German bombing."

"You mean you left London during the Pied Piper operation? Dad told us about that."

"Yes, and it was terrible to leave them. I was an only child. I had a baby brother, David, but he died from pneumonia when he was just four. When Mom and Dad perished in one of the earlier air raids, I had to return to London to take care of Uncle George. And there I was, standing in that long line, holding a bag of coal, waiting for my sugar and Spam, when this young American came tearing around the corner.

"Your brother knocked me down, and my bag opened, spilling chunks of coal everywhere. Other people in line grabbed for pieces of my coal, and Craig went to each one of them and got my coal back for me. When he presented me with a full bag of coal again, his nose and one cheek were completely blackened with coal dust. I busted out laughing, and he stood there, baffled as to what I thought was so funny. I took my hanky out and began rubbing the coal off his face. He was embarrassed and took my handkerchief and finished wiping off his face. He handed it back to me, and I laughed again since he still had some black under his left eye. I looked up into his eyes, and that was it. I knew he should be mine. Later he told me the same thing about looking into my eyes—knowing I should be his."

"Oh, my gosh. What a romantic story and funny, too."

"Yes. I still have to giggle when I remember his black face."

"When was this?"

"Not too long after he arrived in England."

"Oh, so you did get to know each other a little before marrying?"

"Yes, every leave they had while training in England, and the big break they had after D-Day, we spent together. We married September 15, just before the 101st was flown back to Europe."

Ruth saw the speculation in my eyes, and she held her hands up. "Stop thinking that, Abi. We didn't have relations with each other until we married. That first night he came to see me at the ale house where I worked, we got a room but only talked all night. I know a lot about your family, and he mine. Oh, that room was so nice. I was warm for once, in a heated place and hot—your brother has a way of stoking my fire. That made it even more romantic and cozy. I couldn't afford to heat my uncle's house much after he died. When he was gone, I had to work, and I no longer had his ration coupons, so I would go home to a cold house, only starting a fire in the morning."

I impulsively reached out and grabbed Ruth into a hug. "Oh, you poor thing. How in the Sam heck you got through those times, makes me completely respect you. I think I would have fallen apart. No family. No heat, for Christ's sake. Oops, sorry for the swear. No meat. No sweets. And you're so lovely after all that you've been through."

"Except for today—not lovely at all."

"What do you mean?"

Ruth pulled away from me. "You know, the accidental dose of your family's choice in laxatives. What a wanker I am. A bloody wanker. Blimey! And then sitting in the loo all afternoon. Brilliant, just brilliant, Ruth."

I laughed and waved her concerns away. "Don't worry about that. We won't hold that against you. I promise."

We sat in silence—all talked out. I was suddenly tired, and Ruth looked all done in. She had had a tough day. "I think we'd better hit the hay. I'm tired, and you look as worn out as I feel. But this was fun. I've missed having Blair here. Welcome to our family, dear Ruth." I crawled into bed, happy and content, feeling that through Ruth's accounting, I had gotten a bit of Craig back—just for a little while.

Pants or Panties?

Time was bringing us closer to Christmas, and we had not yet received a picture of Gracie. Mom became quieter by the day, and Dad grumpier. Ruth appeared to be settling in. I loved our talks before bedtime. She had a lot on her mind and much to say. I could tell she was homesick because that is what she talked about the most. How green it was in England, how church bells and clocks chimed everywhere, and the people—she missed the crowded streets full of bustling life. Even during war time, the streets of London were full of people. Women, like here in America, had come out of their homes, working men's jobs as well as their traditional ones. The children had begun coming home, and the schools began to fill once more. Ruth teared up when she told me how many more orphans there were in England now, and I thought of Gracie. Where was she? Who had her and was taking care of her? Was she happy? The absence of a new picture on the fridge slapped me in the face each time I opened that door.

We took the train to Missoula, staying overnight at Craig's house. Aileen and her children came, too. We packed that house full of family after Christmas shopping downtown. Kendall stayed home to help Larry take care of the ranch and all our stock. It was a grand time, considering. Yes, in light of our situation, the change in scenery seemed to lift all our spirits, even Mom's. She hadn't wanted to leave and miss two days' mail. Gracie's photo might come while she was gone. But we needed to buy things that had been sold out in the Philipsburg stores. The end of the war was imminent, but manufacturing of common everyday goods was still slow in starting up, and shelves in stores still sat empty. With Rory and the grandchildren growing like bad weeds, needing the next sizes up, Mom and Dad decided a night and a day in the big town was in order.

I think Ruth enjoyed the busy streets and the hustle and bustle of many people moving around, living close together. Mom spoiled us all with her generosity. Ruth kept saying, "No, Nora. No, it's too much." But I could see the sparkle in her eyes as she tried on dresses, shoes, hosiery, and underwear. Ianna had become a five-year-old clotheshorse and squealed with delight when twirling around in front of the three-way mirror, admiring her new dress and patent leather shoes. Rory and John Jacob quickly became bored and were only pacified with promises of riding the carousel horse outside the department store.

We arrived home just four days before Christmas Eve and still no letter from Gracie's captors. Mom broke down and cried after pawing like a maniac through the mail Dad brought home; it had been nearly six years since Gracie had been taken, and I could see that my Mom's belief that Gracie would return had weakened. Dad hugged around on her, and then I took over after he left to do the evening feeding.

Ruth went upstairs to unpack and put her new underwear and stockings away. Mom had insisted that we choose our new things but leave most of them with her so she could wrap them and put them underneath the Christmas tree. I knew she would stay up late every night until Christmas, wrapping presents and baking more Christmas treats, all the while wondering about Gracie, hoping and praying she would soon come home.

That night Ruth and I stayed up with Mom. We both worried about how thin she was getting and thought that a girls' late night might cheer her up. Ruth regaled Mom with stories about her and Craig's times together, and that seemed to help. Dad stayed up, too, listening to music and sipping on his whiskey. He had enough where he became a bit, or a tad, as Ruth would say, obnoxious, coming into the kitchen to tease Mom and joke with Ruth and me—just silly stuff. He finally talked Mom into joining him in the parlor with her own glass of whiskey, and Ruth and I finished cleaning up the kitchen.

We went into town a few nights later to see Ianna play her part in her kindergarten class's Christmas drama, and then we went to Aileen and Kendall's house for a late supper and dessert. It was a good night, especially since Aileen announced that she would have their third child in June. I could see Ruth's eyes mist at that, and I felt sorry for her that she would have to wait and rely on good luck that she could ever tell us she was pregnant. I prayed extra hard that night that all my boys would come home safe, and then Ruth and Craig could start their family.

The next morning dawned sunny and warmer than it had been for days. Ruth had been hinting that she would like to go riding. She had ridden horses at her relatives when she had evacuated to their home in the English countryside. Dad invited Ruth and me to go riding with him after breakfast, which took longer than usual because Ruth inadvertently got into the subject of food and the deprivation she and her fellow British subjects had suffered.

Rory did not want to eat his eggs, which had become a common debate between him and Mom. He only liked them scrambled, but today since Mom had fried them with ham, Rory dug his heels in and refused to eat them. Ruth, trying to help, began telling him how she craved eggs when in England, and that she still couldn't believe she could eat one or two every day here at the ranch. "We were allowed only two eggs a week per person in England. Oh, how I missed eating them every morning. I became tired of Heinz spaghetti and Heinz beans from a tin. We received a lot of tinned food from you Americans."

"Really?" I exclaimed.

"Really. Your government also shipped us Spam, tins of fruit, powdered milk and dried eggs. Everyone fixed Heinz beans on toast, which I hated, and we only had brown bread, that's why I love your bread, Nora—your beautiful, delicious white bread. If I never have to eat another slice of brown bread again in my life, I will be grateful. I hadn't had any meat or butter for over four years until I came to your ranch, and how I craved them. And do you know what they made us kids take to replace iron from the foods we couldn't have? Cod liver oil. Ohhhh, it just makes me ill to think of it. I miss eating bananas. I haven't had a banana since before the war began, and what I wouldn't do for blood bangers. Oh, how I miss blood sausage."

"Blood sausage? Eweeeew! I can't imagine eating something like that." I blurted.

Ruth smiled, rolling her eyes in pleasure at the memory of eating blood sausage. "There's nothing like it." She looked at me and the look of horror on my face. "Well, I guess you have to grow up eating it."

After we finished doing the breakfast dishes, Ruth and I went upstairs to dress for our outing. Ruth now had a few more items in her wardrobe. Mom had bought her some new underpants, bras, and stockings. Ruth wore her new woolen socks over her cotton hose underneath a heavy wool skirt that she and Mom had resurrected from a bag of clothing marked for donation. She pulled on an old sweater which had come from the same bag.

I couldn't help myself and queried, "Why don't you dress like me? It's a lot more comfortable, and maybe warmer."

Ruth answered me airily, "Oh this is fine. I've never worn those things." And she waved her hand to the pair of Ian's pants I had just pulled on.

"Well, suit yourself, Ruthie." I had started calling her Ruthie when she seemed to be a tad stubborn and unbending in her ways. We had come a long way in the last few weeks—we'd become sisters, true sisters in every sense of the word. I loved her, and I believed she loved me.

We went out to the side porch and put on our outerwear, and walked down to the barn, reveling in the warm sun beating on our faces and splashing through the puddles made by the melting snow. It was a glorious day, and I looked forward to riding again after being housebound. Dad had all three horses in the barn. They contentedly chomped on their oats, and he was busy brushing Buck. He had caught Sonny for me, and Lefty for Ruth.

Dad turned to look at us and seeing Ruth's long wool skirt, frowned. He looked her up and down and stormed, "Don't you English girls ever wear pants? What's wrong with you? Too good to wear them?"

Ruth stopped short and retreated a step or two. She just looked at Dad in bewilderment. He returned her look with his famous one of exasperation and said, "Well?"

Ruth stomped her foot, and cried out, "I cannot believe you just said that to me. How would you know if I was wearing pants or not? And what bloody business is it of yours?" Then she turned on her heel and ran back up to the house.

Dad just stood, speechless. "Dad, why do you have to get so gruff at times? You hurt her feelings, and now I won't be able to ride today. Dammit!" And I walked off after stomping my foot. As I strode up to the house, I could hear Dad. "What the hell did I say wrong? Oh, for Christ's sake. Women."

Mom stopped me from going upstairs to check on Ruth. "Abi, what in the world is going on now with that girl? She came through here like a fire storm, spitting mad about something—something to do with your father, I would guess."

"I don't know, Mom. Dad only asked why she won't wear pants. I offered her a pair today but she said she would be fine. I don't understand what the big fuss is at all. Please, Mom, may I go up to talk to her? We get along just fine. In fact, I really like her, and I think she likes me just as much." I lowered my voice. "You like her, don't you?"

"Oh, yes. She's a lovely girl. I can see why Craig fell for her. I just worry about when the war is over, how will they be? For some reason, war brings out a stronger sense of romance." Mom closed her eyes as if trying to come up with a solution to some problem. "Perhaps it's because emotions run so high during wartime. I know the same thing happened during World War I, people got married right and left, and some didn't make it after the war ended. Things were just too different."

"I think they'll be just fine. Ruth misses Craig something awful, and I know she loves him dearly."

"Well, you better go up and see what's got her so upset."

Mom had made a batch of fudge, so I grabbed a napkin and a couple squares and headed for the stairs. As I approached the bedroom, I could hear Ruth blowing her nose. Good, I thought, she's done crying. Ruth was sitting up on her bed, and I could see that she was still angry. She kept shaking her head, but when I offered her a piece of fudge her eyes lit up and she accepted it. In between bites, she asked me, "Why in the world would your father ask me why I don't wear pants? I wear them.

I wear them every day. Does your Dad really believe we British are so barbaric that we don't wear underclothes?"

As soon as I could swallow my bite of fudge, I sputtered. "What do you call these?" And I pointed to Ian's jeans.

Ruth looked at them. "Kecks or trousers."

"Well, then what does the word *pants* stand for in your English?"

"Knickers or now, mostly, we say *pants* when we are talking about our, our . . ." She jumped up, went to the chest of drawers, and pulled out a pair of panties. "These. These are pants in England." She stood in front of me waving her panties around, and I lost it. I started to laugh and I laughed until tears ran down my face. Then Ruth, realizing what the miscommunication had been about, began to laugh, too.

Mom was at the door. "Are you girls okay? I couldn't tell if you were laughing or crying."

I opened the door. "Oh, Mom, you'll never guess what Ruth thought Dad meant when he asked why she never wore pants. Pants in England are what we call our panties." I stopped for a moment for that to sink in, and when Mom looked as if she was getting the point, I went on. "Yes, Mom, can you believe Ruth thought Dad was asking why she never wears panties? No wonder she got pissed off." Mom sat down on the bed and chuckled, shaking her head. And then she turned to Ruth, "It's too bad we can't compare notes on all the other words that will cause more confusion, but that would be impossible."

Ruth nodded. "Yes, just now Abi said something that I figured out means, became angry, but in England it means to be very drunk."

"What was that?" I asked a bit testily.

"Pissed or pissed off means plastered or drunk, and when we say sod off we are saying piss off because we are angry at that person."

Mom sat up and made herself more comfortable and with a twinkle in her eyes, she said, "Tell us more, Ruth. This is hilarious."

Ruth plopped back down on her bed, rolling her eyes, thinking. "Well, there's so much, I don't know where to start." She sat still, thinking. "Okay, I'll begin with some differences that I've already noticed, and then I'll do the more personal, embarrassing, sexual phrases." She looked at Mom, hesitant, and Mom just shrugged her shoulders. "Go ahead, I'm game."

Ruth smiled. "I take it you mean you're okay with that?" Mom nodded, and Ruth began. "You say *damn* and we say *bloody*. You say *idiot* and we say *wanker*, and we also say *tosser*. You say *my goodness* and we say *blimey*. You say *arranged* and we say *sorted*. You say *little bit* and we say *tad*. *Kip* is our word for *nap*. *Jumper* is our word for *sweater*. I have had no idea what you were saying when I've heard you say sweater. But finally, I figured it out."

"What do you call these?" And I cupped my breasts with my hands.

"*Strawberry creams.*"

"*Strawberry creams?*" Mom and I repeated the phrase at the same time. Then I understood. "Oh! I get it. Oh, blimey! How funny."

Mom giggled then, too, and it made me happy to see her smiling and forgetting her worries, and then she asked, "What do you call this?" And she pointed to her woman's part.

"*Fanny.*"

Mom and I, again, both exclaimed, "*Fanny?* We call our behinds, fannies."

"We call our backend an *arse*, or if a person is rude, we call them an *arse*."

Then Mom shocked me by asking, "What do you call a man's part?"

"A *gentlemen sausage* or *twigs and berries*, or simply *bollocks* for balls." Ruth blushed. "Between Craig and I, we straightened out a confusion on those things. Oh, and then there's *John Thomas*, another British word for penis, or another one is *knob*."

Mom just about fell off the bed over that. Now she was blushing, and seeing that, Ruth changed to cleaner phrases and words. Ruth laughed, and pointing to Mom, she said, "If you would have fallen off the bed just now, I would say you *went arse-over-tit.*"

After recovering from a laughing fit brought on by that phrase, Mom said, "We say *ass-over-teakettle* for that one. Why we say teakettle, I have no idea. Well, I'd better get back to the kitchen and clean up my candy mess and start lunch." She stood and turned to go but then turned back, pointing to Ruth, "And you, young lady, can straighten out the confusion on *pants* and *panties* with your dear father-in-law."

Christmas

I t was Christmas Eve, and we hadn't received anything from Gracie's abductors. I could see it was hard on Mom and Dad. That night, we went to mass, and I'm sure there were a lot of prayers said by our family and candles lit, on Gracie's behalf as well as my brothers. Four children gone, and we didn't know where they were, what they were doing, or if they were all right—alive, in one piece, hungry, in pain? All we could hope and pray for was their well-being, and I hoped that would be enough to comfort Mom and Dad.

But the night before, on the twenty-third, Ruth and I had heard Mom and Dad laughing it up in their bedroom, and we assumed that Mom was sharing British phrases and words with Dad. Then suddenly they became quiet, and Ruth had said, blushing, "I think your Mom chatted him up to the point where he was up for it."

"Oh, my God, Ruth, what are you saying now?"

"Chatting up is flirting, and up for it means you're willing to have sex."

I giggled. "How long did Craig have to chat you up before you were up for it?"

Ruth turned red. "I told you. We waited until we had exchanged vows before we shagged." She finished with a grin, and I fell for it.

"Shagged means to have sex, right?"

"Well, actually, it's the nasty word for it in our English, in yours, I think you say screw, and I hate that word. When I worked at the ale house, men would get drunk and obnoxious and ask me if I wanted to screw. Most of them were always on the pull, meaning they were looking for sex, and sex only."

"How horrible for you to have to put up with that."

"I soon established a reputation for not having anything to do with that, unlike that Bess, who, the poor unfortunate girl, became plastered easily. One night she got drunk with a young American soldier, fresh in town from the States. They ended up sleeping together. Now, she's up the duff, stuffed, pregnant from a one-night stand with a poor bloke named Jake. She told me she was lucky he married her because there's no love there at all, but she just couldn't turn him down since marrying him was her way out of England where she had had nothing but a hard life. She's looking forward to living the great American dream everyone talks about."

"So, you're telling me that Jake doesn't really love Bess?"

"Oh, blimey, I'm sure not. Every time I saw them together, he looked miserable."

Suddenly I became very tired, the relief of knowing that I hadn't lost Jake to another woman, not his heart anyway, comforted me and I fell asleep instantly and slept like a baby.

Christmas Day, Mom and Dad seemed deeply sad, and I wished Ruth could somehow come up with one of her jokes or phrases that would cheer them up. Aileen and her family arrived and that helped some. Then there was a knock on the door, and when I answered it, there stood Blair, holding little James. I squealed with delight, and their appearance really helped Mom and Dad brighten up. It was fun to watch Rory, Ianna, John Jacob, and James interact. They acted as if it was just the other day that they had been together; they went to playing as soon as Blair pulled James' coat off him, and I could see Mom and Dad relax and begin to enjoy the day.

We shooed the children out of the dining room where Rory had them playing train. Mom and Aileen placed our Christmas bounty on the table while Ruth and I put the chairs in their places. There was another knock on the door; our neighbor, who had accidentally received some of our mail, handed over the long-awaited envelope with Gracie's picture in it, and a short letter from Craig saying he and Colin were fine but were fighting the Germans again. He ended his short missive by saying, "We love you all. Have a great Christmas. You'll soon hear on the radio where we are. Somebody kiss that sweet wife of mine for me. All our love, Craig and Colin."

Callum surprised us by gathering Ruth into his arms and kissing her on the cheek. Then Rory had to give her a smack. Kendall was next, and after that, we all took our turn at kissing Ruth on her cheek. All she could do was to blush, giggle, and then cry. We settled around the table then, giving her time to recover. Dad prayed a long and special Christmas prayer, not forgetting little Gracie and our dear Ian. That made us all well up, but then Dad poured us each a glass of wine, and we toasted to everyone we loved—the passed-on, the missing, and our 101st Airborne men. The entire day, then, was pleasant, and ended with Dad giving Ruth a package of blood sausage as an apology for the pants mix up, and with Ruth announcing that she would join Aileen in June in giving the family another child to love.

1945

Top Deck's Baby

My fifteenth birthday was disappointing. For some reason, Dad decided he and Mom should take a vacation. They left two days after Christmas without much fuss or forewarning. I felt a bit put out, and couldn't understand how they could do such a thing when four members of our family were out in the big, dangerous world, and we could receive either good news or bad news at any time. I came home to find them gone after working in my classroom, preparing for my new adventure. I had seen many of my teachers' lesson plans over the years and knew how to write them up. What I didn't know was the time frame needed for each new concept I would be teaching children aged six to seven years old. I realized I would be as fresh and green in this undertaking as my students, and I became nervous.

Our house was ominously quiet and still after the commotion of our Christmas celebration. Mom and Dad had taken Rory with them, making me jealous even though I became immediately lonesome for them. Ruth told me they expected to be back home sometime in the first week of January. I went out to help Callum with the chores, and Ruth made supper, which was not that tasty. She had tried making mashed potatoes along with a meatloaf. Ruth admitted that, without a mother to teach her and because of the food shortages during the war, she really wasn't that much of a cook. "My meal preparation was basically just opening tins and heating up the contents." We got through the meal using many shakes of the salt and pepper containers.

Now I had two projects to keep me busy until Mom and Dad returned, teaching Ruth how to cook and getting ready to be a first-grade teacher. I soon came out of my after-Christmas blues, and Ruth and I had a grand time in Mom's kitchen. I taught her how to fry chicken, make biscuits, and make tasty mashed potatoes. We had another much-improved meat loaf along with corn bread smothered in our ranch honey. I showed Ruth how to use a cookbook and our measuring system. She was an absolute natural, Callum and I discovered, because by the time our parents returned, she had surprised us with some new dishes and desserts that were excellent. Once she caught on to how to follow the directions in Mom's cookbooks, cooking and baking became Ruth's way of contributing to our household.

My first day of teaching turned out well, and my nervousness dissipated. The children were a delight, and my enthusiasm for my new venture soared, despite that I knew once they became comfortable with me, certain individuals would test me, try my patience to see what I was made of as a disciplinarian. When I came home that afternoon to find Mom, Dad, and Rory home, I saw it as a great finish to an already good week.

Little did I know it would get better. I was barely in the door when Rory came running and jumped into my arms, kissing me all over, telling me he missed me, and excitedly telling me they had brought a big, big birthday present home for me. Dad came and gave me a bear hug, and Mom kissed me on my cheek, smiling her happiest smile. All I could say was, "Did Gracie come home? Did you bring her back? Where is she?"

Mom and Dad looked crestfallen but soon recovered their high spirits after saying, "No," and sadly shaking their heads. Dad told me to get my ranching clothes on and to meet him out at the horse barn. Puzzled, I just nodded and did as I was told. When I went out to the barn, everyone was there along with a gorgeous chestnut-colored stallion, that wasn't a regular quarter horse, no, I could see he had some thoroughbred in him. He tossed his beribboned head around as if to say, "Yeah, look how magnificent I am and get this damn silly thing off my head."

I was stunned by my good luck. I hugged Dad and then Mom, fighting off tears. "Oh, my goodness, oh, my goodness." Then I grinned at Ruth. "Blimey, what a surprise." It had turned cold again, and Mom took Rory into the house, followed by Ruth, who wanted to finish cooking supper. I knew she wanted to show off her culinary skills.

Dad grinned at me, "I suppose you were disappointed about not having much of a birthday celebration this year."

"I was a bit miffed and, yes, I felt hurt and didn't know what to think."

"Abi, you know me, I couldn't resist the temptation to really surprise you. You like him?"

"Oh, yes, Dad, he's beautiful, and he looks like he's well-bred."

"Well-bred? Well, if having Top Deck as his daddy and Equestrian as his grand sire, and River Queen as his dam, and River Boat as her daddy, then, yes, he has grand breeding. But he's all yours. This summer you can breed him to a beautiful mare I also purchased. But she won't be here until spring after she foals. I think any fifteen-year-old young lady that has the touch with horses as you do, deserves to start her own line of well-bred horses."

"Dad, I love him! Did he really come from the King Ranch in Texas?" Dad received horse-breeding magazines, and I had read enough of them to know where the best horses were being bred, and was somewhat familiar with the top breeding lines in our country.

"Yes, he did." Dad stated proudly.

"Sweet; what possessed you to buy such a high-bred horse for me?"

"Well, like I told you, a young woman with your horse sense needs to learn how to breed horses; it would be a waste of talent if you didn't. Besides, money is good now, and what's the harm in diversifying our operation a bit? We can breed horses just as well as we breed cattle, don't you agree? And I believe you could train one or two more horses each summer."

I just nodded my head in agreement. I was still trying to wrap my mind around this latest opportunity, allowing me to do what I had always dreamed of doing. I slowly approached my magnificent birthday gift. "What's his name?"

"Decker. They call him Decker, and his registered name is simply, Top Deck's Son.

"Hello, Decker, you are going to make nice babies, aren't you?" I said as I rubbed behind his ear.

"What's the mare like?"

"She's a beautiful sorrel, so their offspring will most likely be red, and she is just as sweet natured as Decker."

"What's her name?"

"Melanie, and she's not yet papered so we need to choose a name according to her lineage. But right now, let's get you on your new stud."

Dad helped me saddle Decker and adjust the stirrups and the rest of the tack. Dad told me he measured 16 hands, making him the largest horse on the ranch. I led him out into the corral and put him through the usual paces. I felt intimidated by his size but at the same time enjoyed his smooth gait. Dad told me that Decker's sire, Top Deck, came from a line of racing horses but that when he was young, he was injured, ruining his ability to race, but that didn't stop him from siring horses of great quality with strong traits of ability and speed.

When I brought Decker back into the barn, I knew we were a match and that he was going to be affectionate. As I brushed him he turned to nuzzle me several times as if to say, "Thanks, I needed that," and then he went back to eating his grain, blowing out of his nose occasionally, a sign of his contentment.

Hitler's Last Stand

In December the Germans had begun their last offensive drive in Europe, staging it in the immense Ardennes Forest region, which consisted of the Ardennes mountain range and the Meuse and Moselle Rivers. The Germans launched this attack through the heavily-forested region that lay mostly in Belgium and Luxembourg, but also reached into parts of France and Germany. Their assault was a complete surprise to the Allied forces, with American troops catching the brunt of it. American casualties were higher than any other campaign during the war. But by December 26, our U.S. troops had held Bastogne, stalling the Germans.

We had listened to the war news almost constantly, hoping to hear something that would tell us if our boys were involved in that battle, nicknamed The Battle of the Bulge since the German line of defense took on the shape of a bulge. All we knew was that the Germans also suffered many casualties and couldn't replace these forces, and that they also lost a great amount of their personnel and later, much of their Luftwaffe aircraft.

This engagement finally ended the last week of January, leading many people to believe that Germany would not win the war. But we still had no idea where our boys were, and worry lay like a heavy cloak over both Mom and Dad, and it spread to Ruth. Coming home from teaching school, I often found Mom and Ruth clinging to one another for support after one of them had broken down from the stress of worrying about Craig and, of course, our other two boys, Colin and

Cameron. But the more Ruth's belly expanded, the more optimistic she became, and some of that rubbed off on Mom. They both proclaimed that they would know the instant one of our fighting men was in trouble, hurt, or possibly dead. Dad, usually the pessimist, also had good feelings about his boys. The war was winding down, and for that, we were grateful.

Atrocities

....

While the American forces and their closest allies moved east, the Soviets moved west; soon they were converging on Germany, taking back and freeing countries the Germans had conquered earlier and releasing thousands from concentration camps. Most people believed that Hitler should have surrendered after the Battle of the Bulge. The German Luftwaffe was nearly out of fuel, and German U-boats found it impossible to leave their bases without being sunk, and by February, new recruits to the Nazi army were forced to use either obsolete weapons or share one good weapon between eight men without enough ammunition to be effective.

Hitler would not give up, and his selfish ambition to stay in power caused much suffering for the German people. He ordered a scorched earth policy to be in place once the Allies overran German lands, furthering German citizens' misery. But despite Hitler's stringent orders, many German commanders simply did not act on their Fuhrer's wishes. They thought there should have been a complete German surrender, and had they tailored a peace agreement then, it would have allowed them a better outcome with the Allies, leaving the Reich more intact. Now, it seemed, they would most likely face total annihilation as a country.

At the end of January, the Soviets liberated Auschwitz and Birkenau concentration camps, finding hundreds of newly dead, thousands barely alive, and over a million human remains. In April, U.S. troops reached Buchenwald and found that the prisoners there had liberated themselves, and a few days later, British troops released hundreds of women from the

Bergen-Belsen concentration camp, discovering devastating numbers of corpses.

The Allied forces also reverted to using a horrible means to an end. A Soviet submarine sank a German ship, killing tens of thousands of German refugees and wounded soldiers. In February, they began firebombing Dresden, Germany, killing over 100,000 citizens. And in March, the U.S. began firebombing Tokyo, killing nearly 100,000 people. It struck me that the closer to the end, the more awful the methods to bring the war to a final finish. Radio shows, *Time* magazine and others, as well as newspapers, reported that German citizens preferred dealing with the western allies since the Soviet troops had a reputation of brutality toward captured German POW's and civilians. I only wished it would end so my brothers, Jake, and Blair's Henry could come home safe and sound.

April Showers Bring May Flowers

By April the news sounded hopeful that soon it would be over in Europe; the Allies had surrounded hundreds of thousands of German troops and later captured the German city of Hanover. But the Japanese stubbornly kept on fighting their losing war. News outlets had reported they had suffered many casualties and deaths, and when U.S. troops invaded Okinawa, engaging them in the bloodiest Pacific island battle yet, they still refused to surrender.

On April 12, our president, Franklin Delano Roosevelt, elected four times by the American people, died of a cerebral hemorrhage, and Harry S. Truman became President of the United States. Americans were greatly saddened and shocked to have lost a man who had led them for so long. Hitler, it was said, laughed and jumped up and down, waving his arms, storming around the room, cackling like a mad man.

Meanwhile, Soviet troops captured Vienna, and the Allies captured Arnhem in the Netherlands. Three days later, one of the last remnants of German troops, trapped on the Ruhr River, surrendered. The Soviets entered Berlin April 23, and a few days after that, U.S. and Soviet troops met at the Elbe River in Germany, cutting the remaining German troops in two. April 30 Hitler killed himself after killing his woman, Eva Braun. Joseph Goebbels, Hitler's successor, also committed suicide after having his entire family, his wife and six children, killed.

On May 2, Soviet troops captured Berlin, and German troops in Italy surrendered. Germany then surrendered unconditionally, and after ten bells, the radio announcer proclaimed that victory in Europe had been accomplished, making May 8 V-E Day, nearly a year after the Allies had invaded Europe at Normandy.

Breeding Season

....

Melanie arrived the end of May with her new baby, a filly named Fancy, a lovely palomino with all the right markings—white socks, golden body color, and a nearly white mane and tail. Dad had been teaching me how to tease her to see if she was in heat and at what stage. He had constructed a small, wooden paddock in which we penned Decker each day, and then we scored Melanie's behavior.

Dad taught me his way of scoring a mare and her signs of estrus, explaining that every horse breeder had their own way of doing so, designing their scoring methods specifically for each individual mare since each female comes into heat differently. He told me that once you had a scoring system that worked, you should keep it and use it year after year for that specific mare.

Melanie had been in strong heat for three days, and Dad said it was time to breed her to Decker. She had become completely receptive to him, going up to him in his pen, sniffing on him and then wailing her angst. She continuously had her tail up when she was near him and urinated constantly, squirting it out so he could smell her heat musk. When her tail was up, she did the winking of her vulva, and when she began backing up to Decker, Dad knew she was ready. I was glad the right time had come since both horses had been screaming out their mating calls to one another, breaking our peaceful, sweet, early days of summer with their high-pitched flirts.

Dad and I caught and haltered them, leading them out into the horse corral. I held Melanie and Dad had Decker. We gave them almost all the rope, and they began a funny little mating dance, and every time

Decker got close enough to sniff at her vulva, Melanie twirled around and away from him. Then she teased him, backing up to him, lifting her tail, and winking her vulva, squirting, but she would suddenly turn around when he tried to mount her. Decker let out a frustrated squeal each time. I was about to ask Dad if he was sure she was ready, but then she settled down and allowed him to mount her. He penetrated her, grunting the entire time, and she stilled. Decker rubbed her side with one leg and nibbled on her wither and when he was about to dismount, he rubbed her behind gently with one leg, as if to say, "Thanks."

I went up the hill that afternoon, hoping to see Bear, and there she was with both cubs. When she saw me, she sat down on her behind, waiting. I ran to her and gave her my best bear hug, but her babies were big now and must not have remembered me because they ran away. Bear wouldn't eat her peanut butter and honey sandwich, and soon turned and left. I was hurt and couldn't figure out why she wasn't friendly as always. Perhaps I smelled too much like horse.

But the next time we met, she shook her head, no, on the sandwich. Her cubs hovered in the background, and I slowly approached them but they kept backing up. I threw sandwiches to them, which they ate. As I came back to Bear, I noticed she was very thin and that her fur looked unhealthy, making me think that perhaps she was sick. But what could I do? I had no idea how to help her since I didn't know what ailed her. I didn't see her as much that summer, but she did have her two cubs to take care of, and each time she appeared she seemed to become slower and weaker.

I told myself, you'll need to let her go someday, she's been coming around here for six years now and is probably getting old. While I felt sad about Bear and her condition, I had my horses, and Dad had been right, I could handle training more than two colts a summer. Our neighbors brought me one of theirs to work with, and I made a little money. Dad told me I should put an ad in the paper. What could it hurt? I did, and I ended up with two more colts to work with during that long summer, waiting for our boys to come home.

We had received a letter from Craig saying they were occupying the town of Berchtesgaden, Austria, where Hitler had had his retreat and a meeting house built on top of Mt. Kehlstein. He told us how beautiful it was there and joked about drinking Hitler's champagne. We didn't know if it was just a joke or a boast, but we were just happy to know they were safe and that they wouldn't have to fight any more. Craig ended his letter giving us a phone number where he could be reached when the baby came. He said that it was amazing how quickly the railroad systems, roads, bridges, and communication systems were being rebuilt and were working again.

Ruth was late in giving birth. She might have been so nervous about where and how Craig was that it kept her from going into labor. His letter was the perfect fix for that, it seemed, because Angus Ian MacDougal was born in July on Rory's fifth birthday. Aileen had had another girl in late June, naming her Lacey Fiona O'Leary. Both babies had black, fuzzy heads and bright blue eyes, and looked a little like one another. When Dad called Craig with the news, we heard him yell, "Swell! A son! Oh, I can't wait to get home. Tell Ruth I love her and take good care of them both."

Enola Gay & Bock's Car

Japan with all her treachery and greed remains unsubdued.
Winston Churchill

In June, the U.S. troops finally defeated Japanese troops and captured Okinawa, giving them a secure base from which to attack Japan's mainland, and later in July, the United States, Britain, and China sent the Potsdam Declaration to Japan, giving them the ultimatum to unconditionally surrender immediately or suffer "prompt and utter destruction." They refused to surrender, and on August 6, a plane, called the Enola Gay, flew over Hiroshima dropping an atomic bomb named Little Boy, instantly killing 70,000 Japanese citizens. Two days later, another plane, called Bock's Car, dropped an atomic bomb named Fat Man on Nagasaki, instantly killing 80,000 Japanese people.

News articles would later claim that it was "the most difficult decision" of President Harry Truman's life, and as a young girl, I didn't care one whit for his difficult decision—I thought it was wrong to kill innocent men, women, and children, even after Dad explained that dropping the bomb saved many more lives than if the Americans and Japanese would have fought it out like they had been doing. But as the years went by, and many more Japanese people died from burns and radiation sickness, I still thought it an awful thing for one country to do to another country's population. Had I been a Japanese citizen, I would have rather been vaporized instantly than linger in a slow dying.

But dropping bombs on Japan did coerce the Japanese government to unconditionally surrender on August 14, and President Truman announced our victory over Japan a day later, declaring August 15 V-J Day.

Homecomings

In those days it was no disgrace to be crazy, but, on the other hand, you got no credit for it. We, who had been at the war, admired the war crazies since we knew they had been made so by something that was unbearable. It was unbearable to them because they were made of a finer or more fragile metal or because they were simple and understood too clearly.
Ernest Hemingway

J ake was the first to come home. It was early fall when we heard the Murano family had met him at the train station. He came home because he had been wounded, and came home still on crutches. The Germans had had him for two days, and for some reason, thought he knew more of the Allied plans than he did. Since Germany had surrendered the first week in May, I figured his German captors must have seriously hurt him because it was now September with nearly four months passed. Bess and their baby both died when she went into labor much too early, and she began hemorrhaging after the baby had been born dead.

Despite my unsubstantiated betrayed and jealous feelings, I still felt sorry for Jake and ashamed of myself for having unkind thoughts about his marriage. It was very possible that he had no idea how I felt toward him. I had never told him about my crush on him, and that's all it was, a schoolgirl infatuation. I did think he had tender feelings toward me all these years, and that when we talked or just met in the hall, he sensed my affection for him. Stupid thoughts. There certainly was no solid evidence of him having any romantic thoughts regarding me. I was Ian's little sister, and all we had to draw us together was our lasting grief of losing and missing a person that had been his best friend and my favorite brother.

Dad and Mom chose Baird Construction to build the addition onto our house. They had poured the foundation in August, framed it in, installed plumbing and wiring, and now were setting in the windows and doors. They would have it roofed, shingled, and insulated before cold weather set in, and Mr. Baird promised to have the inside finished and ready to live in by Christmas.

Three weeks after Jake returned, he showed up early one morning after getting back on with Baird's construction. Out of politeness and respect, he stopped in to visit with Mom and Dad before the rest of the crew arrived. Mom sat Jake at our dining room table with a cup of coffee. In her nervousness, Mom insisted I sit down with them. It was awkward. What do you say to someone who has seen so much and lived through God only knows what?

I had dressed in one of Ian's old ranch shirts and pants and had his chinks on, too. I planned to take my newest project for a ride through the woods that day. When I sat down, I saw Jake take them in and recognize them as Ian's. I couldn't meet his eyes, and just sat quiet, while Dad asked him polite questions. Finally, Mom brought up the loss of his wife and child, saying things you say to someone in that situation. He thanked her graciously for her condolences, blushing deeply. I figured he realized that the entire valley probably knew the story behind his marriage, or at least suspected the truth behind his sudden nuptials to a virtual stranger and her showing up pregnant.

Suddenly, I couldn't take the heavy tension hovering over the room and rose to leave. I stopped before him, and he stood up, giving me a clumsy hug. I looked him in the eyes. "I am truly sorry about Bess and your baby. Life just isn't fair sometimes." He shook his head. "No, it isn't." I struggled to keep from running out of the room and out to the porch, and slowly walked out the door. As I donned my leather gloves and my hat, I discovered that tears were racing down my cheeks. The lost look and sadness in Jake's eyes haunted me all day, and I wondered, what will it be like when the rest come home?

It became a sweet agony when Jake came to our place each day. When working with one of the horses out in the corral, I would sneak glances at him and saw how he had changed. His walk was one of defeat, when before he had walked straight, tall, and confident, accompanied with an air that said he was ready to take on the world. He had smiled a lot; not so now, and when he did, it never reached his eyes. I wished I could help him. Our autumn weather that year was warm, sunny, and so beautiful it made your heart ache, especially knowing what was coming later. The *Farmers' Almanac*, my dad's second Bible, and many other forecasts said it would be a long, hard winter, especially in the Northwest.

I didn't know how Jake spent his weekends, and the thought of helping him those days kept creeping into my mind. Ruth had suffered a severe case of baby blues after having little Gus, or Gussie as Rory christened him. Thank goodness Gussie was a good baby and that Ruth nursed him because otherwise I think she would have gone over the deep end. Despite that Ruth got plenty of rest, or should have, since Gussie slept at least six hours per night without needing to be changed or fed, Ruth would snap at people over nothing, her anxiety keeping her up some nights. She was irritable and acted as if just getting through another day overwhelmed her. When she completely lost her appetite, not good for a nursing mother and her child, Mom insisted on taking her to the doctor. He diagnosed her as having postpartum psychosis, which is rare but when it strikes can lead to life-threatening thoughts and actions, even suicide.

We all went into action. Mom took Ruth into see Father Boyle every day except for Saturdays and Sundays, even though Ruth was what she called a C and E. In England C and E stands for the Church of England, which is the one thing about Ruth that still bothered Dad, not having a Catholic daughter-in-law. Ruth had bonded with her baby—no doubt about that since she lit up with a happy smile when nursing or taking care of him. But that was the problem, Gussie was such a good baby, Ruth didn't feel needed like she thought she would.

She continually complained about not being any good for anyone and feeling useless.

Mom put Ruth back to work in the kitchen and added housework to her duties, and that helped, especially when Dad came home with a small cradle for Gussie to sleep in downstairs while Ruth worked. I took her for long rides out in the meadows at first, but later, when she started feeling a little better, we went as far away as up into the deep woods after Ruth finally gave Mom childcare privileges. As our weather became cooler, Ruth would come home from an outing with rosy cheeks and a good appetite, and could sleep all night again. Soon, Ruth began laughing and entertaining us, and when Craig sent a letter saying he would be home by Thanksgiving, Ruth's crisis was over.

I decided to do something to help Jake. Lately, whenever I was out in the corral working, or just in the yard taking Gussie out for some fresh air, I noticed Jake watching me, sometimes out-and-out staring at me for a long time. Then one Friday evening, he came and talked to me when I was finishing up my chores. He casually stood with his arms dangling over the fence and seemed much more relaxed than when I first saw him after returning home. He smiled at me, and this time the smile reached his eyes, and I felt a jolt of electricity run through me. "Say, Abi, would you consider going to the movie with me Saturday night?"

I nearly squealed like Rory over a new toy or adventure. "Yes, yes, Jake, I would like that very much."

He smiled again, showing the endearing gap between his upper front teeth, and I could have cried for joy.

"I'll pick you up about six? I thought we could have a burger and fries before seeing the movie."

"Great. I'll see you then."

When I announced my date with Jake at the supper table that night, Dad, of course, had reservations, but Mom was all for it. She smiled at me and nodded her head in a way that told me she had known about my secret crush on Jake for some time. The next day, I didn't bother too much with my horse duties, doing just the minimal chores. I took a long bath and washed my hair, rinsing it with vinegar to make it shine. Ruth helped me pick out my clothes and helped apply a tiny bit of cosmetics, and for the first time in a long time, I used some of the perfume given to me on my thirteenth birthday. Ruth trimmed my hair a bit on the sides and styled it much like Lauren Bacall wore hers in *To Have and Have Not.*

Waiting for Jake, I suddenly became nervous. Mom sat down in the parlor where I was waiting, smiling. "It's going to be okay Abi, just be yourself, because that is what Jake finds attractive in you, your individuality. Don't worry about your father, he only wants the best for you, and in his mind, he doesn't respect Jake like before because of what happened in England. He's only being negative about Jake because he's not sure he won't hurt you. Dad thinks of him as a much older widower, despite that the boy is only nineteen, just a few years younger than what Ian would be." I nodded, and then there was a knock on the door.

Jake stood inside our porch with a bouquet of lavender. I took a deep whiff and the scent calmed me, and I wondered if Jake had been taking deep breaths all the way here. I ushered him in and put the bouquet in water. Like a gentleman should, Jake opened the door for me and that made me feel wonderful and yet uncomfortable at the same time. And then he even opened the car door for me. But when he sat down behind steering wheel and asked, "Ready?" more like he was asking himself than me, that made me feel better. I could hardly eat my supper at the drive-in, since I had become nervous again. But when we entered the movie theater, Jake gathered my left hand into his right as we walked into the darkened room, making me feel wanted and needed, and my anxiety disappeared. That night on our porch I ventured to ask him, "Would you care to come riding with me tomorrow? I've got two horses I'm working with, and it would be nice if I had another rider so they could learn to trail together."

Jake stilled and was quiet. Finally, he said, "What time?"

"How about eleven. I'll fix a little lunch for us to eat out in the woods."

"Sure." Jake gave me a loose hug and a kiss on the cheek, and clattered down the steps. His lighthearted way of doing that made me feel happy.

The next morning before we went up the mountainside, Jake asked if we could stop at Ian's grave. We did, and after that Jake remained silent, and I just kept it that way. He did comment on what a fine job I had done with the gelding he was riding, and I just nodded in thanks. When we reached the first high-mountain meadow, we stopped for lunch. After we ate, we sat in silence. It was a comfortable one, and I could feel Jake relaxing even more. Suddenly he reached over and gently wiped the side of my mouth with his thumb, and I felt the jolt of electricity again. He just chuckled when I started. "You had a bit of egg salad there."

I laughed and then said, without thinking, "Yes, and if you were British you would have said, a tad of egg salad." His face reddened and I'm sure mine did, too. How stupid of you, Abi, to remind him, I thought. He cleared his throat. "Abi, I need to explain something to you."

I held up my hand in a gesture of pushing away his offer to explain, shaking my head. "You don't need to say a word, Jake. Mom has always stressed that war makes people do very different things than they would otherwise do."

It was his turn to shake his head. "No, Abi, you don't understand. I need to tell you what happened because I want you to know that I had no intention of doing what I did and then end up married to Bess because I have always hoped, even before Ian died, that someday I could marry you."

I had just bitten into an apple and choked. His eyes widened as I struggled to dislodge the chunk that had invaded my windpipe. Before I knew what was happening, Jake was behind me and had his arms around me just underneath my breasts and rib cage, squeezing hard. The apple came up, and I quickly swallowed it, coughed a bit, and I then began to breathe normally. Jake kept his hold on me with one arm and then slowly turned my head, kissing me halfway on my mouth and on the side where he had just rubbed away the smudge of egg salad. I struggled away from him and stood up, his explanation about Bess still between us.

After a moment, I sat down across from him and we looked at each other sheepishly. I finally smiled. "I think I have loved you ever since

I could remember. But I thought it was always just a younger sister's crush on her older brother's best friend."

Jake smiled big, showing the gap in his teeth, and I said with a sigh, "Okay, let's get your explanation over and done with and never talk about it again."

Jake proceeded to tell me, with great embarrassment, how when his unit arrived in England and they had their first weekend leave, they all went into London to make the rounds visiting and drinking in as many ale houses as possible. "I've never been a big partier, you know that, and I got very drunk." He blushed. "The alcohol made me very receptive to this young girl's attentions. We ended up sleeping together in her little apartment, flat she called it, and I left the next morning thinking that would be the end of it.

"The next month when we went back into town, she was there at a public house, watching for me to tell me she was pregnant. At first I thought she might have been lying because she had told me she wanted to come to America in the worst way. But she convinced me she wasn't being dishonest, and we decided to marry for the child's sake and that if things didn't work out after the war, we'd simply get a divorce. My parents, as Catholic as they are, of course were very upset about the plan, but knew I should do the right thing and marry her if she was carrying my baby. Bess and the baby dying will haunt me for the rest of my life, but I never did love her. It was a big mistake."

We sat silent for a while. Then Jake leaned close to me and clasped my face between his hands, looking deep into my eyes. "Abi, I don't want you to ever think I would be so casual and uncommitted with you if we started a relationship. Understand?"

I nodded and leaned forward for the real kiss I knew he would give me. After that he told me how and why he had been wounded and was able to come home early. He had been tending to his dying commander who offered Jake his jacket since he wouldn't need it any longer. The Germans captured Jake, thinking he was an officer and knew more than he did. They shot him in a leg each time they tried getting information from him, and then his unit rescued him. I moaned and commented on how awful that must have been. Jake insisted that it wasn't that bad at first, because he kept passing out. But he admitted that recovering had taken time and had been painful.

In the next month, Jake and I spent many hours together getting to know one another. We had kisses, but left the rest for later. We rode at my place and at his. His horses had been watered and fed while he was gone but their training needed tuning. His little spread was gorgeous. It had a small cabin on it, and Jake planned to begin building a home there soon. It was a happy time for me—a time of finally living and growing up without war hanging overhead. Jake's emotional wounds seemed to be healing as well as his physical wounds. The peace conference and after-war settlements weren't going well, but here in the United States, people began looking forward to a future without war, and the country's optimistic mood soared sky-high. And then Cameron came home.

He came home the day before his birthday. He and Callum would turn seventeen the next day. He, like Jake, had aged; they both looked much older than their years, and had become thin. Cameron wore a beard and a black patch over one eye. He explained that one of the cargo ships he had been on carried a large shipment of mustard gas, which blew up when the ship was bombed. He explained that both eyes and his entire face had suffered burns and that everything had healed but his left eye where he lost his sight completely.

As we celebrated their birthday, Dad asked Cameron what he would like. "Sorry, son, we didn't know you'd be here so we hadn't done anything, yet."

Cameron scratched his beard. "Well, Dad, everyone," and then he looked at me, "I want to go someplace where a man can hunt and trap in peace without being judged." He took another evil look at me. "That's what I want to do."

Dad cleared his throat. "Ahem, okay then, what does that mean exactly? You've already proven you can leave any damn time you want."

Cameron reared up and yelled, pounding his hands on the table. "I want something to drive, money to replace my traps, and I'll get the hell out of here and out of your hair." He stopped and shot me an evil look and went on. "Once I get wheels, I'll take the new military highway from Great Falls and drive to Alaska, where I can once and for all, be alone, in the woods like I like it. I want to be as far away as I can from people, especially this God damn family. I don't fit in here or anywhere; I'm not fit to be amongst humans."

After that we just left him to himself, steering clear of his moods that swung from overly cheerful to dour and down in the dumps. Cameron had been right. He needed to be alone. That's just how he was. Relief flashed across everyone's face when he began talking about leaving. We knew it would be a load off our minds not to worry about Cameron and what he would do next, but we also felt guilty about that thinking. That was the thing about my brother; he made us feel culpable simply because of what he was and how he was—an always unhappy, unsettled person. Trying to bond with him and interact emotionally with him was like befriending a feral cat—a creature that wants you to reach out to it and yet, it strikes at you with its venomous claws the moment you do. I still bear scars from a barn cat that seemed friendly but when I reached out to it, it clawed me and the infected wounds took weeks to heal.

Cameron agreed to stay until after Thanksgiving; he wanted to see Craig if not both of his older brothers. But Colin had been hospitalized because he had developed something they called combat stress reaction. Craig had told us in his most recent letter that Colin probably wouldn't be coming home with him, and that he would explain his condition when he got here, telling us not to worry because the doctors expected him to make a full recovery. Mom and Dad accepted that without too much concern; they were just happy their boys were all safe.

It was the first of November, and I wanted to go up the hill to see if Bear was still around. We had grown apart, it seemed. It was almost as if she was trying to warn me she wouldn't be around much longer. I could feel her love for me but at the same time, she was distant. Her health had improved over the summer, but I was sure that if she survived the winter, she wouldn't come with cubs next year.

Her cubs, while finally accepting me again, coming up close for their sandwiches and allowing me to pet them, were very protective of their mother. One day when Bear seemed energetic, I enthusiastically grabbed her in a big hug, and they both came at me and didn't stop until their mother growled a warning to them. I was glad they were protective since Bear seemed so weak and vulnerable all summer.

The day I saw Bear and her cubs for the last time was one of those days you put into your memory forever. It was lovely and warm—a final sweet kiss from nature before winter set in. The last blaze of Indian summer warmth had brought the bees out. Everything was still, and the only sound I heard was the pounding of nails down in the yard on our addition and buzzing of bees, making me remember the first time I met Bear. I fed my friends their treats and had stepped close to Bear, slow and cautious, to give her one last embrace for the season. I heard a twig snap and sensed a movement behind me. I turned, and there stood Cameron with his gun.

He stood with legs spread wide apart and with his feet firmly planted on the ground like he wasn't going anywhere soon, just staring at me, his eyes turning from their usual light, watery blue to a deep azure, and then they became black. I backed up in front of Bear, holding my arms out, shielding her as much as possible, pleading with Cameron. "Don't shoot. She's my friend. She won't harm you if you don't threaten her. Please don't shoot! Just go."

Cameron sneered. "Finally caught you. Always thought something funny was going on up here. You're crazy, you know that. Hanging out with this ugly, piece of shit wild animal. Look at it. Its coat is a puke white and all scraggly and matted. Wouldn't even want that hide."

His words made my blood run cold, and it seemed as if my heart quit beating. I wasn't worried about me being shot, just Bear. I could hear her cubs creeping closer and began to fear for them. "Cameron, this is insane. Just leave. Go away. These bears will be hibernating soon, and after that, you'll be gone and it won't matter. Stop this, now. It's crazy."

Cameron came close, thrusting the muzzle of his gun into my belly, taking my breath away. "Crazy? You think I'm crazy? That's what they called me in the hospital—*crazy.*" His voice turned into a whiny mimic, *"You have to stay here until we help you. You can't leave like this until we get you healed and you can live a normal, stable, satisfactory life thinking happy, peaceful thoughts."*

Cameron saw my eyes widened at his revelation, and my fear become even larger. His bullying instinct took over. He kept butting me with the end of his gun, all over now, even on my breasts and where my heart barely seemed to be beating. Bear had begun her usual m-m-r-r- . . . sounds, and her cubs hovered behind us. I pleaded again. "Go, Cameron, you're not crazy. Just go and leave us alone. They'll be gone in an instant once you leave." And then I made the mistake of bringing up *crazy* again. "This is crazy, Cameron. I promise nobody will get hurt if you just leave. It makes no sense to shoot them or kill them. Go. Please."

Cameron muttered, his mouth twisted with hate, "Oh, you think I'm thinking about shooting them? Just them? Well, now," and he came close to my face with his, splattering me with his spit. "What makes you think I wouldn't shoot you—first." He cocked his head and finished. "At least you won't see their dying. Would you like it that way?"

I shook my head, trying to keep eye contact, trying to reach him in his furor. I remembered Aunt Peggy and how she got on her knees to plead forgiveness for her awful betrayal when begging for, first Grandpa's forgiveness, and then Dad's. I dropped to my knees, and folding my hands, I pled with Cameron like he was God, himself. He just sneered and turned his gun around, aiming the butt at my head. I started to scramble to my feet, but it was too late. Cameron stood tall and swung at me. I felt the blow and toppled to the ground in what felt like slow-motion. I lay there stunned, sick to my stomach, feeling a wetness in my ear. When I struggled to get up, blackness washed over me until all I could see was a tiny pinpoint of light. The last thing I heard was the sound of a single gunshot ringing through the air.

I woke up feeling the jolting pace of someone carrying me down the hill. I opened my eyes for a bit and saw Jake's concerned face above me, and then everything went black. The next time I woke, Dad's worried face was there. I groaned from the pain radiating from my head, and when I looked again, Dad's image blurred and floated past me. I slept, and when I woke again, Dad was still there.

I kept my eyes closed, my lids feeling too heavy to open. I lay there struggling to remember why I was feeling this way. I opened my eyes a bit and when I tried to move my head, I remembered. Cameron and Bear. What happened to Bear? Where was Cameron? "Cameron," I managed to whisper.

"Just go back to sleep, Abi. You're safe. Cameron will never hurt you again."

I lay still with my eyes closed. It hurt to open them and see the light, and it really hurt when I moved my head. I whispered again. "Bear?"

"Don't worry about Bear. Don't worry about Cameron. Just rest."

The next time I woke, Mom was there. I opened my eyes and saw her worried face and sensed the look of devastation she wore wasn't just about me. I closed my eyes again, trying to think of what could have happened after Cameron knocked me out. I remembered the gun, the look in his eyes, wanting to kill. Bear! I remembered. He threatened her and then me, and I had begged. I struggled to sit up but my head still hurt too much. I settled into the pillows and tested my memory again.

The scene slowly played out in my mind. I remembered going up the hill to say goodbye to Bear and her babies. I was hugging Bear, and Cameron came up behind me. Cameron. He was in an ugly mood, and I could see his face, twisted and mean. His eyes going from his light blue, to dark blue, and then the black of hatred. For me? No. Yes, for me and for Bear. He called her ugly. But that's because she's sick with something. Old age?

Her babies. They were there to protect her. From what? Protect my Bear. Then I remembered what I heard as I struggled in and out of consciousness just after Cameron walloped me. The menacing growling, and then the sound of ripping flesh, like when Dad skins a dead calf so he can put that skin on a motherless one so the mother will accept it as hers. I remember the screaming. Someone screaming, and then silence, and after that Jake picking me up. I couldn't see him but I smelled him and heard him say, "Oh, my God, Abi. Oh, my God." I remembered feeling safe and knowing that, I succumbed to the darkness that I had been fighting.

I opened my eyes, looking at Mom and her shattered appearance. "Cameron. Cameron's dead. Isn't he? Bear's babies killed him. He killed Bear. Shot her. Didn't he?" Mom nodded and broke down crying. She lay her head on my chest, and I kept smoothing her hair, trying to give her comfort for some bad thing happening to our family, again, something that wasn't ever going away. It was bad. It was bad, what happened. Would never go away, it would always make me feel bad. And then it dawned on me—it was all my fault because I loved Bear. I pushed Mom's head off me, and reared up, vomiting. I began screaming and crying, flailing my arms, trying to get up, but I couldn't do it. The doctor was there. I felt someone holding me and a prick in my arm, and I slept.

We buried Cameron up on our hill after a private service at the church. After we had committed Cameron's torn body to the earth, Dad and Callum buried Bear next to Joe, Ian's favorite horse. I tried to explain my unexplainable relationship with Bear. Everyone just shook their heads, not able to wrap their minds around such a thing. Now, without her, I had trouble reconciling with it, too. Our love for one another was completely inconsistent with all laws of nature. Bear hadn't been some circus animal raised by people to be tame, nor was she like the ones raised in a zoo, and sometimes even those turn on their masters and caregivers, attacking them. Our connection had been special, and I will go to my grave believing that and that fate had sent her to me.

My guilt was heavy and difficult to overcome even after everyone babied me and consoled me, saying things like: "no matter what he thought, Cameron shouldn't have threatened to kill you or your bears; don't feel bad, Abi, Cameron was always different; you know what evil he could do; he's in a better place now, don't worry, Abi." All I could do, all anyone could do, was pray that Cameron had finally found peace and happiness in death, something he just could not do in life.

Craig's homecoming helped mitigate some of the sorrow we felt, and though it was never spoken out loud, we all experienced that sense of relief that comes when a problem goes away. We would forever feel the guilt and helplessness that Cameron's existence had always stirred inside us—our problem that could never be solved. The hospital in Europe had tried to help him, but he ran away.

Craig was head-over-heels in love with Ruth; we could see that by the devotion and attention he showered on her, and he was completely infatuated with Gussie. When Craig held him, he would just stare at him in wonder, shaking his head at his good fortune. He looked at Ruth the same way, which made me happy since she had worried that things would be different between them when he returned. Mom and Dad insisted on hosting a wedding reception for them before they moved back to Missoula. In the meantime, we moved them into the new addition.

I missed having Ruth and Gussie in my room, and each time I looked at that empty bed, I thought of the other empty bed in the boy's room, and I was sad. My prayers felt emptier, too. Now the only brother to pray for was Colin. But I still prayed that Gracie would come back; she would fill that empty bed in my room just fine.

Henry had come home to Blair in one piece. But because he had taken care of many "head cases" from war trauma, Henry's terse term for war victims that couldn't sleep, eat, talk, or make sense of things, he had decided to stay in the East and study psychiatry. But they planned on coming home for Christmas, another happy thing to look forward to. Colin remained hospitalized in Europe still coping with his problem, which, according to Craig, was simply that his recurring nightmares made it impossible for him to sleep. He figured Colin hadn't slept more than a few hours a night since after the war, and only a dose of sedatives granted him those hours.

After Thanksgiving, we continued to plan Craig and Ruth's wedding reception. They decided to speak their vows in front of family and friends. Dad insisted that Ruth have a wedding dress, and that they have attendants as well. Mom, Ruth, and I traveled to Butte to shop for the required attire. Ruth had found a way to pump enough breast milk for her boys to get by until she returned. We left one evening and were back the next.

When we walked into the dining room that evening, there sat Colin, looking thin but fit. His eyes were clear and full of emotion. He hugged everyone effusively, showing affection like he never had before. After Mom and I got Rory to bed, and Ruth had settled into her new quarters with Gussie, we joined the men in the parlor. Mom talked Colin into sharing his story about how he was able to come home sooner than expected.

She sat down next to her second-oldest son, joy bouncing off her face. Colin put his arm around Mom, nestled her close, and began. He couldn't help it, he was so proud, and he started at the backend of his story. He had been offered a job writing for the *New York Times* because he had sent them an accounting he had written while convalescing. The *Times* loved it and planned to publish it soon.

Then he circled around to the beginning of his tale. The staff at the hospital were at their wits' end with him because he seemed rational but just couldn't sleep. Each time he dozed off, all he could see in his dreams were reruns from the battles he and the 101st had fought—the most devastating being the Battle of Bastogne where they lost many men and suffered horrible casualties. He said the hospital staff had diagnosed his problem as a traumatic reaction to the stress of the war. But he had been fine until the fighting stopped. Then the horrid nightmares began tormenting him and, after a time, made him fear going to sleep. "I became bitter and didn't even want to talk about it when they urged me to."

One day a young nurse, in hopes of drawing him out of his silence, began asking him about his life before the war. For some reason, he answered her that day. He told her he had been working for a local newspaper in a small town in Montana near the ranch where he had grown up. Shortly after that, the physician that had been supervising his case came to him and suggested that perhaps if he wrote about his war experiences it would help him.

Colin recounted how he began writing and couldn't stop once he started, and that after he had finished, he fell asleep and didn't wake up for nearly forty-eight hours. When he woke, he felt refreshed, hopeful, and hungry. That night when it was time to sleep, he slept again for hours. The nurse that had found out he was a writer, read his story and begged him to send it home to be published. After thinking about it for a while, Craig said he decided to start big. And he did. He sent it to the *New York Times*, and they bought it.

After returning to the United States and going through the hassle of the required examinations and being released from the service, he contacted the *Times* to see if they had received his story. "And," he said with a flourish, "the rest I've already told you. I will be writing for the *New York Times*!" He finished with a *yippee!* So unlike our old Colin, and we all clapped and cheered for him. Our quiet boy and our oldest boy had both survived the war, and astonishingly, had come out the better—Craig with a beautiful wife and child, and Colin with a promising career. Their success and happiness was the salve that helped heal the wound left by Cameron's tragic death.

We continued to prepare for the reception, which would be held on New Year's Day. We agreed that it would be the perfect start for the new year. Mom, with the help of her girls, worked hard cooking, baking, and gathering, not only for the feast we planned to serve after Craig and Ruth renewed their vows, but also for our own Christmas gatherings. It was a crazy-happy time. Mom seemed rejuvenated and looked so happy, I just wanted to cry for her. The lines etched in her face faded a bit, and Dad walked around with a big grin on his face. Everything was as good as could be expected but for the fact that, like last year, Gracie's picture had not yet shown up, and Christmas Eve was only two days away.

We received our package from the bridal store in Butte containing our altered dresses, and that night Ruth, Mom, Aileen, and I had fun trying them on. We also received the three suits we had ordered for our ring-bearers, Rory, James, and little John Jacob. We'd found a little baby-suit for Gussie. Ianna would once again be the flower girl, and we had a matching baby-dress made for Lacey. Oddly enough, they sent two flower girls' dresses instead of just the one, a puzzle we would never figure out. Ianna's dress was of an aqua blue, more blue than green and fit her perfectly, setting off her copper-colored hair. Mom, Aileen, and I would wear dresses of different shades of blue that would blend well with Ianna's.

Mom and Dad had splurged and hired a photographer to take pictures the night of the reception, and wanted the younger married couples to be photographed as well since they had not had professional pictures taken. Aileen, after having three children, worried that her wedding dress from seven years ago wouldn't fit. She brought it to our house that night, and when she tried it on, it still fit her perfectly. Blair's dress hung in Mom's closet. Ruth was the last to put on her wedding dress, which was exquisitely elegant, like her.

Her gown was made of heavy, ivory satin with a low-scooped neckline edged in lace and pearls. It had long fitted sleeves that ended in a V over her hands. It had simple lines, tight at the waist and ending in a full skirt and a forty-eight-inch train edged with the same lace and pearl treatment as the neckline and sleeves. She would wear a simple tiara and veil. She looked lovely, and Mom joked with her. "Now, Ruth, you do have the perfect pants to wear under that dress?" We broke out in laughter, and soon Craig was at the door threatening to come in.

He pounded on the door and demanded to know what was going on in there. The guys had been in the parlor, quaffing Dad's whiskey, and he sounded frisky. "Ruth Anne, if you don't come out soon, I'm coming in. It's time for bed!"

Ruth gasped in embarrassment. "Don't you dare come in, you know you're not supposed to see the bride in her dress until the wedding; it's bad luck if you do."

He returned with, "Well, woman, I would attest to the fact that you're not exactly a blushing, virginal bride any longer."

"Oh, Craig. Hush. Oh, blimey, you're embarrassing me!"

He walked away laughing, and when they retired to their end of the house that night, we could hear him teasing and flirting with her the entire time. I smiled when I watched Dad give Mom the look of desire, making her blush.

I stayed up that night, visiting with Colin. I couldn't believe how conversational he had become compared to the past. He shared his war experiences, concentrating only on the good and funny events. He said sharing life-and-death situations, sleeping close together in barns and outbuildings to keep warm, and splitting your last tin of hamburgers or last cigarette had gotten him over his shy nature. He laughed, and said living in a hospital for six weeks really made a person lose their modesty and restraint.

After hearing him repeatedly bring up the young Austrian nurse, I finally asked him. "What is the story about this nurse you keep talking about?"

Colin smiled, one that went all the way from the corners of his eyes to inside them, making them twinkle.

"Oh, Colin, you're in love with her, aren't you?"

He smiled again. "Well, now that you mention it, I guess I am. After I'm settled in New York and on assignment in Europe, I plan to visit her and ask her to marry me."

"Swell. What's she like?"

"She's beautiful, Abi. She has golden blonde hair and deep blue eyes the color of the sky just before it storms. Her name is Annemarie, and Abi, she is so smart and funny. She saved me, I swear. Once I found that I could write again, and could say exactly what had happened—how, when, where, and how God awful it was for all of us, our enemies and our own troops—I felt free and comforted somehow. Sometimes, especially near the end, we found ourselves helping a stray German more than hurting them, they were in such a bad way, ragged and hungry, and usually battling dysentery. By the end of the war, every one of us over there was tired of the killing, maiming, and seeing gruesome scenes everywhere. Annemarie understood that. She's a great listener, Abi, and she believes in me, like no one ever has. She's the one who convinced me to send my piece on the war to the more influential papers."

I smiled and hugged him. "I'm very happy for you, Colin, and I think she just might be why you have come out of your shell, and I love her for that. Good night, dear brother. I'm so glad you are home safe and sound, even if you will leave us soon and go as far away as New York. Perhaps I can come visit you there, sometime."

"I'd really like that, Abi."

The next day was Christmas Eve, and we still hadn't received anything from Gracie's abductors. Mom had Dad picked up the mail as soon as she saw the postman at our box at the end of our drive. Nothing. But this year, since she had so much to be thankful for, Mom just quietly cleared her throat and returned to her cooking and baking. Just before noon that day, there was a knock at the door. Everybody had settled at the dinner table and were hungry and ready to eat. Rory had recently graduated from his high chair to a booster seat, making Rory feel proud and like a big boy. Taking advantage of his new freedom, Rory jumped down and ran out through the porch to answer the outside door.

He came running back in with eyes wide. "Gracie! Gracie! Gracie's out there with a man." I guess he had heard enough over the years about Gracie to know our situation and how we longed for her return. We had all taken turns pointing out her picture to him, not so much for him to know her, but more for us to remember her and still include her in our family. We all remained seated and Mom, not having sat down yet, calmly took off her apron, and slowly walked out to the porch.

We sat still in dead silence, trying to hear what was being said. Soon, Mom came in and sat down while Dad ushered in Sheriff Monahan, who held the hand of a little redheaded girl. She looked at all of us and smiled. She airily waved her free hand at us. "Hi! I'm Gracie MacDougal, and I guess you are my new family. My mama told me there would be a lot of you and to be friendly and polite." She let go of the sheriff's hand and proceeded to go around the table, shaking everyone's hands, asking our names and nodding like she already had heard them.

Mom remained sitting in her chair. She wept quietly but other than that, she showed no emotion. When Gracie came to me, she noticed my tears and asked me why I was crying. I told her it was because I felt happy, not sad. She wisely nodded. "Yes, Mama Peggy told me you would be the happiest besides Aunt Nora and Uncle Angus." Mom started and came out of her stupor, and Dad finally queried the sheriff. "Patrick, what the Sam hell is going on here? Where did you find her, and how do we know she's Gracie?" I'll never know what made Dad ask such a silly question. This little girl was certainly our Gracie; she looked exactly like she should and appeared to still be the precocious personality she had been as a baby.

The sheriff just shook his head. "The station master called me and said that some lady had gotten off the train with a little girl. She asked him to call you and let you know that there was someone you needed to pick up at the station. Then, she asked him to take good care of her until her parents came for her. He said she left then, after crying and crying her goodbyes. He told me, 'It was enough to break my heart, seeing that. But that little girl did okay. She cried for a while and when she settled down, she asked, 'Well, aren't you going to call them?' "I guess the man called me because he thought I should know about it and that it would be better for me to bring Gracie back home." The sheriff laughed and nodded to Gracie. "She's a little whippersnapper, that one."

Mom stood up shakily and walked around the table, crouching in front of Gracie. She placed her hands gently on each of her little arms, looking intently into her eyes. "Where is . . . where is your mama. Where is she going?"

Gracie cocked her head, looking Mom directly in her eyes, and in a matter-of-fact manner said, "She's been really sick, and now she has to go and be with Mama Mary up in heaven. So she wants me to live here with you. She told me to tell you she's sorry, very sorry for taking me from you. Is that true?" Gracie stopped and screwed up her face all serious. "She took me from you and Uncle Angus? Right? She feels real bad. She cries all the time now, especially after Mama Mary died."

"When did she die, honey?"

Gracie began crying softly. "Mama Mary had 'sumption and died, and uh, uh, well, I don't know when. But it's just been me and Mama Peggy for a while now."

Mom gathered Gracie into her arms, and they clung to each other, crying. Dad thanked the sheriff, barely able to talk, his throat thick with emotion. Sheriff Monahan handed Gracie's small suitcase over to him. "Well, Gus, I'm sure it's Gracie and congratulations on getting her back. Unbelievable. Seven years almost, and one of yours had her. Unbelievable."

Our Christmas Eve that night was the happiest occasion in our family's history. Ianna and Gracie, one little girl with straight-as-sticks copper hair and the other with mounds of copper ringlets, got along as if they had known each other since birth. Rory was a little put out about this development but after the two girls had shared their secrets and all their getting acquainted revelations, they allowed Rory entrance into their little world, and when James arrived, Rory had his own buddy and everyone was happy.

Gift opening that night, consisting of the two younger siblings and five grandchildren, was full of high energy and when it was all over, it looked as if a tornado had whipped through the parlor. Mom brought out the many Christmas and birthday gifts she had wrapped over the years for Gracie. All the children went to work, again, opening those with as much delight as they had their own. But Mom did have Gracie promise she would share with the others.

That night after everyone had gone to bed, Gracie was still up. It had been such a change for her. Going from one person loving and doting on her to nearly a dozen was going to take some adjusting. Mom read to her for a while and then tucked her into the other bed in my room. But as soon as Mom stepped out and shut the door, Gracie came flying across the room and climbed in with me. This made me cry, and again, Gracie wondered why. I told her they were just tears of happiness and not to worry. I told her that we should each share one story with each other about something that happened when we were apart, and then we should sleep.

"Okay. May I go first, Abi?"

"Sure."

Gracie nestled in closer to me, and I had to fight off the tears. I shook my head in wonder, thinking all my dreams had come true. Gracie was back and still as loving and delightful a little girl as she was a baby. Jake had given me a promise ring that night and jokingly told me that I would receive a real engagement ring when he thought I was old enough for one. I laughed, and Gracie wanted to know why. I just told her it was a happy giggle because she was back home. "Now tell me your story, okay?"

Gracie yawned big and began. "I'm going to tell you my most 'barassing story. I still feel bad about it. Well, you know Mama Peggy dressed funny, like a man."

"Uh huh, yes."

"Well, there was this boy at school that wasn't nice, and one day he was making fun of her, and I got mad. We had a fight and we both were in trouble. But guess what, Abi?"

"What?"

"I won. And after that he never made fun of Mama again."

"Wow. He sounds like he was a naughty little boy. So, you're in first grade?"

"Yes. I shouldn't have started yet, but since I can read, write the alphabet and some words, they let me start when I was just five. Soon I'll be six, though."

"So, who taught you how to read?"

"Both my mamas. They read to me all the time. But Mama Peggy cried a lot. I know it was sad for her to look the way she did. Sometimes she could stop crying before I saw her but I still knew. I would pretend I didn't know she had been crying. Sometimes she would just grab me and give me lots of hugs and kisses after she'd been sad and tell me I was worth it. 'You are so worth it, little Gracie,' she would say. Why do you suppose she said that all the time?"

"Because you were worth it."

"What's *it*?"

"Stealing you from us. *It* wasn't right, you know."

"Yes, I know, but I still loved my mamas, and Grandma."

"Grandma MacDougal?"

"Yes. She would come visit. Not often, but always just before Christmas."

I started, thinking. Oh, my God, that's why Aunt Peggy had Grandma lobotomized; she didn't want to take the chance that Grandma would talk about her having Gracie. Grandma had kept that secret safe all those years, but, yes, she may have talked once her dementia became worse. I sighed and accidentally let out a, "Oh, my gosh." Gracie asked what was wrong, and I just told her I was having a hard time thinking of which story to tell her.

Gracie yawned. "Can you tell me your story tomorrow night. I'm really tired, Abi."

"Sure. Did you say your bedtime prayers?" Gracie didn't answer; all I heard was a little snore. My last prayer that night was one of gratitude. I hugged Gracie and kissed the back of her head, and surprisingly, I fell asleep almost as fast as Gracie had.